THE DARKEST MINDS

ALEXANDRA BRACKEN

Quercus

QUERCUS CHILDREN'S BOOKS

First published in 2012 by Hyperion
First published in Great Britain in 2016 by Hodder and Stoughton
This edition published in Great Britain in 2018 by Hodder and Stoughton

3 5 7 9 10 8 6 4

A CIP catalogue record for this book is available from the British Library.

ISBN 978 1 78654 050 8

Typeset by Hewer Text UK Ltd, Edinburgh
Printed and bound in Great Britain by Clays Ltd, Elcograf S.p.A.

The paper and board used in this book are
made from wood from responsible sources.

Quercus Children's Books
An imprint of
Hachette Children's Group
Part of Hodder and Stoughton
Carmelite House
50 Victoria Embankment
London EC4Y 0DZ

An Hachette UK Company
www.hachette.co.uk
www.hachettechildrens.co.uk

For Stephanie and Daniel,
who were in every minivan with me

PROLOGUE

WHEN THE WHITE NOISE WENT OFF, WE WERE IN the Garden, pulling weeds.

I always reacted badly to it. It didn't matter if I was outside, eating in the Mess Hall, or locked in my cabin. When it came, the shrieking tones blew up like a pipe bomb between my ears. Other girls at Thurmond could pick themselves up after a few minutes, shaking off the nausea and disorientation like the loose grass clinging to their camp uniforms. But me? Hours would pass before I was able to piece myself back together.

This time should have been no different.

But it was.

I didn't see what had happened to provoke the punishment. We were working so close to the camp's electric fence that I could smell the singed air and feel the voltage it shed vibrating in my teeth. Maybe someone got brave and decided to step out of the Garden's bounds. Or maybe, dreaming big, someone fulfilled all our fantasies and threw a rock at the head of the nearest Psi Special Forces soldier. That would have been worth it.

The only thing I knew for certain was that the overhead speakers spurted out two warning blares: one short, one long. The skin on my neck crawled as I leaned forward into the damp dirt, hands pressed tightly against my ears, shoulders tensed to take the hit.

The sound that came over the speakers wasn't really white noise. It wasn't that weird buzz that the air sometimes takes on when you're sitting alone in silence, or the faint hum of a computer monitor. To the United States government and its Department of Psi Youth, it was the lovechild of a car alarm and a dental drill, turned up high enough to make your ears bleed.

Literally.

The sound ripped out of the speakers and shredded every nerve in my body. It forced its way past my hands, roaring over the screams of a hundred teenage freaks, and settled at the center of my brain, where I couldn't reach in and rip it out.

My eyes flooded with tears. I tried to ram my face into the ground—all I could taste in my mouth was blood and dirt. A girl fell forward next to me, her mouth open in a cry I couldn't hear. Everything else faded out of focus.

My body shook in time with the bursts of static, curling in on itself like an old, yellowing piece of paper. Someone's hands were shaking my shoulders; I heard someone say my name—*Ruby*—but I was too far gone to respond. Gone, gone, gone, sinking until there was nothing, like the earth had swallowed me up in a single, deep breath. Then darkness.

And silence.

2

ONE

GRACE SOMERFIELD WAS THE FIRST TO DIE.

The first in my fourth grade class, at least. I'm sure that by then, thousands, maybe even hundreds of thousands, of kids had already up and gone the same way she had. People were slow to piece it all together—or, at least, they had figured out the right way to keep us in the dark long after kids started dying.

When the deaths finally came to light, my elementary school put a strict ban on teachers and staff talking to us about what was then called Everhart's Disease, after Michael Everhart, the first kid known to have died of it. Soon, someone somewhere decided to give it a proper name: Idiopathic Adolescent Acute Neurodegeneration—IAAN for short. And then it wasn't just Michael's disease. It was all of ours.

All the adults I knew buried the knowledge beneath lying smiles and hugs. I was still stuck in my own world of sunshine, ponies, and my race car collection. Looking back, I couldn't believe how naive I was, just how many clues I missed. Even big things like when my dad, a cop, started working longer hours and could barely stand to look at me when he finally did come home. My mom started me on a strict vitamin regimen and refused to let me be alone, even for a few minutes.

On the other hand, my parents were both only children. I didn't have any dead cousins to send up red flags, and my mom's refusal to let my dad install a "soul-sucking vortex of trash and mindless entertainment"—that thing commonly known as a television—meant that no scary news broadcasts rocked my world. This, combined with the CIA-grade parental controls set up on our Internet access, pretty much ensured I'd be far more concerned with how my stuffed animals were arranged on my bed than the possibility of dying before my tenth birthday.

I was also completely unprepared for what happened on the fifteenth of September.

It had rained the night before, so my parents sent me to school wearing red galoshes. In class, we talked about dinosaurs and practiced cursive before Mrs. Port dismissed us for lunch with her usual look of relief.

I remember every detail of lunch that day clearly, not because I was sitting across from Grace at the table, but because she was the first, and because it wasn't supposed to happen. She wasn't old like Grandpops had been. She didn't have cancer like Mom's friend Sara. No allergies, no cough, no head injury—nothing. When she died, it came completely out of the blue, and none of us understood what it meant until it was too late.

Grace was locked in deep debate about whether a fly was trapped inside her Jell-O cup. The red mass shivered as she waved it around, inching out over the edge of the container when she squeezed it a bit too tight. Naturally, everyone wanted to give their opinion on whether it was a fly or a piece of candy Grace had pushed in there. Including me.

"I'm not a liar," Grace said. "I just—"

She stopped. The plastic cup slipped from her fingers, hitting the table. Her mouth was open, eyes fixed on something just beyond my head. Grace's brow was furrowed, almost as if she was listening to someone explain something very difficult.

"Grace?" I remember saying. "Are you okay?"

Her eyes rolled back, flashing white in the second it took for her eyelids to droop down. Grace let out a small sigh, not even strong enough to blow away the strands of brown hair stuck to her lips.

All of us sitting nearby froze, though we must have had the same exact thought: she's fainted. A week or two before, Josh Preston had passed out on the playground because, as Mrs. Port explained, he didn't have enough sugar in his system—something stupid like that.

A noon aide rushed over to the table. She was one of four old ladies with white visors and whistles who rotated lunch and playground duty during the week. I have no idea if she had any medical certifications beyond a vague notion of CPR, but she pulled Grace's sagging body to the ground all the same.

She had a rapt audience as she pressed her ear to Grace's hot pink T-shirt, listening for a heartbeat that wasn't there. I don't know what the old lady thought, but she started

5

yelling, and suddenly white visors and curious faces circled in on us. It wasn't until Ben Cho nudged Grace's limp hand with his sneaker that any of us realized she was dead.

The other kids started screaming. One girl, Tess, was crying so hard she couldn't breathe. Small feet stampeded toward the cafeteria door.

I just sat, surrounded by abandoned lunches, staring at the cup of Jell-O and letting terror crawl through me until my arms and legs felt like they would be frozen to the table forever. If the school's security officer hadn't come and carried me outside, I don't know how long I would've stayed there.

Grace is dead, I was thinking. *Grace is dead? Grace is dead.*

And it got worse.

A month later, after the first big waves of deaths, the Centers for Disease Control and Prevention released a five-step list of symptoms to help parents identify whether their kid was at risk for IAAN. By then half my class was dead.

My mom hid the list so well that I only found it by accident, when I climbed on top of the kitchen counter to look for the chocolate she kept hidden behind her baking supplies.

HOW TO IDENTIFY IF YOUR CHILD IS AT RISK, the flyer read. I recognized the flaming orange shade of the paper: it was the sheet Mrs. Port had sent home with her few remaining students days before. She had folded it twice and fastened it with three staples to prevent our reading it. TO THE PARENTS OF RUBY ONLY was written on the outside and underlined three times. Three times was serious. My parents would have grounded me for opening it.

Luckily for me, it was already open.

6

1. Your child suddenly becomes sullen and withdrawn, and/or loses interest in activities they previously enjoyed.
2. S/he begins to have abnormal difficulty in concentrating or suddenly becomes hyper-focused on tasks, resulting in s/he losing track of time and/or neglecting him/herself or others.
3. S/he experiences hallucinations, vomiting, chronic migraines, memory loss, and/or fainting spells.
4. S/he becomes prone to violent outbursts, unusually reckless behavior, or self-injury (burns, bruising, and cuts that cannot be explained).
5. S/he develops behaviors or abilities that are inexplicable, dangerous, or cause you or others physical harm.

IF YOUR CHILD DEMONSTRATES ANY OF THE ABOVE SYMPTOMS, REGISTER HIM/HER AT IAAN.GOV AND WAIT TO BE CONTACTED ABOUT THE LOCAL HOSPITAL TO WHICH S/HE SHOULD BE TAKEN.

When I finished reading the flyer, I folded it back up neatly, put it exactly where I found it, and threw up in the sink.

Grams phoned later that week, and in her usual to-the-point-Grams way explained everything to me. Kids were dying left and right, all about my age. But the doctors were working on it, and I wasn't supposed to be afraid, because

I was *her* granddaughter, and I would be fine. I should be good and tell my parents if I felt anything weird, understand?

Things turned from bad to terrifying very fast. A week after three of the four kids in my neighborhood were buried, the president made a formal address to the nation. Mom and Dad watched the live stream on the computer, and I listened from outside the office door.

"My fellow Americans," President Gray began. "Today we face a devastating crisis, one that threatens not only our children's lives, but the very future of our great nation. May it comfort you to know that in our time of need, we in Washington are developing programs, both to support the families affected by this horrid affliction and the children blessed enough to survive it."

I wish I could have seen his face as he spoke, because I think he knew—he must have—that this threat, the crimp in our supposedly glorious future, had nothing to do with the kids who had died. Buried underground or burned into ash, they couldn't do anything but haunt the memories of the people who had loved them. They were gone. Forever.

And that symptoms list, the one that was sent home folded and stapled by teachers, which was aired a hundred times over on the news as the faces of the dead scrolled along the bottom of the screen? The government was never scared of the kids who might die, or the empty spaces they would leave behind.

They were afraid of us—the ones who lived.

TWO

IT RAINED THE DAY THEY BROUGHT US TO THURMOND, and it went on to rain straight through the week, and the week after that. Freezing rain, the kind that would have been snow if it had been five degrees colder. I remember watching the drops trace frantic paths down the length of the school bus window. If I had been back at home, inside one of my parents' cars, I would have followed the drops' swerving routes across the cold glass with my fingertips. Now, my hands were tied together behind my back, and the men in the black uniforms had packed four of us to a seat. There was barely room to breathe.

The heat from a hundred-odd bodies fogged the bus windows, and it acted like a screen to the outside world. Later, the windows of the bright yellow buses they used to bring kids in would be smeared with black paint. They just hadn't thought of it yet.

I was closest to the window on the five-hour drive, so I could make out slivers of the passing landscape whenever the rain let up for a bit. It all looked exactly the same to me—green farms, thick expanses of trees. We could have still been in Virginia, for all I knew. The girl sitting next to me, the one that would later be classified Blue, seemed to recognize a sign at one point because she leaned over me to get a better look. She looked a little familiar to me, like I had seen her face from around my town, or she was from the next one over. I think all of the kids with me were from Virginia, but there was no way to be sure, because there was only one big rule: and that was *Silence*.

After they had picked me up from my house the day before, they'd kept me, along with the rest of the kids, in some kind of warehouse overnight. The room was washed in unnatural brightness; they sat us in a cluster on the dirty cement floor, and pointed three floodlights toward us. We weren't allowed to sleep. My eyes were watering so badly from the dust that I couldn't see the clammy, pale faces around me, let alone the faces of the soldiers who stood just beyond the ring of lights, watching. In some weird way, they ceased to be whole men and women. In the gray haze of half sleep, I processed them in small, terrifying pieces: the gasoline reek of shoe polish, the creak of stiff leather, the twist of disgust on their lips. The tip of a boot as it dug into my side, forcing me back awake.

The next morning, the drive was completely silent except for the soldiers' radios and the kids that were crying toward the back of the bus. The kid sitting at the other end of our seat wet his pants, but he wasn't about to tell that to the red-haired PSF standing beside him. She had slapped him when he complained he hadn't eaten anything all day.

I flexed my bare feet against the ground, trying to keep my legs still. Hunger was making my head feel funny, too, bubbling up every once in a while to overwhelm even the spikes of terror shooting through me. It was hard to focus, and harder to sit still; I felt like I was shrinking, trying to fade back into the seat and disappear completely. My hands were starting to lose feeling after being bound in the same position for so long. Trying to stretch the plastic band they'd tightened around them did nothing but force it to cut deeper into the soft skin there.

Psi Special Forces—that's what the driver of the bus had called himself and the others when they collected us from the warehouse. *You are to come with us on authority of the Psi Special Forces commander, Joseph Traylor.* He held up a paper to prove it, so I guess it was true. I had been taught not to argue with adults, anyway.

The bus took a deep dip as it pulled off the narrow road and onto a smaller dirt one. The new vibrations woke whoever had been lucky or exhausted enough to fall asleep. They also sent the black uniforms into action. The men and women stood straighter, and their attention snapped toward the windshield.

I saw the towering fence first. The darkening gray sky cast everything in a moody, deep blue, but not the fence. It was glowing silver as the wind whistled through its open pockets. Just below my window were dozens of men and women in full uniform, escorting the bus in at a brisk jog. The PSFs in the control booth at the gate stood and saluted the driver as he navigated past them.

The bus lurched to a stop, and we were all forced to stay deathly still as the camp gate slid shut behind us. The locks cracked through the silence like thunder as they came together again. We were not the first bus through—that had come a year before. We were not the last bus, either. That would come in three more years, when the camp's occupancy maxed out.

There was a single breath of stillness before a soldier in a black rain poncho rapped on the bus door. The driver reached over and pulled the lever—and ended anyone's hope that this was a short pit stop.

The PSF was an enormous man, the kind you'd expect to play an evil giant in a movie, or a villain in a cartoon. He kept his hood up, masking his face, hair, and anything that would have let me recognize him later. I guess it didn't matter. He wasn't speaking for himself. He was speaking for the camp.

"You will stand and exit the bus in an orderly fashion," he yelled. The driver tried to hand him the microphone, but the soldier knocked it away with his hand. "You will be divided into groups of ten, and you will be brought in for testing. Do not try to run. Do not speak. Do not do *anything* other than what is asked of you. Failure to follow these instructions will be met with punishment."

At ten, I was one of the younger kids on the bus, though there were certainly a few kids younger. Most seemed to be twelve, even thirteen. The hate and mistrust burning in the soldiers' eyes might have shrunken my spine, but it only sparked rebellion in the older kids.

"Go screw yourself!" someone yelled from the back of the bus.

We all turned at once, just in time to see the PSF with the flaming red hair launch the butt of her rifle into the teenage boy's mouth. He let out a shriek of pain and surprise as the soldier did it again, and I saw a faint spray of blood burst from his mouth when he took his next, angry breath. With his hands behind his back, there was no way he could block the attack. He just had to take it.

They began moving kids off the bus, one seat of four at a time. But I was still watching that kid, the way he seemed to cloud the air around him with silent, toxic fury. I don't know if he felt me staring, or what, but the boy turned around and met my gaze. He nodded at me, like an encouragement. And when he smiled, it was around a mouthful of bloody teeth.

I felt myself being hauled up and out of my seat, and almost before I realized what was happening, I was slipping down the wet bus steps and tumbling into the pouring rain. A different PSF lifted me off my knees and guided me in the direction of two other girls about my age. Their clothes clung to them like old skin, translucent and drooping.

There were nearly twenty PSFs on the ground, swarming the neat small lines of kids. My feet had been completely swallowed by the mud, and I was shivering in my pajamas, but no one took notice, and no one came up to cut the plastic binding our hands. We waited, silently, tongues clamped between our teeth. I looked up to the clouds, turning my face to the pounding rain. It looked like the sky was falling, piece by piece.

The last groups of four were being lifted off the bus and dropped onto the ground, including the boy with the broken face. He was the last one off, just behind a tall blond girl with a blank stare. I could barely make them out through the sheet of rain and the foggy bus windows, but I was sure I saw the boy lean forward and whisper something into the girl's ear, just as she took the first step off the bus.

She nodded, a quick jerk of her chin. The second her shoes touched the mud, she bolted to the right, ducking around the nearest PSF's hands. One of the PSFs barked out a terrifying *"Stop!"* but she kept running, straight for the gates. With everyone's attention turned toward her, no one thought to look back at the boy still on the bus—no one but me. He came slinking down the steps, the front of his white hooded sweatshirt stained with his own blood. The same PSF who had hit him before was now helping him down to the ground, as she had done for the rest of us. I watched her fingers close around his elbow and felt the echo of her grip on my own newly bruised skin; I watched him turn and say something to her, his face a mask of perfect calm.

I watched the PSF let go of his arm, take her gun out of its holster, and, without a word—without even blinking—stick the barrel inside of her mouth and pull the trigger.

I don't know if I screamed aloud, or if the strangled sound had come from the woman waking up to what she was doing, two seconds too late to stop it. The image of her face—her slack jaw, her eyes bulging out of her skull, the ripple of suddenly loose skin—stayed burned into the air like

14

a photonegative far longer than the explosion of pink, misty blood and clumps of hair against the bus.

The kid standing next to me dropped into a dead faint, and then there wasn't a single one of us that wasn't screaming.

The PSF hit the ground the exact same moment the girl was tackled into the mud. The rain washed the soldier's blood down off the bus windows and yellow panels, stretching the bloated dark lines, drawing them out as they disappeared completely. It was that fast.

The boy was looking only at us. *"Run!"* he yelled through his broken teeth. "What are you doing? *Run—run!*"

And the first thing that went through my mind wasn't *What are you?* or even *Why?*

It was *But I have nowhere else to go.*

He might as well have blown the entire bus up for the panic it caused. Some kids listened and tried to bolt for the fence, only to have their path blocked by the line of soldiers in black that seemed to pour out of the air. Most just stood there and screamed, and screamed, and screamed, the rain falling all around, the mud sucking their feet down firmly in place. A girl knocked me down to the ground with her shoulder as the other PSFs rushed for the boy, still standing in the bus doorway. The soldiers were yelling at us to sit on the ground, to stay frozen there. I did exactly as I was told.

"Orange!" I heard one of them yell into his walkie-talkie. "We have a situation at the main gate. I need restraints for an Orange—"

It wasn't until after they had rounded us back up and had the boy with the broken face on the ground that I dared

15

to look up. And that I began to wonder, dread tickling up my spine, if he was the only one who could do something like that. Or if everyone around me was there because they could cause someone to hurt themselves that way, too.

Not me—the words blazed through my head—*not me, they made a mistake, a mistake—*

I watched with a feeling of hollowness at the center of my chest as one of the soldiers took a can of spray paint in hand and painted an enormous orange *X* over the boy's back. The boy had only stopped yelling because two PSFs had pulled a strange black mask down over the lower part of his face—like they were muzzling a dog.

Tension beaded on my skin like sweat. They marched our lines through the camp toward the Infirmary for sorting. As we walked, we saw kids heading in the opposite direction, from a row of pathetic wood cabins. All of them were wearing white uniforms, with a different colored *X* marked on each of their backs and a number written in black above it. I saw five different colors in all—green, blue, yellow, orange, and red.

The kids with the green and blue *X*'s were allowed to walk freely, their hands swinging at their sides. Those with a faint yellow *X*, or an orange or red one, were forced to fight through the mud with their hands and feet in metal cuffs, a long chain connecting them in a line. The ones marked with orange smears had the muzzlelike masks over their faces.

We were hurried into the bright lights and dry air of what a torn paper sign had labeled INFIRMARY. The doctors and nurses lined the long hallway, watching us with frowns

16

and shaking heads. The checkered tile floor became slick with rain and mud, and it took all of my concentration not to slip. My nose was filled with the smell of rubbing alcohol and fake lemon.

We filed one by one up a dark cement staircase at the back of the first floor, which was filled with empty beds and limp white curtains. *Not an Orange. Not a Red.*

I could feel my guts churning deep in the pit of my stomach. I couldn't stop seeing that woman's face, right when she pulled the trigger, or the mass of her bloody hair that had landed near my feet. I couldn't stop seeing my mom's face, when she had locked me out in the garage. I couldn't stop seeing Grams's face.

She'll come, I thought. She'll come. She'll fix Mom and Dad and she will come to get me. She'll come, she'll come, she'll come . . .

Upstairs, they finally cut the plastic binding that tied our hands, and divided us again, sending half down to the right end of the freezing hallway and half to the left. Both sides looked exactly the same—no more than a few closed doors, and a small window at the very end. For a moment, I did nothing but watch the rain pelt that tiny, foggy pane of glass. Then, the door on the left swung open with a low whine, and the face of a plump, middle-aged man appeared. He cast one look in our direction before whispering something to the PSF at the head of the group. One by one, more doors opened, and more adults appeared. The only thing they had in common aside from their white coats was a shared look of suspicion.

Without a single word of explanation, the PSFs began pulling and pushing kids toward each white coat and its associated office. The outburst of confused, distressed noises that erupted from the lines was shushed with a piercing buzzer. I fell back onto my heels, watching the doors shut one by one, wondering if I would ever see those kids again.

What's wrong with us? My head felt like it was full of wet sand as I looked over my shoulder. The boy with the broken face was nowhere, but his memory had chased me all the way through the camp. Did they bring us here because they thought we had Everhart's Disease? Did they think we were going to die?

How had that boy made the PSF do what she had done? What had he said to her?

I felt a hand slide into mine as I stood there, trembling hard enough for my joints to hurt. The girl—the same one that had pulled me down to the mud outside—gave me a fierce look. Her dark blond hair was plastered against her skull, framing a pink scar that curved between her top lip and nose. Her dark eyes flashed, and when she spoke, I saw that they had cut the wires on her braces but had left the metal nubs glued to her front teeth.

"Don't be scared," she whispered. "Don't let them see."

The handwritten label on the tag of her jacket said SAMANTHA DAHL. It stuck up against the back of her neck like an afterthought.

We stood shoulder to shoulder, close enough that our linked fingers were hidden between the fabric of my pajama pants and her purple puffer jacket. They had picked her up on the way to school the same morning they had come for me. That had been a day ago, but I remembered seeing her dark eyes burning bright with hate at the back of the van they had locked us in. She hadn't screamed as the others had.

The kids who had disappeared through the doors now came back through them, clutching gray sweaters and shorts in their hands. Instead of falling back into our line, they were marched downstairs before anyone could think to get a word or questioning look in.

They don't look hurt. I could smell permanent marker and something that might have been rubbing alcohol, but no one was bleeding or crying.

When it was finally the girl's turn, the PSF at the head of the line forced us apart with a sharp jerk. I wanted to go in with her, to face whatever was behind the door. Anything had to be better than being alone again without anyone or anything to anchor myself to.

My hands were shaking so badly that I had to cross my arms and grip my elbows to get them to stop. I stood at the front of the line, looking at the gleaming span of checkered tile between the PSF's black boots and my mud-splattered toes. I was already tired down to my bones from the sleepless night before, and the scent of the soldier's boot polish sent my head deeper into a fog.

And then they called for me.

I found myself in a dimly lit office, half the size of my cramped bedroom at home, with no memory of ever having walked into it.

"Name?"

I was looking at a cot and a strange, halo-shaped gray machine hanging over it.

The white coat's face appeared from behind the laptop on the table. He was a frail-looking man, whose thin silver glasses seemed to be in serious danger of sliding off his nose with every quick movement. His voice was unnaturally high, and he didn't so much as say the word as squeak it. I pressed my back against the closed door, trying to put space between me, the man, and the machine.

The white coat followed my gaze to the cot. "That's a scanner. There's nothing to be afraid of."

I must not have looked convinced, because he continued. "Have you ever broken a bone or bumped your head? Do you know what a CT scan is?"

It was the patience in his voice that drew me forward a step. I shook my head.

"In a minute I'm going to have you lie down, and I'll use that machine to check to make sure your head is all right. But first, you need to tell me your name."

Make sure your head is all right. How did he know—?

"Your name," he said, the words taking on a sudden edge.

"Ruby," I answered, and had to spell my last name for him.

He began typing on the laptop, distracted for a moment. My eyes drifted back over to the machine, wondering how painful it would be for me to have the inside of my head inspected. Wondering if he could somehow see what I had done.

"Damn, they're getting lazy," the white coat groused, more to himself than to me. "Didn't they pre-classify you?"

I had no idea what he was talking about.

"When they picked you up, did they ask you questions?" he asked, standing. The room wasn't large by any means. He was by my side in two steps, and I was in a full panic in two heartbeats. "Did your parents report your symptoms to the soldiers?"

"Symptoms?" I squeezed out. "I don't have any symptoms—I don't have the—"

He shook his head, looking more annoyed than anything else. "Calm down; you're safe here. I'm not going to hurt you." The white coat kept talking, his voice flat, something flickering in his eyes. The lines sounded practiced.

"There are many different kinds of symptoms," he explained, leaning down to look at me eye to eye. All I could see were his crooked front teeth and the dark circles rimming his eyes. His breath smelled like coffee and spearmint. "Many different kinds of . . . children. I'm going to take a picture of your brain, and it'll help us put you with the others who are like you."

I shook my head. "I don't have any symptoms! Grams is coming, she is, I swear—she'll tell you, please!"

"Tell me, sweetheart, are you very good at math and puzzles? Greens are incredibly smart and have astonishing memories."

My mind jumped back to the kids outside, to the colored X's on the back of their shirts. *Green*, I thought. What had the other colors been? *Red, Blue, Yellow, and—*

And Orange. Like the boy with the bloody mouth.

"All right," he said, taking a deep breath, "just lie back on that cot and we'll get started. Now, please."

21

I didn't move. Thoughts were rushing too quickly to my head. It was a struggle to even look at him.

"Now," he repeated, moving toward the machine. "Don't make me call in one of the soldiers. They won't be nearly as nice, believe me." A screen on the side panel came alive with a single touch, and then the machine itself lit up. At the center of a gray circle was a bright white light, blinking as it set itself up for another test. It was breathing out hot air in sputters and whines that seemed to prick every pore on my body.

All I could think was, *He'll know. He'll know what I did to them.*

My back was flat against the door again, my hand blindly searching for the handle. Every single lecture my dad had ever given me about strangers seemed to be coming true. This was not a safe place. This man was not nice.

I was shaking so hard, he might have thought I was going to faint. That, or he was going to force me onto the cot himself and hold me there until the machine came down and locked over me.

I hadn't been ready to run before, but I was now. As my fingers tightened on the door handle, I felt his hand push through my unruly mass of dark hair and seize the back of my neck. The shock of his freezing hand on my flushed skin made me flinch, but it was the explosion of pain at the base of my skull that made me cry out.

He stared at me, unblinking, his eyes suddenly unfocused. But I was seeing everything—impossible things. Hands drumming on a car's steering wheel, a woman in

22

a black dress leaning forward to kiss me, a baseball flying toward my face out on a diamond, an endless stretch of green field, a hand running through a little girl's hair . . . The images played out behind my closed eyes like an old home movie. The shapes of people and objects burned themselves into my retinas and stayed there, floating around behind my eyelids like hungry ghosts.

Not mine, my mind screamed. *These don't belong to me.*

But how could they have been his? Each image—were they memories? Thoughts?

Then I saw more. A boy, the same scanner machine above him flickering and smoking. *Yellow.* I felt my lips form the words, as if I had been there to say them. I saw a small red-haired girl from across a room much like this one; saw her lift a finger, and the table and laptop in front of her rise several inches from the ground. *Blue*—again, the man's voice in my head. A boy holding a pencil between his hands, studying it with a terrifying intensity—the pencil bursting into flames. *Red.* Cards with pictures and numbers on them held up in front of a child's face. *Green.*

I squeezed my eyes shut, but I couldn't pull back from the images that came next—the lines of marching, muzzled monsters. I was standing high above, looking down through rain-spattered glass, but I saw the handcuffs and the chains. I saw everything.

I'm not one of them. Please, please, please . . .

I fell, dropping to my knees, bracing my hands against the tile, trying to keep from being sick all over myself and the floor. The white coat's hand still gripped the back of

23

my neck. "I'm Green," I sobbed, the words half lost to the machine's buzzing. The light had been bright before, but now it only amplified the pounding behind my eyes. I stared into his blank eyes, willing him to believe me. "I'm Green . . . please, *please* . . ."

But I saw my mother's face, the smile the boy with the broken mouth had given me, like he had recognized something of himself in me. I knew what I was.

"Green . . ."

I looked up at the sound of the voice that floated down to me. I stared, and he stared right back, his eyes unfocused. He was mumbling something now, his mouth full of mush, like he was chewing on the words.

"I'm—"

"Green," he said, shaking his head. His voice sounded stronger. I was still on the floor when he went to shut down the machine, and so shocked when he sat back down at the desk that I actually forgot to cry. But it wasn't until he picked up the green spray paint and drew that enormous *X* over the back of the uniform shirt and handed it to me that I remembered to start breathing.

It'll be okay, I told myself as I walked back down the cold hallway, down the steps, to the girls and men in uniforms waiting for me below. It wasn't until that night, as I lay awake in my bunk, that I realized I would only ever have one chance to run—and I hadn't taken it.

THREE

SAMANTHA—SAM—AND I WERE BOTH ASSIGNED TO Cabin 27, along with the rest of the girls from our bus that were classified as Green. Fourteen in all, though by the next day, there were twenty more. They capped the number at thirty a week later, and moved on to filling the next wooden structure along the camp's perpetually soggy and trampled main trail.

Bunks were assigned based on alphabetical order, which put Sam directly above me—a small mercy, seeing as the rest of the girls were nothing like her. They spent the first night either stunned into silence or sobbing. I didn't have time for tears anymore. I had questions.

"What are they going to do with us?" I whispered up to her. We were at the far left end of the cabin, our bunk wedged in the corner. The walls of the structure had been thrown together so quickly that they weren't completely sealed. Every now and then a freezing draft and sometimes a snowflake whistled in from the silent outdoors.

25

"I dunno," she said quietly. A few beds over, one of the girls had finally dropped off into the oblivion of sleep, and her snores were helping to cover our conversation. When a PSF had escorted us to our new residence, it had been with several warnings: no talking after lights-out, no leaving, no use of freak abilities—intentional or accidental. It was the first time I had ever heard anyone refer to what we could do as "freak abilities" instead of the polite alternative, "symptoms".

"I guess keep us here, until they figure out a cure," Sam continued. "That's what my dad said, at least, when the soldiers came to get me. What did your parents say?"

My hands hadn't stopped shaking from earlier, and every time I tried shutting my eyes all I could see were the white coat's blank ones staring right back into mine. The mention of my parents only made the pounding in my head that much worse.

I don't know why I lied. It was easier, I guess, than the truth—or maybe because some small part of it felt like it *was* the actual truth. "My parents are dead."

She sucked in a sharp breath between her teeth. "I wish mine were, too."

"You don't mean that!"

"They're the ones that sent me here, aren't they?" It was dangerous, how fast her voice was rising. "Obviously they wanted to get rid of *me*."

"I don't think—" I began, only to stop myself. Hadn't my parents wanted to get rid of me, too?

"Whatever; it's fine," she said, though it clearly wasn't and it wasn't ever going to be. "We'll stay here and stick together, and when we get out, we can go wherever we want, and no one will stop us."

My mom used to say that sometimes just saying something aloud was enough to make it true. I wasn't so sure about that, but the way Sam said it, the low burn beneath her words, made me reconsider. It suddenly seemed possible that it could work out that way—that if I couldn't go home, I would still be all right in the end if I could just stick with her. It was like wherever Sam went, a path opened up behind her; all I had to do was stay in her shadow, out of the PSFs' line of sight, and avoid doing anything that would call attention to me.

It worked that way for five years.

Five years feels like a lifetime when one day bleeds into the next, and your world doesn't stretch any farther than the gray electric fence surrounding two miles of shoddy buildings and mud. I was never happy at Thurmond, but it was bearable because Sam was there to make it that way. She was there with the eye roll when Vanessa, one of our cabinmates, tried to cut her own hair with garden shears to look more "stylish" ("For who?" Sam had muttered. "Her reflection in the Washroom mirror?"); the silly cross-eyed face behind the back of the PSF lecturing her for speaking out of turn yet again; and the firm—but gentle—reality check when girls' imaginations started running too wild, or rumors sprung up about the PSFs letting us go.

Sam and I—we were realists. We knew we weren't getting out. Dreaming led to disappointment, and disappointment to a kind of depressed funk that wasn't easy to shake. Better to stay in the gray than get eaten by the dark.

Two years into life at Thurmond, the camp controllers started work on the Factory. They had failed at rehabilitating the dangerous ones and hauled them off in the night, but the so-called "improvements" didn't stop there. It dawned on them that the camp needed to be entirely "self-sufficient". From that point on, we'd be growing and cooking our own food to eat, mucking out the Washrooms, making our uniforms, and even making theirs.

The brick structure was all the way at the far west side of camp, cupped in one end of Thurmond's long rectangle. They had us dig out the foundation for the Factory, but the camp controllers didn't trust us with the actual building of it. We watched it go up floor by floor, wondering what it was for, and what they would do to us there. That was back when all sorts of rumors were floating around like dandelion fluff in the wind—some thought the scientists were coming back for more experiments; some thought the new building was where they were going to move the Reds, Oranges, and Yellows, if and when they returned; and some thought it was where they were going to get rid of us, once and for all.

"We'll be fine," Sam had told me one night, just before they turned the lights out. "No matter what—you hear me?"

But it wasn't fine. It wasn't fine then, and it wasn't fine now.

There was no talking in the Factory, but there were ways around it. Actually, the only time we *were* allowed to speak to

28

one another was in our cabin, before lights-out. Everywhere else, it was all work, obedience, silence. But you can't go on for years together without developing a different kind of language, one that was all sly grins and quick glances. Today, they had us polishing and relacing the PSFs' boots and tightening their uniform buttons, but a single wiggle of a loose black shoelace and a look toward the girl standing across from you—the same one who had called you an awful word the night before—spoke volumes.

The Factory wasn't much of a factory. A better name probably would have been the Warehouse, only because the building consisted of just one huge room, with a pathway suspended over the work floor. The builders had enough thought to install four large windows on the west and east walls, but because there was no heat in the winter or AC in the summer, they tended to let more bad weather in than sunlight.

The camp controllers tried to keep things as simple as possible; they set up rows and rows of tables lengthwise across the dusty concrete floor. There were hundreds of us working in the Factory that morning, all in Green uniforms. Ten PSFs patrolled the walkways above us, each with his or her own black rifle. Another ten were on the ground with us.

It was no more unnerving than usual to feel the press of their eyes coming from every direction. But I hadn't slept well the night before, even after a full day of work in the Garden. I had gone to bed with a headache and woken up with a glossy fever fog over my brain, and a sore throat to match. Even my hands seemed lethargic, my fingers stiff as pencils.

29

I knew I wasn't keeping up, but it was like drowning, in a way. The harder I tried to work, to keep my head above water, the more tired I felt and the slower I became. After a while, even standing upright was taking too much effort, and I had to brace myself against the table to keep from swan-diving straight into it. On most days, I could get away with a snail's pace. It wasn't like they had us doing important work, or that we had deadlines to meet. Every task we were assigned was just glorified busywork to keep our hands moving, our bodies occupied, and our minds dead with boredom. Sam called it "forced recess"—they let us out of our cabins, and the work wasn't difficult or tiring like it was in the Garden, but no one wanted to be there.

Especially when bullies came to the playground.

I knew he was standing behind me long before I heard him start counting the finished, shiny shoes in front of me. He smelled like spiced meat and car oil, which already was an unsettling combination before a whiff of cigarette smoke was added to the mix. I tried to straighten my back under the weight of his gaze, but it felt like he had taken two fists and dug the knuckles deep between my shoulder blades.

"Fifteen, sixteen, seventeen . . ." How was it that they could make mere numbers sound sharp?

At Thurmond, we weren't allow to touch one another, and we were beyond forbidden to touch one of the PSFs, but it didn't mean that they couldn't touch us. The man took two steps forward; his boots—exactly like the ones on the table—nudged the back of my standard white slip-ons. When I didn't respond, he snuck an arm past my shoulder, on the pretense of sorting through my work, and pressed me into his chest. *Shrink*, I told myself, curling my spine down, bending my face to the task in front of me, *shrink and disappear*.

"Worthless," I heard the PSF grunt behind me. His body was letting off enough heat to warm the entire building. "You're doing this all wrong. Look—*watch*, girl!"

I got my first real glance at him out of the corner of my eye as he ripped the polish-stained cloth out of my hand and moved to my side. He was short, only an inch or two taller than me, with a stubby nose, and cheeks that seemed to flap every time he took a breath.

"Like *this*," he was saying, swiping at the boot he had taken. "*Look* at me!"

A trick. We weren't supposed to look them directly in the eyes, either.

I heard a few chuckles around me—not from the girls, but from more PSFs gathered at his back.

It felt like I was boiling from the inside out. It was December, and the Factory couldn't have been warmer than forty degrees, but lines of sweat were racing down the curves of my cheeks, and I felt a hard, stiff cough welling up in my throat.

There was a light touch at my side. Sam couldn't look up from her own work, but I saw her eyes slide over to me, trying to assess the situation. A wave of furious red was making its way up from her throat to her face, and I could only imagine the kinds of words she was holding back. Her bony elbow brushed against mine again, as if to remind me that she was still there.

Then, with agonizing slowness, I felt the same PSF move behind me again, brushing my shoulder and arm with his own as he gently deposited the boot back on the table in front of me.

"These boots," he said in a low, purring voice as he tapped the plastic bin containing all of my finished work. "Did you lace them?"

If I hadn't known what kind of punishment I'd get for it, I would have burst out into tears. I felt more stupid and ashamed the longer I stood there, but I couldn't say anything. I couldn't move. My tongue had swelled up to twice its usual size behind my clenched teeth. The thoughts buzzing around my head were light and edged with a strange milky quality. My eyes could barely focus now.

More snickers from behind us.

"The laces are all wrong." His other arm wrapped around my left side, until there wasn't an inch of his body that wasn't pressed up against mine. Something new rose in my throat, and it tasted strongly of acid.

The tables around us had gone completely quiet and still.

My silence only egged him on. With no warning, he picked up the bin of boots and flipped it over, so dozens of boots scattered across the length of the table with a terrible amount of noise. Now everyone in the Factory was looking. Everyone saw me, thrust out into the light.

"Wrong, wrong, wrong, wrong, *wrong!*" he sang out, knocking the boots around. But they weren't. They were

32

perfect. They were just boots, but I knew whose feet would slide into them. I knew better than to screw it up. "Are you as deaf as you are dumb, Green?"

And then, clear as day, low as thunder, I heard Sam say, "That was my bin."

And all I could think was *No. Oh no.*

I felt the PSF shift behind me, pull back in surprise. They always acted this way—surprised that we remembered how to use words, and use them against them.

"What did you say?" he barked.

I could see the insult rising to her lips. She was rolling it around on her tongue like a piece of hard lemon candy. "You heard me. Or did inhaling that polish kill whatever helpless brain cells you had left?"

I knew what she wanted when she looked over at me. I knew what she was waiting for. It was exactly what she had just given me: backup.

I hung back a step, crossing my arms over my stomach. *Don't do it*, I told myself. *Don't. She can handle it.* Sam had nothing to hide, and she was brave—but every time she did this, every time she stood up for me and I shrunk back in fear, it felt like I was betraying her. Once again, my voice was locked away behind layers of caution and fear. If they were to look into my file, if they were to see the blanks there and start looking into filling them, no punishment they'd give Sam would *ever* compare to the one they'd give me.

That was what I told myself, at least.

The right side of the guy's lips inched up, turning a grim line into a mocking smirk. "We've got a live one."

Come on, come on, *Ruby.* It was all in the tilt of her head and the tightness of her shoulders. She didn't understand what would happen to me. I wasn't brave like she was.

But I wanted to be. I so, so wanted to be.

I can't. I didn't have to say the words aloud. She read it easily enough on my face. I saw the realization come together behind her eyes, even before the PSF stepped forward and took her arm, yanking her away from the table, and from me.

Turn around, I begged. Her blond ponytail was swinging with each step, rising above the shoulders of the PSFs escorting her out. *Turn around.* I needed her to see how sorry I was, to understand the clenching in my chest and the nausea in my stomach had nothing to do with the fever. Every single desperate thought that ran through my head made me feel sick with disgust. The eyes that had been on me lifted two by two, and the soldier never came back to finish his personal brand of torment. There was no one left to see me cry; I had learned to do it silently, without any fuss, years ago. They had no reason to so much as look my way again. I was back in the long shadow Sam had left behind.

The punishment for speaking out of turn was a day's worth of isolation, handcuffed to one of the gateposts in the Garden regardless of the temperature or the weather. I'd seen kids sitting in a mound of snow, blue in the face, and without a single blanket to cover them. Even more sunburned, covered in mud, or trying to scratch patches of bug bites with their free hands. Unsurprisingly, the punishment for talking back to a PSF or camp controller was the same, only you also weren't given food and, sometimes, not even water.

The punishment for a repeat offense was something so terrible, Sam wouldn't or couldn't talk about it when she finally returned to our cabin two days later. She came in, wet and shaking from the winter rain, looking like she had slept no more than I had. I slid off my bunk and was on my feet, rushing to her side, before she had even made it half-way across the cabin.

My hand slipped around her arm, but she pulled away, her jaw clenched in a way that made her look almost fero-cious. Her cheeks and nose had been wind-whipped to a bright red, but she didn't have any bruises or cuts. Her eyes weren't even swollen from crying, like mine were. There was a subtle limp to her walk, maybe, but if I hadn't known what had happened, I would have just assumed she was coming in from a long afternoon of working in the Garden.

"Sam," I said, hating the way my voice shook. She didn't stop or deign to look at me until we were by our bunks, and she had one fist curled in her bedsheets, ready to pull herself up to the top bed.

"Say something, please," I begged.

"You stood there." Sam's voice was low and rough, like she hadn't used it for days.

"You shouldn't have—"

Her chin came down to rest against her chest. Long, tan-gled masses of hair fell over her shoulders and cheeks, hiding her expression. I felt it then—the way that the hold I had on her had suddenly sprung free. I had the strangest sensation of float-ing, of drifting farther and farther away with nothing and no one to cling to. I was standing right beside her, but the distance between us had split into the kind of canyon I couldn't jump across.

"You're right," Sam said, finally. "I shouldn't have." She drew in a shuddering breath. "But then, what would have happened to you? You would have just stood there, and let him do *that*, and you wouldn't have defended yourself at all."

And then she was looking at me, and all I wanted was for her to turn away again. Her eyes flashed, darker than I had ever seen before.

"They can say horrible things, hurt you, but you never fight back—and I know, Ruby, *I know*, that's just how you are, but sometimes I wonder if you even care. Why can't you stand up for yourself, just once?"

Her voice was barely above a whisper, but the ragged quality to it made me think she was either going to scream or burst out into hysterical tears. I glanced down to where her hands were tugging at the edges of her shorts, moving so fast and frantic that I almost didn't see the angry red marks that circled her wrists.

"Sam—Samantha—"

"I want—" She swallowed, hard. Her tears caught in her eyelashes, but didn't fall. "I want to be alone now. Just for a while."

I shouldn't have reached for her, not with fever and exhaustion pressing down on me. Not while I was trembling with a bone-deep hate for myself. But I thought, then, that if I could tell her the truth, if I could explain, she wouldn't look at me that way again. She would know that the last thing—the absolute *last* thing—I ever wanted was for her to be hurt because of me. She was the only thing I had here.

But the second my fingers touched her shoulder, the world dropped out from under me. I felt a fire start at the ends of my hair and burn its way through my skull. The fever I thought I had kicked suddenly painted the world a fuzzy shade of gray. I was seeing Sam's blank face, and she was gone, replaced by white-hot memories that didn't belong to me—a whiteboard at school filled with math problems, a golden retriever digging in a garden, the world rising and falling from the perspective of a swing, the roots of the vegetables in the Garden being pulled free, the brick wall at the back of the Mess Hall against my face as another fist swung down toward me—a quick assault from every side, like a series of camera flashes.

And when I finally came back to myself, we were still staring at each other. For a second, I thought I saw my horrified face reflected in her dark, glassy eyes. Sam wasn't looking at me; she didn't seem to be looking at anything beyond the dust floating lazy and free through the air to my right. I knew that blank look. I'd seen my mother wear it years before.

"Are you new here?" she demanded, suddenly defensive and startled. Her eyes flicked down from my face to my bony knees, then back up again. She sucked in a deep breath, as if coming up for air after a long time beneath dark waters. "Do you have a name at least?"

"Ruby," I whispered. It was the last word I spoke for nearly a year.

FOUR

I WOKE TO COLD WATER AND A WOMAN'S SOFT VOICE. "You're all right," she was saying. "You'll be fine." I'm not sure who she thought she was fooling with her sweet little B.S., but it wasn't me.

I let her bring the wet towel up to my face again, savoring her warmth as she leaned in closer. She smelled of rosemary and past things. For a second, just one, her hand came to rest against mine, and it was almost more than I could take.

I wasn't at home, and this woman wasn't my mother. I started gasping, desperate to keep everything inside me. I couldn't cry, not in front of her, or any of the other adults. I wouldn't give them the pleasure.

"Are you still in pain?"

The only reason I opened my eyes was because she pulled them open herself. One at a time, shining an intense light in each. I tried to throw my hands up to shield them, but they

had strapped me down in Velcro cuffs. Fighting against the restraints was pointless.

The woman clucked her tongue and stepped back, taking her flowery fragrance with her. The smell of antiseptic and peroxide flooded the air, and I knew exactly where I was.

The sounds of Thurmond's infirmary faded in and out in uneven waves. Some kid crying out in pain, boots clipping against the white tile floors, the creak of wheelchair wheels . . . I felt like I was standing above a tunnel with my ear to the ground, listening to the hum of cars passing beneath me.

"Ruby?"

The woman was wearing blue scrubs and a white coat. With her pale skin and white-blond hair she all but disappeared into the thin curtain that had been pulled around my bed. She caught me staring and smiled, so wide and so pretty.

The woman was the youngest doctor I'd ever seen in Thurmond—though admittedly I could count my trips to the Infirmary on one hand. I went once for the stomach flu and dehydration after what Sam called my Gut Puking Spectacular, and once for a sprained wrist. Both times I felt far worse after being groped by a pair of wrinkled hands than I had before I'd come in. Nothing cures a cold faster than the thought of an old perv wearing a cologne of alcohol and lemon hand soap.

This woman—she was unreal. Everything about her.

"My name is Dr. Begbie. I'm a volunteer with the Leda Corporation."

39

I nodded, glancing at the gold swan insignia on her coat pocket.

She leaned in closer. "We're a big medical company that does research and sends doctors in to help care for you guys at the camps. If it makes you feel more comfortable, you're more than welcome to call me Cate and leave off the doctor business."

Sure I was. I stared at the hand she extended toward me. Silence hung between us, punctuated by the pounding in my head. After an awkward moment, Dr. Begbie stuffed her hand back into the pocket of her lab coat, but not before letting it stray over the restraint securing my left hand to the bed's guardrail.

"Do you know why you're here, Ruby? Do you remember what happened?"

Before or after the Tower tried to fry my brain? But I couldn't say it out loud. When it came to the adults, it was better not to talk. They had a way of hearing one thing and processing it as something else. No reason to give them an excuse to hurt you.

It had been eight months since I'd last used my voice. I wasn't sure I even remembered how.

The doctor somehow guessed the question I was barely holding back at the tip of my tongue. "They turned on the Calm Control after a fight broke out in the Mess Hall. It seems that things got . . . a bit out of hand."

That was an understatement. The White Noise—Calm Control, the higher powers called it—was used to settle us down, so to speak, while it did absolutely nothing to them.

40

It was like a dog whistle, the pitch tuned perfectly so only our freak brains could pick it up and process it.

They turned it on for a whole host of reasons, sometimes for things as small as a kid accidentally using their ability, or to stamp out unruliness in one of the cabins. But in both of those instances, they would have piped the noise directly into whatever building the kids were in. If they used it across the camp, blasting it over the speakers for us all to hear, then things must have gotten *really* out of hand. They must have been worried that there was a spark that would have set the rest of us ablaze.

There was no hint of hesitation on Dr. Begbie's face as she unstrapped my wrists and ankles. The towel she had been using to clean my face hung limp on the guardrail, dripping water. Bright red splotches soaked through its white fabric.

I reached up and touched my mouth, my cheeks, my nose. When I pulled my fingers away, I was only half-surprised to see that they were coated with dark blood. It was crusted between my nostrils and lips, as if someone had clocked me right in the honker.

Trying to sit up was the worst idea that crossed my mind. My chest screamed in pain, and I was flat on my back again before I even registered falling. Dr. Begbie was beside me in an instant, cranking the metal bed into an upright position.

"You have some bruised ribs," she said.

I tried to take a deep breath, but my chest was too tight to inhale anything more than a choked gasp. She must not have noticed because she was looking at me with those kind eyes again, saying, "May I ask a few questions?"

41

The fact that she asked my permission was amazing in and of itself. I studied her, searching for the hatred buried beneath the layer of pleasantness on her face, the fear hovering in her soft eyes, the disgust caught in the corner of her smile. Nothing. Not even annoyance.

Some poor kid started to throw up in the stall to my right; I could see his dark outline like a shadow against the curtain. There was no one sitting with *him*, no one holding *his* hand. Just him and his bowl of puke. And here I was, my heart skipping beats out of fear that the fairy-tale princess sitting next to me was going to have me put down like a rabid dog. She didn't know what I was—she couldn't have known.

You're being paranoid, I told myself. *Get a grip.*

Dr. Begbie pulled a pen out of her messy bun. "Ruby, when they turned on the Calm Control, do you remember falling forward and hitting your face?"

"No," I said. "I was . . . already on the ground." I didn't know how much to tell her. The smile on her face stretched, and there was something . . . smug about it.

"Do you usually experience this much pain and bleeding from the Calm Control?"

Suddenly, the pain in my chest had nothing to do with my ribs.

"I'll take that as a no."

I couldn't see what she was writing, only that her hand and pen were flying across the paper, scribbling as though her life depended on it.

I always took the White Noise harder than the other girls in my cabin. But blood? Never.

Dr. Begbie was humming lightly under her breath as she wrote, some song that I thought might have been by the Rolling Stones.

She's with the camp controllers, I reminded myself. She is one of them.

But . . . in another world, she might not have been. Even though she was wearing the scrubs and white coat, Dr. Begbie didn't look much older than I was. She had a young face, and it was probably a curse to her in the outside world.

I had always thought that people born before Generation Freak were the lucky ones. They lived without fear of what would happen when they stepped over the border between childhood and adolescence. As far as I knew, if you were older than thirteen when they started rounding kids up, you were home free—you got to pass Freak Camp on the board game of life and head straight on to Normalville. But looking at Dr. Begbie now, seeing the deep lines carved in her face that no one in their twenties should have had, I wasn't so sure they had gotten off scot-free. They'd gotten a better deal than what we ended up with, though.

Abilities. Powers that defied explanation, mental talents so freakish, doctors and scientists reclassified our entire generation as *Psi*. We were no longer human. Our brains broke that mold.

"I see from your chart that you were classified as 'abnormal intelligence' in sorting," Dr. Begbie said after a while. "The scientist that sorted you—did he run you through all of the tests?"

Something very cold coiled in my stomach. I might not have understood a great many things about the world, I might have only had a fourth grader's education, but I could tell when someone was trying to fish around for information. The PSFs had switched over to outright scare tactics years ago, but there was a time when all of their questioning had been done in soft voices. Fake sympathy reeked like bad breath.

Does she know? Maybe she ran a few tests while I was unconscious, and scanned my brain, or tested my blood, or something. My fingers curled one by one until both hands were tight fists. I tried to work the line of thought through, but I kept getting caught on the possibility. Fear made things hazy and light.

Her question hung in the air, suspended somewhere between truth and lie.

The clip of boots against the pristine tile forced my eyes up, away from the doctor's face. Each step was a warning, and I knew they were coming before Dr. Begbie turned her head. She moved to push herself away from the bed, but I didn't let her. I don't know what possessed me, but I grabbed her wrist, the list of punishments for touching an authority figure running through my head like a skipping CD, each scratch sharper than the next.

We weren't supposed to touch anyone, not even each other.

"It was different this time," I whispered, the words aching in my throat. My voice sounded different to my ears. Weak.

44

Dr. Begbie only had enough time to nod. The slightest movement, almost imperceptible, before a hand ripped back the curtain.

I had seen this Psi Special Forces officer before—Sam called him the Grinch, because he looked like he had stepped straight out of the movie, save for no green skin.

The Grinch cast one look at me, his top lip peeling back in annoyance, before waving the doctor forward. She blew out a sigh and set her clipboard down on my lap.

"Thank you, Ruby," she said. "If your pain gets any worse, call for help, okay?"

Was she on drugs? Who was going to help—the kid throwing up his stomach lining next door?

I nodded anyway, watching her turn to go. The last glimpse I had of her was her hand dragging the curtain back around. It was nice of her to give me privacy, but a little naive, given the black cameras hanging down between the beds.

The bulbs were installed all over Thurmond, lidless eyes always watching, never blinking. There were two cameras in our cabin alone, one on each end of the room, as well as one outside the door. It seemed like overkill, but when I was first brought to camp, there were so few of us that they really could watch us all day, every day, until their brains were ready to burst from boredom.

You had to squint to see it, but a tiny red light inside the black eye was the only clue that the camera had zeroed in on you. Over the years, as more and more kids were brought into Thurmond on the old school buses, Sam and I began to notice that the cameras in our cabin no longer had the blinking red lights—not every day. Same went for the cameras in the laundry, the Washrooms, and the Mess Hall. I guess with three thousand kids spread out over a square mile, it was impossible to watch everyone all the time.

Still, they watched enough to put the fear of God in us. You had a better-than-average chance of being busted if you practiced your abilities, even under the cover of darkness.

Those blinking lights were the exact same shade as the blood-red band the PSFs wore around the upper part of their right arm. The Ψ symbol was stitched on the crimson fabric, indicating their unfortunate role as caretakers of the country's freak children.

The camera above my bed had no red light. The relief that came over me at the realization actually made the air taste sweet. For just a moment, I was alone and unobserved. At Thurmond, that was an almost unheard-of luxury.

Dr. Begbie—Cate—hadn't completely closed the curtain. When another doctor hurried past, the thin white fabric pulled back farther, allowing a familiar flash of blue to catch my eye. The portrait of a young boy, no more than twelve years old, stared back at me. His hair was the same shade as mine—deep brown, nearly black—but where my eyes were pale green, his were dark enough to burn from a distance. He was smiling, as always, his hands clasped in his lap, his dark school uniform without a wrinkle. Clancy Gray, Thurmond's first inmate.

There were at least two framed pictures of him in the Mess Hall, one in the kitchen, several nailed outside of the

Green outhouses. It was easier to remember his face than it was to remember my mom's.

I forced myself to look away from his proud, unwavering grin. He may have gotten out, but the rest of us were still here.

As I tried to readjust my body, I knocked Dr. Begbie's clipboard off my lap and into the crook of my left arm.

I knew there was a chance that they were watching, but I didn't care. Not then, when I had answers inches away from my fingertips. Why had she left it there, right below my nose, if she hadn't wanted me to see it? Why hadn't she taken it with her, like all of the other doctors would have done?

What was different about the White Noise?

What did they figure out?

The fluorescent lights above me were exposed, glowing in the shape of long, angry bones. They gave off a hum, sounding more and more like a cloud of flies swirling around my ears. It only got worse as I flipped the clipboard over.

It wasn't my medical history.

It wasn't my current injuries, or lack thereof.

It wasn't my answers to Dr. Begbie's questions.

It was a note, and it read: *New CC was testing for undetected Ys, Os, Rs. Your bad reaction means that they know you aren't G. Unless you do exactly as I say, they will kill you tomorrow.*

My hands were shaking. I had to set the clipboard down in my lap to read the rest.

I can get you out. Take the two pills under this note before bed, but don't let the PSFs see you. If you don't, will keep your secret, but I can't protect you while you're in here. Destroy this.

It was signed, *A friend, if you'd like.*

I read the note one more time before I ripped it out from under the metal clip and shoved it in my mouth. It tasted like the bread they served us for lunch.

The pills were in a tiny clear bag clipped on top of my real medical chart. Scrawled in Dr. Begbie's dismal handwriting was the note, *Subject 3285 hit her head against the ground and lost consciousness. Nose was fractured when Subject 3286 elbowed her. Possible concussion.*

My eyes were itching to look up, to peer into the black eye of the camera, but I didn't let myself. I took the pills and shoved them into the standard-issue sports bra the camp controllers had bestowed on us when they realized fifteen hundred teenage girls weren't going to stay twelve and flat forever. I didn't know what I was doing; I really didn't. My heart was racing so fast that for a moment I couldn't get any air.

Why had Dr. Begbie done this to me? She knew I wasn't Green, but she had covered it up, lied on the report—was this just a trick? To see if I would incriminate myself?

I pressed my face into my hands. The packet of pills burned against my skin.

. . . they will kill you tomorrow.

Why did they even bother to wait? Why not take me out to the buses and shoot me now? Isn't that what they

48

did with the others? The Yellows, Oranges, and Reds? They killed them, because they were too dangerous.

I am too dangerous.

I didn't know how to use my abilities. I wasn't like the other Oranges, who could spout off commands or slip nasty little thoughts into other people's minds. I had all of the power, and none of the control—all of the pain, and none of the benefits.

From what I'd been able to figure out, I had to touch someone for my abilities to take hold, and even then . . . it was more like I was *glimpsing* their thoughts, rather than screwing with them. I'd never tried to push a thought into someone else's head, and it wasn't like I'd had the opportunity or the desire to try. Every slip of the mind, intentional or not, left my head a jumble of thoughts and images, words and pain. It took hours to feel like myself again.

Imagine someone reaching straight into your chest, past the bones and blood and guts, and taking a nice firm hold on your spinal cord. Now imagine that they start shaking you so fast the world starts bulging and buckling under you. Imagine not being able to figure out later if the thought in your head is really yours or an unintentional keepsake from someone else's mind. Imagine the guilt of knowing you saw someone's deepest, darkest fear or secret; imagine having to face them the next morning and pretend you didn't see how their father used to hit them, the bright pink dress they wore to their fifth birthday party, their fantasies about this boy or that girl, and the neighborhood animals they used to kill for fun.

49

And then imagine the soul-crushing migraine that always follows, lasting anywhere between a few hours and a few days. *That* was what it was like. *That* was why I tried to avoid my mind so much as brushing up against someone else's at all costs. I knew the consequences. All of them.

And now I knew for certain what would happen if they found me out.

I flipped the clipboard over on my lap, and just in time. The same PSF soldier was back at my curtain again, ripping it aside.

"You'll be returning to your cabin now," he said. "Come with me."

My cabin? I searched his face for any sign of a lie, but saw nothing except the usual annoyance. A nod was the only thing I could muster. My entire body was one earthquake of dread, and the moment my feet touched the ground, the back of my head uncorked. Everything spilled out, every thought, fear, and image. I collapsed against the guardrail, holding on tight to consciousness.

The black spots were still gliding in front of my eyes when the PSF barked out, "Hurry it up! Don't think you get to stay another night here just by putting on an act."

Despite the harsh words, I saw the slightest flicker of fear in his face. That moment, the shift from fear to fury, could have summed up the feelings of every soldier at Thurmond. We'd heard rumors that service in the military was no longer voluntary, that everyone between the ages of twenty-two and forty had to serve—most of them in the army's new Psi branch.

I gritted my teeth. The whole wide world spun under me, trying to pull me back down to its dark center. The PSF's words returned to me.

Another night? I thought. How long have I been here?

Still woozy, I followed the soldier into the hallway. The Infirmary was only two stories, small ones. The ceiling crept down so low that even I felt like I was in danger of scraping the top of my head on the doorframes. The treatment beds were on the first floor, but the second was reserved for kids needing to go into what we called Time Out. Sometimes they had something the rest of us could catch, but mostly it was for kids that went completely off their rocker, broken brains broken further by Thurmond.

I tried to stay focused on the movement of the PSF's shoulder blades beneath his black uniform, but it was difficult when most of the curtains had been left open for anyone to peer inside. Most I could ignore, or cast only a brief glance their way, but the second to last stall before the exit doors . . .

My feet slowed of their own accord, giving my lungs time to breathe in the scent of rosemary.

I could hear Dr. Begbie's gentle voice as she spoke to another kid in Green. I recognized him—his cabin was directly across from mine. Matthew? Maybe Max? All I knew was that there was blood on his face, too. Crusted around his nose and eyes, smearing across his checks. A stone dropped in my stomach. Had this Green been marked too? Was Dr. Begbie cutting him the same deal? I couldn't have been the only one to figure out how to dodge the sorting system— who to influence, when to lie.

51

Maybe he and I were the same color beneath our skin.

And maybe we would both be dead by tomorrow.

"Keep up!" the PSF snapped. He didn't try to hide his annoyance as I hobbled after him, but he didn't need to worry; you couldn't have paid me to stay in the Infirmary, not while I was conscious. Not even with the new threat hanging over my head. I knew what they used to do there.

I knew what was under the layers of white paint.

The earliest kids they had brought in, the first guinea pigs, had been subjected to a whole array of electroshock and brain-chop-shop terrors. Stories were passed around camp with sick, almost holy reverence. The scientists were looking for ways to strip the kids' abilities—"rehabilitate" them—but they had mostly just stripped their will to live. The ones who made it out were given warden positions when the first small wave of kids was brought to camp. It was a strange bit of luck and timing that I had come in during the second wave. Each wave grew larger and larger as the camp expanded, until, three years ago, they'd run out of space completely. There were no new buses after that.

I still wasn't moving fast enough for the soldier. He pushed me forward into the hall of mirrors. The exit sign cast its gory light over us; the PSF shoved me again, harder, and smiled when I fell. Anger flooded through me, cutting through the lingering pain in my limbs and any fear I had that he was taking me out somewhere in order to finish the job.

Soon we were standing outside, breathing in the damp spring air. I took a lungful of misty rain, and swallowed the bitterness down. I needed to think. Assess. If he was taking me outside to be shot, and was on his own, I could easily overpower him. That wasn't the issue. But in fact, I had no way of slipping past the electric fence—and no idea where the hell I was.

When they had brought me to Thurmond, the familiarity of the scenery had been more a comfort than a painful reminder. West Virginia and Virginia aren't all that different, even though Virginians would have you believe otherwise. Same trees, same sky, same awful weather—I was either drenched in rain or sticky with humidity. Anyway, it might not have been West Virginia at all. But a girl in my cabin swore up and down that she had seen a WELCOME TO WEST VIRGINIA sign on her ride in, so that was the theory we were working with.

The PSF had slowed considerably, matching my pathetic pace. He fumbled once or twice against the muddy grass, nearly tripping over himself in full view of the soldiers high above on the Control Tower.

The moment the Tower came into view, a whole new weight added itself to the ball and chain of terror I was dragging behind me. The building itself wasn't that imposing; it was only called the Tower because it stuck up like a broken finger in a sea of one-story wooden shacks arranged in rings. The electric fence was the outer ring, protecting the world from us freaks. Cabins of Greens made up the next two rings. Blues, the next two rings. Before they were taken

53

away, the few Reds and Oranges lived in the next rings. They'd been closest to the Tower—better, the controllers thought, to keep an eye on them. But after a Red had blown up his cabin, they moved the Reds farther away, using the Greens as a buffer in case any of the real threats tried to make a run for the fence.

Number of escape attempts?

Five.

Number of *successful* escape attempts?

Zero.

I don't know of one Blue or Green who had ever tried to make a run for it. When kids did stage desperate, pathetic breakouts, it had been in small groups of Reds, Oranges, and Yellows. Once caught, they never came back.

But that was in the early days, when we had had more interaction with the other colors, and before they shuffled us around. The empty Red, Orange, and Yellow cabins became Blue cabins, and newly arriving Greens, the biggest group of all, filled the old Blue ones. The camp grew so large that the controllers staggered our schedules, so we ate by color and gender—and even then, it was still a tight squeeze fitting everyone at the tables. I hadn't seen a boy my own age up close in years.

I didn't start breathing again until the Tower was at our backs and it was clear, beyond a shadow of a doubt, where we were headed.

Thank you, I thought, to no one in particular. The relief lodged in my throat like a stone.

We reached Cabin 27 a few minutes later. The PSF walked me to the door and pointed to the spigot just to the left of it.

I nodded, and used the cold water to wash the blood off my face. He waited silently, but not patiently. After a few seconds, I felt his hand grab the back of my shirt and yank me up. Using his other hand, he slid his access card through the lock on our door.

Ashley, one of the older girls in my cabin, shoved the door open the rest of the way with her shoulder. She took my arm in one hand and nodded in the direction of the PSF. That seemed to be enough for him. Without another word, he took off down the path.

"Jesus Christ!" she hissed as she dragged me inside. "They couldn't have kept you another night? Oh no, they have to send you back early—is that *blood*?"

I waved her hands away, but Ashley pushed past the others and brushed my long, dark hair over my shoulder. At first I didn't understand why she was looking at me like that—with wide eyes, rimmed with a raw pink. She sucked her bottom lip in between her teeth.

"I really . . . thought you were . . ." We were still standing by the door, but I could feel the chill that had taken over the cabin. It settled over my skin like cold silk.

Ashley had been around these parts for far too long to really crack, but I was still surprised to see her so frazzled and at a loss for what to say. She and a few other girls were honorary leaders of our sad, mismatched group, nominated mostly because they hit certain bodily milestones before the rest of us, and could explain what was happening to us without laughing in our faces.

I offered a weak smile and a shrug, suddenly without words again. But she didn't look convinced, and she didn't let go of my arm. The cabin was dark and damp, the usual smell of mold clung to every surface, but I would have taken that over the Infirmary's clean, sterile stench any day.

"Let me . . ." Ashley took a deep breath. "Let me know if you're not, got it?"

And what would you be able to do about it? I wanted to ask. Instead, I turned to the back left corner of our cramped cabin. Whispers and stares followed my zigzagging path around the rows of bunk beds. The pills tucked tight against my chest felt like they were on fire.

"—she was gone," I heard someone say.

Vanessa, who slept on the bottom bunk to the right of mine, had snuck up to Sam's bed. When I came into view, they stopped mid-conversation to stare down at me. Eyes wide, mouths wider.

The sight of them together was still sickening to me, even after a year. How many days and nights had I spent perched up there with Sam, steadfastly ignoring Vanessa's attempts to drag us into some stupid, pointless conversation?

Sam's best-friend slot had been vacant for less than two hours when Vanessa had slithered in—and not a day went by that Vanessa didn't remind me of that.

"What . . ." Sam leaned over the edge of her bed. She didn't look haughty or hostile, the way she usually did. She looked . . . concerned? Curious? "What happened to you?"

I shook my head, my chest tight with all the things I wanted to say.

Vanessa let out a sharp laugh. "Nice, real nice. And you wonder why she doesn't want to be your friend anymore?"

"I don't . . ." Sam mumbled. "Whatever."

Sometimes I wondered if there was a part of Sam that remembered not just me, but the person she used to be before I ruined her. Amazing how I had managed to erase every good part of Sam—or at least, all the parts I loved. One touch, and she was gone.

A few girls asked me what had happened between the two of us. Most, I think, assumed Sam was being cruel when she claimed that we had never, ever been friends and never would be. I tried to play it off with shrugs—but Sam was the only thing that had made Thurmond bearable. Without her, it was no life at all.

No life at all.

I fingered the packet of pills.

Our cabin was brown on brown on brown. The only color was the white of our sheets, and most of those had aged to an ugly yellow. There were no shelves of books, no posters, no pictures. Just us.

I crawled onto my low bunk, dropping face-first into the worn sheets. I breathed in their familiar scent—bleach, sweat, and something distinctly earthy—and tried not to listen to the conversation above me.

A part of me had been waiting, I think—desperate to see if I could fix what I had done to my friend. But it was done. It was over, and she was gone, and the only one to blame was me. The best thing I could do for her was disappear; even if Dr. Begbie was playing me and they really

57

were going to get rid of me, they wouldn't connect us. They wouldn't question or punish Sam because they thought she had helped me hide, like they would if we had still been friends. There were over three thousand of us at Thurmond, and I was the last Orange—maybe in the entire world. Or one of two, if the boy in the Infirmary was like me. It had only been a matter of time before they found out the truth.

I was dangerous, and I knew what they did to the dangerous ones.

The camp routine ran itself through, as it always did, churning us through the Mess Hall for dinner, to the Washrooms, and back to the cabin for the night. The light was dim and fading outside, clinging to the first fringes of night.

"All right, kittens." Ashley's voice. "Ten minutes till lights-out. Whose turn is it?"

"Mine—should I just pick up from where we left off?" Rachel was on the other side of the room, but her squeaky voice carried well.

I could practically hear Ashley's eyes rolling. "Yes, Rachel. Isn't that what we always do?"

"Okay . . . so . . . so the princess? She was in her tower, and she was still really sad."

"Girl," Ashley cut in, "you're going to have to spice this up, or I'm skipping your boring ass and going to the next person."

"Okay," Rachel squeaked. I rolled over onto my side, trying to get a glimpse of her through the rows of bunk beds. "The princess was in terrible pain—terrible, terrible pain—"

"Oh God," was Ashley's only comment. "Next?"

Macey picked up the loose story threads the best she could. "While the princess was locked away in her tower, all she could think about was the prince."

I missed how the story ended, my eyelids too heavy to keep them open.

If there is a single thing I'll miss about Thurmond, I thought as I edged toward sleep, *it's this.* The quiet moments, when we were allowed to talk about forbidden things.

We had to find a way to amuse ourselves because we had no stories—no dreams, no future—other than the ones we created for ourselves.

I swallowed the two pills one at a time, the taste of chicken broth still on my tongue.

The cabin lights had been off for three hours, and Sam had been snoring for two. I unsealed the bag and dropped the little pills into my hand. The clear bag went back into my bra, and the first pill went into my mouth. It was warm from being so close to my skin for so long, which didn't make it any easier to swallow. I popped the next one in before I lost the nerve, and winced as it clawed its way down my throat.

And then, I waited.

FIVE

I DIDN'T REMEMBER FALLING ASLEEP; ONLY WAKING. Of course I did—my body was shaking so hard that I rolled right out of bed and hit my face against the next bunk over.

Vanessa must have jumped out of her skin with the sudden bang and movement of her bed, because I heard her say, "What the hell—*Ruby*? Is that you?"

I couldn't get up. I felt her hands on my face, and registered she was now screaming my name, not just whispering it.

"Oh my *God*!" someone said. It sounded like Sam, but I couldn't open my eyes.

"—emergency button!" Ashley's weight settled over my legs; I knew it was her, even as my brain came in and out of consciousness, and a white hot light was burning behind my eyelids. Someone shoved something in my mouth—rubber and hard. I could taste blood, but I wasn't sure if it had come from my tongue or my lips or . . .

Two pairs of hands lifted me from the ground, dropping me on some other surface. I still couldn't open my eyes; my chest was on fire. I couldn't stop shaking, and my limbs felt like they were caving in on themselves.

And then I smelled rosemary. I felt soft, cool hands pressing against my chest, then nothing at all.

Life came back to me in the form of a hard slap across the face.

"Ruby," someone said. "Come on, I know you can hear me. You have to wake up."

I cracked my eyes open, trying not to cringe as the light flooded in. A door opened and creaked shut somewhere nearby.

"Is that her?" a new voice asked. "Are you going to sedate her?"

"No, not this one," the first voice returned. I knew that voice. It was as sweet as it had been before, only this time it had a sharper edge. Dr. Begbie's hands came up beneath my arms and propped me up. "She's tough. She can handle it."

Something smelled *horrible*. Acidic and rotten all at once. My eyes flew open.

Dr. Begbie was kneeling beside me, waving something beneath my nose.

"What—?"

The other voice I had heard belonged to a young woman. She had dark brown hair and pale skin, but that was all that was remarkable about her. Not realizing I was watching

61

her, she stripped her blue scrubs off and threw them at Dr. Begbie.

I didn't know where we were. The room was small, filled with shelves of bottles and boxes, and I couldn't smell anything besides whatever it was Dr. Begbie had used to wake me.

"Put these on," Dr. Begbie said, pulling me to my feet whether my legs were ready or not. "Come *on*, Ruby, we've got to hurry."

My body felt heavy, cracking at all my joints. But I did as I was told, and pulled the scrubs over my uniform. While I was dressing, the other woman put her hands behind her back and waited as Dr. Begbie wrapped them together with thick silver duct tape. That finished, the doctor moved to tying the other woman's feet together.

"You're meeting them in Harvey. Make sure you take Route two-fifteen."

"I know, I know," Dr. Begbie said as she chewed off another piece of tape and placed it over the woman's mouth. "Good luck."

"What are you doing?" I asked. My throat was scratchy, and the skin around my mouth seemed to crack as I spoke. The doctor pulled my hair back, twisting it up into a messy bun that she secured with a rubber band. The other woman watched as her ID tags were dropped over my neck and Dr. Begbie put a surgical mask over my face.

"I'll explain everything once we're out, but we can't waste time. They'll be doing rounds in twenty minutes," she said. "You can't say anything, understand? Play along."

I nodded and let her push me outside of the dark room and into the dimmed hallway of the Infirmary. Once again, my legs seemed to be failing me, but the doctor took it all in stride. She looped one of my arms over her shoulder and supported most of my weight.

"We're moving," she muttered. "Return the cameras to their normal feeds."

I looked over, but she wasn't talking to me. She was whispering to her gold swan pin.

"Not a word," she reminded me as we turned down another long hallway. We were moving so fast that we rustled the white curtains of the examination stalls as we passed them. The PSFs were black blurs as they stepped out of our way.

"Sorry, sorry!" Dr. Begbie called after us. "I've got to get this one home."

I kept my eyes on the straight lines of tile passing under my feet. My head was still spinning so badly that I didn't realize we were heading outside until I heard the beep of the doctor's card passing through the lock swipe and felt the first drops of cool rain hit my scalp.

They kept the camp's enormous stadium lights on at all hours of the night; the lights stood like giants across the camp, but all they reminded me of were night football games, the smell of fresh cut grass, and the back of my dad's red Spartan sweater as he yelled for his old high school's team to *run some damn offense* at the top of his lungs.

It was a short walk and stumble from the back of the Infirmary to the pebbled parking lot. I actually wasn't sure if

I was hallucinating or not—my sight went in and out of focus, but it was impossible to miss the sound of crunching gravel and the voice that yelled, "Everything okay over there?"

I felt, rather than saw, Dr. Begbie tense. I tried to keep moving, to use her shoulder to prop myself up, but my legs just weren't working anymore.

When I opened my eyes again, I was sitting up, staring at the standard-issue boots of a PSF soldier. He knelt down in front of me. Dr. Begbie was saying something to him, her voice as calm as the first time I had spoken to her.

"—so sick, I offered to drive her home. I put the mask on her to make sure she didn't give the bug to anyone else."

The soldier's voice became clearer. "I hate that we always get sick from these kids."

"Would you mind helping me walk her over to my Jeep?" Dr. Begbie asked.

"If she's sick . . ."

"It'll just take a minute," the doctor interrupted. "And I promise that if you have so much as even the sniffles tomorrow, I'll nurse you back to health myself."

That was the voice I recognized—so sweet that it sounded like little bells. The soldier chuckled, but I felt him lift me up all the same. I tried not to lean against him, to grit my teeth against the jarring motion, but I could barely keep my head from rolling back.

"Front seat?" he asked.

Dr. Begbie was about to respond when the PSF's radio crackled to life. *"Control has you on camera. Do you need assistance?"*

He waited until Dr. Begbie had opened the front passenger side door, and he set me down on the seat before replying. "Everything clear. Doctor . . ." He took my tags in hand, lifting them off my chest. "Dr. Rogers has the virus that's been going around. Doctor . . ."

"Begbie," came the quick reply. She slid into the driver's seat and slammed the door shut behind her. I glanced over, watching as she fumbled to get the key in the ignition. It was the first time I noticed her hands shaking.

"Dr. Begbie is driving her home for the night. Dr. Rogers's car will be here overnight—please inform the morning guards when they do their tally."

"Roger that. Tell them to head straight for the gate. I'll notify the watch patrol to wave them through."

The Jeep sputtered to life in a series of grinding protests. I looked out through the windshield, to the electric fence and the dark, familiar forest behind it. Dr. Begbie reached over to fasten my seat belt.

"Man, she's *out* of it." The PSF was back, leaning against Dr. Begbie's window.

"I did give her some pretty strong stuff." Dr. Begbie laughed. I felt my chest clench.

"So about tomorrow—"

"Come by and say hello, okay?" Dr. Begbie said. "I have a break around three."

She didn't give him a chance to reply. The tires spun against the gravel and the windshield wipers squealed to life. Dr. Begbie rolled up her window with a friendly wave, using her other hand to steer the car back and pull out of the parking space. The little green numbers on the dashboard read 2:45 a.m.

"Try to cover your face as much as possible," she muttered before flicking on the radio. I didn't recognize the song, but I recognized David Gilmour's voice, and the ebb and flow of Pink Floyd's synthesizers.

She turned the volume down, taking a deep breath as she turned out of the lot. Her fingers tapped out a nervous rhythm on the steering wheel.

"Come on, come on," she whispered, glancing down at the clock again. There was a line of two cars in front of us, each waved forward with agonizing slowness. I thought she was going to crawl out of her skin by the time the last car pulled forward into the night.

Dr. Begbie hit the gas too hard and the Jeep lurched forward. The seat belt snapped into a locked position when she slammed on the brakes, knocking the air out of my chest.

She rolled the window down, but I was too tired to be afraid. I pressed my hand over my eyes and sucked in a deep breath. The surgical mask brushed against my lips.

"I'm taking Dr. Rogers home. Let me just get her passes—"

"It's fine. I have you on the schedule for tomorrow at three p.m., is that correct?"

"Yes. Thank you. Please indicate Dr. Rogers will not be in."

"Understood."

I was too tired to try to control my brain's wandering fingers. When Dr. Begbie touched me again, brushing the hair out of my face, an image bloomed to life behind my eyes. A dark-haired man, smiling broadly, with his arms around Dr. Begbie, spinning her, and spinning her, and spinning her, until I could hear her delighted laughter in my ears.

Cate cracked our windows, and the air rushing by brought in the scent of rain and carried me quickly into sleep.

SIX

I<small>T WAS STILL DARK OUT WHEN</small> I <small>OPENED MY EYES.</small>

The AC blew through the vents, batting at the little yellow cardboard tree hanging down from the rearview mirror. Its vanilla fragrance was sickeningly sweet and so overwhelming that it turned my empty stomach. Mick Jagger crooned next to my ear, singing about war and peace and shelter—those kinds of lies. I tried to turn my face away from wherever the song was escaping from, but I only managed to smack my nose against the window and strain my neck.

I sat straight up and almost hanged myself on the gray seat belt.

We weren't in the Jeep anymore.

The night came back like a deep breath, complete and overwhelming all at once. The glow of the green dashboard lit the scrubs I wore, and that was enough to flood my mind with the reality of what had happened.

Smears of trees and undergrowth lined a road that was completely dark, save for the small car's weak yellow headlights. For the first time in years, I could see the stars that Thurmond's monstrous lights had faded into nonexistence. They were so bright, so clear that they couldn't have been real. I didn't know what was more shocking—the endless stretch of road or the sky. Tears pricked at the back of my eyes.

"Don't forget to breathe, Ruby," came the voice beside me.

I pulled the surgical mask down from over my mouth as I looked over. Dr. Begbie's blond hair was around her face, sweeping against her shoulders. In the time it had taken us to get from Thurmond to . . . wherever we were, she had stripped off her scrubs and changed into a black T-shirt and jeans. The night stained the skin under her eyes like bruises. I hadn't noticed the sharp angles that made up her nose and chin.

"You haven't been in a car for some time, huh?" She laughed, but she was right. I was more aware of the forward lurch of the car than I was of my own heartbeat.

"Dr. Begbie—"

"Call me Cate," she interrupted, a bit harsher than before. I don't know if I reacted to the abrupt change of tone or not, but she immediately followed with, "I'm sorry, it's been a very long night and I could use a cup of coffee."

According to the dashboard, it was 4:30 a.m. I had only had two hours of sleep, but I felt more alert than I had all day. All week. All my life.

Cate waited until the Rolling Stones had finished out their song before turning down the radio. "All they play are oldies now. I thought it was a joke at first, or something Washington wanted, but apparently that's all that gets requested these days." She snuck a look at me out of the corner of her eye. "I can't imagine why."

"Dr.—Cate," I said. Even my voice was stronger. "*Where are we?* What's going on?"

Before she could answer, there was a cough from the backseat. I twisted around despite the pain in my neck and chest. Curled up there in a protective little ball was another kid, about my age, or maybe a year younger. *That* other kid. Max—Matthew—whatever—from the Infirmary, and he was looking far better than I felt as he slept on.

"We just left Harvey, West Virginia," Cate said. "That's where we met with some friends that helped me switch cars and remove Martin back there from the medical trunk we had to smuggle him out in."

"Wait . . ."

"Oh, don't worry," Cate said quickly. "We made sure it had air holes."

Like that was my biggest concern?

"They just let you take it out to the car?" I asked. "Without even checking it?"

She glanced at me again, and I was proud of the look of surprise there. "The doctors at Thurmond use those trunks to transport medical waste. The camp controllers started forcing the doctors to dump the waste themselves when the budget got cut. Sarah and I had duty for this week."

"Sarah?" I interrupted. "Dr. Rogers?"

She hesitated a split second before nodding.

"Why did you tie her up—why did she—why are *you* helping us?"

She answered my question with one of her own.

"Have you ever heard of the Children's League?"

"Bits and pieces," I said. And only in whispers. If the rumors were true, they were an antigovernment group. They were the ones the younger kids—the later arrivals to Thurmond—claimed were trying to take down the camp system. The ones that supposedly hid kids so they couldn't be taken. I had always assumed they were our generation's version of a fairy tale. Nothing that good could ever be true.

"*We,*" Cate said, letting that word sink in before continuing, "are an organization dedicated to helping children affected by the government's new laws. John Alban—have you heard of him? He was formerly an intelligence adviser to Gray."

"He started the Children's League?"

She nodded. "After his daughter died and he realized what was going to happen to the kids who survived, he left D.C. and tried to expose all of the testing that was happening at the camps. *The New York Times*, the *Post*, you name it—none of them would run the story, because, by then, things were bad enough that Gray had them under his thumb for 'national security' reasons, and the smaller papers folded along with the economy."

"So . . ." I was trying to wrap my mind around this, wondering if I had misheard her. "So he created the Children's League to . . . help us?"

71

Cate's face lit up in a smile. "Yes, that's exactly right."

Then why did you help only me?

The question sprung up like a lone weed; ugly, and deeply rooted. I rubbed a hand over my face, trying to clear the rumblings in my brain, but I couldn't tear it out. There was a strange feeling rising in my chest that followed—like something heavy was trying to work its way up from my center. It might have been a scream.

"What about the others?" I didn't recognize my own voice.

"The others? You mean the other children?" Cate's eyes were focused only on the road in front of us. "They can wait. Their situation wasn't as pressing as yours was. When the time is right, I'm sure we'll go back for them, but in the meantime, don't worry. They'll live."

I recoiled almost instantly at her tone more than her words. The way she said that—*they'll live*—was so dismissive, I half expected to see a hand come up into the air to wave me off. *Don't worry.* Don't worry at the way they've been mistreated, don't worry about their punishments, don't worry about the guns constantly trained on their backs. God, I wanted to throw up.

I had left them behind, all of them. I had left Sam, even after I promised we'd get out together. After everything she had done to protect me, I had just *left* her there. . . .

"Oh—no, Ruby. I'm sorry, I didn't even realize how that would sound," she said, turning back and forth between me and the road. "I just meant . . . I don't even know what I'm saying. I was there for weeks, and I still can't begin to imagine what it must have been like. I shouldn't act like I know what you went through."

"I just—I left them," I told her, and it didn't matter that my voice was breaking, or that my hands had come up to clutch my elbows to keep from grabbing her. "Why did you only take me? Why couldn't you save the others? Why?"

"I told you before," she said softly. "It had to be you. They would have killed you otherwise. The others aren't in danger."

"They're *always* in danger," I said, and wondered if she had stepped a single foot beyond the Infirmary. How could she not have seen? How could she not have heard it, felt it, breathed it in? The air at Thurmond was so coated in fear that you could taste it like vomit at the back of your throat.

It had taken me less than a day in that place to see that hatred and terror came in circles, and that they fed off each other. The PSFs hated us, so they had to make us fear them. And we feared them, which only made us hate them even more. There was an unspoken understanding that we were at Thurmond because of each other. Without the PSFs there would be no camp, but without the Psi freaks there would be no need for PSFs.

So whose fault was it? Everyone's? No one's? Ours?

"You should have just left me—you should have taken someone else, someone who was better—they'll be punished because of this, I know it. They'll hurt them, and it's my fault for going, for leaving them behind." I knew I wasn't making sense, but I couldn't seem to connect my thoughts to my tongue. That feeling, the heart-swallowing guilt, the

73

sadness that took hold and never let itself be shaken free—how did you tell someone that? How did you put that into words?

Cate's lips parted, but no sound came out for several moments. She took a firm hold of the wheel and guided the car over to the side of the road. Her foot came off the gas and she allowed the car to roll to a hesitant stop. When the wheels finally ceased spinning, I reached for the door handle, a spike of total and complete grief cutting through me.

"What are you doing?" Cate asked.

She had pulled over because she wanted me to get out, hadn't she? I would have done the same thing if our situations had been flipped. I understood.

I leaned back away from her arm as she reached over, but instead of pushing the door open, she slammed it shut and let her fingers linger over my shoulder. I cringed, pressing back against the seat as hard as I could, trying to avoid her touch. This was the worst I'd felt in years—my head was humming, a sure sign I was dangerously close to losing control of it. If she had any thoughts about hugging me, or stroking my arm, or anything my mom would have done, my reaction was more than enough to convince her not to try.

"Listen to me very carefully," she said, and it didn't seem to matter to her that at any moment a car or a PSF could come charging up the road. She waited until I was looking her in the eye. "The most important thing you ever did was learn how to survive. Do not let *anyone* make you feel like you shouldn't have—like you deserved to be in that camp. You are important, and you matter. You matter to me, you matter to the

League, and you matter to the future—" Her voice caught. "I will never hurt you, or yell at you, or let you go hungry. I will protect you for the rest of my life. I will never fully understand what you've been through, but I will always listen when you need to get something out. Do you understand?"

Something warm bloomed in my chest, even as my breath hitched in my throat. I wanted to say something to that, to thank her, to ask her to repeat it again just to be sure I hadn't misunderstood or misheard her.

"I can't pretend like it never happened," I told her. I still felt the vibrations of the fence under my skin.

"You shouldn't—you should never forget. But part of surviving is being able to move on. There's this word," she continued, turning to study her fingers gripping the wheel. "Nothing like it exists in the English language. It's Portuguese. *Saudade*. Do you know that one?"

I shook my head. I didn't know half of the words in my own language.

"It's more . . . there's no perfect definition. It's more of an expression of feeling—of terrible sadness. It's the feeling you get when you realize something you once lost is lost forever, and you can never get it back again." Cate took a deep breath. "I thought of that word often at Thurmond. Because the lives you had before—that we all had before—we can never get them back. But there's a beginning in an end, you know? It's true that you can't reclaim what you had, but you can lock it up behind you. Start fresh."

I did understand what she was saying, and I understood that her words were coming from a true, caring place, but

75

after having my life broken down into rotations for so long, the thought of dividing it up even further was unimaginable.

"Here," she said, reaching inside the collar of her shirt. She pulled a long silver chain up over her head, and the last thing to reveal itself was the black circular pendant, a little bigger than the size of my thumb, hanging from it.

I held out my hand and she dropped the necklace into it. The chain was still warm from where it had been kept against her skin, but I was surprised to find that the pendant wasn't anything more than plastic.

"We call that a panic button," she said. "If you squeeze it for twenty seconds, it activates, and any agents nearby will respond. I don't imagine you'll ever need to use it, but I'd like you to keep it. If you ever feel scared, or if we get separated, I want you to press it."

"It'll track me?" Something about that idea made me vaguely uncomfortable, but I slipped the chain on anyway.

"Not unless you activate it," Cate promised. "We designed them that way so that the PSFs wouldn't be able to accidentally pick up on a signal being transmitted from them. I promise, you're in control here, Ruby."

I plucked the pendant up and held it between my thumb and index finger. When I realized how dirty my fingers were, and how much dirt was still packed under my nails, I dropped it. Me and nice things didn't go well together.

"Can I ask you another question?" I waited until she had finally nudged the car back onto the road, and even then it had taken me a few tries to get the words out. "If the Children's League was formed to end the camps, why did you even bother getting me and Martin? Why didn't you just blow up the Control Tower while you were there?"

Cate ran a hand over her lips. "I'm not interested in those kinds of operations," she said. "I'd much rather be focused on the real issue, which is helping you kids. You can destroy a factory, and they'll just build another. But once you destroy a life, that's it. You never get that person back."

"Do people have any idea?" I squeezed out. "Do the people know that they're not reforming us at all?"

"I'm not sure," Cate said. "Some will always live in denial about the camps, and they'll believe what they want to believe about them. I think most people know there's something off, but they're in too deep with their own problems to call into question how the government is handling things at the camps. I think they want to trust that you're all being treated well. Honestly, there are . . . there are so few of you left now."

I sat straight up again. "What?"

This time, Cate couldn't look at me. "I didn't want to have to be the one to tell you this, but things are much worse now than they were before. The last estimate the League put together said that two percent of the country's population of ten- to seventeen-year-olds were in reform camps."

"What about the rest?" I said, but I already knew the answer. "The ninety-eight percent?"

"Most of them fell victim to IAAN."

"They died," I corrected. "All the kids? Everywhere?"

"No, not everywhere. There have been a few cases of it reported in other countries, but here in America . . ." Cate took a deep breath. "I don't know how much to tell you now, because I don't want to overwhelm you, but it seems like the onset of IAAN or Psi powers is linked to puberty—"

"How many?" They really hadn't learned anything new in all the years I was trapped in Thurmond? "How many of us are left?"

"According to the government, there are approximately a quarter of a million children under the age of eighteen, but our estimate is closer to a tenth of that."

I was going to be sick. I unbuckled my seat belt and leaned forward, putting my head between my legs. Out of the corner of my eye, I saw Cate's hand come down, as if she was going to rest it on my back, but I twisted away again. For a long time, the only sound between us was the tires turning against the old road.

I kept my face down and eyes shut long enough for Cate to worry. "Are you still feeling queasy? We had to give you a high enough dosage of penicillin to induce seizurelike symptoms. Trust me, if we could have done it any other way we would have, but we needed something serious enough for the PSFs to actually bring you back to the Infirmary."

Martin snored behind us until eventually even that faded into the sound of the tires rolling down the old road. My stomach twisted at the thought of asking exactly how many miles we were from Thurmond, how far away the past really was.

"I know," I said after a while. "Thank you—I mean it."

Cate reached over, and before I could think to stop her, her hand ran a smooth path from my shoulder down my arm. I felt something warm tickle at the back of my mind, and recognized its warning trill. The first white-hot flash from her mind came and went so fast, I saw the scene like a photo negative. A young girl with white-blond hair in a high chair, her mouth frozen in a toothless grin. The next image stayed, lingered long enough for me to recognize I was seeing fire. *Fire*—everywhere, climbing the walls of the room, burning with all the intensity of the sun. This . . . memory? It trembled, shuddered hard enough that I had to clench my teeth to keep from getting nauseated. Inside Cate's memory, a silver door with 456B stamped over it in black lettering slid into view. A hand flashed out, reaching for the handle—Cate's pale, slender fingers, outstretched—only to pull away at its molten hot touch. A hand lashed out against the wood, then a foot. The image wavered, curling at the edges as the door disappeared behind the dark smoke that spewed through its cracks and joints.

The same dark door shut, and I jolted back, pulling my arm out from under hers.

What the hell? I thought, my heart racing in my ears. I squeezed my eyes shut.

"Still?" Cate said. "Oh, Ruby, I'm so sorry. When we switch cars, I'll be sure to ask for something to help ease your stomach."

She, like all the others, was oblivious.

"You know . . ." Cate said after a while. She kept her eyes on the dark road, to where it met the brightening sky. "It was brave of you to take the pills and come with me. I knew there was more to you than the quiet girl I met in the Infirmary."

I'm not brave. If I had been, I would have owned up to what I really was, no matter how terrible. I would have worked, eaten, and slept alongside the other Oranges, or at least stepped out of the shadow of the Yellows and Reds.

Those kids had been so proud of their powers. They made a point of harassing the camp controllers at every turn, hurting the PSFs, setting their cabins and the Washrooms on fire, trying to talk their way out of the gate or driving the adults insane by putting images of murdered families or cheating wives in their heads.

It was impossible to miss them, to not step aside and turn away when they passed. I had let myself sit like a coward in the dull, endless stream of gray and green, never drawing attention, never once letting myself believe that I could or should escape. I think that all they wanted was to find a way out, and to do it themselves. They had burned so bright, and fought so hard to get free.

But none of them had made it to sixteen.

There are a thousand ways to tell if someone is lying to you. You don't need to be able to glimpse into their mind to catch all of the little signs of insecurity and discomfort. More often than not, all you have to do is look at them. If they glance to the left while they're talking to you, if they add too many details to a story, if they answer a question with another question. My dad, a cop, taught me and twenty-four other kids about it in second grade, when he gave his presentation on Stranger Danger.

But Cate had no tells. She told me things about the world that didn't seem possible, not until we were able to pick up a radio station and a solemn voice bled through the speakers to confirm it all.

"Yes!" she cried, slapping her palm against the wheel. "Finally!"

"The president has reportedly refused an invitation from Britain's prime minister to discuss possible relief measures for the world economic crisis and how to pump life back into the sagging global stock markets. When asked to explain his decision, the president cited the United Kingdom's role in the UN's economic sanctions against the United States."

Cate fiddled with the tuning again. The newscaster's voice faded in and out. At the first burst of static, I jumped.

". . . forty-five women were arrested in Austin, Texas, yesterday for attempting to evade the birth registry. The women will be detained in a corrections facility until their children are born, after which the infants will be removed for the safety of their mothers and the state of Texas. The attorney general had this to say . . ."

Another voice came through, this one deep and raspy. *"In accordance with New Order 15, President Gray issued an arrest warrant for all persons involved with this dangerous activity. . . ."*

"Gray?" I said, glancing over to Cate. "He's still the president?"

He had only just been elected when the first cases of IAAN appeared, and I couldn't really remember anything about him, other than that he had dark eyes and dark hair. And even that I only knew because the camp controllers had strung up pictures of his son, Clancy, all over camp as proof to us that we, too, could be reformed. I had a sudden, sharp memory of the last time I had been in the Infirmary, and the way his picture had seemed to watch me.

She shook her head, visibly disgusted. "He granted himself a term extension until the Psi situation is, and I quote, *resolved so as to make sure the United States is safe from telekinetic acts of terror and violence*. He even suspended Congress."

"How did he manage that?" I asked.

"With his so-called wartime powers," Cate said. "Maybe a year or two after you were taken, some Psi kids nearly succeeded in blowing up the Capitol."

"Nearly? What does that mean?"

Cate glanced over again, studying my face. "It means that they only succeeded in blowing up the Senate portion of it. President Gray's control of the government was only supposed to last until new congressional elections could be held, but then the riots started when the PSF started pulling kids from schools without their parents' permission. And then, of course, the economy tanked and the country defaulted on its debt. You'd be surprised how little voice you have when you lose everything."

"And everyone just let him?" The thought turned my stomach.

"No, no one just *let* him. It's chaos out here right now, Ruby. Gray keeps trying to tighten his control, and every day more and more people are rioting or breaking whatever laws we have left just to get food on the table."

"My dad was killed in a riot."

Cate turned around to face the backseat so quickly the car actually swerved into the other lane. I had known Martin was awake for at least ten minutes; his breathing had become much lighter, and he had stopped doing his weird little lip licking and grunts. I just hadn't wanted to talk to him, or to interrupt Cate.

"The people in our neighborhood robbed his store for food, and he couldn't even defend himself."

"How are you feeling?" Sugar coated Cate's words, almost as sweet as the vanilla air freshener twirling around in front of us.

"Okay, I guess." He sat up, trying to pat down his floppy brown hair into something presentable. Martin was round all over; his cheeks drooped and his uniform shirt might have been a size too small, but he hadn't started growing like the other kids in his cabin. I had maybe an inch or two on him, and I was short, with an average build. He couldn't have been more than a year younger than I was.

"I'm glad," Cate said. "There's a water bottle back there for you if you need it. We'll be stopping in about an hour to switch cars again."

"Where are we going?"

"We're meeting with a friend in Marlinton, West Virginia. He'll have a change of clothes and identification papers for both of you. We're almost there now."

I thought for sure Martin had dropped right back off into sleep until he asked, "Where are we going after that?"

The radio flashed to life, snatching up bits and pieces of Led Zeppelin, before losing it again to static and silence.

I could feel Martin's eyes burning holes into the back of my neck. I tried not to turn around to stare right back, but it was the closest I had been to a boy my age since we had been sorted. After years of living on opposite sides of the main trail in Thurmond, it was unnerving to suddenly be presented with all his little details. The freckles I hadn't noticed on his face, for instance, or the way his eyebrows seemed to merge into one.

What was I supposed to say to him? *I'm so glad I found you*? *We're the last of us*? One was the truth, and one couldn't be further from it.

"We're going to regroup with the League at their southern headquarters. After we get there, you can decide if you want to stay," she said. "I know you've been through a lot, so you don't have to make any choices now. Just know that you'll be safe if you stay with me."

The feeling of freedom rose in me so fast that I had to chase it down to squash it along with my swelling heart. It was still too dangerous. There was a chance that the PSFs could catch up to us, that I'd be back in camp or dead before we even got to Virginia.

Martin watched me, his dark eyes narrowed. I watched as his pupils seemed to shrink, and I felt a tickle in the back of my mind. The same one I always felt when my abilities wanted to be let out and used.

What the hell? My fingers dug into the armrests, but I didn't turn back around to see if he was still at it. I glanced up into the rearview mirror only once, watching as he leaned back against the seat and crossed his arms over his chest with a huff. A sore at the corner of his mouth looked angry and red, like he had been scratching at the scab.

"I want to go where I can do what I couldn't do at Thurmond," Martin said, finally.

I didn't want to know what he meant by that.

"I'm a lot more powerful than you think," he continued. "You won't need anyone else after you see what I can do."

Cate smiled. "That's what I'm counting on. I knew you'd understand."

"What about you, Ruby?" she asked, turning to me. "Are you willing to make a difference?"

If I said I no, would they let me go? If I asked to go to my parents' house in Salem, would they take me there— no questions asked? To Virginia Beach, if I wanted to see my grandmother? Out of the country, if that's what I really wanted?

They were both looking at me, wearing mirrored looks of urgency and excitement. I wish I could have felt it. I wish I could have shared in the security they were feeling about their choice, but I wasn't absolutely certain of what I wanted. I only knew what I didn't want.

"Take me anywhere," I said. "Anywhere but home."

Martin picked at the sore with grubby nails until blood appeared and he licked it off his lips and the tip of his fingers. Watching me, like he expected me to ask for a taste.

I turned back to Cate, a question dying on my lips. Because for a second, just one, all I could think about was the sight of fire and smoke rising from the sharp lines of her shoulders, and the door she couldn't open.

SEVEN

WE REACHED MARLINTON'S CITY LIMITS AT SEVEN o'clock in the morning, just as the sun decided to reappear from behind the thick layer of clouds. It colored the nearby trees a faint violet, and glinted off the wall of mist that had gathered over the asphalt. By then, we had driven past several highway exits that were barricaded with junk, rails, or deserted cars—done up either by the National Guard to contain hostile towns and cities, or by the residents themselves, to keep unwanted looters and visitors out of already hard-hit areas. The road itself, however, had been silent for hours on end, which meant that we were due for some sort of human interaction sooner or later.

It came sooner, in the form of a red semitruck. I scooted down in my seat as it whipped past us. It was headed clear in the opposite direction, but I had a perfect view of the gold swan painted on its side.

"They're everywhere," Cate said, following my line of sight. "That was probably a shipment to Thurmond."

It was the first true sign of life we'd seen in all of our driving—most likely because we were cruising down Dead Man's Highway in the middle of Butt-Freaking Nowhere—but that single truck was enough to scare Cate.

"Get in the backseat," she said, "and stay down."

I did as I was told. Unbuckling my seat belt, I twisted between the front seats and threaded my legs through them.

Martin watched me with glassy eyes. At one point, I felt his hand slip against my arm, like he was trying to help me. I recoiled, slipping down in the space between the backseat and the front. My back was against the door and my knees were against my chest, but we were still too close. When he grinned, it was enough to make my skin crawl.

There were boys at Thurmond. Plenty of them, in fact. But any activity that involved the commingling of the sexes—whether that was eating together, sharing cabins, or even passing one another on the way to the Washrooms—was strictly forbidden. The PSFs and camp controllers enforced the rule with the same level of severity they did with the kids who—however intentionally or unintentionally—used their abilities. Which, of course, only drove everyone's already hormone-drunk brains crazier, and turned some of my cabinmates into an elite breed of covert stalkers.

Maybe I didn't remember the "right" way to interact with someone of the opposite gender, but I'm pretty sure Martin didn't, either.

"Fun, huh?" he said. I thought he was kidding, until I saw the too-eager look in his eyes. The itching came again, the tingling sensation of yet another attempt to peer inside my head, dread trailing down the length of my spine like a freezing fingertip. I pressed up against the door and kept my eyes on Cate, but it wasn't far enough.

We are nothing alike, I realized. We had been brought to the same place, lived in the same kind of terror, but he . . . he was so . . .

I needed to change the subject and distract him from whatever it was he was trying to do. The AC was on, but you never would have known by the heat he was giving off.

"Do you think Thurmond has noticed we're gone?" I asked, breaking the silence.

Cate switched off her headlights. "I would think so. The PSFs don't have the manpower to launch a full hunt for us, but I'm positive they've put two and two together about what you are."

"What do you mean?" I asked. "That we're Orange? I thought you said they already knew. That was why we had to leave so quickly."

"They were on the verge of finding out," Cate explained. "They were testing the Orange and Red frequencies in that Calm Control. I don't think any of them expected it to work that quickly—*that's* why we had to get you out, and fast."

"Frequencies," Martin repeated. "You mean they added something to it?"

"That's exactly right." Cate smiled at him in the rearview mirror. "The League got wind of their new method of trying to weed out kids who had been labeled incorrectly when they were brought into camp. You know that adults can't hear the Calm Control, I'm sure."

We both nodded.

"The scientists there have been working on frequencies that only certain kinds of Psi youth can pick up and process. There are some wavelengths you all can hear, and others that only Greens, or Blues, or—in this instance—Oranges can detect."

It made sense, but it didn't make it any less horrifying.

"You know, I've been wondering," Cate began. "How *did* you two do it? You especially, Ruby. You went into that camp so young. How did you get around their sorting?"

"I . . . just did," I said. "I told the man who was supposed to run my tests that I was Green. He listened."

"That's weak," Martin interrupted, looking right at me. "You probably didn't even have to use your powers."

I didn't like to think of them as *powers*—that seemed to imply they were something to celebrate. And they were most definitely not.

"I told someone to trade places with me when they started separating all the O's and R's out. Didn't want to go down with them, you know?" Martin leaned forward. "So I took one of the new Greens aside who was about my age, and made him and that warden think he was me. Same for anyone who asked. One by one. Cool, huh?"

The disgust coiled in my gut. He didn't feel sorry about doing any of this, that was clear. Maybe I had lied about what I was, but I hadn't damned another kid to do so. Was that what having control over your Orange abilities turned you into? Some kind of monster—someone who could do whatever you wanted, because no one was capable of stopping you?

Was that what being powerful was like?

"So you can make people believe they're someone they're not?" Cate said. "I thought Oranges could only command someone to do something. Sort of like hypnosis?"

"Nah," Martin said. "I can do much more than that. I get people to do what I want by making them feel what I want them to feel. Like that kid I switched places with? I made him feel too scared to stay in his cabin, made him feel like it would be a good idea to pretend to be me. Anyone who questioned me—I made them feel crazy for doing it. So I can sort of command people to do stuff, but it's more like, if I want someone to hurt someone else, I have to make him feel really, really pissed at the person I want him to attack."

"Huh," Cate said. "Is it the same for you, Ruby?"

No. Not at all, in fact. I looked down at my hands, to the dark mud still caked under my fingernails. The thought of revealing exactly what I could do made them shake in a way I hadn't expected. "I don't throw feelings into someone; I just see things."

At least, as far as I knew.

"Wow . . . I just . . . wow. I know I keep saying this, but you two are really something amazing. I keep thinking of all the things you could do—how much help you'll be to us. Incredible."

Twisting around, I lifted my head just enough to look out to the road. Behind me, I felt Martin grab a few loose strands of my hair and begin to twirl them around his fingers. I could see the reflection of my round face in the rearview mirror—the big eyes that seemed almost sleepy; thick, dark brows; full lips—I could see the revulsion slide over it.

I shouldn't have, but I took the bait. Martin barely had time to brace himself before I whirled around and slapped that same clammy hand back down into his lap. My next breath caught in my throat. *Do* not *touch me*, I wanted to say; *don't think I won't break every single finger on that hand*. But he was grinning at me, his tongue on his cold sore, his hand rising again. Only this time, he wagged his fingers in my direction, taunting. I leaned forward, ready to grab that same wrist, to shut the pig down cold, hard, and fast.

But that was exactly what he wanted. The realization flowed thick and slow through me, inching its way to my guts. He wanted me to show him what I could do, to be willing to fuel my abilities with the same kind of viciousness pumping through him.

I turned my back on him again, my fists tightening with his triumphant chuckles.

Had the anger even been mine, or had he pushed it into me?

"Everything okay back there?" Cate called over her shoulder. "Hang on tight, we're almost there."

Whatever Marlinton normally looked like, it was that much worse under the cover of gray clouds and a layer of misty rain. Strange and terrible enough to distract even Martin from the games he was playing with my head.

The deserted shopping centers with broken store-fronts were disturbing enough before we cut into the first neighborhood of little brown and gray and white houses. We passed a number of empty cars along the street and in driveways, some with bright orange FOR SALE signs still stuck in the back window, but all of them covered in a thick skin of brown, rotting leaves. The cars were surrounded by piles of junk and boxes—furniture, rugs, computers. Entire rooms full of rusting, useless electronics.

"What happened here?" I asked.

"It's a little hard to explain, but do you remember what I told you about the economy? After the attack in D.C., the government was thrown into a tailspin, and one thing led to another. We couldn't pay off our national debt, we couldn't provide money to the states, we couldn't provide benefits, we couldn't pay government employees. Even small towns like this one didn't escape. People lost their jobs when companies failed, and then they lost their homes because they could no longer pay for them. The whole thing is terrible."

"But where is everyone?"

"In tent cities, outside of the big cities like Richmond and D.C., trying to find work. I know a lot of people are trying to go west because they think there's going to be more work and food available, but . . . well, I imagine it'll be safer. There's a lot of looting and vigilante groups roaming about here."

I was almost afraid to ask. "What about the police? Why didn't they stop them?"

Cate bit her bottom lip. "It's like I just told you—the states couldn't afford to pay their salaries, so they were let go. Most of the police work is done by volunteers now, or the National Guard. That's why you need to stay close to me, okay?"

It only got worse when we passed the elementary school.

The pastel jungle gym, or whatever was left of it, was stained black and twisting toward the ground. Clusters of birds were perched along its broken backbone, watching us as we blew past the stop sign and turned the corner.

We passed what must have once been the cafeteria, but the entire right side of the building had crumbled in on itself. The rainbow mural of faces and suns painted on the other side of the building was visible just beyond the tangled web of yellow police tape blocking off the wreckage.

"Someone planted a bomb in the cafeteria, just before the first Collection," Cate said. "Set it off during lunchtime."

"The government?" Martin pressed, but Cate didn't have an answer for him. She switched her blinker on as she made another right, signaling her turn to no one in particular.

A city with no people.

My breath fogged up the window as we left that neighborhood behind and sped toward another strip mall. We passed a Starbucks, a nail salon, a McDonald's, and another nail salon before Cate finally pulled into a gas station.

I saw the other car immediately—a tan SUV, a kind I had never seen before. The man leaning against it wasn't pumping gas. That would have been impossible. All of the gas pumps were beaten in, their hoses and nozzles strewn across the concrete.

Cate honked, but the man had already spotted us and was waving. He was young, too, at least as young as Cate, with a small build and dark brown hair that fell over his forehead. As we got closer, the smile on his face bloomed into something brilliant, and I recognized him then as the man from Cate's thoughts. The one she had pictured in dazzling colors and lights as we left Thurmond.

Cate barely had the car in park before she threw her door open and bolted straight for him. I heard her let out a sharp laugh as she threw her arms around his neck, knocking into him with so much force that the sunglasses flew off his face.

Martin's sweaty palm touched the spot where my neck met my shirt collar, giving me a light squeeze, and that was it for me. I pushed the car door open and stepped outside, whether Cate wanted me to or not.

The air was damp with a thin mist of rain, brightening the trees and grass into an electric green. It clung to my cheeks and hair, a welcome relief after spending the last few hours confined with Martin the Mouth Breather, who seemed to be coated with something perpetually sticky.

"—they found Norah about a half hour after you left," the man said as I walked up. "They sent two units after you. Did you run into any trouble?"

"None." Cate had an arm around his middle. "But I'm not surprised. They're stretched so thin right now. But where are your—"

Rob shook his head sharply, a shadow passing over his face. "I couldn't get them out."

Cate's whole body seemed to slump. "Oh . . . I'm sorry."

"It's fine. Looks like you had more success than I did—is she all right?" Both of them turned to look at me.

94

"Ah—Rob, this is Ruby," she said. "Ruby, this is my . . . this is Rob."

"Such a boring introduction!" Rob clucked his tongue. "They've been hiding the pretty ones at Thurmond, I see."

He held out his hand to me. A large palm, five fingers, hairy knuckles. Normal. By the way I stared, you would have thought his skin was covered in scales. My hand stayed pressed flat against my thigh. I took a step closer to Cate.

There wasn't a gun in his hand, or a knife, or a White Noise machine, but I could see cuts and bruises, some fresh, crisscrossing the back of his hand, all the way to his wrist, where the angry red lines disappeared beneath the sleeves of his white shirt. It was only when he pulled his hand back that I noticed a spray of small red spots on his right shirt cuff.

Rob's face tightened when he saw where I was looking. That same hand disappeared behind Cate's back, tightening around her waist.

"Total heartbreaker, right?" Cate glanced up at him. "She'll be perfect for inside jobs. Who could say no to that face? An *Orange*."

Rob let out an appreciative whistle. "Damn."

People who valued Oranges. Imagine that.

"Is Sarah all right?" I pressed.

Rob only looked confused.

"She means Norah Jenkins," Cate said. "The name Sarah was just her cover."

"She's fine," Rob said, putting a hand on my shoulder. "As far as I know they're still questioning her. I'm sure our eyes in Thurmond will update us if anything changes."

My hands suddenly felt numb. "Is Cate *your* name?"

She laughed. "Yes, but my last name is Conner, not Begbie."

I nodded, only because I didn't know what else to do or say.

"Didn't you say there were two of them?" Rob was staring over my shoulder. On cue, I heard a door open and slam shut behind me.

"There he is," Cate said, clucking like a proud mother hen. "Martin, get over here! I want you to meet your new comrade. He'll be driving with us to Georgia."

Martin strode up and took the man's hand before Rob had the chance to offer it.

"Now," Cate said, clapping her hands together. "We don't have much time, but we need you to wash up and change into something a little less conspicuous."

The SUV let out a steady chime as Rob opened one of its rear doors. As he turned, a few scattered rays of sunlight caught the metal handle of the gun tucked into the waistband of his jeans. I took a step back as he reached for something inside the car that I couldn't see.

It was stupid of me not to have expected one or both of them to be packing some kind of heat, but my stomach tightened all the same. I turned away, looking at the splotches of old oil tattooed on the pavement, and waited for the car door to slam shut again.

"Here you go," Rob said, passing us each a black back-pack. My fellow freak snatched his, checking its contents like it was a party favor bag.

"It looks like the bathrooms in the station still have some running water. I wouldn't try drinking it though," Rob continued. "There's a change of clothes and some necessities in there. Don't take a million years, but feel free to wash that camp off you."

Wash Thurmond off me? Rub it off like a splatter of mud? I may have been able to erase everyone else's memories, but I couldn't scrub away my own.

I took my bag without a word, the beginnings of a headache rumbling at the base of my skull. I knew what that meant well enough to take a step back. My heel caught on the uneven cement, sending me stumbling toward the hard ground. I threw out my arms in a lame attempt to reclaim my balance, but the only solid thing I found was Rob's arm.

He may have thought he was being chivalrous by catching me, but he should have let me fall. My brain released a blissful little sigh as it went tumbling into Rob's thoughts. All at once, the pressure that had been building in the back of my mind released, sending a tingle racing down my spine. I gritted my teeth at the sinking sensation, anger flooding my system as I tried to yank myself away.

Unlike Cate's memories, which came and went like fluttering eyelashes, Rob's thoughts seemed almost lethargic . . . velvety and murky. They didn't piece themselves together so much as seep into one another—like ink dropped into a

97

glass of water, the dark mass stretching and slithering until it finally polluted everything that had once been clean.

I was Rob, and Rob was staring down at two dark shapes—two dark sacks covered their heads, but it was obvious that one was a man and the other a woman. It was the latter that had my heart thrumming in my ears. The strength of her sobbing shook her entire body, but she never stopped struggling against the plastic ties binding her hands and feet.

Rain came down around us like an afterthought, running down through the gutters of the nearby buildings. Through the filter of Rob's mind, it sounded like static. Two enormous black Dumpsters came into focus out of the corner of my eye, and it was only then that I realized we were in an alley, and we were alone.

Rob's hand—my hand—reached out and ripped the hood off the woman, sending her dark hair flying over her face.

But it wasn't a woman at all. It was a girl, no older than I was, wearing a set of dark green clothes. A uniform. A camp uniform.

Tears mixed with rain, dripping down over her cheeks into her mouth. Her colorless lips formed the shape *please* and her eyes seemed to scream *no*, but there was a gun in my hand, silver and shining despite the low light. The same gun that was tucked in the back of Rob's jeans. The same one that was now pointed at the girl's forehead.

The gun jumped in my hand as it went off, but in that instant, the flash lit up her terrified face, an unfinished scream drowned out by the bang. A spray of blood flicked up over my hand as her face seemed to cave in on itself, staining the dark jacket I wore . . . and the edge of the white cuff beneath it.

The boy died the same way, only Rob didn't bother to even take his hood off before he ended his life. The bodies were lifted into the Dumpsters. I shrank back and away from the scene, watching it grow smaller, and smaller, and smaller until the dark, cloudy haze of Rob's mind swallowed it whole.

I tugged myself free, coming up from the inky pool with a sharp gasp.

Rob released my arm instantly, but Cate dove forward and would have taken his place if I hadn't raised both hands to stop her.

"Are you all right?" she asked. "You've gone pale."

"I'm okay," I said, trying to keep my voice calm and steady. "Still feeling a little woozy from the medicine."

Martin let out an annoyed sigh behind me. He was hopping from foot to foot, grumbling impatiently. He slid a suspicious eye in my direction, and for half a heartbeat I was afraid he knew exactly what had just happened. But, no—connections like that were fast, and lasted only a few seconds, no matter how long it felt to me.

I kept my eyes on the ground, carefully avoiding both the adults' faces. I couldn't bring myself to look at Rob, not after seeing what he had done—and I knew if I looked at Cate, I'd give myself away in an instant. She'd ask me what was wrong, and I wouldn't be able to lie, not convincingly. I'd have to tell her that her boyfriend or partner or whatever he was had left the brains of two kids splattered all over an alleyway.

Rob tried to offer me a plastic water bottle from the front seat, his mouth stretched in a thin line. My eyes settled again on the tiny red flecks staining his cuff.

He killed them. The words echoed through my head. It could have happened days, maybe even weeks ago, but it didn't seem likely. Wouldn't he have changed his shirt, or tried to clean it off? *And then he came here—to kill us, too?*

Rob smiled at me, all of his teeth showing. *Smiled.* Like he hadn't just snuffed out two lives at point-blank range and watched the rain carry their blood into the gutters.

My hands were shaking so hard now that I had to fist them around the backpack to keep him from noticing. I thought I had escaped the monsters, that I'd left them locked up behind an electric fence. But the shadows were alive, and they had chased me here.

I'm next.

I swallowed the scream working its way up my throat, and smiled right back at him, my insides twisting. Because I had no doubt, not one single wisp of uncertainty, that if he knew what I had just seen, Cate would spend the next few days bleaching my blood out of his shirt, too.

She knows, I thought, following Martin into the gas station. Cate, who smelled like rosemary, who carried me down the hallway, who saved my life. She must know.

And she kissed him anyway.

The inside of the gas station looked like it had been ravaged by wild animals, and there was a fairly good chance that it had been. Muddy paw tracks in all shapes and sizes created

100

dizzying patterns on the floor, cutting over sticky patches of red and brown to the shelves of food.

The store smelled like sour milk, though the drink cases were still flickering with intermittent electricity. Most of them had been cleared out of sodas and beer, but there was a surprising amount left—and no wonder. The store had marked up milk to ten dollars a carton. The same went for the food. Some shelves had rows of untouched chip bags and candy bars, all priced like they were endangered, precious goods. Others had been picked clean, or were exploding with popcorn and pretzels after their bags had been gutted.

I had a plan before I even realized it.

While Martin entertained himself by fiddling with the soda dispenser, I grabbed a few bags of chips and chocolate bars. A flash of guilt cut through me as I stuffed them in my bag, but, really, who was I even stealing from? Who was going to call the cops on me?

"There's only one bathroom," Martin announced. "I'm using it first. Maybe if you're lucky, I'll leave some water for you."

Maybe if I'm lucky, you'll drown yourself in it.

He slammed the door shut behind him, and any guilt I might have felt about leaving him behind disappeared. Maybe it was cruel of me, maybe I would spend the rest of my life feeling guilty about abandoning him without so much as a warning, but there was no way I could tell him what I was about to do without alerting Cate and Rob. I didn't trust him enough to believe he wouldn't shout for them, or try to hold me there.

I wasted no time in stepping out of what had been Sarah's—Norah's—scrubs, leaving them in a heap on the floor. The uniform I was wearing under them was a dead giveaway to what I was, but the scrubs were too baggy to run in. I needed to get away fast.

Martin must have turned the faucet up all the way, because I could hear the water sputtering as I stepped around some of the broken glass from the store's big windows.

I came around a shelf just in time to see Rob break away from kissing Cate. He patted around his jacket pockets, and out came a cell phone. Whoever it was, he wasn't all that happy to be talking to them. After a minute, he threw the phone at Cate and moved to the driver's side of the car. She turned her back to me, spreading out what looked to be a map over the hood of the SUV. When Rob appeared again, he had a long black object tucked under one arm, and he was holding another by its barrel. Cate took the rifle from him without so much as even glancing at it, and pulled its strap over her shoulder. Like it belonged there.

I recognized them—of course I did. Every PSF officer that walked the perimeter of the electric fence carried an M16 rifle, and I was sure every camp controller that watched us from high up on the Tower had one within reach, too. Is that what they're going to use on us? I wondered. Or are they expecting me to use one, too?

The rational part of my brain finally kicked in, stomping down the chaos of panic and terror that had overtaken me. Maybe there was a reason Rob had killed those kids. Maybe they had tried to hurt him even though they were tied up, or maybe—maybe they had just refused to join up with the League.

The realization rose inside my chest like fire, burning everything in its path. Just the thought, the *image*, of having to touch one of those guns, of being expected to *fire* one of them . . . Is that what it would take to be a part of their family?

Or would I have to be like Martin and become the weapon myself?

My dad had served as a cop for over seven years before he had to shoot someone. He never told me the whole story. I had to hear it secondhand from the kids in my class, who had read about it in the paper. A hostage situation, I guess.

It wrecked him. Dad wouldn't come out of my parents' bedroom until Grams drove out from Virginia Beach to pick me up. When I came back home a few weeks later, he acted like nothing had happened at all.

I don't know what would force me to pick up a weapon like that, but it wasn't a group of strangers.

I had to get out. Get away. To where didn't matter in that moment. I was a lot of things, terrible things, but I didn't want to add murderer to that list.

There was a sound like crunching glass, just loud enough to hear over the bathroom's running water and the buzz of the drink coolers. The water shut off, and it was only then that I heard the rustling again. I whirled around, just in time to see the door with the EMPLOYEES ONLY sign swing open and shut behind the low food shelves.

A way out.

I glanced back out the window one last time, making sure Cate and Rob still had their backs to me, before bolting past the display of beef jerky and heading straight for that door.

It's just a raccoon, I thought. Or rats. Not for the first time in my short life, rats were a preferable option to humans.

But the crinkling came again, louder, and when I pushed the door open, I wasn't staring at a group of rats ravaging a bag of snack food.

It was another kid.

EIGHT

HE—NO, *SHE*—OPENED HER MOUTH, HER LIPS parting in a silent gasp. At first blink I hadn't been able to tell, but she was definitely a girl, and a little one at that. Eight, maybe nine at most, judging by her size. Just a baby, drowning in an oversized Indy 500 shirt, complete with checkered flags and a bright green race car. Even weirder, her hands and arms up to her elbows were covered by bright yellow rubber gloves—the kind my mom used to wear when she scrubbed the bathroom or did the dishes.

The Asian girl's dark hair was shaved down into a buzz cut, and she was wearing baggy boys' jeans, but her face was so pretty she might have been a doll. Her full, heart-shaped lips formed a perfect O of shock, and her skin paled in such a drastic way that the freckles on her nose and cheeks stood out all the more.

"Where did you come from?" I managed to choke out.

The stunned look on her face flashed to one of terror.

The hand she didn't have jammed down into a container of Twizzlers slammed the door shut with a streak of yellow.

"Hey!" I pushed it back open in time to see her dash out the door at the other end of the stockroom, heading out into the rain. I was right behind her, throwing the backpack over my shoulders as I ran past the shelves. The door had caught on a large rock and went flying open as I kicked it and sprinted through.

"Hey!"

Snack-sized bags of pretzels and chips were spilling out from her pockets and beneath her shirt.

She had every right to be terrified of the half-crazed girl chasing after her. I could waste time feeling bad about it later; but, for now, my mind had gotten a whiff of hope, and it wasn't about to let it escape through a parking lot. She had to have come from somewhere, and if she had a way out of this town, or a place to hide until Cate and the others gave up on me, I wanted to know about it.

The gas station's back lot was only four parking spaces wide, and one of them was taken up by an overturned Dumpster. I heard animals tittering inside it as I sprinted after her, keeping my eyes on the back of her gray T-shirt. Her legs were pumping so fast beneath her that she tripped where the lot's loose asphalt met a patch of wild grass. My arms flew out to catch her, but the girl recovered just in time.

I was within two steps of being able to grab the back of her shirt when she suddenly picked up her speed, zipping through the small cluster of trees that separated the station from what looked like another road.

"I just—just want to talk to you!" I called. *"Please!"*

What I should have said was, *I won't hurt you*, or *I'm not a PSF*, or something that would have clued her in to the fact that I was just as screwed in the safety department as she was. But my chest was on fire, and my lungs constricted, stretched tight and useless by the pain in my ribs. The panic button was jumping up into the air, bouncing against my chin and shoulders. I ripped it off so hard, the chain's clasp snapped.

The little girl leaped over a fallen tree trunk, her sneakers squelching through the forest muck. Mine weren't much quieter, but Martin's voice drowned us both out.

"Ruby!"

My blood ran so cold, it seemed to cease pumping through me altogether. I should never have turned back to look over my shoulder, but I did, more out of instinct than fear. I didn't realize that my feet had stopped moving until Martin's round shape appeared on the other side of the trees. He was close enough for me to see the red flush that had overtaken his face, but he hadn't seen me. Not yet.

"Ruby!"

I had expected to find nothing but trees and air waiting for me as I picked up my run, but there she was, a short distance away. The girl had tucked herself behind a tree, not hiding, but also not beckoning me forward. Her mouth was pulled into a tight line, eyes darting back and forth between me and the direction of Martin's voice. When I started toward her, she took off so fast that both feet jumped up from the ground. Scared off like a little rabbit.

107

"Come *on*," I gasped, pumping my arms at my side. "I just want to—"

We broke through the trees, pouring out onto a deserted stretch of road. On the other side of the dead-end street was a line of little ramshackle houses, their windows boarded up like black eyes. I thought for sure that she was heading toward the closest one—the house with the gray fence and green door—but she made a hard right and ran for the minivan parked on the side of the road.

The car was dented beyond repair, not just on the bumpers, but on the side doors and the roof. And that was to say nothing of the shot-out and cracked lights, and the black paint that was flaking off in clumps. The nicest thing about it was the cursive, swirling logo that someone had painted along the sliding door: BETTY JEAN CLEANING.

But it was a *car*. A way out. I wasn't thinking about the logistics at that point—about whether it had gas, or if its engine would even start. I think my heart grew a pair of big, fluffy white wings at the mere sight of it, and nothing was going to shoot it down.

The girl was running so hard, she slammed into the side paneling of the minivan and bounced off it. She landed hard on the ground but recovered faster than I ever would have. With both yellow-gloved hands on the door handle, she ripped the sliding door back with a sound loud enough to shake the birds from the nearby roofs.

I got there just in time for her to close the door and slam her hand down on the lock.

I could see my reflection in the tinted glass—see how she

must have seen me. Eyes that were wide and wild, a tangled mass of dark hair, clothes that would have otherwise been too small if camp hadn't made me so damn skinny I could see bones in my chest I didn't know existed. I ran around to the other side of the car, putting the minivan between me and anyone who'd come charging out of the trees.

"Please!" My voice was hoarse. Martin's bellowing voice was either echoing around in my mind, or it was actually getting closer. The windows' tint was light enough that I could look through them and skim the trees for any flash of his waxy skin. If he was getting closer, then Cate and Rob wouldn't be far behind. They must have heard him yelling by now.

Two choices, Ruby, I thought. *Go back or run.*

My head and heart were in agreement on *run,* but the rest of my body—the parts that had been tormented by White Noise, poisoned, and mistreated by people who claimed they only had the best intentions—stubbornly held its ground. I sagged against the minivan, deflated. It was like someone had crushed my chest in a vise, spinning the handle until every ounce of air and courage had been squeezed out of me.

Years at Thurmond had taught me to stop believing I could ever get away from the life people were so eager to set for me. I don't know why I thought it would be any different on the outside.

I heard footsteps crashing through the trees and under-growth, louder with each second. When I looked up again, Cate's startlingly blond hair was weaving in and out of the trees, glowing under the drizzly clouds like a firefly.

"Ruby!" I heard her call. "Ruby, where are you?"

And then there was Rob, walking right behind her with the gun in his hands. I looked right to the houses on the street's dead end. Farther down the opposite end of the street, I saw signs with symbols I didn't recognize—but that, the unknown, that had to be better than going back to Cate.

The little girl inside of the car looked at me, then turned to look at the trees. Her lips pressed together, pulling down into a frown. One hand was clenched on the door handle, the other on her seat's armrest. She started to stand once, only to sit back down and look one more time in my direction.

I swiped at my face with the back of my hand and took a step back. Hopefully the girl knew well enough to hide herself when Cate and Rob ran after me. I'd lead them as far away as I could—it was the least I could do after scaring a few years off her life.

I hadn't even fully turned to go when I heard the door roll open behind me. A pair of hands reached out and seized the back of my uniform shirt, twisting the fabric for a better grip. When she yanked, I fell back, hitting the closest seat. My neck snapped against the armrest and I rolled onto the rough carpet behind the front passenger seat. The door roared shut behind me.

I blinked, trying to clear the dark spots swimming in my vision, but the other girl wasn't about to wait for me to get settled. She climbed over my tangled legs to get to the rear seat, grabbing my shirt collar and giving it a hard tug.

"Okay, okay," I said, crawling toward her. My fingers slid against the minivan's gray carpets. With the exception of a few stacked newspapers and tied-off plastic grocery bags tucked under the rear seat, the inside of the minivan was pretty well kept.

She motioned for me to crouch down behind one of the middle seats. As I pressed my knees against my chest, I realized that despite the fact that I had followed her order to the letter, she still hadn't spoken a single word to me.

"What's your name?" I asked. She draped herself over the top of the rear seat, her feet kicking at the air as she dug around for something in the back. If she heard me, she pretended not to.

"It's all right; you can talk to me. . . ."

Her face was flushed when she reemerged, a paint-splattered white sheet in hand. She pressed a finger to her lips and I wisely shut my mouth. The girl shook out the folded fabric and threw it over my head. The smell of fake lemon cleaner and bleach assaulted my nostrils as the sheet settled around me. I opened my mouth to protest, reaching up to yank it away from my face, but something stopped me.

Someone was coming—no, more than one person. I caught snippets of their back-and-forth, heard their feet slap against the pavement. The sound of a door opening stopped my heart dead in my chest.

"—I swear to God it was her, Liam!" The voice was deep, but it didn't sound like an adult. "And, look, I told you she'd beat us back. Suzume, did you run into trouble?"

The other car door opened. Someone else—Liam?—let out a relieved sigh.

"Thank God," he said, with a hint of a Southern drawl.

111

"Come on, come on, come on, get in. I don't know what's going on, but I don't want to stay long enough to find out. The skip tracers were bad enough—"

"Why won't you admit that it was her?" the other voice snapped.

"—because we ditched her in Ohio, that's why—"

Above the sound of Liam's voice and the blood pounding between my ears, I heard another voice.

"Ruby! *Ruby!*"

Cate.

I pressed both hands against my mouth and squeezed my eyes shut.

"What in the world?" the first voice said. "Is that what I think it is?"

The first gunshot popped like a firecracker. It might have been the distance, or the army of trees and undergrowth muffling it, but it seemed harmless. A warning. The next one had much sharper teeth.

"Stop!" I heard Cate scream. "Don't shoot—!"

"LEE!"

"I know, I know!" The engine sputtered to life, and the squeal of the tires wasn't far behind. "Zu, seat belt!"

I tried to brace myself, but the car tossed me back and forth between the seats. At one point, my head cracked back against the plastic side paneling and drink holder, but no one was paying attention to the strange noises in the backseat when someone was firing a gun.

I wondered if Rob had given the other rifle to Martin.

—✦—

"Zu, did something happen in the gas station?" the voice identified as Liam pressed. There was an edge of urgency to his words, but not panic. We had been driving for over ten minutes and were well away from the guns. His other companion, however, was a completely different story.

"Oh my God, more skip tracers? What, were they having a freaking *convention*? You realize what would have happened if we'd been caught, don't you?" he railed. "And they were shooting at us! *Shooting!* With a *gun!*"

Somewhere to the right of me, the little girl giggled.

"Well, I'm glad you find it funny!" the other one said. "Do you know what happens when you get shot, Suzume? The bullet rips through—"

"Chubs!" The other boy's voice was sharp enough to cut off whatever gory tale he was about to share. "Settle down, okay? We're fine. That was a little bit closer than I would have liked, but still. We'll just have to try to make better mistakes tomorrow, right, Zu?"

The first voice let out a strangled groan.

"I'm sorry about before," Liam said. His voice was gentle, which was enough for me to put together he was talking to the girl, not the guy who had moved on to moaning in dismay. "Next time I'll go with you to get food. You're not hurt, right?"

The vibrations from the road dulled their voices. A loose penny was clattering around so loudly in the drink holder that I almost reached up from under the sheet to grab it. When the first boy spoke again, I had to strain my ears to hear him. "Did it sound like they were looking for someone to you?"

"No, it sounded like *they were shooting at us*!"

Feeling left my hands, draining from the tips of my fingers.

You're safe, I told myself. They're kids, too.

Kids who had unwittingly put themselves in the line of fire for me.

I should have known this would happen. *This*, not my fear of setting off alone into a deserted town, should have been my first concern. But I had panicked, and it was like my brain had melted into a simmering pool of terror.

"—a number of things," Liam was saying, "but let's try to focus on finding East River—"

I needed to get out now. Right now. This had been a terrible idea, maybe even my worst. If I left now, they still had a chance of escaping Cate and Rob. *I* would still have a chance of escaping them, too.

I looped the straps of the backpack over my shoulders again and kicked the sheet off. Taking in a deep drag of the musty, cool air-conditioning, I used the rear seat to prop myself up.

Two teenage boys were in the front seat, facing the road. It was raining harder now; the fat drops were falling too fast for the windshield wipers to keep up with them, making it look as though we were headed straight into an Impressionist's vision of West Virginia. Silver skies were above and a black road was below—and somewhere in between, the luminescent glow of the trees with their new spring coats.

Liam, our driver, was wearing a beat-up leather jacket, darker across the shoulders where the rain had soaked through. His hair was a light, ashy blond that stood on end when he ran a hand through it. Every now and then he would glance to the dark-skinned teen in the passenger seat, but it wasn't until he cast a quick look into the rearview mirror that I saw his eyes were blue.

"I can't see out of the back window when you—" His words choked off as he did a double take.

The minivan lurched to the right as he spun around in his seat and turned the wheel with him. The other kid let out a strangled noise as the car jerked to the right, toward the side of the road. The girl glanced back over her shoulder at me, her expression somewhere between surprise and exasperation.

Liam slammed on the brakes. Both of the car's other passengers gasped as their seat belts locked over their chests, but I had nothing holding me back from flying between the two middle seats. After what felt like a short eternity, but was likely only a hot second, the tires let off a long squeal of pain before the minivan quivered to a dead stop.

Both boys were staring back at me, wearing two completely different expressions. Liam's tanned face had gone porcelain pale, his mouth hanging open in an almost comical way. The other boy only glared at me through his thin, silver-framed glasses, his lips pursed in disapproval, the same way my mom's used to when she found out I had stayed up past my bedtime. His ears, which were a touch too big for his head, stuck out from his skull; everything between them, from the wide expanse of his forehead down past the thin bridge of his nose to his full lips, seemed to darken in anger. For a split second I was afraid that he was a Red, because judging by the look in his eyes, he wanted nothing more than to burn me to a crisp.

Boys. Why did it have to be boys?

I peeled myself up off the carpets and bolted toward the side door. My fingers squeezed the door handle, but no matter how hard I pulled it, it didn't budge.

"*Zu!*" Liam cried, looking back and forth between us. She merely folded her hands in her lap, rubber gloves squeaking, and blinked at him innocently. Like she had no idea how they had come across the stowaway currently sprawled out by her feet.

"We all agreed—*no strays*." The other boy shook his head. "That's why we didn't take the kittens!"

"Oh, for the love of . . ." Liam slumped down in his seat, pressing his face into his hands. "What were we going to do with a box of abandoned kittens?"

"Maybe if that black heart of yours hadn't been willing to leave them to *starve*, we could have found them new, loving homes."

Liam gave the other boy a look of pure amazement. "You're never going to get over those cats, are you?"

"They were innocent, defenseless kittens and you left them outside someone's mailbox! A *mailbox*!"

"Chubs," Liam groaned. "Come *on*."

Chubs? That had to have been a joke. The kid was as skinny as a stick. Everything about him, from his nose to his fingers, was long and narrow.

116

He leveled Liam with a withering stare. I don't know what amazed me more, the fact that they were arguing about kittens, or that they'd managed to forget that I was in the car.

"Excuse me!" I interrupted, slamming my palm against the window. "Can you please unlock the door?"

That shut them up at least.

When Liam finally turned back toward me, his expression was entirely different than before. He looked serious, but not altogether unhappy or suspicious. Which is a lot more than I could have said for myself if our situations had been reversed.

"Are you the one they were looking for?" he asked. "Ruth?"

"Ruby," Chubs corrected.

Liam waved his hand. "Right. Ruby."

"Just unlock the door, please!" I yanked at the handle again. "I made a mistake. This was a mistake! I was selfish, I know that, so you have to let me go before they catch up."

"Before who catches up? Skip tracers?" Liam asked. His eyes darted over me, from my haggard face down my forest green uniform to my mud-stained shoes. To the Psi number that had been written on their canvas toes in permanent marker. A look of horror flickered over his face. "Did you just come from a camp?"

I felt Suzume—Zu's—dark eyes on me, but I held Liam's gaze and nodded. "The Children's League broke me out."

"And you ran away from them?" Liam pressed. He looked back at Zu for confirmation. She nodded.

"What does that have to do with anything?" Chubs interrupted. "You heard her—unlock the stupid door! We already have PSFs and skip tracers after us; we don't need to add the League to the list! They probably think we took her, and if they put in the call that there are freaks roaming around in a beat-up black minivan . . ." He couldn't bring himself to finish.

"Hey," Liam said, holding up a finger, "don't talk about Black Betty that way."

"Oh, *excuse me* for hurting the feelings of a twenty-year-old minivan."

"He's right," I said. "I'm sorry, please—I don't want any more trouble for you."

"You want to go back to them?" Liam was facing me again, his mouth set in a grim line. "Listen, it's none of my business, Green, but you have the right to know that whatever lies they fed you probably aren't true. They aren't our angel network. They have their own agenda, and if they plucked you out of camp, it means they have a plan for you."

I shook my head. "You think I don't know that?"

"Okay," he returned in a calm voice. "Then why are you in such a hurry to get back?"

There was nothing judgmental or accusatory about the question, so why did I still feel like an idiot? Something hot and itchy bubbled up in my throat, drifting up until it settled behind my eyes. Oh God, the kid was looking at me with all the sympathy and pity required of someone watching a stray puppy being put down. I didn't know if the emotion swelling inside me was anger or embarrassment, but I didn't have time to sort it out.

118

"No, but I can't—I didn't mean to drag you into—I mean, I did mean to, but . . ."

I saw Zu move out of the corner of my eye, reaching for me. I jerked away, sucking in a harsh breath. A hurt expression crossed her face, staying long enough for me to feel guilty about it. She had been trying to help me—to be kind to me. She didn't know what kind of monster she had saved.

If she had, she would never have unlocked the door.

"Do you want to go back to them?"

Chubs was looking at Liam, and Liam was looking at me. He had caught me again with his eyes, and I hadn't even realized it.

"No," I said, and it was the truth. "I don't."

He didn't say anything, only shifted the minivan out of park. The van rolled forward.

What are you doing, Ruby? I willed my hand to reach for the door, but it seemed too far and my hand too heavy. *Get out. Get out now.*

"Lee, don't you dare," Chubs began. "If the League comes after us . . ."

"It'll be okay," Liam said. "We're just taking her to the nearest bus station."

I blinked. That was more than even I was expecting. "You don't have to."

Liam waved me off. "It's fine. Sorry we can't do more. Can't risk it."

"Yes, you're right," Chubs said. "So explain to me why we aren't taking her to one of the train stations, which are closer?"

119

When I looked back up, Liam was studying me, his light eyebrows pulled tight together by some unspoken thought. I tried not to squirm under his gaze. "Remind me again— Ruby, right? I'm sure you've caught on by now, but I'm Liam, the lovely lady behind me is Suzume."

She smiled shyly. I turned and raised a brow in the direction of the other boy. "I'm guessing your name isn't actually Chubs?"

"No," he sniffed. "Liam gave me that name at camp."

"He was a bit of a porker." Liam had a small smile on his face. "Turns out field labor and a restricted diet are better than fat camp. Zu can back me up on this one."

But Zu wasn't paying attention, not to any of us. She had pulled her hoodie up over her ears and twisted around in her seat so that she was staring over the top of it, out the back window. Her lips were parted, but she couldn't bring the words to them. The color drained from her round face.

"Zu?" Liam said. "What's wrong?"

She didn't need to point. Even if we hadn't seen the tan SUV speeding straight for us, it would have been impossible to miss the bullet that blew through the back window and shattered it.

NINE

THE SINGLE BULLET CUT A PATH STRAIGHT DOWN THE center of the minivan, exiting out through the windshield. For a moment, none of us did anything but stare at the hole and the spreading spiderweb of cracks radiating out from it.

"Holy sh—!" Liam threw the car into forward, slamming his foot down all the way on the gas. He seemed to have forgotten that we were in a Dodge Caravan and not a BMW, because it went from zero to sixty in what felt like thirty minutes. Black Betty's body began to shake, rattling from more than just the holes and cracks in the road.

I whirled around, searching for Rob's SUV, but the car behind us was a bright red pickup truck, and the man leaning out of the passenger window of the truck, rifle in hand, was not Rob.

"I told you!" Chubs yelled. *I told you they were skip tracers!*

"Yes, you were right," Liam yelled right back. "But could you try to be useful, too?"

He jerked the car left, just as the man fired off another shot. It must have gone wide, because it never hit the car, not that I could tell. He fired again, and that bullet had far better luck; it slammed into Black Betty's bumper. We felt the hit like a brick to the back; every single one of us let out a sharp gasp. In Chubs's case, he moaned and crossed himself.

Zu was slouched down in her seat, her chest pressed against her knees. Her hood hid her face, but it couldn't mask the way her entire body shook. I put a hand on her back, holding her down.

Another bang sounded behind us, but this time, it wasn't a gunshot.

"What in the . . ." Liam risked a look back over his shoulder. "Are you kidding me?"

My heart fell like a stone into my stomach. The red truck jolted forward, and I saw the driver—a dark haired woman with glasses—tug the wheel to the side, trying to shake the truck free from the tan SUV that had rammed into it. I didn't need to see who was driving it to know who *that* vehicle belonged to: Cate and Rob. But, then, who was in the pickup truck?

"It *is* her!" Chubs cried. "I told you! She found us!"

"Then who's the guy with the gun?" Liam cried. "Her boyfriend?"

The man who had fired at us turned his attention to taking out the SUV behind him, twisting around in the window. He lasted half a breath. A gunshot from the SUV clipped him in the chest and sent an explosive spray of blood into the air. The crack of the next bullet sent the shooter's lifeless body sliding out of the passenger window of the truck. The driver—the woman—didn't so much as look back at him.

I watched the red truck finally break away from the SUV's front bumper. With both of its back tires blown out, it swerved into the other lane, spinning out, until it came to a jolting stop on the shoulder of the highway.

"That's one," I heard Liam say. I turned back, fully expecting to see Rob's gun trained on me through the blown-out back windshield of our van. Only, Rob was behind the wheel.

Cate was the one in the passenger seat, a rifle steady between her hands.

"Please, just let me go," I said, grabbing Liam's shoulder. "I'll go back with them. No one has to get hurt."

"Yes!" Chubs said. "Pull over, let her out!"

"Both of you shut up!" Liam said, throwing Black Betty into the right lane and then back into the left. The SUV followed us, more than keeping up. I couldn't tell if we had slowed down, or if they had somehow gunned it harder, because in the next breath, the SUV rammed into us, and not even the seat belts could keep us from jerking forward.

Liam muttered something under his breath, which was lost in the sudden onslaught of heavy rain. He rolled down his window and threw a hand outside, as if to motion for the SUV to go around us.

"Do something!" Chubs shouted, bracing his hands against the steering wheel.

"I'm trying!" he said. "I can't concentrate!"

He's trying to use his abilities. The realization crept up through my terror.

The fat droplets splattering the window blurred the trees around us, but Liam didn't bother with the wipers. If he had, he might have seen the other car blazing toward us from the opposite direction. Its horn screeched to life and woke Liam from his trance.

The minivan swerved back into the right lane, narrowly missing a head-on collision with the sedan. If that little car hadn't slammed on its brakes, the SUV would have plowed right into it, too. Both Zu and I whirled around just in time to see the SUV swerve back into the right lane. Rob managed to recover quickly, and they were speeding toward us again before we had a chance to catch our breaths.

"Liam," I begged. "Please, just pull over. I won't let them do anything to you!"

I don't want to go back.

I don't want to go back.

I don't want to . . .

I squeezed my eyes shut.

"Green!' Liam's voice cut into my thoughts. "Can you drive?"

"No—"

"Can you see better than Chubs?"

"Maybe, but—"

"Great!" he said, reaching back for my arm. "Come on up to the captain's seat."

He snorted, even as another bullet pinged against Black Betty's metal skin. "Come on, it's just like riding a bike.

124

Right pedal is gas to go, left is brake, steer with wheel. That's all you need to know."

"Wait!" But apparently, I didn't get a say in the matter. He swerved back into the left lane just as the SUV came up for another tap. Instead of speeding up, his foot came down hard on the brake. Black Betty skidded to a halt, and the SUV blew right by us.

It happened too fast for me to put up any kind of fight. He unsnapped his seat belt and pulled me toward the driver's seat just as he stood from it. The car rolled forward on its own accord and I panicked, slamming my foot down on what I thought was the brake pedal. Black Betty leaped forward, and this time I was the one that screamed.

"Brake is on the left!" Liam flew against the dashboard as the SUV recovered. I heard its tires scream as Rob turned the truck around and kicked up the speed. "Hit the gas!"

"Why can't he drive?" I asked in a strangled voice.

Chubs pushed the passenger's seat back far enough for him to climb over it into the back, and Liam took Chubs's seat.

"Because," he said, rolling down the window, "he can barely see five feet in front of him. Trust me, you don't want him to drive, darlin'. Now—*hit the gas!*"

I did as I was told. The car sprung forward again, sending my heart up into my throat. The wheels spun against the wet asphalt.

Liam was half hanging out of the window, half sitting on it. "Faster!" he said.

The rain fell thick and heavy, but the SUV's headlights pierced the mist as I drove the van straight toward them. We were going so fast that the steering wheel shook in my hands, jerking around like it had a life of its own. I bit back a frustrated scream and tried to let up on the gas, but Liam wasn't having it.

"No, keep going!"

"Lee," Chubs was hunched over in his seat. "This is insane—what are you doing?"

He had been so quiet that I'd almost forgotten he was in the van. With the speedometer creeping past eighty, ninety, ninety-five, I wasn't remembering much at all.

And that's when it went to hell.

There was a horrible bang—a thousand times worse than the sound of a balloon exploding—and the van was spinning, the wheel dancing right out of my hands.

"Straight!" Liam was shouting, "Straighten out!"

"Sh—!" The wind was knocked out of my chest by my seat belt, but I fought against the natural turn of the wheel long enough to get us heading straight again. The car tilted back, leaving a trail of sparks on the road behind us. We were staring the SUV down again, making a second head-on pass at them.

"Keep going toward them—don't stop!" Liam yelled.

But the tire, I thought, my hands strangling the steering wheel, *the tire . . .*

Chubs had reached for Liam's legs, steadying him before he could go flying out the window. "Let go!" he snapped. "I'm fine, I've got it now!"

I didn't know what Liam had meant by "it," not until I looked up into the rearview mirror and saw the dark body of a tree come hurtling out of the woods, guided in front of the SUV, by nothing other than a flick of Liam's hand.

With his attention focused on the minivan barreling toward them, Rob didn't have time to jerk the car out of the tree's path. I spun my hands around the wheel blindly, until we were facing away from the wreckage. I heard the sound of shattering glass and crunching metal as Rob tried to veer, only to overcorrect. When I looked back in the side mirror, the SUV was on its side in a smoking heap. Beside it was the splintered body of a tree, still rolling to a stop after the collision.

"What did you do?" I had to yell over the chatter of the wind and road. "I thought—"

Chubs was the one to answer, his face ashen. "Now do you get it? They weren't going to stop."

Liam slid back inside of the window, plopping down with a long sigh. His hair was standing up on all ends, dusted with leaves and little twigs.

"Okay, Green," he said, keeping his voice steady, "they blew the back tire out, so you're driving on the rim. Just keep heading straight and start to slow down. Get off on the next ramp."

I clenched my jaw so hard that it ached.

"You all right, Zu?" he asked. The girl gave him two thumbs-up, her yellow gloves the only bright spot of color in the van.

"Well, I'm fine, thanks for asking," Chubs said. His little glasses were crooked on his face as he smoothed his blue button-down shirt. For good measure, he leaned forward and smacked the back of Liam's head. "And by the way, are you out of your freaking mind? Do you know what happens when a body is thrown from a car at high velocity?"

"No," Liam interrupted, "but I imagine it's not pretty or appropriate for an eleven-year-old's ears."

I glanced back at Zu. Eleven? That couldn't be right. . . .

"Oh, so you can throw her in the path of bullets, but she can't hear a scary story?" Chubs crossed his arms over his chest.

Liam reached down and pulled his seat back upright. When he sat back, it was with a grimace and clenched fists. There was a fresh cut above his eye. Blood dripped from his chin.

I saw the green highway sign through the haze of rain. It didn't matter what town or exit number it said. I just wanted to get off the road and out of the driver's seat.

My entire body was numb, exhausted, as I took my foot off the gas. The minivan followed the curve of the ramp with only the slightest nudging, and by the time we reached the road, it came to a natural stop. I pressed a hand to my chest to make sure my heart hadn't given out on me.

Liam reached over and put the parking brake on.

"You did a good job," he began. His voice was quieter than I expected. Unfortunately, it did nothing to calm the pissed off snake that was coiled tight around my stomach.

I reached over and punched him in the arm. *Hard.*

"Ow!" he cried, pulling away from me with wide eyes. "What was that for?"

"That was *not* like riding a bike, you asshole!"

He stared at me a moment, his lips twitching. It was Suzume who burst out into a fit of silent laughter, an endless stream of gasping and shaking that turned her face bright pink and left her breathless. Seconds passed with her laughter as the only sound able to float up above the rain—at least until Chubs put his face in his hands and let out a long groan.

"Oh yeah," Liam said, popping his door open, "you're gonna fit in real nice."

The rain had slowed to a drizzle by the time Liam got to work on the back tire. I had stayed exactly where I was in the driver's seat, mostly because I wasn't sure what I was supposed to be doing. The other two kids had jumped out of the car after him, Suzume heading to the back of the van with Liam, and Chubs in the exact opposite direction. I watched through the cracked windshield as he made his way toward a sign pointing us in the direction of the Monongahela National Forest. After a minute, he pulled something—a paperback book—out of his back pocket, and sat down at the edge of the road. Feeling more than a little envy, I squinted, trying to make out the book's title, but half of the cover was missing, and the other half covered by his hand. I don't know if he was actually reading or just glaring at the text.

I had pulled us over into Slaty Fork, West Virginia, if the road signs were to be trusted. What I thought had been some hickville back road had actually been Highway 219, in the middle of nowhere. Marlinton might have lost its people, but it didn't look as though Slaty Fork had any to begin with.

I stood up from the driver's seat and made my way to the back of the minivan. My hands were still trembling, as if trying to shake out that last bit of adrenaline singing in my blood. The black backpack that Rob and Cate had given me had been thrown into the backseat, covered in a few loose sheets of newspaper and an empty bottle of Windex.

I brushed the backpack off and set it down next to me on the seat. The newspaper was over three years old and stiff with age. There was a half-page ad for a new face cream someone had oh-so-cleverly called Forever Young.

I flipped the sheet over, looking for any actual news. I skimmed over an opinion piece that celebrated the rehabilitation camps and was more amused than offended that Psi kids were now being openly referred to as "mutant time bombs." There was also a short article on rioting that the reporter claimed was "the direct result of escalating tensions between the West and East government on new birth legislation." At the very bottom of the page, past some fluff story about the anniversary of some train conductors' strike, was a picture of Clancy Gray.

"President's Son Attends Children's League Hearing," is what the headline beneath it said. I didn't need to read more than the first two or three lines to get the basic gist: the president was too big of a coward to come out of hiding after a failed assassination attempt, so he sent his freak baby to do the dirty work for him. How old was Clancy now? I wondered. The pictures at Thurmond were identical to this one, and I had never thought of him as anything older than eleven or twelve. But he must have been eighteen or close to by now. Practically an old geezer by our standards.

I tossed the paper aside in disgust and reached for my backpack again. Rob had said there was a change of clothes inside, and if that was the case, I was getting out of my Thurmond uniform once and for all.

A plain white shirt, a pair of jeans, a belt, and a zip-up hoodie. I could handle that.

The knock on the window startled me enough that I nearly bit my tongue clean off. Liam's face appeared there, drawn in tense lines. "Can you bring those clothes to me for a sec? I need to show you something."

The very second I knew his eyes were on me, every bone, muscle, and joint in my body snapped to attention. With the faint taste of blood in my mouth, I jumped out of the sliding door, taking in the sight of the van. If it were possible, the car looked worse than before—like a toy that someone had wedged down the sink and run through the garbage disposal. My fingers came up to trace one of the fresh punctures on the side paneling where a bullet had slammed through the thin metal.

Liam knelt beside Zu, who was holding on to the spare tire with everything she had, and went to work cranking the van up on the jack and off the demolished back right tire. I came to stand behind them just in time to watch Liam wave his hand in front of the hubcap. The nuts twirled out on his command, collecting in a neat pile on the ground.

Blue, I registered. Liam was Blue. What did that make the others?

"Okay," he began. He blew a strand of his light hair out of his eyes. "Take out the shirt you were about to change into."

"I'm—I'm not changing out here," I said.

He rolled his eyes. "Really? You're worried about your modesty when we're going to have League agents on our tail in a matter of hours? Priorities, Green. Take out the shirt."

I watched him for a moment, but even I wasn't sure what I was looking for.

"Feel around the collar," Liam said. He set another nut on the ground by his feet. "You'll find a bump."

I did. It was small, no bigger than a pea, sewn into the otherwise nondescript shirt.

"Chubs has a little fancy lady kit under the front seat," he said. "If you're going to change into it, you need to cut the tracker out of that shirt."

The "little fancy lady kit" turned out to be a box of thread, scissors, and a tiny piece of embroidery. On a scrap of fabric, someone—Chubs?—had sewn a perfect black square. I stared at the mark, rubbing my thumb over its raised surface.

"Anyway, you should probably change out of the uniform," Liam continued. "But be sure to check the pants and the sweater, too. I wouldn't put it past them to use more than one."

He was right again. I found one sewn into the waistband of the jeans, one in the hem of the hoodie, and even one glued inside the belt buckle—four trackers for one girl, plus one that had been sewn into the lining of the backpack itself.

Liam finished replacing the tire with the spare faster than I thought possible. Zu helped him place the nuts back in their sockets and slowly crank the car back down. When he handed the tools to her, she knew exactly where to put them in the trunk.

"Here," he said, holding his hand out to me. "I'll take care of them." My hands trembled as I handed the trackers to him. He threw them on the ground, and crushed them beneath the heel of his shoe.

"I don't understand. . . ." I began. But I did, in a way. They wouldn't have gone to all that trouble breaking me out if they hadn't had a method of keeping tabs on me if I got recaptured or separated from them.

Liam's hand came out toward me, and the sheer panic at the thought of his touch had me jumping back, trying to put as much air between us as I could. It still wasn't far enough; his hand dropped between us, but I felt the warmth of his upturned palm brush my shoulder as if it had actually rested there. My arms came up and crossed over my chest, and some mangled mess of anxiety and guilt rose up from deep in my guts. I tried to focus on the Psi identification numbers on the top of my shoes to keep from jumping away again.

You are acting like a nervy five-year-old, I told myself. *Stop it. He's just another kid.*

"They tell you a lot of lies in the Children's League, the biggest being that you're free," he said. "They talk about love and respect and *family*, but I don't know any family that puts

133

a tracking device on someone and then sends them out to be shot up and blown away."

"But we didn't have to kill them," I said. My fingers tightened around the backpack straps. "There was another kid inside. Martin. He didn't . . . he didn't deserve to . . ."

"You mean—" Liam wiped the grease and dirt from his hands off on the front of his jeans. "The kind of—" He made a vague motion with his hands, which I think was supposed to indicate Martin's plump stature. "That guy?"

I nodded.

"The tree didn't actually hit them," Liam said, leaning against the minivan's sliding door. "They might still be alive."

Liam guided me back toward the passenger seat and whistled to get Chubs's attention. Somewhere behind me, I heard Zu climb back into Black Betty.

"Look," he continued, "they all wear the trackers. I'm sure another League agent will be along in a little while to help them. You can go back if you want, or we can take you to the bus station like I said we would."

My hands were still by my side, my face as blank as a clear sky, but I wasn't fooling him. He tuned in to my guilt like I had been wearing it plain as day on my face. "It doesn't make you a bad person, you know—to want to live your own life."

I looked back and forth between the road and his face, more confused now than ever. It didn't make sense for him to want to help me, not when he already had two other people counting on him. That he wanted to protect.

Liam opened the back door for me, tilting his head toward the empty seat inside. But before I could even consider the cost of staying with them, if just for a short while, Chubs's arm shot out and he ripped the sliding door shut in front of my face.

"Chubs—" Liam warned.

"Why," Chubs began, "were you with the Children's League?"

"Hey now," Liam said. "This is a don't-ask-don't-tell operation. Green, you—"

"No," Chubs said, "*you* decided that. You and Suzume. If we're going to be stuck with her, I want to know who this person is and why we got chased down by gun-toting lunatics trying to get her back."

Liam lifted his hands in surrender.

"I . . ." What could I tell them that wouldn't sound like a complete and total lie? My head felt light; I was almost too exhausted to think. "I was . . ."

Zu gave me a nod of encouragement, her eyes bright.

"I was a runner in the Control Tower," I blurted. "I saw the access codes to the computer servers the League wants access to. I have a photographic memory, and I'm good with numbers and codes."

That was probably overkill, but apparently I had sold it.

"What about your friend? What's his deal?"

The longer they stared at me, the harder it became to not fidget. *Get a grip, Ruby.*

"You mean Martin?" I said, my voice sounding high to my own ears. "Yesterday was the first time I had ever seen him. I don't know what his story was. I didn't ask."

I wished I didn't know what Martin's story was.

135

Chubs slapped the side of the minivan. "Don't tell me you believe that, Lee. We knew everyone by the time we broke out."

Broke out. They actually escaped? Shock left me speechless for several moments until I asked, finally, "Really? All three thousand of them?"

The boys took a step back at the same time.

"You had three thousand kids at your camp?" Liam asked.

"Why?" I looked between them, unnerved. "How many were in your camp?

"Three hundred at most," Liam said. "Are you sure? Three *thousand*?"

"Well, it's not like they gave us an official number. There were thirty kids per cabin and about a hundred of those. There used to be more, but they sent the Reds, Oranges, and Yellows away."

Apparently, I had blown his mind. Liam let out a strangled noise at the back of his throat. "Holy crap," he finally managed to squeeze out. "What camp was it?"

"It's none of your business," I said. "I'm not asking you where you were."

"We were in Caledonia, Ohio," Chubs said, ignoring a sharp look from Liam. "They stuck us in an abandoned elementary school. We broke out. Your turn."

"Why, so you can report me to the nearest PSF station?"

"Yeah, because, *clearly*, we'd be able to stroll up and lodge a sighting report."

After a moment, I blew out a harsh breath. "Fine. I was in Thurmond."

The silence that followed seemed to stretch on longer than the road beneath us.

"Are you serious?" Liam asked, finally. "Crazy Thurmond, with the FrankenKiddies?"

"They've stopped testing," I said, feeling strangely defensive.

"No, I just—I just . . ." Liam raced through the words. "I thought it was all filled up, you know? That's why they bused us to Ohio."

"How old were you when you went into camp?" Chubs's voice was measured, but I saw his face fall all the same. "You were young, right?"

The answer popped out before I could stop myself. "The day after my tenth birthday."

Liam blew out a low whistle, and I wondered exactly how much of Thurmond's reputation had leaked out in the time I had been there. Who were the ones talking about it—the former PSFs assigned there?

And, if people knew, why hadn't anyone come to help us?

"How long were you guys in Caledonia?"

"Suzume was there for about two years. I was there for a year and a half, and Lee was there for a year or so."

"That's . . ." A small, ugly voice inside my head whispered, *That's it?* even as the better part of me knew full well that it didn't matter if they had been there for one year or one day—a minute in one of those camps was enough to smash you into pieces.

"And you're what, sixteen? Seventeen?"

"I don't know," I said, and the thought nearly knocked me back against the van. I really *wasn't* sure—Sam had claimed it was six years, but she could have been wrong. We didn't keep track of time at Thurmond in the usual way; I recognized seasons passing, but somewhere along the line I had stopped trying to mark it. I grew bigger, I knew every winter that I must be another year older, but none of it . . . it just hadn't seemed to matter until now. "What year is it?"

Chubs snorted, rolling his eyes heavenward. He opened his mouth to say something, but stopped once he got a good look at my face. I'm not sure what kind of expression I was wearing, but it erased his exasperation in two seconds flat. His narrowed eyes widened into something that looked very much like pity.

And Liam . . . his expression seemed to dissolve entirely.

I felt the hair on my neck begin to prickle, my fingers twist the fabric of my uniform shorts. The absolute last thing—*the last thing*—I wanted was to be pitied by a bunch of strangers. Regret washed down through me, flooding out even my anxiety and fear. I shouldn't have said anything at all; I should have lied or dodged the question. Whatever they thought Thurmond was like, whatever they believed I'd gone through, it was bad enough to mark me as pathetic in their eyes. I could see it in their faces, and the irony stung more than I expected it to. They'd taken in a monster, thinking it was a mouse.

"Sixteen, then," I said, once Liam had confirmed the year. Sam had been right after all.

Something else was bothering me. "They're still creating new camps and sending kids to them?"

"Not so much anymore," Liam said. "The younger set—Zu's age—they were hit the hardest. People got scared, and the birthrate dropped off even before the government tried banning new births. Most of the kids that are still being sent to camps are like us. They escaped detection during collections or tried to run."

I nodded, mulling this over.

"At Thurmond," Chubs began, "did they really—"

"I think that's enough," Liam interrupted. He reached past Chubs's outstretched arm and opened the sliding door for me again. "She answered your questions, we answered hers, and now we've gotta hit the road while the going is still good."

Zu climbed in first, and, without looking at either boy, I followed, heading to the rear seat, where I could stretch out and hide from any more unwanted questions.

Chubs took the front passenger seat, throwing one last look back at me. His full lips were pressed so tight together they were colorless. Eventually, he turned his attention to the book in his lap and pretended that I wasn't there at all.

Black Betty purred as Liam hit the accelerator and my entire body vibrated with her. She was the only one willing to speak for a long time.

The rain was still coming down, casting a gray light around the car. The windows had fogged, and for a minute I did nothing but watch the rain. Car headlights were flashing through the front windshield, but it was nowhere near dark.

Chubs eventually turned the radio on, filling the quiet space with a report about America's gas crisis and the drilling that was happening in Alaska as a result. If I wasn't already halfway to sleep, the droning from the humorless newscaster would have put me there.

"Hey, Green," Liam called back. "You have a last name?"

I thought about lying, about making myself into someone that I wasn't, but it didn't seem right. Even if I let these people in, they'd forget about me soon enough.

"No," I said. I had a Psi number and the name I'd inherited from my grandmother. The rest didn't matter.

Liam turned back to the road, his fingers drumming on the steering wheel. "Got it."

I dropped back down on the seat, pressing my hands against my face. Sleep came for me eventually, just as the storm clouds peeled back to reveal a pristine night sky. Without the sound of rain, I could just make out the quiet song floating from the car speakers, and Liam's deep voice as he sang along.

TEN

CHUBS WAS THE ONE TO WAKE ME. IT WAS A QUICK slap to my shoulder, like he couldn't bring himself to touch it long enough to put the effort into shaking me, but it was enough. I had been curled like a shrimp on one of the cramped seats, but at his touch, I bolted out of it, knocking my head against the window. I felt its cold touch on the back of my neck as I all but tumbled in the narrow space between the front seat and mine. For a single, foggy instant, I couldn't remember where I was, never mind how I had gotten there.

Chubs's face crossed back into my line of sight, one eyebrow arched at my tangle of limbs. And then it all came back to me, like a punch to the throat.

Damn it, damn it, damn it, I thought, trying to smooth my dark hair out of my face. I had only meant to rest my eyes for a few minutes—and who knows how long I'd been conked out? Judging by Chubs's expression, it hadn't been a short nap.

"Don't you think you've slept long enough?" he huffed, crossing his arms over his chest. The van felt warmer, and I didn't realize why until I sat up and saw the dark blue fabric that had been strung up to cover the rear windshield.

The reality of the situation struck me at once, with a sharp twist in my side. I'd left myself wide open in a van of strangers—so wide open, in fact, that Chubs had been able to put a hand on me. God, I didn't know which of us had come out luckier in the end—him, for not having his brain wiped clean, or me for avoiding yet another potential disaster. How stupid could I be? The second they knew what I was, they'd throw me out, and then where would I be? Speaking of which . . .

"Where are we?" I pulled myself back up into the seat. "Where are the others?"

Chubs sat in one of the middle seats, dividing his time between the book in his lap and the world of trees just outside the tinted car window. I moved, trying to follow his gaze, but there was nothing to see.

"Somewhere near the lovely city of Kingwood, West Virginia. Lee and Suzume are checking something out," he said.

I had leaned forward without realizing it, trying to see what he was reading. It'd been years since I'd even seen a book, let alone read from one. Chubs wasn't having it, though. The moment my shoulder brushed his, he snapped the book shut and turned to give me the nastiest stink eye he could muster. Even with his too-small glasses and my knowledge of his little fancy lady kit under the front seat, I reminded myself there was a distinct possibility he was capable of killing me with his brain.

"How long did I sleep?"

"A day," Chubs said. "The general wants you up and ready to report to duty. He's in one of his go-go-go moods. You may only be a Green, but he's expecting you to help."

I chose my next words carefully, ignoring the smug look on his face. Let him think that if it made him feel better. He was smarter; there was no debate about that. He probably had years of education on me, had read hundreds more books, and could remember enough math to actually be useful. But as small and stupid as he made me feel, there was no ignoring the fact that all it would take is one touch, and I could have read him the contents of his brain.

"Liam's a Blue, right?" I began. "Are you and Zu both Blue, too?"

"No." He frowned, and it took him several moments to decide whether or not to reveal his next bit of information. "Suzume's Yellow."

I sat up a little straighter. "You had Yellows at your camp?"

Chubs grunted. "No Green, I just lied to you—*yes*, we had Yellows."

But that didn't make sense—after all, if they took the Yellows out of Thurmond, why wouldn't they have taken them from all the camps?

"Did . . ." I began, unsure of how to ask this. When she first pulled me into the van, I thought she was just shy and skittish around strangers. But I hadn't heard her utter a single word in the entire time I had been with them. Not to me, not to Chubs—not even to Liam. "Did they . . . do something to the Yellows? To her?"

The only way the van's atmosphere could have electrified faster was if I had thrown a live wire into a full bathtub.

Chubs turned toward me sharply, drawing his arms up, crossing them in front of his chest. The look he leveled at me over his glasses would have turned a weaker soul to stone.

"That," he said slowly—precisely, I thought, to make sure I understood, "is absolutely none of your business."

I held up my hands, retreating.

"Were you even thinking about what could happen to her when you followed her?" he pressed on. "Do you even care that your friends in the green SUV would have gladly scooped her up?"

"The people in the green SUV—" I began, and would have finished, had the door not suddenly rolled open behind us. Chubs let out a noise that could only be described as a squawk and just about flew into the front passenger seat. By the time he had settled himself down, his eyes were almost as wide as Zu's, who stood watching him from the door.

"Don't *do* that!" he gasped, clutching his chest. "Give us a little warning, will you?"

Zu raised an eyebrow in my direction, and I raised one right back at her. After a moment, she seemed to remember the reason she had come and began waving us outside, her bright, sunny-color glove flashing.

Chubs unbuckled his seat belt with an aggravated sigh. "I told him this was a waste of time. They said *Virginia*,

144

not *West Virginia*." He turned his gaze back toward me. "By the way," he added, "that SUV was tan. That's some photographic memory you have."

An excuse leaped to my throat, but he cut me off with a knowing look, and slammed the door behind him.

I jumped out of the van and followed Zu. As my feet sunk into the mud and sad, yellowed grass, I had my first good look around.

A large wooden sign, leaning back like someone had nearly run it over, said EAST RIVER CAMPING GROUNDS, but there was no river, and it certainly wasn't your typical camping ground. If anything, it was—or once was—an old trailer and RV park.

The farther we walked from the minivan, the more nervous I felt. It wasn't raining, but my skin felt clammy and cold to the touch. All around us, as far as my eyes could see, were the burned-out silver and white husks of former homes and vehicles. Several of the larger, more permanent trailers had entire walls ripped or charred away, revealing kitchens and living rooms with their insides still intact, if not waterlogged and infested with animals and slowly rotting leaves from the nearby trees. It was like a mass grave of past lives.

Even though screen doors had been ripped off or warped, even though some RVs knelt on whatever tires had been slashed, there were still signs of life all around. Walls were decorated with pictures of happy and smiling families, a grandfather clock was still counting time, pots were still on stoves, a small swing set remained undisturbed and lonely on the far end of the grounds.

Zu and I navigated around an RV that was now on its side, following a path of deep footsteps in the mud. I took one look at the RV's rusted bones and immediately turned away, my hand tightening around Zu's gloves. She looked up at me with a questioning look, but I only shook my head and said, "Spooky."

When the rain came, it hammered against the metal bodies around us, rattling a few of the weaker roofs and screens. I jumped back with a yelp when a trailer's door fell into our path. Zu only jumped over it and pointed ahead, to where Chubs and Liam were locked in conversation.

It had taken me a second to recognize Liam. Under his jacket, he wore a blue sweatshirt with the hood pulled up over what looked like a Redskins hat. I had no idea where he managed to find them, but a pair of aviator sunglasses obscured a good portion of his face from view.

"—isn't it," Chubs said. "I *told* you."

"They said it was at the east edge of the state," Liam insisted. "And they could have meant West Virginia—"

"Or they could have been screwing with us," Chubs finished for him. He must have heard us approaching, because he jumped and turned around. The moment he locked eyes with me, he scowled.

"Mornin', sunshine!" Liam called. "Sleep okay?"

Zu darted out ahead of me, but I could feel my feet begin to drag with an invisible weight as I came toward them. I crossed my arms over my chest, steadying myself enough to ask, "What is this place?"

This time, it was Liam who blew out a sigh. "Well, we were hoping it was East River. *The* East River, I mean."

"That's in Virginia," I said, looking down at my shoes. "The peninsula. It empties into the Chesapeake Bay."

"Thank you Detective Duh." Chubs shook his head. "We're talking about the Slip Kid's East River."

"Hey." Liam's voice was sharp. "Lay off, buddy. We really didn't know anything about it until we were out of camp, either."

Chubs crossed his arms over his chest and looked away. "Whatever."

"What is it?"

I felt Liam turn his attention back to me, which immediately prompted me to turn my attention back to Zu, who mostly just looked confused. *Get a grip*, I ordered myself, *stop it*.

I wasn't afraid of them, not even Chubs. Maybe a bit when I thought too hard about how easily I could ruin their lives, or pictured their horrified reactions if they were to figure out what, exactly, I was. I just didn't know what to say or how to act around them. Every movement and word on my part felt uncomfortable, shrill, or sharp, and I was beginning to worry that the feelings of hesitancy and awkwardness were never going to lift. I already felt like the freak of freaks without the added realization that I lacked the basic ability of communicating normally with other human beings.

Liam sighed, scratching the back of his head. "We first heard about East River from some kids in our camp. Supposedly—and I mean *supposedly*—it's a place where any kids on the outside can go and live together. The Slip Kid, who runs the show, can get you in touch with your folks without the PSFs finding out about it. There's food, a place to sleep—well, you get the picture. The problem is finding it. We think it's somewhere in this area, thanks to a few fairly unhelpful Blues we ran across in Ohio. It's the kind of thing that . . ."

"If you're in the know, you're not supposed to talk about it," I finished. "But who's the Slip Kid?"

Liam shrugged. "No one knows. Or . . . well, I guess people *know*, they just don't say. The rumors about him are pretty incredible, though. The PSFs gave him that nickname because he—*supposedly*—escaped their custody a good four times."

I was too stunned to say anything to that.

"Kind of puts the rest of us to shame, huh? I was feeling really bad about myself until someone told me the rumors about him." Liam shuddered. "Supposedly he's one of those—an *Orange*."

That single word thundered down around me, freezing me in place. Liam went on to say something else, with a lot less disgust, but I couldn't hear him over the roar in my ears. I didn't hear a word of what he was saying.

Slip Kid. Someone who could help kids get home, if they had a home to return to, and parents who remembered them and wanted them. A life to reclaim.

And, potentially, one of the last Orange kids out there.

I squeezed my eyes shut, pressing the heels of my palms against them for good measure. I didn't qualify for his help, not in the traditional way. Even if I could get in touch with my parents, it wasn't like they would welcome a girl they considered a stranger back with open arms. There was Grams, but I had no way of knowing where she was now. After finding out what I had done, would she even want me?

"Why do you even need this guy's help?" I interrupted, still feeling light-headed. "Can't you just go home?"

"Use your brain, Green," Chubs said. "We can't go home, because PSFs are probably watching our parents."

Liam shook his head, finally taking his sunglasses off. He looked exhausted, the skin under his eyes baggy and bruised. "You'll have to be really careful, okay? Do you even want me to drop you off at a bus station? Because we'd be happy—"

"*No!*" Chubs said. "We most certainly *would not*. We've already wasted enough time on her, and she's the reason we have the League after us, too."

A sharp pain sprouted on the left side of my chest, just above my heart. He was right, of course. The best option for everyone would be to drop me off at the nearest bus station and be done with it.

But it didn't mean I didn't want to, or need to, find this Slip Kid as badly as they did. But I couldn't ask to stay. I couldn't impose on them anymore than I already had, or risk ruining them with the invisible fingers that seemed bent on tearing apart every single connection I managed to make. If the League caught up to us and took them in, I'd never forgive myself. Never.

If I was going to find the Slip Kid, I was going to have to do it by myself. You'd think I'd be used to the thought of taking on each day with no one beside me, that it'd be some kind of relief not to be in constant danger of sliding into someone else's head. But I didn't want to. I didn't want to step out under the gray overcast sky alone and feel its chill work its way under my skin.

"So," I said, squinting at the nearest trailer. "This isn't East River."

"It might have been, once," Liam said. "They could move around from time to time. I hadn't really considered it."

"Or," Chubs groused, "they could have already been taken back into PSF custody. Maybe this was East River, and now there is no more East River, and we're going to have to find a way to deliver Jack's letter and get home by ourselves, only we won't ever, because of the skip tracers, and we'll all be thrown back into camp, only this time they'll—"

"Thank you, Chuckles," Liam cut in, "for that rousing burst of optimism."

"I could be right," he said. "You have to acknowledge that."

"But you could also be wrong," Liam said, dropping a reassuring hand on Zu's head. "In any case, that's what we're going with now: this was just a false alarm. Let's see if we can find anything useful, then we'll hit the road."

"*Finally.* I'm sick of wasting time on things that don't matter." Chubs shoved his hands into his trouser pockets and stalked toward me. If I hadn't jumped out of the way, his shoulder would have knocked into mine and sent me stumbling back.

I turned, my eyes following his path as he kicked rubbish and rocks out of his way. Liam was suddenly standing next to me, his own arms crossed over his chest.

"Don't take it personally," he said. I must have made a sound of disbelief, because he continued. "I mean . . . okay, the kid is basically a grumpy seventy-year-old man trapped in a seventeen-year-old's body, but he's only being this insufferable to try to push you out."

Yeah, well, I thought, *it's working*.

"And I know it's not an excuse, but he's as stressed and freaked out as the rest of us and—I guess what I'm trying to say is, all of this acid he's throwing your way? It's coming from a good place. If you stick it out, I swear you won't find a more loyal friend. But he's scared as hell about what'll happen, especially to Zu, if we're caught again."

I looked up at that, but Liam was already walking away toward a far row of battered trailers. For one crazy second I thought about following him, but I'd caught Zu out of the corner of my eye, her bright yellow gloves swinging at her sides. She jumped in and out of the trailers, stood on her toes to peer into the smashed windows of the RVs, and even, at one point, started to crawl into wreckage of an RV that looked like it had been split in half by a tornado. The metal roof, which was hanging on by what looked like two flimsy joints, was swaying and bouncing under the combined forces of rain and wind.

Although she had the hood of her oversized sweatshirt pulled snug over her head, I watched as one of Zu's gloved hands came up and brushed the side of her face—as if she was pushing a strand of hair out of her eyes. It didn't strike me as strange until she did it again, only to pale slightly as she caught herself.

The conversation I had tried to have with Chubs in the van came crashing back to me.

"Hey, Zu . . ." I began, only to stop short. How were you supposed to ask a little kid if someone had played slice and dice with her brain without trampling over an already painful memory?

The truth of it was, they only shaved kids' heads at Thurmond when they wanted to do some poking around inside of their skulls; they had all but stopped by the time I arrived, but it had taken a while for the older kids' hair to grow back out. Somewhere in the back of my mind, I had wondered if this wasn't the case with her after all—if the reason she couldn't speak was because they had crossed a few wires they shouldn't have, or gone a step too far in the name of finding a "cure."

"Why did they cut your hair?" I asked, finally.

I knew plenty of girls that would have preferred shorter hair—myself included—but aside from an annual haircut for the girls, we didn't have much say in the matter. The way that Zu seemed to stroke her ghost hair made me think she hadn't had much say, either.

If she had been upset by my question, she didn't show it. Zu brought her hands up to her head and began to scrub at it, making a face of acute discomfort. Seeing that I wasn't getting it, she slipped one hand out of its glove and went to work scratching at her scalp.

"Oh," I said. "*Oh!* You mean your group had lice?"

She nodded.

"Yikes," I said. It made sense, but it still didn't explain

152

why she couldn't open her mouth and answer me. "I'm so sorry."

Zu lifted a shoulder in a half-hearted shrug, then turned and bounded up into the nearest RV.

The door wobbled and protested as I followed her in, squealing as its hinges worked. Zu made a face, and I made one back at her in agreement. The whole home smelled sweet, but . . . not pleasant. Almost like rotten fruit.

I started in the small, central living space, opening and closing the pale cabinet doors. The seat cushions were done up in an obnoxiously bright purple, but they, like the small TV hanging on the wall across from them, were coated with dust and dirt. The only thing out on the counter was a single coffee mug. The back sleeping area was equally spare—a few cushions, a lamp, and a closet with a red dress, a white button-down shirt, and a whole fleet of empty hangers.

I had only just reached for the shirt when I saw it at the edge of my vision.

Someone had attached it to the RV's windshield in place of a rearview mirror. It was nothing that would have seemed odd from the outside, looking in, or drawn attention unless you were really, truly staring at it. But inside, standing only a few feet away from it, I was close enough to see the red light at the base of it, close enough to see that camera inside was pointed toward everything and everyone that passed by on the road in front of it.

And if I could see Betty from where I was, so could it.

The camera's shape was slightly different from the ones they had at Thurmond, but close enough to make me think

153

the same people were behind it. I looked down at Zu and she looked up at me.

"Stay right here," I said, reaching for the coffeepot on the table.

I crossed the RV in three steps, the coffeepot out in front of me like a sword. I kicked aside a few empty boxes and trash, and saw, mixed in with the litter of plastic bags, a small red glove. Too small for any adult's hand.

I didn't realize the pot was still in my hand until I brought it down against the device and smashed it. The cheap glass body broke off and fell to the ground, leaving me holding its handle. The black bulb stayed perched exactly where it was, only now, the camera's eye rotated to face me.

It's on, I thought through the haze of panic, searching for something else to smash it with. It's recording.

I didn't remember calling for her, but Zu appeared at my side in an instant, stuffing something under the front of her oversized sweatshirt. She must have recognized it, too, because before I could even get another word in, she was pulling off one of her yellow rubber gloves and reaching toward it.

"Don't—!"

I'd never seen a Yellow use their abilities before. I'd suffered the aftereffects, of course—power outages across the camp, White Noise when the camp controllers thought one of them had done it on purpose. But they had been gone so long at Thurmond that I had stopped trying to imagine what it must have been like for them to speak the mysterious language of electricity.

154

Zu's fingers had only brushed against it, but the camera began to let out a high-pitched whine. There was a bolt of white-blue that seemed to leap from her bare finger to the camera's outer shell. That same crackling line whipped down over the plastic, causing it to smoke and warp under its heat.

Without warning, all of the lights in the RV flashed on, glowing so molten hot that they shattered. The vehicle began to cough and sputter, shaking under our feet, as its engine found itself miraculously revived after a long sleep.

Zu jammed her hand back into its glove and crossed her arms over her chest. She squeezed her eyes shut, as if willing it all to stop. But we didn't have time to wait around and see if it would. I moved toward the door, grabbing the front of her sweatshirt to all but drag her out of the RV. She was still stumbling as I pulled her around to the end that faced the road, and Black Betty.

"Come on," I said, not letting her slow. The brightness was gone from her face, blown out like a candle. "It's okay," I lied. "We just need to get the others."

There was a camera installed in the front windshield of every trailer in that front row; I spotted them one by one as we ran back toward Betty. There was no point trying to get rid of them now. Whoever was going to see us had likely already seen us. We just had to get out of there, and fast.

They could be old, I tried telling myself, throwing Betty's door open. They could have been installed years ago, in case of robberies. Who knew where the video they recorded was being sent? Maybe nowhere at all.

And at the same time, my heart was beating out a completely different track. *They're coming, they're coming, they're coming.*

I thought about yelling for the others, but they could have been anywhere in the park. I climbed into the van after Zu and did the only other thing that seemed to made sense in that moment: I banged the heel of my palm against the wheel. The high whine of Betty's horn shook the sleepy landscape awake. A cluster of birds flew up from the nearby trees, hitting the sky at the same moment I began beating out a faster, more insistent rhythm.

Chubs appeared first, booking it down one aisle of RVs, and Liam a second later, a few rows over. When they saw that it was still just us, they both slowed down. An annoyed look crossed Chubs's face.

I leaned out of the open driver's side window and shouted, "We have to go—*now*!"

Liam said something to Chubs that I didn't hear, but they did as they were told. I stayed crouched between the two front seats as they boys jumped inside.

"What?" Liam was almost out of breath. "What's wrong?"

I pointed to the nearest trailer. "They have cameras installed," my voice rasped. "In every one of them."

Chubs sucked in a sharp breath.

"You're sure?" Liam's voice was calm—too calm. I could tell he was forcing it, even as his fingers fumbled to put the keys in the ignition.

The van's back tires spun against the mud as he threw

156

it into reverse. I went tumbling on to my backside with the force of his acceleration.

"Oh my God," Chubs was saying, "I can't believe it. We got Hansel and Greteled. Oh my God—do you think it was her?"

"No," Liam said. "No. She's sneaky for a skip tracer, but this—this is something else."

"They could have been there for a while," I said, just as we found the highway again. It was empty and open in front of us, a gaping mouth ready to swallow us whole. "They could have been spying on the people that lived there. Maybe that really was East River. . . ."

Or it was just a trap, for kids looking for the real East River.

Liam propped his elbow against the door panel and his chin against his palm. When he spoke, the hundreds of snaking cracks in the windshield cut up his reflection. He pushed the minivan up into a faster speed, causing the wind to whistle through the bullet hole. "Just keep your eyes open and let me know if you see anyone or anything acting suspect."

Define suspect. The rows of shuttered houses? A shot-up minivan?

"I knew we should have waited until it was dark," Chubs said, tapping his fingers against the passenger seat window. "I *knew* it. If those cameras were on, they probably got the license plate number and everything."

"I'll take care of the plates," Liam promised.

Chubs's lips parted, but he said nothing, only resting his head against the window.

"Should I be looking for PSFs?" I asked, as we drove over another railroad track.

"Worse." Chubs sighed. "Skip tracers. Bounty hunters."

"The PSFs are stretched pretty thin, by all accounts," Liam explained. "Same with the National Guard and what's left of the local police. I don't know that they'd send a unit all the way out here on a tip. And unless they just so happen to have a resident bounty hunter in this neck of the woods, we're going to be fine."

Those were famous last words if I had ever heard them.

"The reward for turning in a kid is ten thousand dollars." Chubs twisted around to look at me. "And the whole country is broke as a joke. We are *not* going to be fine."

I heard a train in the distance, its horn so similar to the ones that had passed by Thurmond at all hours of the night. It was enough for me to dig my fingernails into the skin of my thighs and squeeze my eyes shut until the nausea passed. I didn't even realize the conversation had rolled on without me until I heard Liam ask, "You okay, Green?"

I reached up and wiped my face, wondering if the wetness there was from the rain, or if I'd been crying without realizing it. I didn't say anything as I crawled to the rear seat. I didn't jump into their conversation about where they would need to look next for East River, though I wanted to. There were hundreds, thousands, millions of places the Slip Kid could have set up camp, and I wanted to help them puzzle it out. I wanted to be part of it.

But I couldn't ask, and I needed to stop lying to myself. Because every second I stayed with them was another chance for them to discover that skip tracers and PSFs weren't the real monsters of the world. No. One of the real ones was sitting in their backseat.

For once, the music was off.

It was the silence from the speakers that unnerved me, more than the deserted roads or the empty shells of repossessed houses. Liam was a constant stream of motion. Looking around the abandoned small towns we drove through, glancing at the gas level, fiddling with the turn signal, fingers dancing on the steering wheel. At one point, his eyes flashed toward mine in the rearview mirror. It was just for an instant, but I felt the small twinge in my stomach as sharply as I would have if he had taken a soft finger and run it down the length of my open palm.

My face was flushed, but something inside of me had gone very cold. It had been half a second, no more, but it was plenty long enough to notice the way his eyes had darkened with something that might have been frustration.

Chubs was in the front seat folding and unfolding something in his lap, over and over again, almost like he didn't realize he was doing it.

"Will you cut that out?" Liam burst out, agitated. "You'll rip it."

Chubs stopped immediately. "Can't we just . . . try? Do we need the Slip Kid for this?"

"Do you really want to risk it?"

"Jack would have."

"Right, but Jack . . ." Liam's voice trailed off. "Let's just play it safe. He'll help us when we get there."

"*If* we get there," Chubs huffed.

"Jack?" I didn't realize I had said it aloud until Liam's eyes looked up at me in the rearview mirror.

"It's none of your business," Chubs said, and left it at that.

Liam was only a little more forthcoming. "He was our friend—in our room at camp, I mean. We're trying . . . we're just trying to get in touch with his dad. It's one of the reasons we need to hit up the Slip Kid."

I nodded toward the sheet of paper. "But before you guys broke out, he wrote a letter?"

"The three of us each did," Liam said. "In case one of us backed out at the last minute and didn't want to come or . . . didn't make it out."

"Which Jack did not." Chubs's voice could have cut steel. Behind him, house after gorgeous colonial house passed in rapid-fire succession, their colors winking at us through her window.

"Anyway." Liam cleared his throat. "We're trying to put his letter in his dad's hands. We tried going to the address Jack gave us, but the house had been repossessed. He left a note saying he was going to D.C. for work, but no new address or phone number. That's why we need the Slip Kid's help—to find where he is now."

"You can't just mail it?"

"They started scanning mail for this exact reason about two years after you went to Thurmond," Liam explained. "The government reads all, speaks all, and writes all. They've crafted a lovely little story about how we're all being saved and reprogrammed back into sweet little darlings at camp, and they don't want anyone to get wind of the truth."

I honestly had no idea what to say to that.

"Sorry," I mumbled. "I didn't mean to give you a shake-down about it."

"It's okay," Liam said, after the silence had stretched to the point of breaking. "It's fine."

There wasn't a way to explain how I knew. Maybe it was the way Liam's hands tightened on the steering wheel, or how he kept glancing in his side mirror throughout the conversation, long after a silver car had passed us from the other direction. It could have been the way his shoulders sagged, sloping down in a way that was so defeated. I just knew, long before I caught his worried eyes in the rearview mirror.

Slowly, without disturbing Zu and Chubs as they watched an endless stream of forest pass by the side windows, I crouched between the two front seats again.

Liam met my gaze for a split second, nodding in the direction of his side mirror. *See for yourself,* he seemed to say. So I did.

Trailing behind us, back about two car lengths, was an old white pickup truck. With the rain fogging up the air between the two cars, I couldn't tell if there were one or two men inside. They looked like little more than two black ants from where I was sitting.

"Interesting," I said, keeping my voice even.

"Yep," he said, his jaw clenched. The muscles of his neck strained. "Gotta love West Virginia. Glorious Mountain State. Land O'Many John Denver Songs."

161

"Maybe . . ." I began slowly, "you should pull over and look at a map?"

It was one way of feeling out the situation. Liam was about to turn onto George Washington Highway—slightly wider than the twisting road we were leaving. If the truck was following us, they wouldn't be able to stop without revealing it. In any case, whoever was driving the truck wasn't being aggressive about it. If he was a bounty hunter, as Liam apparently thought, they were probably feeling us out, too.

We continued up Gorman Road, following its natural curve. Black Betty slowed in anticipation of the upcoming turn. Liam hesitated half a second before flipping his turn signal on. I looked in the mirror, my heart lifting when I saw the truck turn its other blinker on. They were turning right. We were going left.

Liam blew out a long sigh, finally sitting back against his seat as the minivan reached the intersection of the highway and the road. There was another car turning off the highway, a small silver Volkswagen; both Liam and I threw up a hand to block the intense glint of the sun against its windows.

"Okay, Old Man River." Liam gave the car an impatient wave. "Go ahead and turn before the next century. No, take your time, shave, contemplate the universe . . ."

Lynyrd Skynyrd was blasting through the pickup truck's open windows as it pulled up alongside us, creaking and groaning in the way all old cars seem to do. "Free Bird." Of course. It had to be Dad's favorite. Two seconds into the damn song, and it was like I was back in the front seat of his squad car, cruising around town. That was the only time I got to listen to the good music—when it was just the two of us, cruising. Mom hated the stuff.

A laugh bubbled up inside of me as I watched the driver bob his head in time with the music. He howled the words at the top of his lungs, exhaling each lyric with a puff of cigarette smoke.

And then it was replaced by a different sound—a shriek of sorts. I looked up just in time to see the Volkswagen slam on its brakes right in front of us, jolting to a stop and sending another blinding glare of sunlight our way.

"You have got to be kidding me!" Liam made as if to press his hand down on the horn, but not before the driver of the Volkswagen rolled down his window and pointed something black and gleaming at us.

No. The world went into sharp focus. Sound evaporated around me. *NO.*

I reached up and slapped Black Betty's radio button on, turning it up as loud as it would go. Liam and Chubs both started yelling, but I knocked Liam's hand away before he could switch it off.

The White Noise cut straight through the music from the speakers, tearing at our ears. Not as loud or as powerful as I was used to, and not even close to as bad as it had been last time, but still there, still agonizing. My radio trick couldn't drown it out, not completely.

The others crumbled around me, shriveling at the first piercing shriek.

Liam fell forward against the wheel, mashing his hands up against his ears. Chubs knocked his head into the passenger seat window, as if trying to ram the noise out of his head. I felt Black Betty began to drift forward, only to jerk to a stop when Liam hit the brakes instead of the gas.

The door opened beside me, and a pair of arms circled Chubs's waist, trying to untangle him from the seat belt. I pulled myself up off the floor and lashed a hand out, catching the man's cheek and raking my fingernails down as hard as I could. It was enough to startle the truck driver, the same one that had been nodding his head to "Free Bird" two seconds before, into dropping Chubs. He was left half hanging in his seat, half hanging out.

The driver stumbled back against the bed of his truck, his words drowned out by the thunderstorm of noise that had settled over the three cars. It was only then that I saw the badge hanging around his neck on a silver cord, and the bright red Ψ stitched there. They weren't skip tracers.

Psi. PSF. Camp. Thurmond. Capture.

The man from the Volkswagen had opened the driver's side door of the van and was trying to unhook Liam's seat belt. He wasn't large in any sense of the word—he looked like he could have been an accountant, with thick glasses and hunched shoulders from spending too many hours at a desk. But he didn't need strength, not when he was holding the black megaphone in his hands.

Some of the PSFs at Thurmond carried the noise machines around with them, blasting them at small, rowdy groups, or just to see a few kids squirm. What did they care? They couldn't hear it.

Every nerve in my body was singing, but I launched my elbow into the chest of the pickup truck driver. He fell back again, and I pulled the door shut and locked it. I only had a second to look back at Zu as I dove across Liam's body, fist-first. I nailed Volkswagen in the glasses, knocking them off his face. Somewhere behind me, Pickup Truck had moved on to the sliding door, and this time he wasn't empty-handed.

Zu didn't flinch as the rifle was pointed in her face—by the way she was moaning, her eyes scrunched up and her yellow gloves curled over her ears in agony, I don't think she was seeing straight.

I didn't know what to do. My hands were on Liam, trying to shake him back into consciousness. His eyes flashed open, clear and so blue, but it was only for an instant. The megaphone was suddenly two inches from my face, and the White Noise sunk into my brain like an ax. My bones went to jelly. I didn't register the fact I had fallen over Liam until I was there. The only thing louder than the White Noise, than the radio, than Chubs's screams, was the sound of Liam's heart racing.

I squeezed my eyes shut again, my fingers curling into the soft leather of Liam's coat. Half of me wanted to push away, put enough distance between us that I had no chance of sliding into his mind—but the other half of me, the desperate part, was already trying to push through, to anchor myself to him and will him to *move*. If I could hurt someone, shouldn't that mean I could help them, too?

Get up, I begged, *get up, get up, get up, get up* . . .

There was a high-pitched wail, a sound that couldn't have possibly come from a human. I forced my eyes open.

165

Pickup Truck had his rifle in one hand and the collar of Zu's shirt in the other, and he was tugging both in the direction of the truck. I tried to scream for her, even as I felt Volkswagen's hands in my hair, yanking me up and out of the door. He let me hit the ground hard, the loose gravel cutting open my legs and palms.

I rolled onto my side, trying to twist away from the PSF's reach. From under Betty, I saw flutters of yellow dropping to the road like two small birds, and heard a door slam.

"Stewart—confirm Psi number 42755 spotted—" Volkswagen wrenched the driver's side door open again, pulling something bright orange from his pocket. I swiped at my eyes, trying to force the double image of him I was seeing back into one. The orange device in the PSF's free hand was no bigger than a cell phone, easy enough to maneuver in front of Liam's face from where it was pressed against the minivan's steering wheel.

Taking a swipe at the PSF's ankle with my hand was pointless—he was so involved with whatever it was he was doing that he didn't so much as notice.

Liam! My mouth wasn't moving, it wasn't working. *Liam!*

The orange device flashed, and a moment later, above even the wailing of the White Noise, I heard Volkswagen say, "That's a positive ID on Liam Stewart."

Something hot and sharp cut through the air, billowing out under Betty like a stinging cloud of sand. I felt it rub up against my bare skin and had to turn my face away from the blinding light that came next—a flash burn that erased anything and everything that stood in its way. I heard Volkswagen cuss from above me, only to be drowned out by the sound of metal screeching against metal, glass exploding so hard, so fast, that tiny shards dropped like hail onto the ground in front of me.

And then it was gone. The White Noise cut out sharply as something clattered to the ground and landed a short distance away. The megaphone.

I stretched my arm out, hand groping for the megaphone's handle. Volkswagen was screaming something that I couldn't hear over the ringing in my ears, and I was too focused on getting the bullhorn to actually give a damn and listen. A hand wrapped around my bare ankle and tugged me back across the ground—but not before my fingers closed around the handle.

"Get up, you piece of—!" There was a digital squeak, like an alarm, and the man immediately dropped my leg. "*This is Larson, requesting immediate backup—*"

I pushed myself up on my knees with a grunt, then my feet. The man had his back turned to me one second too long, and when he finally realized his mistake and looked over his shoulder, he was rewarded with a face full of metal as I swung the megaphone.

His radio clattered to the asphalt, and I kicked it out of his reach. Both of his hands went up, trying to shield his face from another hit, but I wasn't going to go easy on him. I wasn't going to let him take me back to Thurmond.

My hand closed over his exposed forearm, and I yanked it, forcing him to look down at me. I watched his pupils shrink in his hazel eyes before blowing back out to their normal size. The man had a foot of height on me, but you never

167

would have known by the way he dropped to his knees in front of me. He hadn't even been able to catch his breath, let alone keep me from walking straight into his mind.

Leave! I tried to say. My jaw was clenched, the muscles there seized as though the White Noise was still running through them like a current of pulsing electricity. *Leave!*

I had never done this before, and there was no way to know if it would actually work—but what did I have to lose now? His memories flooded over me, wave after wave lapping at my brain, and all I could think was, *I'm going to do this. It is going to work.*

Martin had said that he *pushed* feelings into people, but my abilities didn't work that way, and they never had. I only saw images. I could only muddle, sort, and erase images.

But I'd never tried to do anything else. I had never wanted to, before this moment. Because if I couldn't help these kids, if I couldn't save them, then what good was I? What point did I even have? *Do it. Just do it.*

I imagined the man picking up his radio—every detail, from the way he would fumble for it without his glasses to the way his jeans would wrinkle. I imagined him canceling the request for backup. I imagined him walking down the rocky hill that kissed the edge of the road, into the wild.

And when I released my fingers from his arm, one by one, that's exactly what he did. He walked away, and each step brought a new jolt of shock. I had done that. *Me.*

I turned to where black smoke spilled out over the road, coating the hill's grass and hidden edges in a thick, ugly blanket. Then, I remembered.

Zu.

I could see the wreckage clearly now as I limped forward. The pickup truck, which at one point had been parked beside Betty, was now several hundred feet away, resting in the empty green field. The smaller silver Volkswagen was on its side in front of it, a heap of twisted metal that I barely recognized. It was smoking wildly, belching out thick smoke, as if it were only one small spark away from exploding.

It rammed it, I realized. The truck rammed it out of the way.

I followed the trail of tire marks and glass, but I only found Truck Driver. What was left of him.

His body was tangled up in itself in the wild grass; I couldn't tell where one limb began and the other ended. None of them seemed to be in their right place. His elbows stuck up from the ground like two broken wings. He had been rammed, too.

Something cold and brittle wrapped itself around my chest, forcing me back out of the haze of smoke once I confirmed Zu wasn't in either car. I waited until I cleared the heaviest of the smoke before falling to my knees and throwing up what little food I had in my stomach.

It was only when I looked up that I finally saw her, sitting on the road just beside Betty, her back slumped forward, her head bowed, but alive—*alive* and *safe*. My mind clung to those two words as I tried calling for her again. Zu looked up, panting. As I stumbled closer, the smoke revealed her in pieces: bloodshot eyes, a cut on her forehead, tears streaming down her dirt-stained cheeks.

My head throbbed in time with my heartbeat as I knelt down in front of her, and for several agonizing seconds, it was all that I could hear.

"O . . . kay?" I asked, my mouth feeling like mush.

Her teeth chattered as she nodded.

"What . . . happened?" I squeezed out.

Zu curled down on herself like she was trying to vanish from my sight. Her yellow gloves were beside her on the ground, and her bare hands were still up and facing forward, as if she had only touched the truck a second before.

I didn't know what to say to get her to calm down—I didn't even know how to calm myself down. This girl, this Yellow—she'd destroyed two vehicles and one life in a matter of seconds. And, by the looks of it, she'd done it with a single touch.

But even knowing that, she was still Zu, and those hands? They were the ones that had pulled me to safety.

I lifted her back into Betty with shaking arms. Zu was hot, well past the point of feeling feverish. Dropping her into the closest seat, I pressed my hands against her cheeks, but her eyes couldn't focus on me. I was about to roll the door shut when she grabbed my wrist and pointed toward her gloves on the ground.

"Got 'em," I said. I tossed them to her, and then turned to confront a heavier load.

Chubs was still passed out in the passenger seat, his body hanging out of the open door. The truck driver hadn't been able to maneuver his long limbs farther than that, thank God—otherwise Chubs probably would have been in the

170

grass with the driver. His limp sack of bones smacked against the door as I slammed it shut behind him.

I tripped over the tips of my tennis shoes as I made my way around the front of the van. With a cloud of bright spots bleaching out my sight, I pulled the driver's door open the rest of the way. Liam was also still out cold, and no amount of shaking was able to stir him up into consciousness. Zu began to whimper, her cries muffled as she pressed her face against her knees.

"You're okay, Zu," I said. "We're all okay. We're gonna be fine."

I untangled Liam's arms from the gray seat belt and half pushed, half rolled him off the driver's seat. I wasn't strong enough to deposit him into one of the back seats, not right then. So he ended up on the ground, wedged between the two front seats. With his face turned up toward me, I could see the muscles around his mouth twitch, every so often turning the corners of his lips up in an unnatural smile.

I stared at the wheel, trying to bring to mind the right steps to getting the van to work. Trying to remember what Liam had done, what Cate had done, what my father used to do. Sixteen, and I couldn't even figure out where the goddamn parking brake was, let alone if it was actually on.

In the end, it didn't matter. I could drive with it on or off, apparently, and all I really needed to know was that the right pedal was go, and the left was stop, and there really wasn't a whole lot more to it than that.

Betty tore through the thickest heart of the smoke, and chased it down the open road until we were finally, finally, *finally* free of the wreckage, and the air coming through the vents no longer carried the echo of the White Noise into our heads, or smell of smoke into our lungs.

ELEVEN

I GOT MAYBE TEN MILES BEFORE THE BOYS BEGAN TO rouse. With Zu still crying in the backseat and me having no idea where we had been headed in the first place, to say I was relieved was an understatement.

"Holy crap," Liam croaked. He pressed a hand against the side of his head and startled, sitting straight up. "Holy crap!"

His face had been inches away from Chubs's feet, so his hands went there first, yanking at them like he was making sure they were still attached to something. Chubs let out a low moan and said, "I think I'm going to be ill."

"Zu?" Liam crawled toward her, earning another yelp out of Chubs as he kicked his leg. "Zu? Did you—?"

She only cried harder, burying her face in her gloves.

"Oh my God, I'm sorry—I'm so sorry—I—" Liam sounded agonized, like his guts were being torn straight out of him. I watched him press his fist against his mouth, heard him try to clear his throat, but he couldn't get another word out.

"Zu," I said, sounding strangely calm to my own ears. "Listen to me. You saved us. We wouldn't have made it without you."

Liam's head jerked around, as if just remembering I was there. I winced, but how could I be upset that he would check on his real friends first?

I felt his eyes on the back of my neck as he worked his way back up to me. When he reached the driver's seat, he collapsed into it, his face drawn and pale. "Are you all right?" he asked, his voice rough. "What happened? How did you get us out?"

"It was Zu," I began, already well aware of the narrow line I'd have to walk between the truth and what I could actually tell them—both for myself and for Zu's sake. I wasn't sure how much she actually remembered from what happened, but I wasn't about to confirm any of her fears. In the end, all I said was, "She sent one car crashing into the other. It knocked one of the guys out and sent the other one running."

"What was"—Chubs was having a hard time breathing—"that horrible noise?"

I stared at him, my mouth trying to push the words past my disbelief. "You've never heard that before?"

The boys both shook their heads. "Jesus," Liam said, "that was like hearing a cat go through a blender while being electrocuted."

"You really didn't have White Noise? Calm Control?" I demanded, surprised by the anger licking at my heart. What camp had these kids been in? Candy Land?

"And you did?" Liam shook his head, probably trying to clear the ringing.

"They used it at Thurmond to . . . disable us," I explained. "When there were outbursts or problems. Keeps you from being able to think long enough to use your abilities."

"Why are you all right?" Chubs wheezed, half suspicious, half jealous.

That was the question of the day, wasn't it? My long, sordid history with the White Noise included several episodes of fainting, vomiting, and memory loss, not to mention my most recent experience with bleeding profusely out of my eyes and nose. I guess once you'd had a taste of the worst, pretty bad isn't all that terrible. If it was their first time dealing with it, that would at least explain why they wilted like dead grass after only a few seconds.

Liam was searching my face, and I wondered what he was seeing. All of it? I thought of how his jacket had felt against my cheek, the curve of his spine, and something calm and warm settled in my chest.

"I'm used to it, I guess," I said. "And Greens aren't as affected as Blues and the others." I remembered to add this. A truth and a lie.

Liam offered to trade seats as soon as his face lost that familiar pinched look, and a healthy color began to return to his cheeks. The kid deserved a round of applause for how well he was hiding the tremors in his hands and legs from the others, but I had a trained eye. I recognized the nasty after-bites of the White Noise as the old friends they were. He needed a few more minutes.

"Come on," he said as the dashboard clock clicked off another minute. "You've done . . ." His voice trailed off.

I looked down at him, only to realize he was looking at me—or, more accurately, my bony, busted knees. A moment later, after I returned my gaze to the road, I felt something warm hovering just above my leg and jerked away.

"Ah—sorry," Liam whispered, pulling his hand back. I watched the tips of his ears go a bright cherry red. "It's just—you're all cut up. Please, can we stop for a second? We should regroup. Figure out where we are."

But I didn't want to just pull over alongside some random stretch of fence and pasture; I waited until we had found an old rest stop, complete with its red-brick colonial-style finish, and turned the van off the road and into the deserted parking lot.

Chubs took the opportunity to try to empty the contents of his stomach onto the ground but accomplished little more than some enthusiastic dry heaving. Liam stood and patted his back. "Will you help Ruby when you're done?"

Chubs might have hated me, or wanted to scare me off, but he at least recognized I had played some small part in saving his skin. He didn't say yes, though, only crossed his arms over his chest and blew out a long, martyred sigh.

"Thanks," Liam said. "You're the best, Mother Teresa."

He went out the sliding door behind my seat and made a beeline for the small cluster of silver water fountains that stood between him and the restroom entrances. Zu followed him out, bounding across the distance with a pink duffel bag in hand. By the time I turned my attention back to him,

Chubs had collected himself enough to start poking and prodding me.

"Easy!" I gasped when his finger brushed my elbow. He jabbed a finger against one of the overhead lights and it snapped on at his command. I finally saw that the skin from my elbow down to my wrist had been rubbed raw by the road.

"Turn toward me." Chubs looked like he was fighting with all the strength he had left in him not to roll his eyes at me. "*Now*, Green, before I grow a beard."

I twisted myself around so my legs were facing toward him in the passenger seat. Unsurprisingly, they looked just about as pretty as my arm did. Both knees were skinned and already scabbing over in places, but aside from a few stray scratches and bruises that had nothing to do with the attack, they were in much better shape than my hands.

Chubs pulled what looked like a briefcase out from under his seat and popped the clasps on it open. I was only able to sneak a quick glance inside before he pulled out four white square packets and shut it again.

"God, how did you even manage to do this?" he muttered as he ripped the first one open. I smelled the antiseptic and tried to squirm away.

Chubs glowered at me from over the rims of his glasses. "If you're going to make yourself at home, could you at least try to take better care of yourself? It's hard enough as it is to keep the other two in one piece without you flinging yourself at danger, too."

"I didn't *fling*—" I began, then thought better of it. "Sorry?"

"Yeah, well," he huffed. "Not as sorry as you'll be if any of these cuts get infected."

He brought my right hand up close to his face in order to get a better look, and I tried not to wince as he began to swipe at it with one of the disinfecting wipes about as tenderly as a wolf shredding apart its dinner. The sting that followed snapped me out of the hazy, numb stupor I was falling into. Suddenly aware of his touch, I wrenched my hand away from his and took the cold wet cloth from his hand. It didn't hurt any less when I cleaned the small bits of asphalt out myself.

"You should go check on Lee and Zu," I said.

"No, because then they'll be all pissed off I'm not taking care of you." After a moment he admitted, somewhat reluctantly, "Besides, you did seem to . . . well, you're worse off than the rest of us, at least. They can wait." He must have seen the corner of my mouth twitch, because he added, "But don't think you're going to get all the bandages—these are superficial wounds at best."

"Yes, sir," I said, tossing the disinfectant wipe out of the window. He handed me a new one for my other palm, eyes still narrowed, but maybe, just maybe, softening at the edges. I felt myself relax a bit, but I wasn't suffering under any delusion that we were about to start braiding friendship bracelets for each other.

"Why did you lie?"

My head shot up at his question, suddenly feeling very light. "I didn't—what are you—I'm not—"

"About Zu." He glanced back over his shoulder. His voice was quiet when he continued. "You said she only knocked that guy out, but . . . that wasn't the case, was it? He was killed."

I nodded. "She didn't mean to—"

"Obviously not," he said, sharply. "I was wondering why no one was coming after us, and I got worried, knowing what it would do to her . . . and, well, I guess you have some common sense after all."

It came to me then as I looked at him—one of those rare, perfect crystallizations of understanding. He wanted me out because he saw me as a threat to them. He wouldn't ever trust me until I proved myself otherwise—and after my slip in messing up the color of the SUV, that was likely to be half past never.

"What's the world with one less skip tracer, anyway?" He bent down to retrieve his briefcase again, replacing the unused supplies in it.

That's right, I thought, sitting up straighter. I didn't tell them.

"They weren't skip tracers. They were PSFs."

At that, Chubs actually barked out a laugh. "And I'm guessing their uniforms were stuffed under their plaid shirts and jeans?"

"One of them was wearing a badge," I said. "And the orange device they were using—I saw one at Thurmond, once." Chubs didn't look convinced, but we didn't have the time—and I certainly did not have the energy—to be running circles around the truth for the next hour. "Look," I continued, "you don't have to believe me, but you should know that one of them radioed in a Psi number—42755. That's Liam, right?"

179

I gave the story from my end and left the rest for him to fill in from his side. By the time I got to a description of the orange device, he had heard quite enough. He sucked in a deep breath, his lips drawing together to a point, until he looked more ferret than human. I held my own breath as he rolled down his window and proceeded to relate, down to the exact words, what I had just finished telling him, like he didn't trust me to do it myself.

"I told *you* the PSFs would catch up to us!" he kept repeating, like we hadn't heard him shout it the first ten times. "We're just lucky it wasn't *her*."

I wondered who he meant but knew better than to ask.

Liam ignored him and kept his back to us, still bent over the silver drinking fountain. Zu stood next to him, dutifully holding the button down so he could use both hands to scrub his face in the stream of water shooting out of it.

I used the last of the wipes to clean the dirt off my own face. "I just want to know how that PSF recognized him, even before he used this orange *thing*. It flashed, but he knew the number off the top of his head. He didn't need to wait for it to tell him that."

Chubs stared at me a moment, then brought a hand up to pinch the bridge of his nose. "Everyone had their photo taken when they were processed. Didn't you?"

I nodded. "So they put together a network for searching the photos?" I asked.

"Green, how the hell am I supposed to know that?" he said. "Describe it to me again."

The orange gadget must have been some sort of a camera or scanner—that was the only explanation I could drum up that Chubs didn't shoot down as being moronic.

I pressed my hands against my eyes, trying to fight back the urge to vomit.

"It's bad news if that's all it takes for them to ID us," Chubs said, rubbing a hand over his forehead and smoothing out the wrinkles there. "If we weren't already screwed—they probably know we're looking for East River now, which means they're going to have more patrols out, which means they're going to be watching our families even closer, which means it'll be even harder for the Slip Kid . . ."

He never finished his train of thought. He didn't have to.

I let out a humorless laugh. "C'mon. They're going to send out a whole armada for a few freaks?"

"First of all, armadas are comprised of ships," Chubs said. "And second, no, they wouldn't send one out for a few freaks."

"Then what's the—"

"But they *would* send one out to get Lee."

He didn't wait for me to piece it together.

"Green, who do you think was the mastermind behind our camp's breakout?"

When the others were ready to return to the minivan, we played a silent game of musical chairs. Chubs took the middle seat on the passenger side, and Zu, her usual perch behind the driver's seat. I had two options at that point: crawl into the rear seat or tough it out in the front seat, while trying to act like everything was all hunky-dory and pretending that Chubs hadn't just told me Liam was responsible for what might have been the only successful camp breakout ever.

In the end, exhaustion won out. I managed to collapse into the passenger seat feeling about as lovely as a wilted head of lettuce, just as Liam climbed into the driver's seat.

He grinned. "Must be tiring being the big hero."

I waved him off, trying to quiet the small, ridiculous buzz of happiness in my chest that came with his words. He was just trying to be nice.

"Good thing we had the ladies there to take care of business," he continued, turning to Chubs. "Otherwise you and I would be rolling around in the bed of a truck, halfway back to Ohio."

Chubs only grunted, his coloring still faintly gray.

Liam looked a little better, at least. His face was tinged pink from the shock of cold fountain water, and his fingers still seemed to be twitching every so often, but his eyes had lost that cloudy, unfocused look. Considering it was his first time being ear-tased by the White Noise, Liam had recovered fast.

"All right, team," he said, slowly. "Time for a Betty vote."

"No!" Chubs startled back to life. "I know exactly where you're going with this, and I know I'm going to be over-ruled, and I—"

"All those in favor of letting our girl wonder stay with us for the time being, raise your hand."

Both Liam and Zu raised their hands immediately. Zu looked at me with a smile that seemed particularly bright next to Chubs's glowering face.

"We don't know anything about her—hell, we don't know that what she *has* told us is even true!" he objected. "She could be a psychopath who kills us in our sleep, or calls her League buddies in just when we let our guard down."

"Gee, thanks," I said dryly, half flattered he thought I was capable of that level of scheming.

"The longer she stays with us," he added, "the more likely it is the League will catch up to us, and you *know* what they do to their kids!"

"They won't catch up with us," Liam said. "We took care of that already. If we stay together, we'll be fine."

"No. No, no, no, no, *no*," Chubs said. "I want to register my nay vote, even though the two of you always win."

"Well, don't be a bad sport about it," Liam said. "This is democracy in action."

"Are you sure?" I asked.

"Of course I am," Liam said. "What I wasn't okay with was the thought of dropping you off at some back-of-beyond Greyhound station with no money, no papers, and no way of knowing for sure you got where you're going safe and sound."

There it was again—that smile. I pressed my hand against my chest, trying to keep things at bay. Locked inside. To keep my hand from reaching out to brush the one he had put on the armrest of my seat. It seemed so sick, so wrong, but all I wanted to do was slip inside his mind and see what he was thinking. Why he was looking at me like that.

You really are a monster, I thought, pressing a fist tight against my stomach.

I wanted to protect him—at that moment, it was suddenly clear to me exactly what I wanted: to protect them, all of them. They had saved me. They had saved my life and hadn't expected a single thing in return. If the showdown with the undercover PSFs had shown me anything, it was that they needed someone like me. I could help them, protect them.

I didn't think I could ever begin to repay them for taking me in and letting me stay as long as I had, but if I could control myself long enough, it would be a start. It was the best I could do with what I had.

"Where are you trying to go, anyway?" Liam tried to keep his voice casual, but his eyes had darkened, obviously troubled. "Could you even get there on a bus if you tried?"

I told them the feeble plan I'd half-baked inside of the gas station. I fingered the ends of my long, tangled hair, and was surprised to feel some of the tightness in my chest ease up long enough for me to take a deep breath.

"What's in Virginia Beach?"

"My grandmother, I think," I said. "I hope."

Yes, Grams, I reminded myself. Grams was still an option. She remembered me, didn't she? If I could help them find the Slip Kid—and if he could help *me*—then wasn't there a real chance I could see her again? Live with her?

It was a lot of *ifs*. *If* we found the Slip Kid. *If* he was an Orange. *If* he could help me figure out how to control my abilities. *If* he could help us contact our families.

Once I had tapped into the vein of doubts, the rest came flooding in.

What if Grams—the thought was crushing—had passed away? She was seventy when I was taken, which meant she'd be inching closer to eighty. I had never even considered it a possibility, because I couldn't remember a time that she didn't look glowing and ready to take on the world with little more than her silver hair, a neon fanny pack, and matching visor.

But if I wasn't the same person I had been six years ago, how could I expect her to be? If she was alive, how could I ask her to take care of her freak granddaughter—protect me and hide me—when there was a chance she couldn't take care of herself?

It was too much to think about now, too much to consider and agonize over in a logical way. My brain was still thrumming from the effects of the White Noise, but my weak heart made the choice easy for me.

"All right," I said. "I'll stay."

And hope that none of us regret it.

The deep wrinkle that had appeared between Liam's brows eased but didn't disappear. I knew he was studying me, his light eyes flicking over my face. Trying to figure out, maybe, why I had hesitated so long to agree. Whatever conclusion he came to made him sit back with a sigh and adjust the mirrors in silence.

Liam had the kind of face that you could read and instantly know what he was thinking—it made it easy to trust that whatever he was saying was true. But there was a practiced quality to his expression now, an intense concentration to keep his face blank. It looked unnatural on someone who seemed to always have a grin tucked in the corner of his mouth. I leaned back, trying to ignore the throbbing in my head and the pitiful dying animal noises coming from Chubs once he remembered how much pain he was in.

Liam silently passed him a half-empty water bottle from under the driver's seat. I glanced back at Zu out of the corner of my eye, but the twilight had lulled her to sleep. A thin sheen of sweat coated her forehead and the skin above her lips.

The car rumbled back to life. Liam exhaled as he cut a diagonal path through the parking lot. He didn't seem to know which direction to turn when we finally found the road.

"Where are we going?" I asked.

He was silent for a moment, scratching his chin. "We're still headed to Virginia, if I can find it. I think we crossed the state line a while back, but I don't know where we landed. Not too familiar with this area, to be honest."

"Use the damn map," Chubs groused behind him.

"I can figure it out without it," Liam insisted. He kept swiveling his head back and forth, like he expected someone to appear and guide him in the right direction with road flares and fanfare.

Five minutes later, the map was spread out over the steering wheel, and Chubs was gloating in the backseat. I leaned over the armrest, trying to make sense of the pastel colors and crisscrossing lines on the flimsy, ripped paper.

Liam pointed out the boundaries of West Virginia, Virginia, Maryland, and North Carolina.

"I think we're about . . . here?" He pointed to a tiny dot that was surrounded by a rainbow of crisscrossed lines.

"I don't suppose Black Betty has GPS?" I said.

Liam blew out a sigh, patting the steering wheel. He had decided we were going right. "Black Betty may drive the straight and true path, but souped up, she is not."

"I told you we should have taken that Ford SUV," Chubs said.

"That piece of—" Liam caught himself. "That box on wheels was a death trap—not to mention its transmission was shot to hell."

"So, naturally, the next choice was a minivan."

"Yep, she called to me from the parking lot of abandoned cars. The sun was shining through her windows like a beacon of hope."

Chubs groaned. "Why are you *so weird*?"

"Because my weird has to be able to cancel out *your* weird, Lady Cross-stitch."

"At least what I do is considered an art form," Chubs said.

"Yes, in ye olde medieval Europe you would've been quite the catch—"

"Anyway," I cut in, now in full possession of the map, "we have to be close to Winchester." I pointed to a dot on the western end of Virginia.

"What makes you say that?" Liam began. "Are you from this area? Because if—"

"I'm not. I just remember driving past Keyser and Romney while the two of you were out. And with all the Civil War Trails signs, we should be near one of the battlefields."

"Those are some good detective skills, Nancy Drew, but, unfortunately, those signs pretty much mean nothing in this part of the country," Liam said. "You can barely go fifty feet without hitting a historical marker for the place this army crossed, or that guy died, or where James Madison lived—"

"That's in Orange," I interrupted. "We're nowhere near that."

The soft blue light of evening gathered around his blond hair, stripping it of color. He studied me for a minute, scratching his chin again. "So you *are* from Virginia, then."

"I'm not—"

He held up a hand. "Please. No one outside of this state gives a crap about where James Madison's house is."

I sat back. *Walked right into that one.*

It was my mom's fault. As a high school history teacher, it had been her personal mission to cart Dad and me around to every major historical site in the area. So while my friends got to have pool parties and sleepovers, I got to walk around one battlefield after another, posing for pictures with cannons and Colonial reenactors. Fun times, made even more fun by the thousands of bug bites and peeling sunburns I always showed up with on the first day of school. I still had scars from Antietam.

Liam smiled at the dark road, keeping the minivan's headlights off. I thought it was fairly brave—or stupid—considering the commonwealth of Virginia had never considered it a priority to install lights on its highways and roads.

"I think we should stop for the night," Chubs said. "Are you going to find a park?"

"Relax, buddy; I got this," Liam said.

"You keep saying that," Chubs muttered, sitting back, "and then it's, *Oh, sorry team, let's huddle together for warmth,* while the bears try to break in and eat our food."

"Yeah . . . sorry about that," Liam said. "But hey, what's life without a little adversity?"

That had to have been the fakest attempt at optimism since my fourth grade teacher tried reasoning that we were better off without the dead kids in our class because it'd mean more turns on the playground swings for the rest of us.

I lost track of their conversation after that. It wasn't that I had no interest in hearing all about the bizarre traditions and habits they'd managed to form in the two weeks since escaping their camp; I was exhausted with trying to figure out why, exactly, those two were able to cling to the thin thread that bound their friendship together.

Eventually Liam found Highway 81, and Chubs found a shallow, restless sleep. The endless stream of old trees, only a few fully dressed for spring, passed by my window. We were going too fast, and we were too far into twilight, for me to make out the patchwork of leaves that had grown in. Wherever we were, there were still traces of the dead leaves from the fall before staining the highway's cement. Almost as though we were the first car to drive the road in quite some time.

I leaned my forehead against the cool glass, reaching over to point the AC vent directly at my face. My headache was still there, pinching the space behind my eyes. The freezing air would help keep me awake, and, if nothing else, alert enough to catch my mind blindly groping for Liam's.

"You okay?"

189

He was trying to watch both the road and me. In the dark, I couldn't do much else besides make out the curve of his nose and lips. A part of me was glad I couldn't see the bruises and cuts there. It had only been a few days, a blink in my collective sixteen years of life, but I didn't need to see his face to know soft concern would be there. Liam was a great many things, but mysterious and unpredictable weren't included in that deck of cards.

"Are *you* okay?" I countered.

The car was quiet enough for me to hear his fingers drumming on the steering wheel. "Just need to sleep it off, I think." Then, after a moment, he added, "Did they really use that on you at Thurmond? A lot?"

Not a lot, but enough. I couldn't tell him that, though, without fanning the flames of his pity.

"Do you think the PSFs figured out where you're going?" I asked instead.

"Maybe. We could have just been at the wrong place at the wrong time."

Chubs woke behind us with a loud yawn.

"Not likely," he said sleepily. "Even if they weren't intentionally tracking us, I'm sure they are now. They were probably forced to memorize your ugly mug and Psi number. We already know you're a tasty treat for the skip tracers"

"Thank you Mr. Sunshine and Smiles," Liam gritted out.

"For what it's worth, the guy seemed surprised that it was actually you," I said. "But . . . who is this person you keep talking about? The woman?"

"Lady Jane," Liam said, as if that explained everything.

"Excuse me?"

"It's what we call one of the more . . . persistent skip tracers," he continued.

"First, it's what *you* call her," Chubs said. "And second, persistent? Try she's been on us like a shadow ever since we got out of Caledonia. She shows up everywhere, at any time, like she can guess what we're going to do before we do it."

"The lady is good at what she does," Liam confirmed.

"Can you please not compliment the person trying to drag our asses back to camp?"

"Why do you call her Lady Jane?" I asked.

Liam shrugged. "She's a rare British lass in a crop of bloodthirsty Americans."

"How did *that* happen?" I asked. "I thought they closed all the borders."

Liam opened his mouth to answer, but Chubs got there first. "I don't know, Green; why don't you hit her up for a chat and tea next time she comes around to capture us?"

I rolled my eyes. "Maybe I will if you tell me what she looks like."

"Dark hair up in a bun, glasses—" Liam began.

"—long, sort of hooked nose?" I finished.

"You've seen her?"

"In Marlinton. She was the one driving the red truck, but . . ." Cate and Rob had taken care of that. She had been left behind. "Well, she wasn't there this time," I finished. "Maybe we lost her for real."

"Fat chance," Chubs grumbled. "The woman is a Terminator."

We passed one rundown motel after another, some occupied more than others. I sat up in my seat when Liam turned into an old Comfort Inn's parking lot, only to immediately back out of it with a low whistle. There were no cars in the parking lot, but a dozen or more men and women were hanging around outside of their rooms, smoking, talking, fighting.

"We saw this a lot driving through Ohio," he explained without me having to prompt him. "After people lost their houses, they'd go to the nearest closed hotel and try to fight over the rooms there. Gangs and all that crap."

The motel he settled on was a Howard Johnson Express, one with a quarter of its parking lot filled with different makes and models of cars and the blue VACANCY sign on. I held my breath as he navigated around the outer ring of rooms, careful to avoid driving past the office. He picked a spot at the very edge of the lot, surveying the line of rooms in front of us. Two were easily ruled out—we could see the glow of the TV through the windows and curtains—but the others weren't as obviously occupied.

"Wait here a sec," he said, unbuckling his seat belt. "I'm going to scope out the area. Make sure it's safe." And it was just like before; he didn't bother to wait for any of us to protest. He just jumped out of the car, glanced into each room he passed, and began to jimmy the door of his choosing.

Chubs and I were left to divide up the last of the food we had gathered from the gas station in Marlinton. Our inventory was down to a bag of Cheetos, peanut butter crackers, some Twizzlers, and a snack pack of Oreos, plus the candy I had managed to stuff into my backpack. It was every six-year-old's dream feast.

We worked silently, avoiding each other's gaze like champions. Chubs's fingers were quick and nimble as he opened the peanut butter crackers and started in on them. The same ratty book was on his lap, the pages open and smiling up at him. I knew he couldn't actually be reading them—not with eyesight as bad as his, at least. But when he finally decided to talk to me, he didn't so much as glance up from it.

"Enjoying our life of crime yet? The general seems to think you're a natural."

I reached over to wake Zu, ignoring whatever it was he was trying to imply. I was too exhausted to deal with him, and, frankly, none of the comebacks warring at the tip of my tongue at the moment were likely to win him over.

Before I could step out of the van, my backpack and food in hand, Chubs's hand reached out and slammed the door shut again. In the dim light of the hotel, he looked . . . not angry, exactly, but certainly not friendly, either. "I have something to say to you."

"You've already said quite a bit, thanks."

He waited until I had looked back at him over my shoulder before continuing. "I'm not going to pretend like you didn't help us today, or that you didn't spend years living in a glorified shit hole, but I'm telling you now—use tonight to think seriously about your decision to stay, and if you decide to slip out in the middle of the night, know that you probably made the right choice."

I reached again for the door, but he wasn't finished. "I know you're hiding something. I know you haven't been completely honest. And if you think for some insane reason that we can protect you, think again. We'll be lucky to make it out of this mess alive *without* whatever crisis you're bringing to the table."

I felt my stomach clench, but kept my face neutral. If he was hoping to read some clue in my face, he was going to be disappointed; I'd spent the better part of the last six years schooling my expression into perfect innocence under the threat of guns.

Whatever he suspected couldn't have been the truth, though, otherwise he wouldn't be giving me one last chance to duck and run. He would have personally punted me out of the van, preferably at a high speed, in the middle of a deserted highway.

Chubs rubbed a thumb across his lower lip. "I think . . ." he started. "I hope you get to Virginia Beach, I really do, but—" He pulled the glasses off his face and pinched the bridge of his nose. "This is ridiculous, I'm sorry. Just think about what I said. Make the right choice."

Liam began waving at us from the door of the room, keeping it propped open with his foot. Zu put a hand on Chubs's shoulder. He jumped, blinking in surprise at the touch of yellow rubber. She had been so silent, I had forgotten she was there, too.

"Come on, Suzume," Chubs said, dropping a hand on her shoulder. "Maybe if we're lucky, the general will deign to let us take showers. And, maybe if we're *really* lucky, he'll actually take one himself."

Zu followed him out the side door, casting an anxious look my way. I waved her off with a forced smile and reached in the backseat for my black backpack.

I didn't notice it until I was already outside, the darkening sky sapping away the last bit of the van's warmth from my skin. One of my hands reached out to hold the sliding door open as I leaned back into the minivan and pulled the book out of the passenger seat's back pouch. It was the first and only time I had seen it free from Chubs's hands.

The flat, empty M&M's bag he was using as a bookmark was still in place. I flipped the book open to that page, and didn't need to look at the spine to know instantly what book it was. *Watership Down*, by Richard Adams. No wonder he had gone to such great lengths to hide what he was reading. The story of a bunch of rabbits trying to make their way in the world? Liam would have a field day.

But I loved that book, and apparently Chubs did, too. It was the same old edition my dad used to read to me before bed, the one I used to steal from his study and put on my shelf for when I couldn't sleep at night. How had it come to me just when I needed it the most?

My eyes drank in each word, worshipping their shape until my lips started forming them and I was reading aloud for everyone and no one to hear. *"All the world will be your enemy, Prince with a Thousand Enemies, and whenever they catch you, they will kill you. But first they must catch you, digger, listener, runner, prince with the swift warning. Be cunning and full of tricks and your people shall never be destroyed."*

I wondered if Chubs knew how the story ended.

TWELVE

THE HOT WATER WAS ENOUGH TO MAKE ME FORGET I was standing in an old motel shower, washing my hair with shampoo that reeked of fake lavender. In the entire compact bathroom, there were only six things: the sink, the toilet, the towel, the shower, its curtain, and me.

I was the last one in. By the time I finally walked through the motel room door, Zu had already been in and out and Chubs had just barricaded himself in the bathroom, where he spent the next hour scrubbing himself and all of his clothing until they stank of stale soap. It seemed pointless to me to try to do laundry in a sink with hand soap, but there was no bathtub or laundry detergent for him to use. The rest of us just sat back and tuned out his impassioned speech on the importance of good hygiene.

"You're next," Liam had said, turning to me. "Just make sure you wipe down everything when you're done."

I caught the towel he threw to me. "What about you?"

"I'll take one in the morning."

With the bathroom door shut and locked behind me, I dropped my backpack on the toilet seat cover and went to work sorting through its contents. I pulled out the clothes they had given me and dumped them on the floor. Something silky and red spilled out on top of the pile, causing me to jump back in alarm.

It took several moments of suspicious inspection to figure out what it was—the bright red dress from the trailer's closet.

Zu, I thought, passing a tired hand over my face. She must have grabbed it when I wasn't looking.

I poked at it with a toe, nose wrinkling at its faint scent of stale cigarette smoke. It looked like it was going to be a size too large for me, not to mention the somewhat icky feeling that came with knowing where it had been.

But, clearly, she had wanted me to have it—and wearing it, loath as I was to admit it, was smarter than running around in my camp uniform. I could do this for Zu; if it made her happy, it'd be worth the discomfort.

There was no shampoo, but the Children's League had thought to give me deodorant, a bright green toothbrush, a pack of tissues, some tampons, and hand sanitizer—all travel-sized and zipped up tight in a plastic bag. Under that was a small hairbrush and water bottle. And there, at the very bottom of the bag, was another panic button.

It must have been there the entire time, and I just hadn't realized it. I'd thrown the first one Cate had given me away, leaving it behind in the mud and brush. The thought that this one had been in my bag all this time—the *entire time*—made my skin crawl. Why hadn't I thoroughly searched the bag before now?

I picked it up between two fingers and dropped it into the sink like it had been a piece of hot coal. My hand was on the faucet, ready to drown the stupid thing in water and fry it for good, but something stopped me.

I'm not sure how long I stared down at it before I picked it up again and held it toward the light, trying to see if I could peer inside of the black outer shell. I looked for a red blinking light that would tell me if it was recording. I held it up to my ear, listening for any kind whirring or beeping that would tell me if it was activated. If it was on, or if it really was a tracker, wouldn't they have caught up to us by now?

Was it so bad to keep it—just in case? Just in case something happened again, and I couldn't help the others? Wouldn't being with the League be better than being thrown back into Thurmond? Being *killed*—wasn't anything better than that?

When I put the panic button back in the pocket of the backpack, it wasn't for me. If Cate had seen me she would have smiled, and the thought only made me angry all over again. I couldn't even believe in my own ability to protect these kids.

Stepping under the shower's perfect warm spray was already surreal enough without having to hear the *click-click-click-beep* of Thurmond's automatic timer to keep my wash time under three minutes. It was a good thing, too, since the dirt seemed to come off me in slow layers. A good

198

fifteen minutes of scrubbing and it felt like I had turned every inch of my skin inside out. I even tried using the bubblegum pink razor that had been included in the hotel's small pack of soap and shampoo, opening up old and new scabs on my shins and knees.

Sixteen years old, I thought, and this is the first time I've been able to shave my legs.

It was stupid—so stupid. I didn't know what I was doing, and I didn't care. I was old enough. No one was going to stop me.

My mom always came back to me in flashes. Sometimes I'd hear her voice, just a word or two. Other times, I'd have a memory so real it was like reliving the moment altogether. And now, as I kept at it, all I could think of was that conversation we'd had about this very thing, and her smile as she repeated over and over again, "Maybe when you're thirteen."

Eventually, I washed the razor off and threw it in the direction of my bag. I didn't think anyone else would want to use it now. With blood running down my legs, I turned my attention to the nest on my head. My hair was still too tangled for me to run my hands through it. I had to work through it knot by knot, using more of the shampoo than I had ever meant to, and by the time I was finished, I was crying.

I'm sixteen.

I don't know what brought it out. One minute I was fine, and the next it felt like my chest had collapsed in on itself. I tried to take in a deep breath, but the air was too hot. My hands found the wall's white tile first, a second before the rest of my body collapsed against it. I sat down on the rough, fake stone floor of the shower, and pressed my hands to my chest, grateful for the noise of the running water and overhead vent, which hid the sound of me breaking into pieces. I didn't want them to hear me like this, especially not Zu.

It was stupid, so stupid. I was sixteen—so what? So what, I hadn't seen my parents in six years? So what, I might never see them again? It's not like they remembered me anyway.

I should have been happy that it was over, that I was out of that place. But inside or out, I was alone, and I was beginning to wonder if I always had been, if I always would be. The water pressure wavered, its temperature spiking as someone in the next room over flushed the toilet. It didn't matter. I could barely feel it blasting against my back. My fingers went to my bleeding knees and pressed down, but I couldn't feel that, either.

Cate had told me that I needed to divide my life into three acts and close the first two behind me—but how did someone do that? How were you just supposed to *forget*?

There was a knock on the door. Faint, almost tentative at first, but more insistent when I didn't answer right away.

"Ruby?" I heard Liam's voice call. "You okay?"

I took a deep breath and reached back, hand feeling through the air for the faucet. The water overhead faded to a mere drizzle, and then a drip, and then nothing at all.

"Can you—uh—open the door? Just for a sec?" He sounded nervous enough to make *me* nervous. For one terrifying split second I thought something had happened. I reached for the towel and wrapped it around myself. My fingers flicked the lock over and were turning the doorknob before my brain caught up.

A blast of icy air was the first thing to hit me. Liam's wide eyes were the second. The pair of big white socks in his hand, the third.

He glanced around the bathroom over my shoulder, his mouth pressed in a grim line. The motel room was darker than it had been when I first walked in; we must have been well into night now. So I couldn't be sure, not in any real way, but I thought I caught a hint of color flooding the tips of his ears.

"Is everything all right?" I whispered. He stared at me, letting the warm fog from the bathroom wash over him. "Liam?"

The socks were thrust in my direction. I looked down at them and then up at him, hoping I didn't look as flabbergasted as I felt.

"Just wanted to . . . give you these," he said, giving them a little shake. He thrust them again in my direction. "You know, for you."

"Don't you need them?" I asked.

"I have a couple extra pairs, and you have none, right?" He looked like he was in some kind of pain now. "Seriously. Please. Just take them. Chubs says your extremities or whatever are the first things to get cold, so you need them, and—"

"Oh my God, Green," I heard Chubs say from somewhere in the room. "Just take the damn socks and put the kid out of his misery."

Liam didn't wait for me to hold out a hand. He reached past me and deposited them on the counter, right next to the sink.

"Um . . . thanks?" I said.

"Great—I mean, no problem," Liam turned to walk away, only to turn back again, as if thinking of something else. "Okay. Great. Cool—well, so you—"

"Use your words, Lee," Chubs called. "Some of us are trying to get some sleep."

"Oh, right. Sleep." Liam made a vague motion toward the room's bed. "You and Zu are going to share. I hope you don't mind."

"Of course not," I said.

"Okay, great!" He put an abnormally bright smile on his face. I wondered what he was waiting for me to do or say—if this was one of those moments that being trapped in a cabin with dozens of girls for six years had failed to prepare me for. It was like we were speaking in two different languages.

"Yeah, um, great," I repeated, more confused now than ever. That seemed to do the trick, though. Liam turned and walked away without another word.

I picked up my new socks from the counter, examining them. Just before I shut the door, I heard Chubs's voice, tinged with his usual *told-you-so*.

"—hope you're pleased with yourself," he was saying. "You should have just left her alone. She was fine."

But I hadn't been, and somehow Liam had known.

—◆—

202

It took me several long moments to realize it was Zu's dream.

She and I were on the room's queen-sized bed, huddled together for warmth. The boys were on the floor with the blankets, using extra towels stolen from a cleaning cart as pillows. The collective brain trust of Chubs and Liam hadn't been able to figure out how to turn down the air-conditioning unit, which insisted on spitting out its frosty breath every time the room so much as dared to spike to sixty degrees.

I had been hovering around the sweet, milky edges of sleep for hours when I felt the itch at the back of my mind. There was a part of me that had been expecting it; even though my body had settled onto the bed like a slab of concrete, my brain was still buzzing around in circles, processing what had happened with the PSFs, wondering if I could do what I had done to that man again, when Zu's bare feet brushed against mine, and that was all it took. I was pulled into her dream headfirst.

I was Zu and Zu was in a small bed, staring up at the underbelly of a brown mattress. Darkness blurred around us until finally some recognizable shapes emerged. Stacks of bunk beds, a chalkboard, bright blue cabinets that stretched from floor to ceiling, large windows boarded up with plywood, and strange square discolorations on the wall, where posters must have once hung.

I couldn't tear away. That was the dangerous thing about dreams—how quickly you became tangled in it all. People naturally let their guard down when they slept, so much so that sometimes, if the dream was frightening enough, I didn't even need a touch to be drawn into it.

I couldn't smell the smoke, but I saw it right away, gliding beneath the old classroom's door like spilled milk racing across the ground. A moment later, I jolted up, rolling until I was off the bed completely. I watched in slow, dawning horror as a dozen girls jumped down from their bunks and gathered in a buzzing huddle at the center of the room.

One girl, who must have been a good head taller and four years older than the others, tried to get them to crouch in a line beneath the windows, with no success. Her arms were waving through the air, the long sleeves of her simple, mustard-yellow uniform blurring.

And then, the alarms went off and the door at the far end of the room swung open.

The sound the bell made was nearly as excruciating as the White Noise, its pitch stretched and distorted by the dream. I was jostled forward as the other little girls made a break for the door. It didn't seem to matter to them that the smoke was suffocating, or that it didn't have a visible source.

In the place of neat, orderly lines was mass chaos. Kids with green, navy, and yellow uniforms spilled out into the white-tiled hallway. The emergency lights were on, fire alarms flashing red and yellow along the wall. I was thrown into the crushing river of bodies, all headed in the same direction—the direction of the smoke.

My vision blurred with tears and forced the breath out of my chest. One glance over my shoulder was enough to see some of the older kids, both boys and girls, dragging out the blue cabinets from their room and knocking them over in front of the silver double doors at the other end of the hallway.

We weren't evacuating at all. We were escaping.

My vision was swimming in black by the time we were pushed through the other set of doors and into the cramped stairway. The smoke was thickest there, rising not from shimmering flames but two small black canisters—the kind PSFs kept hooked on their belts, waiting to be thrown into a crowd of unruly kids.

So the PSFs set them off? No, that wasn't possible. It was much more likely a few kids had nabbed them, to get the alarms going and the doors open. That was probably the extent of their emergency protocol.

We were trapped in that stairwell, our bodies pressed against everyone else's in one shivering mass of nerves and exhilaration. I tried to keep my eyes forward and feel for the steps under my feet, but it was hard not to see what the darkness and flashing lights were doing to the other kids. Some were crying hysterically, some looked on the verge of passing out, but some were laughing. *Laughing*, like it was a game.

I don't know how I spotted the other small Asian girl under the tide of hands and heads. She was wedged in the bottom left corner of the stairwell landing, standing on her toes, her green uniform barely visible. Her hair was gleaming black under the emergency lights, and her arm was above her head, outstretched—toward me?

The minute I made eye contact with her, her face lit up in recognition. I saw her mouth form Zu's name. I tried to reach out, to grab her hand, but the swarm of people around me pushed me down, jostling forward. By the time I turned around, she had disappeared, too.

205

I didn't see one PSF or camp controller—not until we were at the base of the stairwell, stepping over, but mostly on, the three prone black figures on the ground. Their faces were swollen into bruised masks. Blood collected on the ground under them.

Someone, probably a Blue, had ripped the doors from their hinges and sent them flying outside, into what looked like a wasteland of white snow. The ground was unnaturally bright under the moonless sky—partly from the dream, partly from the searchlights that switched on as the pitch of the alarm changed from a trill to a warning siren.

Once we were out those final doors, we were running.

The snow was knee-deep, and most of the kids weren't wearing anything beyond their paper-thin uniforms—most of them hadn't even remembered to put on their shoes. Tiny flakes floated into the deep intersecting lines of footprints, and for a moment I felt myself slow, watching the way the snow was neither flying nor falling. Just hovering there, like a held breath. Lighting up like a thousand fireflies under the camp searchlights.

And then the spell was broken, shattered with the first gunshot.

And then it was bullets flying over us, not snow.

The screams ripped jagged and piercing from the throats of hundreds of kids. Five—ten—fifteen—it was impossible to count the kids that suddenly pitched forward, falling face-first into the snow, screaming and howling in pain. A nightmarish red began to creep through the snow like spilled ink spreading, expanding, devouring. I reached up to my cheek, to the wetness there, and when I pulled my hand away, my brain finally connected that I had run straight through a spray of blood. I was covered in it—someone else's blood was dripping down my cheeks and off my chin.

We ran harder, faster, toward the back right corner of the chain-link fence surrounding the old school. I threw a look back over my shoulder to the brick school building, to the dozens of black figures on top of its gray slate roof, to the dozens more pouring out from the first story windows and doors. When I turned back, the field in front of me was covered in heaps of every color—Yellow, Blue, Green. And red. So, so much red. They formed lines, unwilling barriers that others had to jump over to keep going.

I fell forward, barely catching myself on the snow. Something—someone had caught my ankle. A Green girl on her stomach, crawling toward me, her eyes open, her mouth gulping at the air. *Help me*, she was sobbing, blood bubbling up over her lips, *help me*.

But I got back up and ran.

There was a gate at this edge of the camp; I could see it now that I was within a few hundred feet of it. What I couldn't see was what was causing the backup of kids, why we weren't dashing through the gate to get to freedom. With a jolt, I realized there were almost three times as many kids down in the snow behind me than there were in front of me.

The cluster of kids surged forward with a unified wail, hundreds of hands straining forward. My size made it easy for me to slip through legs and fight my way up to the front, where three older boys in blue uniforms were struggling to keep the crowd of kids back from both the gate itself and the one-man watch booth beside it, which was currently playing host to three people: an unconscious PSF, Liam, and Chubs.

I was so shocked at the sight of them, I nearly missed the blur of green that was a little kid rushing for the fence. He darted around the teenagers in his path and threw himself against the bright yellow bars holding the gate firmly in place.

He had only just touched it when all of the hair on his head seemed to stand on end, and a burst of light flashed under his fingers. Instead of releasing it, his hand only seemed to clamp down harder, frozen in place as thousands of volts of electricity sent his body into a frenzied fit of shuddering.

Oh my God.

The gate was still on. Liam and Chubs were trying to turn it off.

I felt my own scream bubble up in my throat when he collapsed to the ground, finally still. Liam yelled something from the booth that I couldn't hear, not above the screams from the kids around me. The sight of that boy burst the temporary bubble of calm in a heartbeat.

The PSFs were closer now; they had to be, because when they started firing again, it was like shooting fish in a barrel. Each layer of kids fell down and away, peeling back to reveal a new, fresh layer for the kill—I couldn't see the snow beneath them anymore.

Kids turned and bolted in every direction, some heading back toward the school, others following the edges of the electrified fence, looking for another way out. I heard

208

dogs bark and the growling of engines. Combined, the noises sounded like a monster straight out of hell. I turned to look at the trail the animals and snowmobiles were blazing toward us, when something hard slammed into me from behind, throwing me into the thick snow.

I'm shot, I thought, half in shock.

No—that wasn't right. The blow had come from an elbow to the back of the head. The Blue girl hadn't even seen me as she turned and ran back toward the camp. I rolled over just in time to see her with her hands in the air, a clear surrender, and still—still—they shot her. She shrieked in pain and crumbled to the ground.

It wasn't just the girl who hadn't spotted me in the snow—no one did. I felt my arms, stinging with the cold, strain as I tried to push myself up and out of its freezing touch, but every time I made progress, another foot came slamming down across my shoulders and back. I had enough time to cover my head, but that was it. There was no getting air to my chest—I was screaming and no one could hear.

Rage and despair ripped through me. The crush of stampeding kids pushed me deeper and deeper into the snow, and I kept thinking, can you drown like this? Can you suffocate in the freezing dark? Would it be better to die this way?

Hands reached around my waist. Freezing air flooded my lungs in a single, painful gasp as I was lifted up and out of the snow.

The gate was open now, and the kids who had been steady and calm enough to remain—who had been lucky enough not to be hit—poured through, running for the dense cluster of trees ahead. There couldn't have been more than twenty—of the hundreds of kids who had flooded through the halls of the old school—*twenty*.

I felt warm, impossibly warm. The arms holding me tightened. When I looked up, it was into Liam's bright eyes.

Hang on tight, okay?

Zu woke with a gasp, coming up from her nightmare for a long drag of air.

I was thrown out of the dream, sent hurtling back into the freezing hotel room. Through the topsy-turvy vertigo that slammed into me, I turned toward Zu, my eyes adjusting just enough to make out her silhouette.

When I reached for her, I found someone else's hands already there.

Liam shook his head, trying to snap himself out of sleep's lingering grasp. "Zu," he whispered. "Hey, Zu . . ."

I stayed perfectly still.

"Hey," Liam said gently, "you're okay. It was just a bad dream."

My gut twisted when I realized she was crying. I heard a scraping sound, wood against wood, like he had taken something out of the nightstand.

"Write it down," Liam said. "Don't force yourself."

It must have been the hotel stationery. I shut my eyes, waiting for him to switch on the cheap nightstand lamp, but he kept to his rule: no lights outside the bathroom.

"What are you sorry for?" he whispered. "The only one that needs beauty sleep is Chubs."

She let out a shaky laugh, but her body was still tense next to mine.

"Was it . . . the same one as before?" The bed dipped as Liam sat down.

"A little different?" he repeated after a moment. "Yeah?"

The silence stretched a little longer this time. I wasn't sure she was still scribbling in the darkness until Liam cleared his throat and said, in a rough voice, "I could never forget that. I was . . . I was really worried you had tried to touch the gate before Chubs figured out how to switch it off." And then, so soft that I might have imagined it, he said, "I'm so sorry."

The guilt and misery that coated the words were like a kick to the chest. I felt myself shift forward on the bed, drawn to the pain there, desperate to reassure him that what had happened there in the snowy field hadn't been his fault. It scared me, knowing how well I understood him in that moment.

But I couldn't. This was a private conversation, just like her memory had been private. Why was I always trespassing into places I didn't belong?

"Chubs isn't the only one that thinks it's too dangerous. But I think Ruby's tough enough to make it without us if she wants to. Why?"

More scribbling.

"The only thing Chubs wants is for us to be safe," he said, still whispering. "Sometimes that gets in the way of him doing what's good for others—seeing the big picture, you know? It's only been two weeks since we got out. You got to give him more time."

211

He sounded so confident then that I felt a small part of me give. I believed him.

"Oh, man." I could practically see him running a hand through his hair. "Never be ashamed of what you can do, you hear me? If you hadn't been there, we wouldn't be here."

The room settled back into a peaceful quiet, save for Chubs's wheezing snores.

"You feeling better?" he asked. "Need anything from Betty?"

She must have shaken her head, because I felt the bed shift again as Liam stood. "I'll be right here. Just wake me up if you change your mind, okay?"

I didn't hear him say good night. But instead of lying down, I saw him sit, back flush against the bed, watching the door and anything that might come through it.

A few hours later, with the moon still visible in the gray-blue morning sky, I gently untangled Zu's fingers from the front of my dress and slipped out of the bed. The red glow of the alarm clock on the nightstand burned the time into my mind: 5:03 p.m. Leaving time.

None of us had really unpacked our things, on Liam's insistence, but I had to collect my toothbrush and toothpaste from where I had left them next to Chubs's in the bathroom. There was one set of HoJo toiletries left out by the sink, next to the world's ugliest coffeemaker. I stuffed them into my bag, along with one of the smaller hand towels.

Outside, it was only a few degrees warmer than it had been in the room. Typical bipolar Virginia spring weather.

It must have rained the night before, too. A feathery white fog threaded through the cars and nearby trees. The minivan, which last night had been parked on the far end of the lot, was now stationed directly in front of the hotel room. If I hadn't walked right by Black Betty, running my hand against her bruised side, I don't think I would have seen Liam at all.

He was kneeling beside the sliding door, slowly scraping off the last of the BETTY JEAN CLEANING sign with his car keys. At his feet was the Ohio plate that had, at one point, been screwed into place. My feet drifted to a stop a few feet short of him.

There were dark circles under his eyes. His face was drawn in thought, his mouth set in a grim line that didn't suit him at all. With his damp hair combed back and his face clean-shaven, he could have looked a good two or three years younger than he had the day before, but his eyes told a different story.

My shoes scuffed the loose asphalt, catching Liam's attention. He started to rise. "What's wrong?"

"Huh?"

"You're up early," he explained. "I usually have to drag Chubs into the shower and blast him with cold water to get him going."

I shrugged. "Still on Thurmond's schedule, I guess."

He rose to his feet slowly, wiping his hands on the front of his jeans. The way his eyes flicked toward me made me think he wanted to say something, but, instead, he only gave me a small smile. The Ohio license plate was tossed into the

213

backseat, and in its place was a West Virginia plate. I didn't have a chance to ask where it had come from.

I dropped my backpack at my feet and leaned against the minivan's door. Liam disappeared around the back of the car, reappearing a few minutes later with a red gas can and a chewed up black hose in hand. With my eyes closed and ear pressed against the cool glass, I soaked up the honeyed singsong radio commercial for a local grocery store. When the broadcaster came back on, it was with a grim forecast of whatever was left of Wall Street. The woman read the stock report like a eulogy.

I forced my eyes open, letting them fall where Liam had been standing only a second before.

"Liam?" I called before I could stop myself.

"Over here," came the immediate reply.

With a quick glance to the row of aquamarine motel doors, I shuffled around the back of the van until I was a few feet behind him. I stood on my toes, leaning to the right to get a better look at what he was doing to the silver SUV parked next to the van.

Liam worked silently, his light eyes focused on the task at hand. One end of the hose was shoved deep into the belly of the SUV's gas tank. He looped the excess length of the unruly hose around his shoulder, and let the other end fall in the red can.

"What are you doing?" I didn't bother to hide my shock.

His free hand hovered over the length of the hose, gliding it back in our direction. It was almost like he was tugging in a line, or at least motioning someone forward. A few drops of pungent liquid began to drip from the free end of the hose.

Siphoning gas, I realized. I'd heard about people doing this during the last gas shortage, but I'd never actually *seen* it done before. The liquid began to fill the can in a smooth pour, filling the space between us with a sharp odor.

"Gas crisis," he said with an unapologetic shrug. "Times are a little desperate, and we were running on fumes for a while yesterday."

"You're Blue, right?" I said, nodding toward the hand guiding the gas into our red can. "Could you just move Betty along without it?"

"Yeah, but . . . not for long." Liam sounded shy. When he pressed his lips together, they turned an unnatural shade of white and highlighted a small scar at the right corner.

When I realized I was staring, I squatted down beside him—more to hide my embarrassment than actually help. Stealing gas was, surprisingly, not all that complicated.

"I guess I'm just impressed you can use your abilities at all."

A part of me wondered, then, if I hadn't had it backward this entire time. The way things were at Thurmond . . . the camp controllers were so vigilant about making sure that we were terrified of getting caught using our abilities, and we were made to understand from the beginning that what we were, and what we could do, was dangerous and unnatural. Mistakes and accidents were not excuses, and punishment was not avoidable. There was to be no curious testing, no stabbing at limits to see if there was a way to push through them.

215

If Liam was so accomplished with his abilities, it probably meant he had taken years to practice, most of those spent outside of camp walls. It never occurred to me to think that other kids, safe at home, hiding out—that the *others*, who had never seen the inside of a cabin, experienced the grave and still *nothing* that was life at camp—might have managed to teach themselves amazing things. They weren't afraid of themselves; they weren't crippled by the weight of what they didn't know.

I had the strangest feeling—like I had lost something without ever really having it in the first place—that I wasn't what I once was, and wasn't at all what I was meant to be. The sensation made me feel hollow down to my bones.

"The whole thing's pretty straightforward for us Blues," Liam explained. "You look at something, concentrate hard enough to imagine that object moving from point A to point B, and it just . . . does," he said. "I bet a lot of the Blues at Thurmond figured out how to use their abilities. They just chose not to. Maybe something to do with that noise."

"You're probably right." I hadn't had enough interaction with the Blue kids to know.

Liam jerked the hose back and forth as the stream of gas slowed to a measly drip. I glanced up, searching the parking lot and motel doors for signs of life, and didn't settle back down until I was sure we were alone.

"Did you teach yourself?" I asked, testing my theory.

He glanced my way. "Yeah. I went into camp pretty late and had plenty of time alone, bored out of my mind, to figure things out."

Naturally, the next question was: Were you in hiding? But I wouldn't be able to ask that without him asking about my history and how I was caught.

This had to stop. My hands were shaking like he had just told me he was about to strangle the life out of me. Nothing he had done up until now had proven him to be anything other than nice. Hadn't he shown me, time and time again, that he was willing to be my friend if I was willing to let him?

It had been so long since I'd even wanted a friend that I wasn't sure I even remembered how to go about making one. In first grade, it had been stupidly simple. Our teacher had told us to write down our favorite animal on a sheet of paper, and then we had to go around the room until we found someone with a matching animal. Because making friends was supposed to be that easy, apparently—finding someone else who liked elephants.

"I like this song," I blurted out. Jim Morrison's voice was soft and barely reached us from where it was filtering through Betty's speakers.

"Yeah? The Doors?" Liam's face lit up. "'Come on baby, light my fire,'" he crooned in a low voice, trying to match Morrison's. "'Try to set the night on fire. . . .'"

I laughed. "I like it when *he* sings it."

Liam clutched his chest, like I had wounded him, but his recovery was quick. The radio DJ announced the next song; it was like Liam had won the lottery. "Now this is what *I'm* talking about!"

"The Allman Brothers?" My eyebrows were inching up my face. Funny, I had pegged him for a Zeppelin fan.

"This is the music of my soul," he said, nodding his head in time with the music.

"Have you ever actually listened to the lyrics?" I asked, feeling the anxiety lift off my shoulders. My voice was growing steadier with each word. "Was your father a gambler down in Georgia that wound up on the wrong end of a gun? Were you born in the backseat of a Greyhound bus?"

"Hey now," he said, reaching over to flick my hair. "I said it was the music of my *soul*, not my life. For your information, my stepdad is a mechanic down in North Carolina and, as far as I know, still alive and well. But I *was* born in the backseat of a bus."

"You're joking." I honestly couldn't tell.

"Am not. It made the newspapers and everything. I was the Miracle Bus Boy for the first three years of my life, and now I'm—"

"'Trying to make a livin' and doin' the best I can'?" I finished.

He laughed, the tips of his ears tinged with a faint pink. The song went on, filling the air between us with its rapid pulse and relentless guitars. Every piece fit together effortlessly; not quite country and not quite rock and roll. Just warm, fast, Southern.

I liked it even better when Liam started singing along.

When the flow of gas had stopped, he carefully pulled the hose free and replaced the gas cap. Before he stood, Liam knocked his shoulder into mine. "Where in the world did you get that dress?"

I snorted, picking at the skirt. "Present from Zu."

"You look like you want to throw it into a fire."

"I can't promise there won't be an unfortunate accident later on," I said, very seriously. When he laughed again it felt like a small victory.

"Well, Green, it was nice of you to put it on," Liam said. "Though be careful. Zu's so starved for girl time that she might turn you into her own personal dress-up doll."

"Kids these days," I said. "Think the whole world belongs to them."

He grinned. "Kids these days."

We moved from car to car, working our way down the parking lot. He didn't ask for my help, and I didn't ask him any more questions. We could have stayed together in that comfortable silence for hours, and it still wouldn't have been enough for me.

THIRTEEN

CHUBS AND ZU WERE NOT HAPPY TO BE WOKEN UP at five thirty a.m., and even less enthusiastic about Liam forcing them to make the bed while we freshened up the bathroom and replaced the used towels. Not exactly clean of us, but it was better than alerting the management they had hosted a bunch of squatters for the night.

Chubs took one look at me as he marched out to the minivan and stopped dead in his tracks. He wore his thought plain as day on his face: *You're still here?*

I shrugged. *Deal with it.*

He shook his head and let out another one of his sighs.

Once we were settled, Zu and Chubs in the middle seats, we all watched as Liam closed the hotel room door, cup of crappy hotel coffee in hand.

That's right, I thought, glancing at Zu out of the corner of my eye. She had curled up on her seat and was using her gloved hands as a pillow. Didn't get much sleep, did he?

Liam ran through his usual routine of checking the mirrors' position, adjusting the recline of his seat, buckling himself in, and turning the keys in the ignition. But Liam's next order of business upon returning to the minivan wasn't to answer any of the number of questions Chubs threw his way about where we were going. He waited until his friend was good and snoring before calling back to me, "Can you read a map?"

The embarrassment and shame that washed through me painted my face red. "No. Sorry." Wasn't that something your dad was supposed to teach you eventually?

"No problem." Liam patted the empty passenger seat. "I'll teach you later, but for now I just need someone to watch the signs for me. Come on up to the copilot chair."

I jerked a thumb in the direction of Chubs.

Liam only shook his head. "Are you kidding me? Yesterday he thought a mailbox was a clown."

I unbuckled my seat belt with a sigh. As I climbed over Chubs's outstretched legs to the front, I glanced over my shoulder, my eyes going to his too-small glasses. "Is his eyesight really that bad?"

"Worse," Liam said. "So, right after we got the hell out of Caledonia, we broke into this house to spend the night, right? I woke up in the middle of the night hearing the most awful noise, like a cow dying or something. I followed the wailing, clutching some kid's baseball bat, thinking I was going to have to beat someone's head in for us to make a clean getaway. Then I saw what was sitting at the bottom of the drained pool."

"No way," I said.

"Way," he confirmed. "Hawkeye had gone out to relieve himself and had somehow missed the giant gaping hole in the ground. Twisted his ankle and couldn't climb out of the deep end."

I tried so hard not to laugh, but it was impossible. The mental image was just too damn good.

Liam reached over and switched on the radio, letting me choose the station. He seemed satisfied with my decision to stay with the Who.

With the window down all the way, I leaned out, resting my chin on my hands. The morning air was warm, licked by the first rays of sunlight. When I looked up past the very tip-top of the wild trees, there was nothing but blue sky.

A small sound, a ghost of a sigh, was released behind us. Both Liam and I turned to look at Zu's sleeping face.

"Did we wake you up last night?" he asked.

"I caught a little of it," I said. "Does she have a lot of nightmares?"

"In the few weeks I've known her, it's been an every other night thing. Sometimes she dreams about Caledonia and I can talk her down, but I never know what to say about her family. I swear, if I ever meet her parents, I'm going to . . ."

His voice trailed off, but the anger coating them had given the air a palpable charge.

"What did they do to her?"

"Gave her away, because they were afraid of her," he said. "Like, me and Chubs? Our folks tried to keep us hidden,

222

and that's why we went to the camp late. Zu's parents actually *sent* her away when she short-circuited her dad's car in the middle of a freeway."

"Oh, God."

"They sent her during the first official Collection." He propped an elbow along the door panel and leaned his face against his hand. His Redskins cap hid his eyes from view. "I forgot you missed this."

I waited for him to explain.

"It was after most people our age had already been taken or were in hiding. The government issued a notice that any parents who didn't feel safe or capable of taking care of their kiddos could send them to school on a specific morning, and the Psi Special Forces would be there to collect them for rehabilitation. Kept it all very hush-hush to avoid *upsetting* the children or *inciting them to misbehave*."

I rubbed my forehead, trying to force out the images flittering through my mind. "Did she actually tell you this?"

"*Tell me*—tell me, you mean?" He kept his eyes straight ahead, but I saw his hands choke the wheel. "No. She wrote it out in bits and pieces. I haven't heard her say a single word since . . ."

"Since the breakout?" I finished. I felt relieved in spite of everything I knew. "It's a choice, then, not something they did to her."

"No, it has everything to do with what they did, and it's not a choice," Liam said. "I think maybe the most frustrating feeling in the world is to have something to say but not know how to put it into words. To have lived through something but not be able to get it out of you before it festers. I mean, you're right—she *can* talk, and maybe one day she will. After everything I've put her through, after what happened . . . I just don't know."

It *was* the most frustrating feeling in the world, second only to the inherent helplessness that came with being trapped in a camp, all of your decisions made for you. After what had happened with Sam, I didn't say a word for almost a full year; there was just no way to vocalize that kind of pain.

The radio jumped as we lost the station's signal, switching through a Spanish language channel, then to one with classical music, before finally settling on the dry, nasally voice of a man reading the news.

"*. . . to inform you that initial reports indicate that four separate explosions were set off this morning in Manhattan's subway . . .*"

Liam's finger shot out to switch the channel, but I changed it right back.

"*—though confirmation has been slow to come out of the city, we believe these explosions were not nuclear or biological in nature, and were concentrated around midtown, where President Gray was rumored to be in hiding after the most recent attempt on his life.*"

"League, West Coast, or fake?" Chubs's sleepy voice floated up behind us.

"*Our sources indicate that President Gray and his cabinet believe this to be the work of the Federal Coalition.*"

"Federal Coalition?" I repeated. "West Coast," the boys answered together. Chubs elaborated. "Based out of Los

224

Angeles. They're the section of the government that survived the D.C. bombings and weren't crazy about the idea of Gray disregarding that whole two-term limit they had set up. They're mostly talking heads since the military sided with Gray, obviously."

"Why is Gray in New York and not Washington?" I asked.

"They're still rebuilding the Capitol and the White House, only it's not going so well since, you know, they defaulted on all of their debt," Liam said. "He spread the government out between Virginia and New York for its *protection*. To make sure none of the fugitive Psi groups or the League got any ideas about wiping it all out at once."

"So the Federal Coalition . . . they're against the camps? The reform program?"

Chubs sighed a little. "Hate to break it to you, Green, but something you'll learn pretty fast is that we're not exactly a priority to *anyone* right now. Everyone's more focused on the fact that the country is broke as a joke."

"Who *do* we like, then?" I pressed.

"We like us," Liam said after a while. "And that's about it."

There were, apparently, only two restaurant chains left in the state of Virginia, or at least the western half of it: Cracker Barrel and Waffle House—and one wasn't open before nine o'clock in the morning.

"Thank goodness," Liam said in a solemn voice as he parked a short distance away from the Waffle House. "I don't know how we would have chosen between these two fine culinary establishments."

He had nominated himself to order whatever food he could afford with twenty bucks, but refused when I asked if he wanted me to go with him.

Zu held up a small notebook, waving it to get his attention as he stepped outside.

"Done already?"

She nodded.

"Why don't you have Chubs check your answers? No, don't make that face. He's better at math than I am, anyway."

"You're damn right I am," Chubs said, without looking up from his book.

Zu flipped the flimsy notebook open to a blank page and scribbled something down. When she held it up for him to see, Liam grinned.

"Whoa, whoa—*long division?* I think you're getting ahead of yourself, ma'am. You still haven't conquered your double-digit multiplying."

I watched him hop out of the minivan, a flare of annoyance shooting up from my core. All of this would have been so much easier if he wasn't the only one of us who looked old enough to pass for twenty—at least I'd feel a lot better knowing one of us could be out there watching his back. Liam must have felt my gaze burning through the back of his jacket, because he stopped and turned to wave before disappearing around the corner.

"You really have to stop encouraging him," Chubs was

saying to Zu. I glanced back, watching as he used the blunt end of her pencil to follow lines of numbers on the page. "He needs to accept reality at some point."

Zu's face scrunched up, twisting like a piece of hard lemon candy was stuck on her tongue. She punched him in the shoulder.

"I'm sorry," he said, but clearly wasn't. "It's just a waste of time and energy to teach you this stuff when you're never going to get the chance to use it."

"You don't know that," I said. Flashing Zu a reassuring smile, I added, "You'll be ahead of everyone else your age by the time things go back to normal."

When had I started believing in "normal," anyway? Everything I had been through up to that point could only be used as support for Chubs's argument. He was right, even if I didn't want to admit it.

"You know what I'd be doing if things were *normal*?" Chubs said. "I'd be picking which college I was going to attend later this fall. I'd have taken my SATs, gone to football games and prom, taken chemistry . . ."

His voice trailed off, but I picked up the frayed ends of his thought all the same—how could I not? These were the exact things I thought about when I let myself get to that dark place of should-be and could-have-been. My mom said once that education was a privilege not afforded to everyone, but she was wrong—it wasn't a privilege. It was our right. We had the right to a future.

Zu sensed the shift of mood. She looked between us, lips moving silently. We needed a change of subject.

"Pffft," I said, crossing my arms over my chest and leaning back against the seat. "Like you would have ever gone to a football game."

"Hey, I resent that!" Chubs handed Zu her notebook. "Here, you need to work on your nines." When he turned back to me, it was with a disapproving look. "I can't believe you of all people fell for his cotton candy dreams."

"What's that supposed to mean?"

"You were in Thurmond for what—five years?"

"Six," I corrected. "And you're missing the point. It's not that I believe in what Lee's saying; it's that I hope he's right. I really, really hope he's right, because what's the alternative? We're stuck hiding out until their generation dies off? We flee to Canada?"

"Good luck with that," Chubs said. "Both Canada and Mexico have built walls to keep us out and them in."

"Because they thought IAAN was a contagious disease."

"No, because they've hated us all along and were only looking for the right excuse to keep our fat asses and fanny packs out of their countries forever."

Liam chose that exact moment to reappear, four Styrofoam containers balanced between his hands. He was moving fast, almost at a run. I leaned over and popped the door open for him, and he all but dumped the containers on my lap.

"Oh God, what now?" Chubs cried.

"Whoa—" I began, trying to keep the hot food from spilling all over my legs and the seat. Betty's engine started with a snarl, and suddenly we were rocketing backward. With the sheet blocking the back window, Liam had to rely on using the side mirror to navigate us down the road and up into the small back alley that divided the Waffle House from an abandoned jewelry consignment store. I braced an elbow against the door as he steered the old minivan past the Dumpsters to the cramped employee parking lot tucked away in a dead-end around the corner. The minivan lurched to a stop, throwing all four of us forward.

"We're . . . going to stay here for a little while," he announced to our terrified faces. "Don't panic, but I think I saw . . . I mean, it'll just be safer here for a bit."

"You saw her." It wasn't a question; Chubs already knew the answer before he asked. "Lady Jane."

Liam rubbed the back of his neck as he leaned forward. He had left the nose of the minivan out far enough so we could peer around Waffle House's wall to see down the alleyway. "Yeah. I'm pretty sure."

How was it possible that she had caught up with us?

"Holy *hell*," Chubs squawked. "*Pretty* sure or *definitely* sure?"

After a moment Liam answered, "Definitely sure. She's got a new set of wheels—a white truck—but I'd recognize that smug face anywhere."

"Did she see you?" I asked.

"I don't know," he said. "Probably not, otherwise she and whoever her new boy toy is would have tried to run me down. They drove by just as I was leaving."

I craned my neck forward, trying to see far enough past the wall of the restaurant to the alley opening. As if on cue, a glinting white truck rolled by, two dark figures in the front seats. Liam and I flew back against our seats at the exact same moment, looking at each other in alarm. I don't think either of us took a breath until we were sure no one was coming down the alley to investigate.

He cleared his throat. "Um . . . how about you pass out the food? I'll just check—"

"Liam Michael Stewart," Chubs's voice thundered from the backseat, "if you step one foot out of this minivan, I will order Green to run you down with it."

"Don't think I won't," I warned, knowing exactly what Liam wanted to do: go out and risk his neck by walking down the alley to make sure the coast was clear. When I handed him a Styrofoam container, he slumped back in his seat, accepting defeat.

Liam had ordered each of us a simple meal of scrambled eggs, bacon, and two pancakes without syrup. The others dug in with gusto, inhaling the meal in five bites. I gave my pancakes to Zu, before Liam had the chance to.

After some semblance of calm had settled back over us, he pulled his map up and spread it out over the wheel. The dashboard clock beside him said 7:25 a.m., and when he turned to face us, it was with an expression of determination I had never seen someone wear so early in the morning.

"Okay, team," he began. "We need to get back on the right track. I know our last East River was a total bust, but we have to keep looking. So let's review the facts those Blues gave us: Eddo."

It was only after a full minute of silence that I realized that was the extent of the "facts".

"We should have tried to bribe them for more information," Chubs said.

"With *what*?" Liam said, setting the map down. "They wouldn't take you, Chubs, and you're our most precious commodity."

Chubs, unsurprisingly, did not find that funny.

"Did they spell Eddo out for you? Was it one 'd' or two?" I asked. "Because if it's an actual clue, that could make a difference."

The two boys shared a look.

"Well . . . crap," Liam said, finally.

I felt a sharp tug on my arm, and turned toward Zu, who was holding up her notebook for us to see. She had written the letters *E-D-O*.

"Nice job, Zu," Liam said. "Good thing one of us was listening."

"And that was it?" I said.

"The only other thing they coughed up was that if we hit Raleigh we'd gone too far south. And we had to beg for even *that*," Liam confessed. "It was really pathetic."

"They could have been pulling our legs, too," Chubs said. "That's what irritates me the most. If East River is so great, why were they leaving?"

"They were going home; remember, the Slip Kid—"

While they were arguing, I slipped the map out from under Liam's hands and squinted at it, trying to make sense of the lines. He had given me a very vague rundown of how to route a path from point A to point B, but it was still overwhelming.

231

"What are you guys thinking?" I asked. "What theory were you working with?"

"We ran across the kids right around the Ohio state line," Liam said. "They were coming from the east, headed west. If you add that to the other bit about D.C. and Raleigh, the likely candidates become West Virginia, Virginia, or Maryland. Zu said Edo is another name for Tokyo, but it seems a little far-fetched he'd be there."

"And *I* think it's a code," Chubs said. "A cipher of some kind." He sat up a little straighter, turning to face me fully. The way the smile spread over his face made me think of a nature documentary we watched once in school, about the way crocodiles flash their teeth as they skim through the water toward their prey. "Speaking of codes, didn't you say the League broke you out because you were a world-class code breaker?"

Crap.

"I didn't say *world-class* . . ."

"Oh yeah!" Liam's face lit with the most heartbreaking expression of excitement. "Can you take a stab at it?"

Double crap.

"I—er, I guess," I said, careful to keep my face neutral. "Zu, can I see the notebook again?"

They were all staring at me; they might as well have been sitting on my chest for how paralyzing it was. It was near freezing in the van without the heat on, but my body felt heavy with hot, sticky panic. I was holding on to that notebook like it was a prayer from heaven.

I knew there were kids out there who could plug in a few dozen letters into their brain and spew out complex

232

coordinates or immediately spot a riddle hidden in a puzzle, but I definitely was not one of them.

Chubs snorted. "Looks like the League picked a lemon."

"Hey," Liam said, his tone sharp. "We've been mulling over the damn thing for two weeks and have figured out exactly nothing. You can't even give her an hour to think about it?"

Could I sub out the letters *EDO* for numbers? 5-4-15? God, what other kinds of codes were there? A railroad code? No—that wasn't right. Or was it not a code? That would make a hell of lot more sense, actually. The riddle had to be something that kids both in and out of camps could figure out, and it couldn't be *too* difficult, otherwise no one would ever get it.

Lie, I thought, reaching up to smooth a stray piece of hair back from my face. Just lie. Just do it. Just say *something*! What did three-digit numbers usually represent? A price, a time, an area code—

"Oh!" If I was right, *Oh God* was more like it.

"Oh?" Liam repeated. "Oh what?"

"I'd forgotten—well . . ." I corrected myself. "I could be remembering it wrong, so don't get too excited, but I think it's a Virginia area code."

"There's no area code that's four digits," Chubs said. "Five-four-fifteen doesn't work."

"But five-four-zero *does*," I said. "People sub out *O* for zero when they talk sometimes, right?"

Liam scratched the back of his head and looked over at Chubs. "Five forty? Does that sound familiar to you?"

I turned toward Chubs, suddenly seeing him in a new light. "You're from Virginia?"

He crossed his arms and looked out his window. "I'm from *Northern* Virginia."

Well, that figured. "Five forty is western Virginia," I explained to Liam. "I'm not sure how far north and south it extends, but it should be right around this area, I think." I showed him on the map. I didn't just *think*, I knew. 540 had been my area code when I lived with my parents in Salem. "There are a number of cities and towns, but there's also a lot of undeveloped land—not a bad place to hide out."

"Is that a fact?" Liam kept his eyes on the road and his voice even, but there was something maybe a little bit too casual about it. "Did you grow up near there?"

I looked down at the notebook in my hands again, feeling something clench in my chest. "No, I didn't."

"Virginia Beach, then?"

I shook my head. "Not any place you've been or heard of."

I heard Chubs's tongue cluck as he opened his mouth to say something, but there was a sharp cough from the driver's seat. The topic had been dropped, and no one was willing to try picking it up again, least of all me.

"Well, it's as good of a lead as any, though I wish the area was a little smaller." He glanced my way. "Thanks, Ruby Tuesday."

A not unpleasant warmth rushed up from my center. "Don't mention it." *And if I'm wrong* . . . I let the thought trail off. It *was* a good lead.

234

With one last glance down the alley to make sure it was clear, Liam refolded the map and tossed it back into the open glove box. Betty came back to life with a low growl.

"Where are we going?" Chubs asked.

"It's a place I know." Liam gave a one-shoulder shrug. "Someplace I stayed before. The drive shouldn't take us that long—maybe two hours. If I get lost, though, one of you Virginians is going to have to step up to the plate and help me out."

It had been a very long time since someone had labeled me like that—as a person with a home. It was true, I had been born here, but Thurmond had been my home for nearly as long as it hadn't. Gray walls and concrete floors had bleached out almost every memory of my parents' house, stripping away first the small details—the smell of my mom's honey-soaked biscuits, the order of the pictures lining the staircase wall—before going on to devour the bigger ones, too.

I used to wonder—at night when it was quiet enough in the cabin to think, when I let myself get to the point of wishing for *home*—if the *home* in my heart was supposed to be the place where'd I'd been born, or if it was the place that was raising me. If I got to choose it, or if it had somehow already claimed me.

The truth was, when I looked at my reflection in the window, I couldn't see any bit of the Ruby that had lived in a little white house at the end of a lane, honey sticking to her fingers and hair falling from her braids. And it made me feel empty in a way—like I had forgotten the words to my favorite song. That girl was gone forever, and all that was left was a product of the place that had taught her to fear the bright things inside of her heart.

We passed exit after exit to Harrisonburg and the turnoffs for James Madison University. Driving down a major highway with nothing more than a prayer that no one would pull us over wasn't exactly my idea of a good time, but, for now, the risk seemed worth it—at least for the view.

I loved the Shenandoah Valley, every inch of its gorgeous spread. When I was little, my parents used to pull me out of school early for a long weekend of hiking or camping. I never brought books or video games for the drive—I didn't need them. I would just stare out the window and drink it all in.

You know in movies, the ones set in older times, when the shot freezes on the hero or heroine gazing out over the forest, or river, and the sun catches the leaves at just the right slant, and the music begins to swell? That's exactly how I felt as we entered the Shenandoah Valley.

It didn't hit me until that moment, until the first glimpse of the gauzy blue mist surrounding the mountains, that we really *were* in western Virginia. That if we stayed on the highway, we'd be two hours away from my parents in Salem. Two hours.

I didn't know how to feel about that.

"Ugh," Liam groaned, pointing toward the temporary road sign up ahead: 81 CLOSED BETWEEN HARRISONBURG AND STAUNTON. USE LOCAL ROADS.

By nine o'clock in the morning, we were finally deep enough into Harrisonburg to find its pulse of life. Here and there we saw restaurants opening their doors to the morning light. We passed a few older adults pedaling away on their bikes, balancing precariously on two wheels with their briefcases or bags, their heads bent toward the sidewalk. They didn't even look up as we passed.

No JMU students, though. None that I could spot.

Chubs sighed at the sight of them, leaning his forehead against the window.

"You okay, buddy?" Liam asked. "Need to stop and smell the scholasticism?"

"What's the point?" Chubs shook his head. "It's closed like all of the others."

I whirled around in my seat. "Why?"

"Lack of students, mostly. If you're old enough to go to college, you're old enough to be drafted. Even if that wasn't the case, I doubt people can really afford it anymore."

"Jesus, that's depressing," I said.

"The offer still stands," Liam told his friend. "You know I'm happy to break into a classroom for you if you need to sit in one of those cramped seats and stare at a whiteboard for a while. I know how much you like the smell of dry erase markers."

"I appreciate that," Chubs said, folding his hands in his lap, "but it's not necessary."

We passed what I thought must have been a black wrought iron fence, but it was almost impossible to see, trapped as it was beneath what looked to be a raggedy, patchwork blanket. It wasn't until we got closer that I realized what we were actually looking at: hundreds, maybe thousands of sheets of paper that had been tied and taped onto the fence or stuck between the thin bars.

Liam slowed the car, tilting his sunglasses down to squint at them.

"What do they say?" Chubs asked. "I can't . . ."

Zu only put her head back down and shut her eyes.

They were "Missing" posters with the faces of little kids and teenagers, photographs, signs whose wording had been smeared away by rain—the biggest of these being a banner that said nothing more than MATTHEW 19:14. It hung crookedly, almost like someone had tried to rip it down, only to have someone else come along and halfheartedly string it back up. The wall of faded paper took a beating as the wind blew through the fences, ripping some of the more decrepit sheets free and making others flutter like hummingbird wings. And where there was room, we saw stuffed animals and flowers and blankets and ribbons.

No, not missing, I thought. Those kids had been taken, or really were gone forever. Their parents and families were searching for them, posting their pictures, because they wanted them back. Needed them.

"God." Liam's voice sounded strained. "Where did they say we could pick the eighty-one back up again?"

The ash trees lining the lonely one-lane back road were just coming into their lovely young skin, but in the afternoon light their shadows couldn't have been longer.

238

FOURTEEN

I SLIPPED OFF INTO SLEEP SOMEWHERE BETWEEN Staunton and Lexington, and woke up just in time to get a perfect view of the towering white warehouse that was Roanoke, Virginia's former Walmart.

Sure, the blue sign was still clinging desperately to the side of the building, but that was about the only recognizable thing about the Supercenter. A number of stray carts wandered across the parking lot aimlessly, carried this and that way depending on each moody gust of wind. With the exception of a few abandoned cars and green Dumpsters, the enormous blacktop parking lot was empty. Against the tangerine blush of the afternoon sun, it looked like the apocalypse had already touched down in Virginia.

And we were only a stone's throw away from Salem. A ten-minute drive. My stomach clenched at the thought.

Once again, Liam insisted on going in alone to check it out. I felt Zu's rubber glove on my arm and didn't need to look at her face to know what kind of expression I would find there. She didn't want him charging into what looked like an honest-to-God hellhole alone anymore than I did.

This is why you stayed, I reminded myself. To take care of them. And, in that moment, the person that needed me most was the one walking away.

I jumped out of Betty, my hand gripping the door handle.

"Honk the horn three times for trouble," I said, and slid the door shut. Liam must have heard, because he waited for me, leaning against one of the rusted shopping cart stalls.

"Any way I could convince you to go back to Betty?"

"Nope," I said. "Come on."

He fell in step beside me, fists dug deep in his pockets. I couldn't see his eyes, but the way he was slouching toward the demolished doors was telling enough.

"You asked me before how I knew about this place. . . ." he said, when we were nearly to the entrance.

"No—no, it's okay. I know, none of my business."

"Green," Liam said. "It's okay. I just don't know where to begin. You know Chubs and I were both in hiding? Well, it wasn't exactly pleasant for either of us. He at least got to stay at his grandparents' cabin in Pennsylvania."

"Ah, but you had the pleasure of holing up in this fine American establishment."

"Among other places." Liam said. "I . . . don't like to talk about that time in front of Zu. I don't want her to think that that's what her life is going to be."

"But you can't lie to her," I said. "I know you don't want to scare her, but you can't pretend that her life isn't going to be hard. It's not fair."

"Not fair?" He sucked in a sharp breath, closing his eyes. When he spoke again, his voice had returned to his usual soft tones. "Never mind, forget it."

"Hey," I said, taking his arm. "I get it, okay? I'm on your side. But you can't act like it's going to be easy. Don't do that to her—don't set her up to be crushed. I was in camp with thousands of kids who grew up thinking Mommy and Daddy were always going to be there for them, and they— *we*—are all coming out of this seriously damaged."

"Whoa, whoa," Liam said, all traces of anger gone. "You are *not* damaged."

That, I could have protested until I was blue in the face.

Whoever had unhooked Walmart's glass sliding doors from their tracks hadn't done a good job of finding a safe place to store them. Shards of glass coated the cement floor, blown out dozens of feet from the black metal frames. We stepped over and through their mangled shapes, entering that small, strange space where the greeter would have been.

Next to me, Liam's foot slipped against the sallow dust collected on the floor. I shot an arm out to brace him as he grunted in surprise. Even as I helped him right himself, his eyes remained fixed on the ground, where a dozen footprints fanned out in the dust.

Every shape and size, from the jagged pattern of the sole of a man's hiking boot to the decorative swirly curls left behind by a young child's tennis shoe, all stamped out there like cookies cut from a fresh spread of dough.

"They could be old," I whispered.

Liam nodded but didn't pull away from my side. I hadn't fooled either of us.

The store's power had been shut off some time ago, and it was clear it had been open to the wild for too long. There was only a second between when we first heard the rattling in the nearby shelves and when Liam jumped in front of me. "It's—" I began, but he silenced me with a shake of his head. We watched the shelves, waiting.

And when the deer, a gorgeous, sweet thing with a silky caramel coat and big black eyes, came prancing out from behind the overturned magazine racks, Liam and I looked at each other, dissolving into shaky laughter.

Liam pressed his finger to his lips and waved me forward, his eyes scanning the dark fleet of identical cash registers in front of us. Someone had taken the carts from the store and tried stuffing them in the lanes, as if to create a kind of forti-fied wall against any unwanted visitors. Carefully, without disturbing the pileup of plastic baskets, we climbed up and over the nearest register's conveyer belt. Standing on top of it, I could see where more shelves had been lined up in front of the other exit. It looked as though something huge had come slamming through it at one point, bursting through the makeshift barricade.

What did that?

I think there's some part of everyone, Psi or not, that's tuned into the memories of a place. Strong feelings, especially terror and desperation, leave an imprint on the air that echo back to whoever's unlucky enough to walk through that place again. It felt like the darkness was stroking beneath my chin with a beckoning finger, whispering to me to lean forward and know its secrets.

Something terrible happened here, I thought, feeling a cold drip down my spine. The wind whistled through the broken doors, playing us the kind of screeching song that made the hair on the back of my neck stand on end.

I wanted to leave. This was not a safe place. This was not a place to bring Zu or Chubs—so why was Liam still going forward? Overhead, the emergency lights flickered on and off, buzzing like boxes of trapped flies. Everything beneath them was cast in a sickly green light, and as he moved farther and farther down the first aisle, it seemed like the darkness waiting at the end of it would swallow him whole.

I sprung forward into the sea of empty metal shelves, half of which were knocked flat on their backs or leaning against others in slanted lines, their shelves buckling under some invisible weight. My sneakers squeaked as I wove through the sea of lotions, mouthwash, and nail polish on the floor. Things that seemed so necessary in the past, so vital to life, wasted and forgotten.

When I caught up to him again, my fingers closed around the soft, loose leather of his jacket's sleeve. At the slightest tug, Liam turned, his blue eyes lit up in surprise. I took a step back and pulled my hand back to my side, shocked at myself. It had felt natural to do it—I hadn't been thinking at all, only feeling a very sharp, real need to be close to him.

"I think we should leave," I whispered. "Something about this place doesn't feel right." And it had nothing to do with the strange crying of the wind, or the birds high up in the old store's rafters.

"We're okay," he said. His back was to me, but he slipped his hand from his pocket. It drifted back toward me, floating up through the darkness. I didn't know whether he meant to motion me to move forward, or for me to take it, but I couldn't bring myself to do either.

We walked side by side toward the back right corner of the store; it seemed that this section of the store, with all of its hardware and lightbulbs, had been left somewhat alone, or at least hadn't seemed as useful to the people who had picked the other shelves to the bone.

I saw where we were headed immediately. Someone had set up their own little camp, using bright blue pool rafts as mattresses. A few empty boxes of graham crackers and Hostess cupcakes were piled on top of a cooler, and on top of that was a small wireless radio and lantern flashlight.

"Wow, I can't believe this is still here." Liam stood a foot behind me, his arms crossed over his chest. I followed his gaze down to the dozens of indentations in the cracked white tile. They were almost enough to distract me from the patchwork of old bloodstains on the ground beneath his feet.

My lips parted.

"It's old," Liam said, quickly, like that would make me feel any better.

Liam reached toward me, forcing a smile. I blew out the breath I had been holding and reached up to take his hand.

At almost the exact moment our hands touched, I saw it. The emergency light above that section of the back wall snapped back to full glare like a spotlight, illuminating the enormous black Ψ painted there, along with a very clear message: GET OUT NOW.

The thick, uneven letters looked like they were weeping. The light crackled and went back out with a loud pop, but I still threw myself forward, out of Liam's grip, straight for the spray-painted message. Because that smell . . . the way the words drooped . . . I pressed my fingers against the Psi symbol and they came away sticky. Black.

Fresh paint.

Liam had only just reached me when I felt the strangest sensation of burning, right at my core. I looked down, expecting to see a spark igniting the front of Zu's ridiculous dress, and then I was falling, and Liam was falling on top of me. Bulldozed right over, as if we had been nothing more than two daisies poking up through the cracks in the tile.

Liam's shoulder rammed into my chest, knocking the air out of our lungs. I tried to lift my head to see exactly what had happened, but there was this weight—this solid, invisible slab of stone—keeping me on my back, and Liam flat against me.

The floor was freezing at my back, but my entire focus was on the solid press of his shoulder against my cheek. Our hands were caught between us, and for a moment I had the uneasy sensation of not knowing where one of us began and the other ended. He swallowed hard, the pulse in his throat close enough for me to hear it.

Liam moved to lift his head, straining the muscles that lined the strong column of his spine. "Hey!" he shouted. "Who's there?"

The only response was another shove from the invisible hands. Suddenly we were shooting across the ground, Liam's leather jacket squealing against the dusty floor as we slid. I watched the emergency lights beyond Liam's head pass with dizzying speed, tracking together like a single beam. Riotous laughter followed us down the aisles, seeming to come from below us, above us, on either side. I thought I saw a dark shape move out of the corner of my eye, but it looked more like a monster than a person. We tore through ribbons of ripped shower curtains, the body lotion, the bleach, to the line of cash registers at the front of the store.

"Cut it out!" Liam yelled. "We're—"

There are some sounds you hear once and never forget. A bone breaking. An ice cream truck's song. Velcro. A gun's safety clicking off.

No, I thought, Not now—not here!

We slid to a painful stop at the checkout lanes, the impact with the metal jarring every sense out of my body. There was a single moment of agonizing silence before the once-dead store lights surged into brightness. And then, the cash register flashed on, conveyer belt sputtering to life— first one lane, then the next, and the next. Every single one, falling to order like soldiers. The numbered signs above blinked between yellow and blue, like a dozen warning signals, faster than my eyes could follow.

At first I thought it was White Noise; all at once, the building's security alarms, intercom system, and televised displays went off, a hundred different voices screaming at us. Block after block of ceiling lights snapped on, electricity pouring through them after years of existing as nothing more than hollow, dusty veins.

Liam and I turned to see Zu, her bare right hand splayed out against a checkout lane. Chubs was next to her, his face ashen.

After only a few seconds of Zu's power surge, the lights on the registers began to pop like firecrackers, dropping streams of blue-white sparks and glass to the ground.

She had only meant for it to be a distraction, I think; a flash and a bang to draw the attention of our attackers away from us long enough for an escape. Out of the corner of my eye, I could see her waving us toward her, but the machine under Zu's other hand had heated to a terrifying molten glow. I felt the invisible grip on me slacken suddenly, but fear kept me still as the dead. She wasn't letting go. Liam and I must have had the same thought—the same scorching fear— because we pushed to our feet, shouting for her to stop.

"Turn her off!" someone managed to shout over the alarms.

"Zu, let go!" Liam stood and stumbled over cans of sunscreen and bug spray from a nearby display. I saw him lift his arms, ready to yank Zu away with his abilities, but Chubs was faster. He tugged the glove off Zu's other hand and pulled it over his own, then all but ripped her arm away from the metal.

The lights went out. Just before the overhead bulbs exploded, I saw Zu's face as she came out of whatever trance she had been locked in. Her big eyes were rimmed with red, her short black hair on end, freckles standing out against the full flush of her oval face. The sudden darkness gave Liam the opportunity to knock both her and Chubs to the ground.

And then, by some small miracle, the emergency lights flicked back on.

The first sign of movement didn't come from us. I saw our attackers clearly now, climbing over the mangled heaps of white shelves. Four of them, each dressed in layers of black, each with a gun raised and ready. My first thought, as it almost always was when I saw anyone in a black uniform, was to run. To get the others and bolt.

But these weren't PSFs. They weren't even grown-ups.

They were kids, like us.

FIFTEEN

As they came closer, I saw their mismatched dark clothes and the grime on their faces. They were all thin limbs and hollow cheeks, as if they had stretched out a great deal in a short period of time.

All boys, about my age.

All easy to take, if we had to.

"Christ on a cracker," the one closest to me muttered, shaking his mop of red hair. "I told you we should have checked the van first."

Liam's blond head popped up from the wreckage.

"What the *hell* are you fools trying to pull?" he snarled. There was another sound, too, like the mewling of a kitten. Or a little girl crying.

I climbed over a bin of bargain DVDs to get to them. Zu sat on the floor, her pink palm facing up toward Chubs's squinting eyes. Without the glasses perched on his nose, he looked like a different person. "She's all right," he said. "No burns."

Liam was suddenly standing beside me, using my shoulder for balance as he climbed over one of the overturned shelves.

"You okay?" he asked.

"Fine," I said. "Pissed. You?"

"Fine. Pissed."

I thought for sure I was going to have to hold him back as we came closer to the cluster of boys, but his fury seemed to fall away from him with each step. The other kids had regrouped beside an overturned display of neon-colored pool noodles. The tallest one, his cloud of frizzy brown hair hovering around a pencil-thin neck, stepped in front of the others—the ginger kid who had spoken before, and two big-shouldered blonds that looked like brothers.

"Look, man, I'm sorry," he said.

"Do you always do crap like this?" Liam said. "Attacking folks without even checking to see if they're armed—if they're like you?"

The leader bristled. "You could have been skip tracers."

"And it was your Yellow that did all of—*this*." The ginger kid gestured toward the shelves. "The girl needs a leash."

"Watch your mouth," Liam snapped. The blond brothers took a step forward, their eyes lighting at the challenge. "She wouldn't have panicked if you hadn't pulled guns on us."

"We wouldn't have had to use them if you'd paid attention to our warning back there and just left."

"Because you gave us so much time to get away—" Liam snapped.

250

"Look, we could go back and forth forever and it won't solve a damn thing," I interrupted. "We were hoping to spend the night here, but if you've claimed it or whatever, then we'll go. That's the only reason we came—for shelter."

"For shelter," the leader repeated.

"I'm sorry, did I stutter?"

"No, but my ears are still bleeding from your Yellow's meltdown," he snarled. "Maybe you should say it again, baby, for good measure."

Liam shot out an arm, cutting off my warpath before it could start.

"We just want to stay here a night. We're not looking for any trouble," he said flatly.

The leader gave me the once-over, his eyes drifting to a stop where my hands were fisted at my side, bunching up my dress.

"Looks like you already found it."

The leader's name was Greg, and he hailed from Mechanicsville, Virginia. The nervous ginger-haired kid refused to introduce himself but was called Collins by the others. I caught that he was from some town in Pennsylvania, but that was as much as he was willing to share with anyone. The blonds—who were, as I guessed, brothers—were Kyle and Kevin. The only thing the ramshackle group had in common, outside of their pool of food and an alarming pile of firearms and knives, was their camp in New York, which they lovingly referred to only as "Satan's Ass Crack."

They told the incredibly dramatic—and highly improbable—tale of their escape from PSF custody over our shared meal of fruit snacks, stale Pringles, and Twinkies.

"Let me get this straight," said Chubs, his face etched with disbelief. "You were being moved from one camp to another?"

Greg leaned back against one of the glass freezer doors. "They weren't taking us to another camp. They packed up as many guys as they could and said we were being brought to a testing facility in Maryland."

"Only guys?" Chubs asked.

"We didn't have girls there." Greg's voice was heavy with disappointment. That explained a lot—particularly why he still seemed to be inching toward me, no matter how far I scooted away. "Otherwise I'm sure they would have been loaded up, too."

"I'm surprised they even told you that much," I said, trying to steer the conversation back on track. "Do you think that's actually where they were bringing you?"

"No," Collins cut in. "It was pretty clear that they had orders to get rid of us."

"And a storm flooded the road, flipping the bus and allowing you to escape?"

That was the part of the story I had problems with, too. It was that easy for them? A simple intervention of Mother Nature, and they were saved, washed out to freedom and a new life Biblical-style? Where was the detail of PSFs traveling with them?

"We've been holed up ever since. It took something like six months to get word to my dad that I was out and

252

safe, and another three to get some kind of response from him."

Chubs leaned forward. "How, exactly, did you get in touch with them? The Internet?"

"Nah, man," Greg said. "After that terrorist business, you can't even search for recipes online without the PSFs snooping and breaking down your door. All they need is one whiff of trouble."

"What terrorists?" I interrupted.

"The League," Chubs said. "Don't you remember—ah." He seemed to realize his mistake a second late, and, with more patience than I thought he possessed, explained, "Three years ago, the League hacked into the government's Psi databases and tried posting information about the camps online for everyone to see. Other groups took that as their cue to hack into banks, the stock exchange, the State Department . . ."

"So they cracked down on it?"

"Right. Most of the social networking sites are gone, and all of the e-mail services are required to monitor the e-mails being sent on their servers." He turned to the other boys, who were staring at me with varying degrees of interest and curiosity. I don't think Kevin—or was it Kyle?—had stopped staring at me the entire time I had sat there.

"How, then?"

"Easy," Greg said, with a highly unnecessary wink in my direction. "We used what was left. I put an ad in my hometown paper with a message only my brother would get."

I didn't need to look to know that Chubs had narrowed his eyes. He tensed beside me. "And who paid for this ad?

The editors didn't just let you put that in there for free, did they?"

"No, the Slip Kid paid," Greg said. "He set everything up for me."

I sat up straight, kicking aside some of the empty foil wrappers. "You've actually been in contact with the Slip Kid?"

"Oh yes. He's like . . . a god," Collins said, his breath rushing out. "He gathered all of us together. Kids from all over New England and the South. Every color. Older kids, young ones, too. They say that the PSFs stay away from his court in the woods because they're afraid of him. That he set his camp on fire and killed all the PSFs sent to bring him back."

"Who is he?" I asked.

The four of them grinned at one another, the jumping shadows from the emergency lights making them look even smugger.

"What else?" Chubs said, sucking all of this down eagerly. "How was he able to send the money for the ad? What's East River like—where is it?"

I glanced back over my shoulder to Liam, who stood behind me, leaning against what used to be a TV dinner freezer. He'd been strangely quiet the entire time, his lips pressed tight together, but his face otherwise perfectly devoid of emotion.

"They have a sweet setup at East River," Collins said. "But if you want to get to East River, you have to find it for yourself."

"Sounds that way," Liam said, finally. "Are there a lot of kids there?"

The four of them had to think about this. "More than a hundred, but not, like, in the thousands," Greg said. "Why?"

Liam shook his head, but I was surprised to see a hint of disappointment there. "Just wondering. Most never were in camps, I take it?"

"Some." Greg shrugged. "And some found it after dodging skip tracer or PSF custody."

"And the Slip Kid—he doesn't have . . ." Liam seemed to struggle to figure out how to ask his question. "He doesn't have plans for them, does he? What's his endgame?"

The others seemed to find the question as strange as I did. It wasn't until Greg said, "No endgame. Just livin', I guess," that I realized I hadn't once thought about the reason why Liam would be looking for the Slip Kid. I'd just assumed that he and the others wanted to find him to get home and to deliver Jack's letter—but if that really was the case, what had sparked the fire in Liam's eyes? His hands were stuffed in his jacket pockets, but I could see the outline of them curling into fists.

"What about directions?" I asked.

"Well, now." Something changed in Greg's expression; a slick smile took over his face as his free hand landed on my foot. The brothers, Kyle and Kevin, hadn't said a word since we'd sat down in their makeshift encampment in the freezer aisles, but now looked at each other with identical expressions of knowing. I tried to gulp back the revulsion rising in me.

255

"I'm sure they'd be happy to have you," Greg said, his fingers sliding up from my shoe to stroke my ankle. I started to push away but stopped when he added, "It's in a really great location near the coast, but there just aren't a whole lot of girls. They could use something so . . . nice to look at."

His fingers moved again, tracing a line up my calf. "You should go. It's safer than getting caught by one of the tribes. There's a group of Blue kids that hangs out around Norfolk—they're nasty. Steal the clothes right off your back. There was a tribe of Yellows around here for a while, but a kid we were in camp with claims they were all taken in by PSFs."

All of this tribe stuff was new to me. Kids banding together and roving the countryside, trying to avoid getting caught, taking care of one another? Amazing.

Greg's warm, fleshy palm continued its ascent until it swallowed up my knee and squeezed—and that was as far as he was ever going to get. I felt the trickle at the back of my mind, the buzz that pushed past even my anger, and had to close my eyes at the flash of images that followed. A glimpse of a shining yellow shell of a school bus coming down a dirt road. A woman's blurry face, her mouth moving in silent song. A campfire flaring up into the night sky. The faces of Kevin and Kyle leaning close to what looked like a clock radio, in the middle of a trashed electronics store; the numbers on the clock's face were climbing, but not counting time. They lit an electric green glow in the dark—310, 400, 460, 500, until it finally stopped on—

My hand clenched into a fist as I started to detach from both Greg and his silky swarm of memories, but Chubs was

256

already there. He reached across my lap and began to peel Greg's fingers off, one by one, with a look of pure disdain. For his part, Greg only looked slightly dazed, his eyes glassy, unaware of what I had just done. I glanced around wildly, my heart lodged somewhere between my mouth and chest, but no one seemed to have noticed my slip. The only one who moved was Chubs, and it was just to scoot closer to me.

Damn it, I thought, squeezing my eyes shut again. One hand drifted up to press against my forehead, as if I could hold back the invisible fingers there by force. Too close. That was way too close.

"What was that kid's name again? The Yellow who worked with us in the kitchen? Fred? Frank?" Collins lay back on his sleeping bag, folding his hands over his chest.

"Felipe—Felipe Marino?" Greg's eyes came back into full focus and continued up my legs, past where his hand had been allowed.

"Felipe?" Liam interrupted, as if coming out of a trance. "Did you say Felipe Marco?"

"You know him?"

Liam nodded. "We traveled together for a while."

"Must have been before he got his ass caught here," Greg said. "He was the one that told us about this place. Said he was here with his friend—that you?"

"Yeah. What happened to him?" Liam knelt, wedging himself between Greg and me. "They brought us to separate camps."

Greg shrugged. "He was in one of the earlier buses they were taking to Maryland. Who knows?"

So the Yellows at their camp had been removed, too. They must have only been taken from the bigger camps, not the smaller ones that had been cobbled together farther west.

"I miss that kid. He was smart. Knew how to use his powers—better than your pet, at least. Might as well send her back for all the good she's going to do for you." Greg nodded toward Zu, who was sitting with her back to us, working through the pages of multiplication problems Liam had made for her.

And that was about as much as I could take.

"You have two seconds to tell me you're kidding," I said, "or I'm punching you in the face."

"Do it," Chubs hissed beside me.

But Liam put a firm hand on my shoulder, effectively shutting down any chance I had of making good on my threat. He kept his face passive, easygoing, but his breath hitched in his throat. He stretched his fingers out, brushing them against mine on the floor. I jolted at the touch but couldn't bring myself to pull away.

Greg held up his hands. "All I'm saying is there's something off about her. She's not like the others, is she?" He leaned closer. "Is she retarded? Did they do testing on her?"

"She's mute, not deaf," Liam cut in smoothly. "And I promise you, she's probably five times smarter than the seven of us put together."

"I'm not so sure about *that*," Chubs began. "I'm—"

Liam silenced him with a look and brought his lips down next to my ear. "Take Zu?"

I nodded, my fingers tapping his to show that I understood. I pushed myself up off the ground, feeling calmer now.

When I reached Zu, I held out my hand to her. She raised hers without looking up, blindly reaching for mine. I stared at the yellow glove in front of me, streaked with dirt and black grime, and, despite what had happened a few minutes before, pulled it right off her little fingers.

I couldn't say why I had done it; maybe being so close to Liam and not losing control had made me stupidly brave, or maybe I was just sick of the reality that forced her into them. All I knew for sure was that if I never saw Zu wear those gloves again, it would be too soon.

Zu jerked when she felt the warm skin of my hand against hers, and tried to tug away. Her eyes went wide, but I couldn't tell if it was from worry or wonder.

"Come on," I said, squeezing her hand. "Girl time."

Her face brightened, but she didn't smile.

"Don't go too far," Liam called after us.

"Don't go too far," the other boys echoed, then burst out into laughter.

Zu's nose wrinkled in disgust.

"I know what you mean," I said, and took her as far away from them as I could.

For the first ten or so minutes we spent walking around the store, Zu kept turning to look at our linked hands, as if she couldn't believe what she was seeing. Every now and then, some bin of unwanted DVDs or an aisle endcap of

259

pointless knickknacks would catch her attention, but her dark eyes would always wander back to where our hands swung between us. We had just turned down one of many ravaged cleaning supply aisles when she gave my arm a tug.

"What's wrong?" I asked, kicking aside a stray mop.

Zu pointed at the glove I was twirling around with my free hand.

I lifted our hands between us. "What's so bad about this?"

She blew out the breath she had been holding, and it was evident I had missed the point. I was dragged all the way to the other end of the aisle, where she let go of my hand to snatch a white box from the shelf. Zu went to work tearing the box open, tossing aside the foam and plastic stuffing to get the old-fashioned silver toaster inside.

"I'm not sure we're going to need that," I started slowly.

She pinned me with a look that very clearly said, *Quiet, please.*

Zu tugged the other glove off her hand and spread all ten fingers out along either side of the appliance. After a moment, I saw her shut her dark eyes.

The metal piping that served as the toaster's innards heated to a glowing red. A long black cord dangled near her feet, unplugged. The cheap little thing only lasted another minute before its insides started to melt together. I made her put it down at the first sign of smoke.

See? she seemed to be saying. *Get it?*

"But you can't do that to me," I said, reaching for her hand again. "You don't have to worry about hurting me, because you never could."

I know how it feels, is what I really should have been saying. *I know what it's like to be scared of what you can barely control.*

I had forced myself to stop thinking about what I had done to that undercover PSF. I didn't let myself wonder if I could do it again, let alone test it out. But how, I wondered, were either of us ever going to learn to control ourselves if we couldn't practice? If we couldn't stretch and test boundaries?

"Let's see if we can find something useful," I said, slipping my fingers around hers again. I waited until I felt her hand close against mine before leading her back down the aisle. "What do you think—"

I'm not even sure what I was about to ask her, but she wasn't paying attention to me. Zu stopped so suddenly and gripped my hand so damn hard, that I stumbled back a few steps. My eyes followed the line of her outstretched arm to the upended clothing and shoe racks.

More specifically, to the lone hot pink dress dangling from an otherwise empty rack.

Zu took off at a run, blitzing down the aisles of extension cords and buckets. I tried to keep up with her, but it was like the wind had caught her heels and was propelling her forward. She stopped just short of the rack. I watched, fascinated, as one of her hands reached out to stroke the fabric, only to pull back at the last second.

"Beautiful," I told her. The dress itself flared out at the waist, with a big ribbon bow at the place where the sleeveless top met the pink and white striped skirt. She looked like she wanted nothing more than to pull it down, hug it to her chest, and press her face against the satiny fabric.

I could think of about a thousand things I missed while I was at Thurmond, but dresses were not on that list. My dad's favorite story to tell strangers and indulgent relatives was the day he and Mom tried to button me up into a blue one for his birthday party when I was three. Because the buttons were so small and impossible for me to reach, I shredded the fabric by hand, bit by gauzy bit. I spent the rest of the party proudly parading around in Batman underwear.

"Are you going to try it on?" I asked.

She looked back up at me and shook her head. Her hands dropped from where they were hovering over the plastic hanger's shoulders, and it took me a moment to recognize what was happening.

Zu thought she didn't deserve it. She thought it was too nice, too new, too pretty. I felt a sweltering hate rise in me, but I didn't know where to direct it. Her parents, for sending her away? Her camp? The PSFs?

I pulled the dress off the silver rack with one hand and took Zu's arm in the other. I knew she was looking at me again, her dark eyes wide with confusion, but instead of explaining—instead of trying to force her to understand the words I wanted to say—I led her over to the dressing rooms in the center of the clothing section, thrust the dress into her hands, and told her to try it on.

It was like tugging a boat in to dock on a thin line. The first few times I handed it to her, she would put it down and I'd have to pick it back up again. I don't know if her desire

262

finally won out, or if I'd managed to exhaust even her wariness, but by the time she appeared, peeking out from around her dressing room's door, I was so relieved I almost cried.

"You look *amazing*." I turned her back around, so she could see herself in the room's tall mirror. When I finally coaxed her to look, I felt her shoulders jerk under my hands—saw her eyes go huge and bright, only to droop again a moment later. Her fingers began to pluck at the fabric. She was shaking her head, as if to say, *No, no I can't.*

"Why not?" I asked, turning her so she was looking at me. "You like it, right?"

She didn't look up, but I saw her nod.

"Then what's the problem?" At that, I caught her sneak another look at herself in the corner of the mirror. Her hands were smoothing the fabric of the skirt, and she didn't seem aware of it in the slightest.

"That's right," I said. "There is no problem. Let's see what else we can find."

After, she wanted to find something for me. Unsurprisingly, the adult section had been decimated by looters; my choices seemed limited to hunting gear and industrial jumpsuits. After several patient explanations about why I didn't need the silky cornflower blue nightgown or the skirt with daisies on it, she—with a look of total and complete exasperation—accepted that I was only ever going to try on jeans and plain T-shirts.

And then she pointed to the bra rack, and a part of me wanted to crawl under the discarded piles of kids' pajamas and die. The letters and numbers might as well have been in Chinese for how much sense I could make of them, and I half expected Zu to start laughing when the first touch of frustrated tears welled up in my eyes.

There were not many times I'd stop and think, *I wish Mom were here*. I understood now, at least, that what I had done to her I could never fix. She would never look at me again and recognize me, and I would never be able to think of anything other than the look in her eyes when she saw me that morning. It was strange how my feelings about her seemed to change by the minute; that one moment I could remember what it felt like for her to brush my hair, and the next, be furious that she had abandoned me. That she hadn't taught me how to live in my own skin and be a girl, like she was supposed to.

But whose fault was that, really?

Zu's lips puckered in thought, her eyebrows knitting together as she surveyed the Everest of undergarments in front of us. She began to pluck one of every size, tossing them back toward me until both of us were laughing ourselves silly for no real reason at all.

Eventually, I found what I thought might have been the right fit for me. It was hard to tell; they had all been so damn uncomfortable with their wires and pinching straps. While I changed out of my dress, Zu happily pulled together an outfit for herself that looked like something out of a store catalog—the pink dress, white leggings beneath it, and a jean jacket that was one or two sizes too big for her. The rest of the things she found were stuffed into a flower patterned backpack I pulled down off a display for her. Now that she

264

had found her own things, she wanted to go the whole hog and pick out things for the boys, too.

When I found her a new pair of tennis shoes with rosy laces, she actually wrapped her arms around my waist and hugged me, like she could squeeze the thanks into me. And while Zu was not especially impressed by the pair of short black boots I found for myself in the men's section, she didn't try to force any of the ribbon flats or towering high heels on me.

Zu was in the process of neatly folding a button-down shirt she had chosen for Chubs when I remembered something.

"I'll be right back," I told her. "Wait right here, okay?"

It took me a few minutes to find the aisle again. Liam and I had walked past it so quickly as we made our way toward the back of the store, I wasn't altogether sure that I hadn't imagined seeing them. But there they were, just above the cleaning supplies—a pair of bright pink rubber gloves dangling amid a sea of traditional yellow ones.

"Hey, Zu," I called as I made my way back to her. I dangled them out in front of me and waited for her to turn around. When she did, her mouth actually fell open. She was so dazzled by her new gloves that she walked with her hands stretched out in front of her—the way a princess examining the collection of fine jewelry around her fingers and wrists would. I watched her curtsy and twirl in her new dress as we lapped the store, all the while her feet dancing over the evidence of what had happened at the checkout lanes. Watching her, feeling the exhilaration swelling in my chest, I couldn't say I was all that aware of the broken glass and flickering monitor displays, either. We turned down the dimly lit corridor of cosmetics, and I could barely keep the grin off my face.

Liam found us there a short while later, just as Zu was tying off the braid she'd woven in my hair with a glittery hair tie. I sat on the tile and she sat on the shelf behind me like some fairy queen. "Magnificent!" I told her, when she held a broken mirror out in front of my face. "You are incredible."

And my reward for that was the feeling of her arm's birdlike bones twining around my neck. I twisted around so that I was facing her, because I wanted her to see my face—I wanted her to see how serious, how sincerely I meant it when I repeated myself. "You are *incredible*."

"You two have been busy, I see."

Liam leaned against the aisle's endcap, eyebrows raised. Zu bounded toward him, scooping up the shirts and socks she'd picked for him.

"Thank you—oh God, Chubs is going to piss his pants when he sees this!" His hand came down to rest on top of her head. "Jeez, I leave you two alone for a little while and you clean out the joint. Good job."

I pushed myself up off the floor, helping them gather up the clothes and supplies we'd managed to scrounge up. That done, we started our slow, reluctant shuffle back to the others. All three of us seemed to be aware that once we left that peaceful moment, it would be behind us forever.

Zu had only just darted out a few steps ahead of us when Liam turned to me and said, "Thanks for doing this. I'm glad you got what I meant." He gave my braid a little playful tug. "I just wanted to ask them a few more questions."

"And you didn't want"—I nodded toward Zu—"to hear?"

He looked down at his feet, and when he looked back up, his ears were pink. "Yeah, but also . . . you were kind of distracting them."

"What? I'm sorry I threatened them or whatever, but—"

"No—*distracting* them," Liam repeated. "With your . . . face."

"Oh." I recovered quickly. "Did you get anything useful out of them?"

"The names of a few of the friendlier tribes, a few cities under lockdown for insurrection—stuff like that. I just wanted to get a sense of what was happening in Virginia."

"I meant about the Slip Kid," I said, maybe a little too eagerly.

"Nothing we didn't have before. Apparently everyone takes some sacred oath not to reveal more information than that. Totally ridiculous."

"They really wouldn't give you any more information?" I said.

Liam looked down at the ground. "Greg made us an offer—a trade—but we turned him down."

"What did he want?" What was so valuable that they wouldn't trade it for the one thing that would reunite them with their families? Black Betty?

"Doesn't matter," Liam said, and there was finality in his voice. "If those numbnuts managed, I'm sure we can find East River ourselves. Eventually."

"Yeah," I said, with a light laugh. "True."

Out of the corner of my eye, I watched him hoist the pile of clothes onto his shoulder, his gaze never leaving where Zu was hopping and skipping through the field of cans and old magazines. I glanced down at a blond movie star's face as we passed it, my eyes falling over the words SHE FINALLY TELLS ALL printed under her face.

"Can I ask you something?"

"Of course," he said. "What's up?"

"Why are you looking for the Slip Kid?" I asked. I felt his eyes on me, and I knew what explanation was coming. "I mean, besides wanting to help Chubs and Zu get there, and trying to deliver Jack's letter. Is it because you want to go home, or . . . ?"

"Any reason in particular you're asking?" His voice was even. Testing.

"The questions you were asking them about the camp," I explained. "It just seemed like you were trying to figure something out."

Liam didn't reply for a long while, not until the tents they'd set up for the night were in sight. Even then, it wasn't an answer. "Why do *you* want to find the Slip Kid?"

"Because I want to be able to see my grandmother." *Because I need to understand how to control my abilities before they destroy everyone I care about.* "But you didn't answer my question."

Zu dashed through our tent flap, and the lantern in the tent lit up Chubs's delighted face. When she handed his new things over, he folded her into an enormous hug, lifting her off her feet with the force of it.

"It's . . . the same as you," he said. "I just want to get home."

"Where's that?"

"See, that's the funny thing," he said. "It used to be North Carolina, but I'm not so sure anymore."

We stood staring at each other for a moment, nearly toe to toe, and when he lifted the flap of the tent for me, I couldn't help but wonder if he had picked up on my half-truth as easily as I had picked up on his.

SIXTEEN

I<small>T WAS AN HOUR, MAYBE MORE, BEFORE</small> L<small>IAM'S</small> breathing evened out and he began to snore. He slept flat on his back, his hands resting against the soft flannel of his shirt. His face, which earlier had seemed marked by old, bruising shadows, looked young again. He might have been able to pass as a twenty-year-old with his facial scruff and solid build, but he didn't fool anyone while tucked away in sleep.

His face was turned toward Zu, who slept between us under a mountain of blankets and was currently the only thing that was keeping me from inching closer to him; from slipping my hand under his bigger one and learning the contents of his dreams.

But the distance between us was there for a reason. Imagining a future in which I didn't exist, in which I had unwittingly erased myself from his memories, kept my hands pinned under my legs and my mind, for once, in check.

When I heard Greg and his pals stir in their tents next to ours, I finally gave up all pretense of sleep. Their voices began as a low murmur indistinguishable from one another, and grew louder as the minutes ticked by. Finally, they turned their lantern on to the lowest setting, just enough to be visible through our own green tent's shell.

I slipped out the other side of the tent, careful to keep my footsteps soft against the concrete. Their whispers grew in volume and urgency the closer I came.

"—them," Greg mumbled. "We don't owe them anything."

My hands clenched at my side, all of the anxiety and distrust that had been swelling up inside of me over the past few hours coming to a head. For a single second, I wished that I had brought my backpack inside the store with me. The panic button was there, waiting to be used if the situation blew up fast and ugly. *Stupid Ruby*, I thought. *Stupid.*

I wasn't worried about taking care of Greg and his friends. Even with their guns, we still had a chance. But if they tried to pull something while we were asleep, or if they called in reinforcements—

My feet stopped mid-stride.

Chubs had beaten me to guard duty.

He sat facing the tents, his long, spidery legs crossed in front of him, and Zu's workbook in his lap. He was leaning toward the others' tents, concentrating so hard on picking up their conversation that he missed my approach and nearly jumped out of his skin when I appeared.

"Zu?" He squinted in my direction.

271

"Zu?" I whispered back. *"Really?"* I mean, *really?*

I took Zu's workbook and pencil out of his hands and flipped the page without looking at whatever he had been writing.

WHAT ARE YOU DOING? I wrote, showing it to him. He rolled his eyes and refused to respond when I tried to put the pencil back in his hand.

DO YOU THINK THEY'RE GOING TO TRY SOMETHING?

After a moment, he sighed and finally nodded.

ME TOO, I scribbled. COME WITH ME?

By the way his shoulders slumped, Chubs seemed to think he didn't have much of a choice. He stood quickly and quietly, wiping his palms against the front of his khaki pants.

"I have a bad feeling about this," Chubs said when we were out of earshot. The tents were in our line of sight, but we weren't in theirs. "About them."

"Do you think they're going to try to rob us?"

"I think they're going to try to take Betty, actually."

There was a long pause; I felt Chubs's eyes slide over to me, but my own were fixed on the tents, watching for trouble.

"You should go back to sleep." There was a gruff edge to his voice as he crossed his arms over his chest. But there was also something about the way he said it that made me wonder if he was waiting to see what I would reply. "What are you even doing up?"

"Same as you, I guess," I said. "Making sure no one gets brutally mugged, beaten, or murdered in their sleep. Watching to see if those kids are the assholes I think they are."

Chubs snorted at that, rubbing his hand over his forehead. It took some time in silence, but I felt the air between us ease from a guarded hostility to something that felt to me like acceptance. His shoulders were no longer bunched up with tension, and when he tilted his head toward me, I saw it for the subtle invitation it was. I took a step closer.

"It was bad enough he had to come back here," Chubs mumbled, more to himself than to me. "God . . ."

"Liam?" I asked. "This is where he and his friend were captured, right?"

Chubs nodded. "He's never told me the whole story, but I *think* what happened was that he and Felipe were traveling and ran into a tribe of Blues. Instead of recruiting them like Lee hoped, the tribe beat the hell out of them and stole everything they had—food, packs, family pictures, you name it. They came here for a few days to regroup, but they were in such bad shape that they couldn't get away when the skip tracers finally showed up."

Something hard settled in my throat.

"Lee thinks that that tribe probably called them in," Chubs continued. "That they got a cut of the reward."

I didn't know what to say. The thought of a kid, of any of us, turning against our own kind made me want to smash the shelf we were leaning against into a heap of metal.

"I trust Liam," I said slowly. "He's such a good person, but he's so easy for others to read—and *they* don't have the best intentions."

"Exactly," Chubs said. "He's so busy looking inside people

273

to find the good that he misses the knife they're holding in their hand."

"And even then he'd probably blame himself for the person having the knife to begin with, and apologize for being such a tempting target."

That was what troubled me the most about Liam—if he was any more trusting and good-hearted, he would have been a Boy Scout. It was either an amazing feat of stubbornness or naiveté, I thought, for someone who had seen so much death and suffering to still believe so unconditionally that everyone was as stand-up as he was. It was something that inspired both exasperation and a fierce sense of protectiveness in me—and Chubs, too, it seemed.

"I think we both know he's far from perfect, no matter how hard he tries," Chubs said, settling himself down on the ground and leaning back against the empty shelf. "He's never been a big thinker, that one. Always rush, rush, rushing to do whatever his gut tells him to, and then drowning in his own self-pity and guilt when things blow up in his face."

I nodded, absently fiddling with a tear in the sleeve of my new plaid shirt I hadn't noticed before taking it. After hearing Liam with Zu, I knew that he felt an intense guilt over what had happened the night of their breakout, but it sounded like it might run even deeper than that.

"I can fix that for you later." Chubs nodded toward the torn fabric. His long fingers were splayed out over his knees, tapping against the bones. "Just remind me."

"Who taught you how to sew, anyway?" I asked. Apparently it was not the right question to ask. Chubs's back went stiff and straight, like I had dropped an ice cube down the back of his shirt.

"I don't know how to *sew*," he snapped, "I know how to *stitch*. Sewing is for decoration; stitching is for saving lives. I don't do this because I think it's pretty or fun. I do it for practice."

He stared at me over the rims of his glasses. Waiting to see if I got what he was trying to say.

"My dad taught me how to stitch before I went into hiding," he said, finally. "In case of emergencies."

"Is your dad a doctor?" I asked.

"He's a trauma surgeon." Chubs didn't bother to hide the pride in his voice. "One of the best in the D.C. area."

"What does your mom do?"

"She used to work for the Department of Defense, but got fired when she refused to register me in the IAAN database. I don't know what she's doing now."

"They sound great," I said.

Chubs snorted, but I could see him warm to the compliment.

The minutes dragged by, and the conversation waned. I found myself reaching for Zu's notebook and flipping it open to the beginning. The first few pages were mostly sketches and doodles, but those gave way to page after page of math problems. Liam's handwriting was neat and precise, and, surprisingly, so was Zu's.

—*Betty traveled 118 miles in three hours. How fast was Lee driving?*
—*You have five Snickers bars to share with three friends. You cut them in half. How many will each friend*

get? How can you make sure the leftovers get shared
equally so Chubs doesn't complain?

And then I got to a page with completely different hand-writing. Messy and smeared. The letters were darker, as if the writer had been pressing down on the paper too hard.

I'm not sure what else can be said about this book that hasn't already been said. I'm out of clever things to say, I'm afraid. Jonathan Swift has always been a favorite, but I can't get over how clever his wordplay is throughout the novel. I really can't get over how similar it is to Robinson Crusoe at times, especially when he's on the ship to Lilliput. Though his interaction with the Lilliputians wasn't the strongest section, you would be hard pressed to find equally clever interplay of parody and originality. I can see why the book has been studied so carefully by scholars over the years. We meet Gulliver as a dreamy young man in search of adventure, trying to get anywhere that would involve sea travel, and see him evolve masterfully. If I had to name the best section of the book, it would probably be the Laputians section, a place I would greatly like to visit, because my own head is often stuck in the clouds, and to be able to study philosophy and mathematics all day—a dream. There was a time or two over the course of the novel that I felt Swift had gone overboard and missed some opportunities to drive home his idea of what the ideal society should be. You, as the reader, are left to figure it out for yourself. This book is perfect if you love thought-provoking literature from an objective, rational viewpoint, or if you dream about one day traveling the world yourself.

"Umm . . ." I held the page up for him to see. "This yours?"

"Give me that," he said. His face was wild with panic. Not just panic—by the way his nostrils flared and his hand shook, it was almost like I had scared him half to death. Guilt shot through me. I passed it back to him and watched him tear that sheet of paper out.

"Hey, I'm sorry," I said, worried about the tinge of green coloring his face. "I didn't mean anything by it. I'm just wondering why you'd practice writing essays when you said you didn't think we'd ever get to go back to school."

He continued to stare at me for several seconds, until something in his stony expression finally gave. Chubs blew out the breath he'd been holding.

"I'm not practicing for school." Instead of tucking the sheet of paper inside the briefcase, he laid it out between us. "Before . . . before camp, my parents thought the PSFs were investigating them, which, you know, they were. They sent me up to my grandparents' cabin to hide, and—you remember what I said about the Internet being policed? We had to find a way around it, especially when they started putting pressure on Mom at work."

I glanced down at the sheet of paper again. "So you used to send book reviews?"

"I had a laptop and a few wireless Internet cards," he said. "We would post book reviews online. It was the only way we could think of to talk without them catching on."

He leaned over, covering the paper so only the first column of words was visible. *I'm out can't get to you can meet anywhere name place and time missed you love you.*

"Oh."

277

"I wanted to write it out now," Chubs said. "In case I can get online, but only have a few minutes."

"You're pretty genius," I said slowly. "Your whole family."

I got a snort in response. *Duh.*

The question I really wanted to ask him was inching its way up my throat when he pulled a deck of cards out of his briefcase.

"Want to play a few games?" he asked. "We're going to be here a while."

"Sure . . . but I only know Old Maid and Go Fish."

"Well." He cleared his throat. "We don't have the right deck for Old Maid and, unfortunately for you, I excel at Go Fish. I won the Go Fish tournament in fifth grade."

I grinned, waiting for him to deal my cards. "You are a star, Chubs, a—" His nose wrinkled at the name. "I can't call you by anything else if I don't know your real name."

"Charles," he replied. "Charles Carrington Meriwether IV, actually."

I tried to keep my face as straight as possible. Of course he would be named something like that. "Okay, Charles. Charlie? Chuck? Chip?"

"Chip?"

"I don't know, I thought it was kind of cute."

"Ugh. Just call me Chubs. Everyone else does."

I figured it out.

It must have been half past five in the morning, well after several delirious games of cards and charades that had been brought on by too much candy and too little sleep. Both of us had been waiting for the other shoe to drop, to be proven right about the other boys. We kept the baseball bat beside us and never once turned our backs to the tents. When exhaustion finally set in, we took turns curled up on the ground, trying to steal a few minutes of sleep here and there.

I picked up Zu's notebook again in an attempt to avoid being lulled to sleep by Chubs's rhythmic snores, and added a few clouds and stars to the first page of doodles. The pages fanned out under my fingers as I flipped through the notebook again, not catching until I found what I was looking for.

540.

It *was* an area code for this part of the state, I was sure of it. Grams had lived down near Charlottesville for a time, and I had a very vague memory of standing in the kitchen of my parents' house, staring at her number printed on a notepad beside the phone. But the area it covered—that was no small bit of land, and there was no real guarantee that it was supposed to represent an area code in the first place.

It was easier to think of it now without three eager sets of eyes on me, but slightly complicated by the fact that I was running on fumes, sleepwise. With more than enough time to kill, I started in again—rearranging them, trying to create anagrams, substituting different letters for others.

The feeling snuck up on me slowly, crawling back up through the crowded, tired portions of my brain. The other number—540—where had I seen that? Why did it feel like—?

When it came to me, I almost laughed. Almost.

I had seen the number on the radio in Greg's memory only a few hours earlier, burning brightly through even the murkiest clouds of his thoughts.

It was 540 AM—a radio station.

Shaking Chubs back awake wasn't enough for me, not when I thought I would actually burst at the seams with excitement. I all but pounced onto Chubs's back, both scaring him senseless and kneeing him in the kidney in the process. I'm not sure what sound he made when I landed, but I was fairly certain it wasn't human.

"Wake up, wake up, wake up!" I hissed, hauling him huffing and puffing and cursing to his feet. "When they gave you EDO, did they say anything else?"

"Green, if I can still walk tomorrow, so help me God—"

"Listen to me!" I hissed. "Did they say anything about tuning in, or picking it up?"

He fixed me with a baleful look. "All they said was to check out Edo."

"Check out?" I repeated. "Those exact words?"

"Yes!" he said, exasperated. "Why?"

"I was wrong before," I said. "I don't think the number has anything to do with a phone number. We were right before. The last letter isn't a letter at all—it was supposed to be a zero. Five forty. It's some kind of radio station."

"How in the world did you reach that conclusion?"

Ah. The tricky part in all of this. How to B.S. the fact I had cheated and seen the answer, rather than being in possession of brain power to actually work it through. "I was trying to think of what else uses three digit numbers, when I remembered hearing them—Greg and the others, I mean—talk about needing to find a radio here. I should have mentioned it to you guys before, but I didn't think anything of it until now."

"Oh my God." Chubs was shaking his head, mildly stunned. "I don't even believe it. We have honestly had such shit luck this entire trip I thought at least two of us were going to end up dead in a ditch somewhere before we figured it out."

"We need a radio," I said. "I think I'm right, but if I'm not . . . we need to test it before telling the others."

"Betty?"

"No!" I wasn't about to leave the tent unguarded, even for fifteen minutes. "I thought I saw a radio in the back—let me go grab it."

The store was rushing around me in dark streams and fading colors as I ran, but I wasn't afraid of what was lurking there, not now. I hadn't imagined the radio after all. It was back in the small cluster of rafts and blankets that Liam and his friend had set up the last time he was here.

Chubs was pacing in front of the shelves by the time I got back. I set the small device up on a shelf that was about eye level and began to fuss with its buttons, searching for the ON switch.

I had to be the one to start it up—and the one to fumble with the volume knob when it just about blew our eardrums out with static. The thing was ancient, a beat-up silver box, but it worked. The speakers jumped between voices, commercials, and even a few old songs I recognized.

"It has to be AM," Chubs said, taking the radio in his hands. "FM frequencies don't go up past 108 or so. Here we go—"

My first thought was that Chubs had somehow tuned it to the wrong station. I had never heard a sound like the one sputtering through the speakers—a low growl of static pierced by what sounded like a tub of broken glass being tossed around. It wasn't painful like the White Noise, but it wasn't pleasant, either.

But Chubs was still grinning.

"Do you know what this is?" he asked, and was all too happy to explain when I shook my head. "Have you heard that there are certain frequencies and pitches that only kids with a Psi brain can pick up?"

I braced a hand on the shelf to keep from doubling over. I had. Cate had told me as much, when she explained the camp controllers had embedded a certain frequency in the White Noise to root out any of the dangerous ones still hiding out in the other cabins.

"It's not so much that others can't hear the noise, it's that their brains translate the sounds differently than ours do—really fascinating stuff. They did some testing with it at Caledonia, to see if there were any pitches that certain colors couldn't pick up and others could, and it always sounded like this when we couldn't—"

No sooner had the words left his mouth, than there was another sharp *click*, and the noise cut off altogether, replaced by a soft, male voice whispering, *"If you can hear this, you're one of us. If you're one of us, you can find us. Lake Prince. Virginia."*

282

Orange – one of the dangerous ones

Chubs, Zu and Liam

Ruby and Liam on the run

Infirmary visit

Welcome to East River

Children's League agents Cate and Rob

You and me? Inevitable

Alexandra Bracken with the cast, producer, and director

Amandla Stenberg and Jennifer Yuh Nelson

That same message, three times, before it clicked again and switched back to the frequency we had heard before. For a long time, Chubs and I could only stare at one another, speechless.

"Oh my God!" Chubs said, *"Oh my God!"* And then we were saying it together, jumping up and down, arms flung around one another like two damn fools—like we had never, ever wanted to reach over and slap each other multiple times on multiple days. I hugged him without any kind of fear or self-consciousness, fiercely, with a rush of emotion that almost brought tears to my eyes.

"I could kiss you!" Chubs cried.

"Please don't!" I gasped out, feeling his arms tighten around my ribs to the point of cracking them.

Either by his internal clock or Chubs's excited squeaks, Liam woke first. I saw him out the corner of my eye, his head of tousled blond hair sticking out of the tent. He looked between us once and retreated back into the tent, only to reemerge a second later looking torn between confusion and worry.

"What's wrong?" he asked. "What's going on?"

Chubs and I glanced at each other, wearing identical grins.

"Get Zu," I said. "You guys are going to want to hear this."

SEVENTEEN

ACCORDING TO CHUBS, JACK FIELDS WAS THE SECOND son in a family of five kids, and the only one to survive Idiopathic Adolescent Acute Neurodegeneration. His father had owned an Italian restaurant, and his mother died of cancer when he was young. Jack was unremarkable in appearance, the kind of kid you would pass in a school hallway and not think twice about. But he was stealth cool, the only one in their room that knew what Liam was talking about when he started in on Japanese horror flicks or articles from back issues of *Rolling Stone*. Apparently, he liked to tell stories in weird voices and spent years scratching out a replica of New York City's skyline on the converted classroom's blackboards. The PSFs assigned to their room had been so impressed with the sheer detail of his work that they actually let him finish.

More importantly, Jack took great pleasure in antagonizing the camp controllers by using his abilities to lift things off their belts and out of their pockets, or to throw things into their paths so that they'd trip and fall in front of everyone. To hear Chubs talk, you would have thought Jack Fields was a saint walking on earth, a disciple of Awesome, preaching the proper way to use their Blue abilities after spending years figuring it out for himself.

Which was probably why he was the first one the camp controllers shot in the back of the head the night the kids tried to make their escape.

Liam was silent as we approached Petersburg's outer city limits, only nodding once or twice to confirm that the craziest parts of Chubs's tale were true. He had been just as excited as the two of us when we dragged him over to listen to the broadcast, but slowly, over the course of a few hours, his mood had deteriorated. When Chubs's stories died out, so did all conversation in the van.

"It's supposed to be really beautiful there," I said, suddenly, then winced at how awkward it sounded. "Lake Prince, I mean."

Liam didn't looked stressed so much as profoundly sad. That was what worried me—that he was sinking into something that not even our breakthrough could pull him out of.

"I'm sure you're right," he said, quietly. He handed me the half-folded map. "Can you put this back in the glove box?"

I certainly hadn't been looking for it when I opened the small compartment, but there they were, nested on top of a pile of crumpled napkins.

Truthfully, I had been expecting envelopes, or at the very least lined notebook paper. Which was stupid and didn't make any sense, because it's not like their camp had arts and crafts days. It's not like they were just *given* the paper and pens. Still, I had been expecting the letters to be something . . . heavier. For Chubs and Liam to be carrying theirs with them.

Jack's letter was on top, written on half of what looked like a computer printout, folded over several times. He had managed to squeeze his father's name in tight capital letters on the back of the paper, between the large black words: AREA RESTRICTED.

Instead of putting the map away, I took the letter out, only vaguely aware of the argument Liam and Chubs had gotten into over the best route to Lake Prince. I wasn't thinking much of anything as my fingers slid over the wrinkled surface, smoothing it out as I unfolded it. No date in the upper right-hand corner, just a hasty, straight to the point *Dear Dad*.

I didn't get to take in another word. Liam reached over and ripped the paper out of my hand, crumpling it slightly in his fist.

"What are you doing?" he demanded.

"I'm sorry, I just . . ."

"You just *what*?" he barked. I felt my body jerk in response. "It's personal! It's none of your business what it says."

"Lee . . ." Chubs said, sounding every bit as surprised as I felt. "Come on."

"No, this is serious. We don't read each other's letters!"

"Never?" I said. "What if you can't find his dad and the letter has some clue about where he might be?"

Liam was shaking his head, even as Chubs said, "She has a point."

He said nothing, but his hands trembled on the steering wheel. It was his silence that stung, and when I couldn't take another second of it, I reached over and turned on the radio, sending up a prayer that an Allman Brothers' song would be on. Instead, Betty picked up a news talk show.

"—*children are in containment for their own good, not just the safety of the American public. My well-placed sources in the Gray administration have informed me that all instances in which a child has been removed from rehabilitation early have resulted in their untimely death. There is simply no way to reproduce the routine of medication, exercise, and stimulation these rehab centers are using to keep your children alive.*"

Liam punched a knuckle against the volume button, trying to turn it off. Instead, the tuner jumped to the next available station, and this time it was a woman's voice delivering the bad news. "*Sources are reporting that two Psi fugitives were picked up on the Ohio–West Virginia border, traveling on foot—*"

Betty turned so hard and fast into the empty rest stop that I swore she did it on two wheels. Liam parked diagonally across three different spaces, throwing the brake on with a fast, "Be right back." One minute he was beside me, and the next, we were watching the back of his red flannel shirt as he jumped over a puddle of stale rainwater and headed for the Colonial-style brick building and vending machines.

"That was . . . dramatic."

I turned to look at Chubs over the seat, but he was just as confused as I was.

"You should probably follow him," Chubs said.

"What should I say?"

Chubs gave me one of his looks. "Really? You need me to spell it out for you?"

I had no idea what he meant, but I went anyway, tracing Liam's trail of anger and frustration past the restrooms, past the abandoned sitting area, to the other side of the building, where there was wild long grass, trees, and absolutely no way we could have seen him from Betty.

He stood with his back toward me, sagging against the rest stop's wall. Arms crossed over his chest, hair standing on end. I thought I was being quiet like a fox, but he knew the moment I stepped behind him. His grief hung around us like humidity, seeping into my skin. I felt the invisible fingers at the back of my mind awaken. Howling, like a feral cat that'd been caged too long.

I kept my distance.

"Lee?"

"I'm okay. Go back to the van." Again, with the forced, bright voice.

He dropped to a crouch, then completely to the ground. But I didn't move, not until he leaned forward and stuck his head between his knees, looking like he was about to throw up everything in his stomach.

I stared long and hard at the place where his light hair curled against his neck, at the exact spot an old bruise disappeared down his shirt collar. My hand lifted at my side to push the soft fabric away. I wanted to see how far the ugly mark extended. To see what other old wounds he was hiding.

288

You touched him before, a little voice whispered at the back of my mind, *and nothing happened then. . . .*

Instead, I took a step back and away, so I was no longer standing directly behind him, but off to the side. Distance. Distance was good.

"You're right, you know," he said quietly. "I don't want to find the Slip Kid just to deliver Jack's letter. I don't even want to use him to help me find my family. I know where they are and how to reach them, but I can't go home. Not yet."

Somewhere behind us, I heard one of Betty's doors slide open, but it didn't break the stillness of the moment. "Why not? I'm sure your parents miss you."

Liam rested his arms over his knees, his back still to me. "Did Chubs tell you . . . did he say anything to you about me and the League?"

He couldn't see it, but I still shook my head.

"Harry—my stepdad—he knew from the start that the Children's League was bad news. Said they would use us worse than Gray ever would, and wouldn't shed one damn tear if we died helping them. Even after . . . even after Claire—Claire is, was, my little sister." He cleared his throat. "Even after she was gone, he used to remind me that no amount of fighting was ever going to bring her back. Cole had already joined up with them, and he came back to get me to go with him. To fight."

Was. Was my sister. *Was* gone. Another victim of IAAN.

"I bought into it. I was so angry, and I hated everyone and everything, but there wasn't anyone to direct it at. I was there with them for weeks, training, letting them turn me into this weapon. Into the kind of person that would take an innocent

289

person's life just because it served their needs and what *they* wanted. My brother was like a stranger; he even kept this— this thing he called a kill chart in our room. And he'd add to it, every time he killed someone important. Every time he completed a mission. And I would come in after training all day, and I'd look at it and think, How many of those people had families? And how many of those people had people who needed them like we needed Claire? And that's just it—they all did, Ruby, I'm sure of it. People don't live like islands."

"So you got out."

He nodded. "Had to run during a training simulation outside. I was trying to get back to Harry and Mom when the PSFs picked me up." He finally turned so he was looking at me. "I can't go back to them yet, not until I earn it. Not until I make it right."

"What are you talking about?"

"While I was with the League I realized that the only people that were ever going to help us were ourselves. So when I figured out a way to break out of Caledonia . . ." Liam's voice trailed off. Then he said, "It was horrible. *Horrible*. I totally failed them, even after I promised it would work out in the end. So why—" His voice caught. "You heard what that newscaster said. Only a few of us got out, and they just keep picking us off like rabbits in hunting season. So *why* do I want to do it again? Why can't I shake it? All I want is to help more kids break out of Caledonia—out of Thurmond—out of every single camp, one by one."

Oh, I thought, feeling vaguely numb. *Oh*. I had only ever wanted to find the Slip Kid to help myself, to figure out how

290

to tame my abilities. But all along, Liam had wanted to find him because he was sure he'd be able to help others. That, together, they could figure out a way to save the kids we'd all been forced to leave behind.

"It's just so unfair, you know? All this morning, I kept thinking, it's so goddamned unfair that I'm here, so close to finding East River, and the rest of them are gone." He pressed the back of his hand to his eyes. "It makes me feel sick. I can't shake it. I can't. Those kids they were talking about on the radio—I'm sure they were from Caledonia. I just . . ." He took in a ragged breath. "Do you think . . . do you think they regret following me?"

"Not for a second," I said. "Listen to me. You didn't force them to follow you. You only gave them what the PSFs and camp controllers took away from them—a choice. You can't live in a place like those camps and not know what the consequences might be. If those kids followed you out, it was because they *chose* to. They believed you when you said we'd all get home someday."

"But most of them didn't." Liam shook his head. "In some ways, it would have been safer for them to stay in the camps, right? They wouldn't have been hunted. They wouldn't have had to see how afraid everyone is of them, or felt like they don't have a place out here."

"But isn't it better to give them that choice?" I asked.

"Is it?"

My head was pounding, and my shoulders ached. By the time I finally thought of something to say, Liam was climbing up onto his knees.

291

"What are you still doing here?" Not upset or angry. Not anymore.

"Watching your back."

He shook his head, a sad smile on his face. "You've got better things to worry about."

"I'm really sorry." The words tumbled out of me in a breathless rush. "I shouldn't have opened his letter. It was none of my business. I wasn't thinking."

"No—*no*, I'm the one that's sorry. I didn't mean to blow up at you. God, it was like Dad was talking through me. I'm so, so sorry."

Liam looked down, and when he looked back at me, his lips were pressed tight together. I thought he might cry or scream, and felt myself sway forward at the same time he took another dangerous step toward me. It made me feel boneless to meet his gaze straight on, but I wanted the truth from him even as I worried the intensity of his gaze would burn me.

"Come on, let's go back." He shook his head. "I'm fine. I shouldn't have left those two alone again."

"I think you need another minute," I said. "And I think you should take it. Because when you get back in that car, you'll have people depending on you."

He tried to reach for my arm, but I took a step back.

"I don't know what you're—" he began. God, I wanted to take his hand when he offered it. Mine were frozen, needled with pain.

"Here—" I motioned between us. "This is a place where you don't need to lie. I meant what I said before, but I can't help you if you don't tell me what's really going on inside your head. If you need to talk or vent or scream, do it with me. Don't just get up and *go* like that again—like you always do. I know you think you're protecting us, but, Lee, what happens if one of these days you go off and don't come back?"

He took a step toward me, his eyes darkening with something I didn't recognize. It never occurred to me how tall he was, but he seemed to tower over me then, leaning down until our faces were level with each other. I could see what I would have done if our situation had been different. If I had been in control of myself. I could see what he wanted.

What *I* wanted.

My foot slipped against a rock as I stepped away, my back scraping against the wall, my head sending me spiraling into panic. It was trilling in anticipation, relishing how close he was. Maybe his anger had evaporated, but whatever he was feeling now was stronger than before, stronger than pain or frustration or fury. The words *Get away from me* and *Don't* were stuck in my tight chest, wedged between terror and want. Liam's lips formed my name, but there was nothing outside of the blood rushing in my ears.

I tried one last time to wrench myself away, but my knees, the traitors, buckled under me. Spots in every shade of the rainbow popped and burst in front of my eyes.

And that's when he grabbed me, only this time it was to hold me up, not pull me to him. It didn't matter. The moment his hands circled my waist, he was gone.

EIGHTEEN

My eyes were shut, but I could imagine what must have happened. How his pupils must have shrunk and then dilated, open and vulnerable. Waiting for a command.

Liam's mind was a blur of colors and lights. One moment I was standing next to a young, blond boy in overalls, clutching a woman's hand. Then I was balancing on the front bumper of an old car as a gentle-faced man with strong arms pointed out the engine. I saw the face of a kid rocket back as I punched him in the nose, heard a roar of approval from a circle of boys formed around us. I stared at Chubs's long legs as they hung over the edge of the top bunk, and then I was standing in front of Black Betty, watching Zu climb into the backseat, looking frail and hungry.

And then I was seeing me.

I was seeing me with the sunlight reflecting off my dark hair, laughing my fool head off in the passenger seat. I didn't know I could look like that.

No.

No.

No! I don't want to see—

I slapped him across the face. The sound echoed up through the tree branches. Pain flared in my hand, spreading quickly up my arm to the center of my chest. I heard something else, too—a *snap*, like a dried-out wishbone being pulled apart. I reeled back, as if he had been the one to hit me. I almost wished he had, because the pain would have distracted me from the dizzy disorientation that came next.

I panicked. I knew from countless experiences at Thurmond that the best way to break a connection was to do it slowly, carefully. Unravel the invisible threads linking us together one by one. Wasn't this exactly what had happened with Sam? One wrong touch and I had pulled back so hard and so fast from her mind that I ripped away every single trace of me.

Wasn't it?

Wasn't it?

The pain lessened, the farther I dragged myself away from him.

"Ruby?"

Why did I always have to do this? Why couldn't I just hold it together *for once*?

Liam was staring at me. *At* me, not through me. He looked focused, if not completely bewildered. My eyes fell on the red welt forming on his cheek.

Had I heard that right? My name?

"What the hell just happened?" He let out a strangled laugh. "I feel like I just got hit by a linebacker."

295

"I slipped—" What could I possibly say? The truth was on the tip of my tongue, dangling there, but if he knew, if he knew what I had just done to him . . . .

"And there I was, trying to be all valiant and stuff by catching you?" He chuckled, using the closest tree to help him stand. "Lesson learned! You're falling next time, darlin', because, *man*, you have a hard head. . . ."

"I'm sorry." I whispered. "I'm so, so sorry. . . ."

Liam stopped laughing. "Green . . . you know I'm just kidding, right? Really, it takes a special kind of guy to get knocked out by the same person he's trying to catch. Aside from bringing back a few humiliating memories of school sports, I'm fine, honestly—what?"

Do you even remember what we were talking about?

"Oh my God," he said, all of a sudden noticing I was still on the ground. "Are *you* okay? I can't believe I didn't even ask—are you hurt?"

I avoided the hand he offered. It was too soon.

"I'm fine," I said. "I think we should head back now. You left Betty running."

My voice sounded calm, but inwardly I was such a desert. All of the hope that had sprung there, growing and spreading and yielding like a stream, had dried up in an instant. I had slipped up, but he didn't know. They never did.

This couldn't happen again—I was lucky this time; he still remembered *me*, even if he couldn't recall what I had done, but there was no guaranteeing that luck would hold.

No more touching. No more fingers brushing against arms, or shoulders pressed against shoulders. No more taking his hand, no matter how warm or big it was.

That alone was a reason to find this Slip Kid. To beg him to help me.

"Yeah . . . yeah." He nodded, but I didn't miss the way his brows furrowed when he looked my way again, or the grinding ache in my chest when he passed by and didn't let his hand reach for mine.

I stayed five steps in front of him as we made our way back around the rest stop, past the water fountains, through the silver benches and tables under the overhang. I moved faster, practically jogging as I came around the corner. I half expected to see Chubs and Zu outside trying to rig the vending machines into burping up whatever snacks they had left.

But it wasn't Chubs waiting there for me, and it certainly wasn't Zu.

Dark hair, darker eyes. A man that couldn't have been older than twenty-five, with a scar that began just under his right eye and raced up to his hairline, where the shiny pink skin had prevented any hair from growing back. My brain processed his features one by one, in agonizing slowness. I watched as his face twisted, turning his narrow nose up in disgust.

Liam called my name in a panic, his feet thundering against the cement. *Run*, I wanted to scream to him, *What are you doing? Run!* I turned back to face the man—the skip tracer, in his wrinkled blue Windbreaker—just in time to see the butt of his rifle flying down toward my face, knocking every thought clear out of my skull.

—✦—

Pain blinded me, flashing white beneath my eyelids. But I was down, not out. When the man tried to haul me up by the front of my shirt, I swung a leg around and caught him by the ankles. He landed on the ground with a grunt, his gun clattering against a nearby patch of rocks. I kicked until I made contact with something solid. I knew it wasn't enough.

I tried pushing myself up to my feet, but the world swung wild and loose under me. My head throbbed, and something hot and wet poured down over my right eye—blood. I could taste it then, just as plainly as I felt the air move as Liam lifted the man clear off the ground with a wave of his hand. He threw him like a rag doll into the sharp edges of the picnic tables, knocking the skip tracer out in a single blow.

Zu, Chubs, Zu, Chubs, my mind was stuck on a loop. I pressed a hand against my forehead, to the place where the gun had burst the skin in a jagged line.

I don't know what happened next. It felt like my head was skipping seconds as we moved. At one point, I think Liam must have tried to help me up, but I pushed him away with clumsy, slow hands.

Run! I tried to say. *Get out of here!*

"Ruby—*Ruby*." Liam was trying to get my attention, because he hadn't seen what was up ahead.

Zu and Chubs were sitting on the ground, outside of Betty. Their hands were handcuffed behind their backs, and their feet tied straight out in front of them with a length of bright yellow rope. Standing over them was none other than Lady Jane.

This was the first time I had seen her up close—close enough, at least, that I could make out the beauty mark on

298

her cheek and the sunken quality to her eyes behind the black frames of her glasses. Her dark hair was down around her shoulders and curling with the humidity, but her skin still looked as though it had been pulled taut over the sharp angles of her face. Her black shirt was tucked neatly into her jeans, and a black utility belt was there to keep them both in place. I recognized the countless devices hanging from the belt. The orange identifier, a Taser, handcuffs . . .

"Hello, Liam Stewart," the woman said, her accent cold and silky.

Next to me, Liam braced his feet and threw his arms up—to knock her back, I think. The woman only tsk-tsked, nodding a head toward her outstretched left arm. My eyes followed its angle downward, to the gun pointed at Zu's head.

"Lee—" Chubs's voice was unnaturally high, but it was the look in Zu's eyes that planted me in place.

"Come here," the woman said. "Slowly, with your hands on top of your head—*now*, Liam, otherwise I can't be sure that my finger won't slip." She cocked her head to the side.

Panic, I thought. The panic button—where? My backpack was somewhere tucked under the front passenger seat. If I could get to it, if I could reach the door—

"Yeah?" Liam spat. "And what's the going rate for me these days? How much did it get cut back when it took you three weeks to finally catch up to us?"

Her smile faltered, but returned with far more teeth than before. "You're still at a healthy two hundred and fifty thousand dollars, love. You should feel proud of that. You barely fetched me ten thousand the first time around."

Liam was vibrating with rage, too choked up to speak. I heard his breath catch in this throat. I suddenly understood how he had known so much about her—this was the same woman who had captured him before.

"You can't imagine my surprise when your name popped back up in the bounty database—and with that kind of reward? It seems that you've gotten yourself in a fair bit of trouble since we last met."

"Yeah, well," Liam said, his voice rough. "I do my best."

"But, darling, how could you be stupid enough to go back to that place? Didn't you think I'd look for you there?" The woman tilted her head again. "Your friends were only too willing to tell me where you were headed and why in exchange for letting them go. Lake Prince, is it?"

My pain gave way again to fear. *If she finds East River . . .* God, I couldn't even imagine the consequences.

Liam could, from the look of it. His knuckles were white with the effort it took him to keep his fingers clutched in his hair.

"If I can pull in that much for you, imagine what I'll get for a whole *camp* full of kids," she said. "Enough to finally buy my way home, I think, so thank you for that. You have no idea what kind of funds it takes to get an official to look the other way and admit someone from a disease-ridden country."

The next second of silence that passed was deafening, only because I knew exactly what he would say next.

"If you let them all go, you can have me," he said, both hands still on his head. "I won't give you any trouble."

"No!" Chubs shouted. "Don't—"

The woman didn't even need a moment to consider it. "You think I'm going to do *you* any favors? No, Liam Stewart, I'm going to take all of you, even that girl of yours—maybe you should consider her condition before you try to bargain?"

His eyes slid my way, taking in the blood streaking down my face. I tried to keep my vision straight as I took the tiniest step forward.

"I don't know where you came from, little girl, but I can assure you that where you're going won't be nearly as pleasant."

I'm not going back.

None of us were. Not if I could help it.

"Come here," she said, her eyes on me but her gun still trained on Liam. "You first, little girl. I'll take special care of you."

I went one step at a time, ignoring Liam's sharp intake of breath and the buzzing in my ears. My eyes went from Chubs, to Zu, to the woman's all-too-pleased face. Everyone was watching me.

Everyone will know.

And no one would be willing to have me after that.

"Turn around," the woman barked. Her eyes flickered over to where her partner was still hidden behind a tangle of picnic tables. I saw her grip relax ever so slightly on her handgun with her focus torn, and I took my chance.

My knee flew up, nailing her just under her chest. The gun clattered to the ground, and I heard Liam take two running steps in my direction, but somehow I was faster. Blood was alive and warm on my face, dripping from my chin. The

301

woman's eyes widened as my hand closed over her exposed throat, slamming her back against Betty's door. When her gaze met mine, I knew I had her. The pain that exploded behind my eyes told me so.

Slipping into her head was as easy as releasing a sigh. Seeing her pupils shrink and explode back out to their normal size, it felt as though someone had wrapped a line of barbed wire around my brain and was tightening it with every passing second.

Chubs's face appeared at the corner of my vision, eyes wide. When he tried to stand, I knocked him back down with my foot. No. It wasn't safe. Not yet.

The woman looked around, her eyes wide and unfocused. That's when the pounding began in my ears. *Da-duh, da-duh, da-duh, da-duh* . . . I couldn't tell if it was my heart or hers.

"Hand him your gun," I said, tilting my head toward the place I knew Liam was standing. When she didn't move, I pushed the image of her doing it through the bubbling black shapes of her mind. I couldn't bring myself to look at his reaction as the black weapon was placed in his outstretched hand.

"Listen to me very carefully," I said. The blood was bitter in my mouth. "You are going to turn and walk back across the highway. You are . . . going to walk into that forest and keep walking until an hour passes . . . and you are going to sit down in the middle of it and not move. You're not going to eat . . . or sleep . . . or drink, no matter how much you want to. You're not going to move."

Imagining that into her mind, pushing the thought of her doing exactly that, was becoming more difficult. Not because my grip on her was slipping, but because my grip on consciousness was.

You can do this, I told myself. It didn't matter that no one had ever taught me, or that I had never practiced. In the end, it was all instinct. Like I had known all along.

I closed my eyes and went to work sorting through the darkened memories bubbling up behind her eyes. I found myself driving down the highway, one hand on the wheel, the other pointing to the rest stop up ahead. I parked the car a ways back, half hidden by the trees, and began to walk toward the lone black van in the parking lot. I stayed with this memory, taking in the scent of rain and grass, feeling the light breeze, until her partner reached the van, his rifle up and ready to fire.

I forced the memory out of her mind, imagining nothing but air where Black Betty had been in the parking lot. I traced the line of memories back to the boys at Walmart, to the secret they had revealed about East River. The images slipped away in smears of light, like raindrops racing down a car window.

"Now, you're . . . you won't remember any of this, or any of us."

"I won't remember any of this. . . ." she parroted, as though the thought had just occurred to her.

I let go of her neck, but my pain didn't go away. Her eyes regained some of their focus. The pain didn't go away. She turned sharply on her heel and started to make her way toward the deserted highway.

The pain didn't go away.

No, it got worse. A trickle of sweat began at my temple and worked its way down the length of my spine. I was drenched. My hair clung to my face. My shirt was a second skin. I dropped into a crouch. If I was going to faint, it was better to stay close to the ground.

God, I don't want to faint. Don't faint. Do. Not. Faint. . . .

I heard Liam say something. His foot came into my line of sight, and I leaned away.

"Don't—" I began. *Don't touch me. Not right now.*

And it was strange, because the last thing I saw before I closed my eyes wasn't the old asphalt, it wasn't the sky, or even my reflection in Betty's panels. It was a glimmering memory of my own. Of a few days before, when Liam had been in the driver's seat, singing along to Derek and the Dominos' "Layla" at the top of his lungs, so off-key that it had even Chubs laughing. Zu had been sitting right behind him, moving in time with the music, her entire body rocking out to the wailing electric guitar. And it had been so easy then, to laugh and pretend, even if just for a second, that we would be okay. That I belonged with them.

Because they hadn't known—none of them had known, and now that they did, it was over. It was all over now, and I would never have that back.

I wished that I had gone for the panic button. I wished that Cate could come and take me away from them, back to the only people who would ever embrace me for the monster I was.

NINETEEN

WHEN I WAS ABOUT TO TURN TEN YEARS OLD, THE most significant thing about that number was that it was double-digits. It didn't really feel much like a birthday, anyway. At dinner, I sat bookended by my parents at the table, moving peas around my plate, trying to ignore the fact that neither of them were speaking—to each other, or to me. Mom's eyes were rimmed with red and glassy because of the argument they'd had a half hour before; she was still valiantly trying to gather up kids for a surprise birthday party for me, but Dad forced her to call and cancel. Said it wasn't the kind of year to be celebrating, and, as the last kid alive on my block, it would be cruel of us to hang the birthday banner and tie up the usual cluster of balloons outside. I heard the whole thing from the top of the stairs.

I didn't really care about the birthday either way. It wasn't like I had anyone left I really wanted to invite. What was more important to me was the fact that, at ten, I was suddenly *old*—or rather, would be old *soon*. I'd start to look like the girls in the magazines, be forced to wear dresses and high heels and makeup—go to *high school*.

"In ten years from tomorrow, I'll be twenty." I don't know why I said it out loud. It was just this profound realization, and it had to be shared.

The silence that followed was actually painful. Mom sat straight up and pressed her napkin to her mouth. For a moment I thought she might stand up and leave, but Dad's hand came down to rest on top of hers, settling her like an anchor.

Dad finished chewing on his barbecued chicken before giving me a smile that quivered at the edges. He leaned down a ways so our identical green eyes met. "That's right, Little Bee. And how old will you be ten years after that?"

"Thirty," I said. "And you'll be . . . fifty-two!"

He chuckled. "That's right! Halfway to the—"

Grave, my mind whispered. *Halfway to the grave*. Dad realized his mistake before the word fully left his mouth, but it didn't matter. All three of us knew what he meant.

Grave.

I knew what death was. I knew what happened after you died. At school, they brought in special visitors to talk to the kids that came back. The one assigned to our room, Miss Finch, gave her presentation two weeks before Christmas, wearing a bright pink turtleneck and glasses that covered half of her face. She wrote everything out on the whiteboard, in thick, capital letters. DEATH IS NOT SLEEPING. IT HAPPENS TO EVERYONE. IT COULD HAPPEN AT ANY TIME. YOU DO NOT COME BACK.

When people die, she explained, they stop breathing. They do not have to eat, they no longer speak, and they cannot think or miss us like we miss them. They do not, ever, *ever* wake up. She kept giving us more examples, like we were too stupid or little to understand—like the six of us left hadn't sat there and watched Grace's lights go out. Dead cats cannot purr, and dead dogs cannot play. Dead flowers—Miss Finch pointed to the bundle of dried flowers on my teacher's desk—do not grow or bloom anymore. Hours of this. Hours of being asked, *Do you understand?* But for all of her answers, she never got around to the one question I had wanted to ask.

"What does it feel like?"

Dad looked up sharply. "What does what feel like?"

I looked down at my plate. "To die. Do you feel it? I know that it's not the same for everyone, and that you stop breathing and your heart stops beating, but what does that feel like?"

"Ruby!" I could hear the horror in Mom's voice.

"It's okay if it hurts," I said, "but are you still in your body after things stop working? Do you know that you've died?"

"Ruby!"

Dad's bushy eyebrows drew together as his shoulders slumped. "Well . . ."

"Don't you dare," Mom said, using her free hand to try to pry his big one off her other trembling fingers. "Jacob, don't you *dare*—"

I kept my hands clenched together under the table, trying not to stare at Mom's face as it paled from a deep red to a stark white.

"No one . . ." Dad began. "No one knows, sweetheart. I can't give you an answer. Everyone finds out when it's their time. I guess it probably depends—"

"*Stop it!*" Mom said, slapping her other hand down on the table. Our plates jumped in time with her palm. "Ruby, go to your room!"

"Calm down," Dad told her in a stern voice. "This is important to talk about."

"It is not! It absolutely is not! How dare you? First you cancel the party, and when I told you—" She strained against his grip. I watched, my lips parting, as she picked up her water glass and threw it at his head. In ducking, he lifted his hand from the table, just enough for her to wrench away and stand. Her chair clattered to the ground a second after the glass shattered against the wall behind Dad's head.

I screamed—I didn't mean to, but it slipped out. Mom came around to my side of the table and grabbed me by the elbow, hauling me up, nearly taking the tablecloth with me.

"Cut it out," I heard Dad say. "*Stop!* We have to talk to her about it! The doctors said we needed to prepare her!"

"You're hurting me," I managed to choke out. Mom startled at the sound of my voice, looking down at where her nails were digging into the soft skin of my upper arm.

"Oh my God . . ." she said, but I was already in the hallway, flying up the stairs, slamming my bedroom door shut and locking it behind me, closing out the sound of my parents screaming at each other.

I dove under my heavy purple bedcovers, knocking the row of carefully arranged stuffed animals to the ground. I

308

didn't bother to change out of the clothes I had worn to school, or turn off the lights, not until I was sure my parents were still in the kitchen, and far away from me.

An hour later, breathing the same hot air under the comforter in and out, listening to the rattle of the air vent, I thought about the other significant thing about turning ten.

Grace had been ten. So had Frankie, and Peter, and Mario, and Ramona. So had half of my class, the half that never came back after Christmas. *Ten is the most common age for IAAN to manifest*, I had overheard a newscaster saying, *but the affliction can claim anyone between the ages of eight and fourteen.*

I straightened my legs out and pressed my arms in at my sides. I held my breath and shut my eyes, staying as still as possible. *Dead.* Miss Finch had described it like a series of stops and nots. Stopped breathing. Not moving. Stopped heart. Not sleeping. It didn't seem like it should have been that simple.

"When a loved one dies, they don't get to wake up," she had said. "There are no comebacks or do-overs. You may wish they could come back, but it's important that you understand they can't, and they won't."

Tears slipped down the side of my face, dripping into my ears and hair. I turned to the side, smashing a pillow over my face, trying to block out the screaming match downstairs. Were they coming up to my room to yell at me? Once or twice I heard heavy footsteps on the stairs, but then Dad's voice would float up to me, booming and terrible, yelling words I didn't like or understand. Mom sounded like she was being gutted.

I drew my legs up to my chest and pressed my face against my knees. For every two breaths I was taking in, I was lucky to get one out. Inside my chest, my heart had been racing for what felt like hours, jumping with every shatter or thud from downstairs. I stuck my head over the covers just once, to make sure that I had locked the door. That would make them even angrier if they tried it, but I didn't care.

My head felt light and heavy all at once, but worst of all was the pounding. The *dum-dum-dum* at the back of my head, like something was inside of me knocking against my skull, trying to break out.

"Stop it," I whispered, squeezing my eyes shut against the pain. My hands were shaking so hard I couldn't keep them over my ears. "Please, please *stop!*"

Hours later, when my feet carried me downstairs, I found them in their dark bedroom, deep into sleep. I stood in the sliver of light coming through their open doorway, waiting to see if they would wake up. I had half a mind to climb into bed between them like I used to do, into that small space between them that I knew was warm and safe. But Dad had told me I was too big to be doing such silly things.

So instead, I walked over to my Mom's side of the bed and kissed her good night. Her cheek was slick with rose-mary-scented cream, cool and smooth to the touch. The instant I pressed my lips there, I jumped back, a flash of white burning inside my eyelids. For one strange second, the image of my own face had leaped to the front of a long series

310

of jumbled thoughts, then disappeared, like a photo drifting into dark water. Her blanket must have shocked me—the jolt traveled all the way up to my brain, flashing it white for a second.

She must not have felt it, because she didn't wake up. Neither did Dad, even when the same strange thing happened.

As I made my way back upstairs, the tightness in my chest vanished, lifting away with the comforter as I kicked it to the floor. The head-splitting pain released its grip on my brain, leaving me feeling like my tank had run empty. I had to close my eyes to block out the sight of my room swaying in the darkness.

And then it was morning. My alarm went off at seven exactly, switching over to the radio, just as Elton John's "Goodbye Yellow Brick Road" was starting. I remember sitting straight up in bed, more surprised than anything. I touched my face, my chest. The room seemed unnaturally bright for so early in the morning, despite the curtains being closed, and within only a few minutes, the headache had crept back in, claws out.

I rolled out of bed and onto the floor, my stomach turning with me. I waited until the dark spots had stopped floating in my eyes, and tried to swallow to ease my dry throat. I knew this feeling—I knew what the clenching in my guts meant. *Sick*. I was sick on my birthday.

I stumbled out of bed, changing into my Batman pj's on the way to the door. Mom would be even angrier at me if she knew I had slept in my nice button-down shirt; it was wrinkled and drenched in sweat, despite the cold clinging to my bedroom window. Maybe she'd feel bad about the night before and let me stay home to show how sorry she was.

I wasn't even halfway down the stairs when I saw the wreckage in the living room. From the landing, it looked like a pack of animals had gotten in and had a field day throwing around pillows, overturning an armchair, and smashing every single glass candleholder that had been on the now-cracked coffee table. Every picture on the fireplace mantel was facedown on the ground, as were the line of school portraits my mom had placed on the table behind the couch. And then there were the books. Dozens of them. Mom must have emptied out every book in the library in her anger. They littered the ground like rainbow candy.

But as scary as that room was, I didn't feel like throwing up until I reached the last step and smelled bacon, not pancakes.

We didn't have many traditions as a family, but chocolate pancakes on birthdays was one of them, and the one we were least likely to forget. For the past three years they'd forgotten to leave out milk and cookies for Santa, somehow forgotten their pact that we would go camping every Fourth of July weekend, and even, on occasion, forgot to celebrate St. Patrick's Day. But forgetting the birthday pancakes?

Or maybe she was just mad enough at me not to make them. Maybe she hated me after what I had said last night.

Mom had her back to me when I walked into the kitchen and shielded my eyes from the sunlight streaming through the window above the sink. Her dark hair was pulled back into a low, messy bun, resting against the collar of her red robe. I had a matching one; dad had bought them for Christmas the month before. "Ruby red for my Ruby," he had said.

She was humming under her breath, one hand flipping the bacon on the stove, the other holding a folded newspaper. Whatever song was stuck in her head was upbeat, chipper, and, for a moment, I really did think the stars had aligned for me. She was over last night. She was going to let me stay home. After months of being angry and upset over the tiniest things, she was finally happy again.

"Mom?" Then again, louder. "Mom?"

She turned around so quickly, she knocked the pan off the stove and nearly dropped the gray paper into the open flame there. I saw her reach back and slap her hand against the knobs, twisting a dial until the smell of gas disappeared.

"I don't feel good. Can I stay home today?"

No response, not even a blink. Her jaw was working, grinding, but it took me walking over to the table and sitting down for her to find her voice. "How—how did you get in here?"

"I have a bad headache and my stomach hurts," I told her, putting my elbows up on the table. I knew she hated when I whined, but I didn't think she hated it enough to come over and grab me by the arm again.

"I asked you how you got in here, young lady. What's your name?" Her voice sounded strange. "Where do you live?"

Her grip on my skin only tightened the longer I waited to answer. It had to have been a joke, right? Was she sick, too? Sometimes cold medicine did funny things to her.

Funny things, though. Not scary things.

"Can you tell me your name?" she repeated.

"Ouch!" I yelped, trying to pull my arm away. "Mom, what's wrong?"

She yanked me up from the table, forcing me onto my feet. "Where are your parents? How did you get in this house?"

Something tightened in my chest to the point of snapping.

"Mom, Mommy, why—"

"Stop it," she hissed, "stop calling me that!"

"What are you—?" I think I must have tried to say something else, but she dragged me over to the door that led out into the garage. My feet slid against the wood, skin burning. "Wh-what's wrong with you?" I cried. I tried twisting out of her grasp, but she wouldn't even look at me. Not until we were at the door to the garage and she pushed my back up against it.

"We can do this the easy way or the hard way. I know you're confused, but I promise that I'm not your mother. I don't know how you got into this house, and, frankly, I'm not sure I want to know—"

"I live here!" I told her. "I live here! I'm *Ruby*!"

When she looked at me again, I saw none of the things that made Mom my mother. The lines that formed around her eyes when she smiled were smoothed out, and her jaw was clenched around whatever she wanted to say next.

314

When she looked at me, she didn't see *me*. I wasn't invisible, but I wasn't Ruby.

"Mom." I started to cry. "I'm sorry, I didn't mean to be bad. I'm so sorry, I'm so sorry! Please, I promise I'll be good—I'll go to school today and won't be sick, and I'll pick up my room. I'm sorry. Please remember. *Please!*"

She put one hand on my shoulder and the other on the door handle. "My husband is a police officer. He'll be able to help you get home. Wait in here—and don't touch anything."

The door opened and I was pushed into a wall of freezing January air. I stumbled down onto the dirty, oil-stained concrete, just managing to catch myself before I slammed into the side of her car. I heard the door shut behind me, and the lock click into place; heard her call Dad's name as clearly as I heard the birds in the bushes outside the dark garage.

She hadn't even turned on the light for me.

I pushed myself up onto my hands and knees, ignoring the bite of the frosty air on my bare skin. I launched myself in the direction of the door, fumbling around until I found it. I tried shaking the handle, jiggling it, still thinking, hoping, praying that this was some big birthday surprise, and that by the time I got back inside, there would be a plate of pancakes at the table and Dad would bring in the presents, and we could—we could—we could pretend like the night before had never happened, even with the evidence in the next room over.

The door was locked.

"I'm sorry!" I was screaming. Pounding my fists against it. "*Mommy, I'm sorry! Please!*"

Dad appeared a moment later, his stocky shape outlined by the light from inside of the house. I saw Mom's bright-red face over his shoulder; he turned to wave her off and then reached over to flip on the overhead lights.

"Dad!" I said, throwing my arms around his waist. He let me keep them there, but all I got in return was a light pat on the back.

"You're safe," he told me, in his usual soft, rumbling voice.

"Dad—there's something wrong with her," I was babbling. The tears were burning my cheeks. "I didn't mean to be bad! You have to fix her, okay? She's . . . she's . . ."

"I know, I believe you."

At that, he carefully peeled my arms off his uniform and guided me down, so we were sitting on the step, facing Mom's maroon sedan. He was fumbling in his pockets for something, listening to me as I told him everything that had happened since I walked into the kitchen. He pulled out a small pad of paper from his pocket.

"Daddy," I tried again, but he cut me off, putting down an arm between us. I understood—*no touching*. I had seen him do something like this before, on Take Your Child to Work Day at the station. The way he spoke, the way he wouldn't let me touch him—I had watched him treat another kid this way, only that one had a black eye and a broken nose. That kid had been a stranger.

Any hope I had felt bubbling up inside me burst into a thousand tiny pieces.

"Did your parents tell you that you'd been bad?" he

316

asked when he could get a word in. "Did you leave your house because you were afraid they would hurt you?"

I pushed myself up off the ground. *This is my house!* I wanted to scream. *You are my parents!* My throat felt like it had closed up on itself.

"You can talk to me," he said, very gently. "I won't let anyone hurt you. I just need your name, and then we can go down to the station and make some calls—"

I don't know what part of what he was saying finally broke me, but before I could stop myself I had launched my fists against him, hitting him over and over, like that would drive some sense back into him. "I am your *kid*!" I screamed. "I'm *Ruby*!"

"You've got to calm down, Ruby," he told me, catching my wrists. "It'll be okay. I'll call ahead to the station, and then we'll go."

"No!" I shrieked. "No!"

He pulled me off him again and stood, making his way to the door. My nails caught the back of his hand, and I heard him grunt in pain. He didn't turn back around as he shut the door.

I stood alone in the garage, less than ten feet away from my blue bike. From the tent that we had used to camp in dozens of times, from the sled I'd almost broken my arm on. All around the garage and house were pieces of me, but Mom and Dad—they couldn't put them together. They didn't see the completed puzzle standing in front of them.

But eventually they must have seen the pictures of me in the living room, or gone up to my mess of the room.

317

"—that's not my child!" I could hear my mom yelling through the walls. She was talking to Grams, she had to be. Grams would set her straight. "I have no child! She's not mine—I already called them, don't—*stop it!* I'm *not crazy!*"

I had to hide. I couldn't let him take me to the police station, but I also couldn't dial 911 to get them help. Maybe if I waited it out, they'd get better on their own? I dashed toward the storage tubs on the other side of the garage, squeezing past the front of Mom's car. One, maybe two steps more, and I would have jumped inside the closest tub and buried myself under a pile of blankets. The garage door rolled open first.

Not all the way—just enough that I could see the snow on the driveway, and grass, and the bottom half of a dark uniform. I squinted, holding a hand up to the blinding blanket of white light that seemed to settle over my vision. My head started pounding, a thousand times worse than before.

The man in the dark uniform knelt down in the snow, his eyes hidden by sunglasses. I hadn't seen him before, but I certainly hadn't met all the police officers at my dad's station. This one looked older. *Harder,* I remembered thinking.

He waved me forward again, saying, "We're here to help you. Please come outside."

I took a tentative step, then another. *This man is a police officer,* I told myself. *Mom and Dad are sick, and they need help.* His navy uniform looked darker the closer I got, like it was drenched straight through with rain. "My parents . . ."

The officer didn't let me finish. "Come out here, honey. You're safe now."

It wasn't until my bare toes brushed up against the snow, and the man had wrapped my long hair around his fist and yanked me through the opening, that I even realized his uniform was black.

When I finally came to in the gray light, I knew by the curve of the rear seat and the smell of fake lemon detergent that I was back in Betty.

The van wasn't on and running, and the road wasn't passing underneath me, but the keys had been left in the ignition and the radio was on. Bob Dylan whispered the opening verse of "Forever Young" through the speakers.

The song cut off abruptly, replaced by the DJ's flustered voice.

"—*sorry about that.*" The man let out a nervous, breathy laugh. *"I don't know why the system brought that one up. It's on the no-play list. Uh . . . back to . . . the music. This one's a request from Bill out in Suffolk. Here's 'We Gotta Get Out of This Place' by the Animals."*

I opened one eye and tried to sit up, with zero success. The throbbing in my head was so brutal, I had to clench my teeth to keep from getting sick all over myself. A good five minutes must have passed before I felt strong enough to reach up and touch the pain's epicenter on my right temple. My fingers brushed against the jagged, raised surface of my skin, feeling each coarse stitch holding it together.

Chubs.

I pulled my right arm in front of me. It flopped around, useless and asleep, until the blood began to fill it again. Then it was fire and needles. But the pain was good. It roused the rest of me from its stubborn sleep.

It didn't let me forget.

I should go, I thought. Now, before they get back. The thought of seeing any of their faces made my chest feel like it was going to explode.

They know.

They know.

I did start to cry then. I wasn't proud of it, but I knew I couldn't go through this again and come out of it in one piece.

Footsteps sounded outside.

"—saying it's too dangerous." Chubs. "We need to consider getting rid of her."

"I don't want to talk about this right now." Liam sounded agitated.

I used one of the seat belts to pull me upright. The sliding door was wide open, giving me a perfect view of where Chubs and Liam stood in front of a small fire, which was ringed by a series of mismatched stones. The sky was dipping into night.

"When *are* we going to talk about it, then?" Chubs said. "Never? We're just going to pretend like it never happened?"

"Zu will be back soon—"

"Good!" Chubs shouted. "Good! This is her decision, too—this is all of our decision, not just yours!"

Liam's face was as red as I had ever seen it. "What the hell are we supposed to do, just *dump* her here?"

Yes, I thought. That's exactly what you should do. And I had started to climb over the middle seats to tell them that much when Chubs lurched forward, throwing Liam onto his back without touching him. Unfazed, Liam pressed his mouth into a tight line, raised his hand, and literally pulled the ground out from under his friend's feet. Chubs hit the dirt with a sharp gasp, too stunned to do anything but lie there.

Liam stayed on the ground, too, pressing his fists against his eyes.

"Why are you doing this to us?" Chubs cried. "Do you *want* to get caught?"

"I know, I know," Liam said. "This is my fault. I should have been more careful. . . ."

"Why didn't you just *tell* me?" Chubs continued. "Did you know this whole time? Why lie about it? Do you even want to get home, or—?"

"Charles!"

His name cracked as it left my throat. I didn't think I sounded anything like myself, but the boys recognized my voice at once. Chubs's face lost some of its heat as he turned to where I stood clutching the minivan's sun-warmed frame. Liam pushed himself up off the ground.

"I'm gonna go, so you—don't fight anymore, okay?" I said. "I'm sorry I lied to you. I know I should have left, but I wanted to help you get home because you had helped me, and I'm sorry, I'm so, so, sorry—"

"Ruby," Chubs said. Then again, louder. "Ruby! Oh, for the love of . . . we were talking about Black Betty, not your Orange ass."

I froze. "I just . . . I thought . . . I understand why you would leave me behind. . . ."

"Huh?" Liam looked horrified. "We left the radio on in case you woke up, so you'd know that we *didn't* leave you."

God help me, that only made me cry harder.

When a girl cries, few things are more worthless than a boy. Having two of them just meant that they stared at each other helplessly instead of at me. Chubs and Liam stood, up to their ears in awkward, until Chubs finally reached out and patted my head like he would have patted a dog.

"You thought that we wanted to get rid of you because you're not really Green?" Liam sounded like he was having a hard time wrapping his head around that. "I mean, I'm not thrilled you didn't trust us enough to tell us the truth, but that was your secret."

"I trust you, I do," I said, "but I didn't want you to think that I had forced my way in or manipulated you. I didn't want you to be afraid of me."

"Okay, first?" Liam said. "Why would we think that you pulled a Jedi mind trick on us to let you stay? We voted—*we* asked *you*. Second, what in the name of God's green earth is wrong with being Orange?"

"You have no idea—" *What I'm capable of.*

"Exactly," Chubs cut in. "We have no idea, but it's not like we're going to win any awards for normalcy anytime soon. So you get into people's heads? The two of us can throw people around like toys. Zu once blew up an AC unit, and all she did was walk by it."

It wasn't the same, and they didn't understand that.

"I can't always control it like you can," I said. "And sometimes I do things—*bad* things. I see things I shouldn't.

322

I turn people into things they aren't. It's horrible. When I'm in someone's head, it's like quicksand; the more I try to pull free, the more damage I do."

Chubs started to say something, only to stop. Liam leaned down so his face was level with mine, so close that our foreheads were nearly touching. "We want you," he said, his hand slipping through my hair to cup the back of my neck. "We wanted you yesterday, we want you today, and we'll want you tomorrow. There's nothing you could do to change that. If you're scared and you don't understand your crazy abilities, then we'll help you understand—but don't think, not for one second, that we would ever just leave you."

He waited until I was looking him in the eye before continuing. "Is this why you acted that way when I said the Slip Kid might be an Orange? Is that really why you want to find him, or do you just want to go to your grandmother's? Because either way, darlin', we'll get you there."

"Both," I said. Was it so wrong to want both?

I had stopped crying, but my lungs felt sticky, heavy, and getting in even an ounce of air was too much effort. I don't know why my brain was as still as it was, but I was trying not to think about it. Liam and Chubs both took an arm. I was lifted out of the van, guided over to the crackling fire.

"Where are we?" I asked finally.

"Somewhere between North Carolina and the Great Dismal Swamp, I hope," Liam said, his hand still on my back, now rubbing circles there. "Southeast Virginia. Now that

323

you're awake, I need to check on Zu. You two stay put, okay?"

Chubs nodded; we watched Liam go in silence, then Chubs turned to me. "Ruby," he began, voice perfectly serious. "Can you tell me who the president is?"

I blinked. "Can you tell me why you're asking this question?"

"Do you remember what happened?"

Did I? The memory was milky and distorted, like I was glimpsing someone else's dream. "Angry man," I said. "Rifle. Ruby's head. Ouch."

"Cut it out; I'm being serious!"

I winced, touching the stitching in my forehead again. "Can you keep your voice down? It feels like my head is about to cave in."

"Yeah, well, serves you right for scaring the hell out of all of us. Here, keep drinking this," he said, handing me what was left of our water bottle. It didn't matter that the water was stale or warm; I finished it off in one gulp. "I mean, my dad used to say that head wounds look worse than they actually are, but I legitimately thought you were a corpse."

"Thanks for stitching me up," I said. "I'm looking a little Frankenstein, but I guess it's appropriate, all things considered."

Chubs gave me a weary sigh. "Frankenstein is the name of the doctor that *created* the monster, not the monster itself."

"Couldn't let that one go, could you?"

"Don't get on my case about it. You're the one that doesn't know her classic literature."

"Funny, I don't think they had that one in Thurmond's library." I hadn't meant for it to come out as sharply as it did, but it wasn't a pleasant experience being reminded that your education level equaled that of a ten-year-old.

He had the decency to look apologetic as he let out a deep sigh. "It's just . . . take it easy, will you? My heart can only take so much stress."

All along, while listening to Chubs and Liam try to talk me down, some part of me had been trying to work through the argument I had overheard. I could understand, as horrifying as it was, the need to leave Betty behind. The PSFs and skip tracers all seemed to know to look for her now. But there had been something else underlying their words—something else that had them at odds. I had a feeling I knew exactly what it was, but I couldn't ask Liam. I wanted the truth, not a sugarcoated version of it. The Team Reality take. Only Chubs could give that to me.

But I hesitated, because next to his feet, on the ground between us, was Chubs's copy of *Watership Down*. And I kept thinking about this one line, the one that had made me so angry the first time I read it as a little kid.

Rabbits need dignity and, above all, the will to accept their fate.

In the book, the rabbits had come across this warren— this community—that accepted food handouts from humans in exchange for accepting that some of them would be killed by the same humans in return. Those rabbits stopped fighting the system, because it was easier to take the loss of freedom, to forget what it was like before the fence kept them in, than to be out there in the world struggling to find shelter and food. They had decided that the loss of some was worth the temporary comfort of many.

"Will it always be this way?" I asked, drawing my knees up to my chest and pressing my face against them. "Even if we find East River and we get help—there's always going to be a Lady Jane around the corner, isn't there? Will it even be worth it?"

The will to accept their fate. In our case, that fate was to never see our families again. To always be hunted and chased down to every dark pocket of earth we tried to hide inside. Something had to give—we couldn't live that way. We weren't made to.

I felt him drop a heavy palm on the back of my head, but it was a long time before he could piece together his thoughts.

"Maybe nothing will ever change for us," he said. "But don't you want to be around just in case it does?"

I don't know if it was the smoke from the campfire that calmed me, or the sudden reappearance of Zu, who had come back from scouting a nearby campsite, making sure it was deserted. As she wrapped her arms around my waist, the boys began to pool together what was left of the food in Betty.

"So that's how you figured out the clue," Liam said. "You saw a memory of it?"

I nodded. "Not so impressive now, is it?"

"No—*no*, that's not what I meant," Liam said, adding quickly, "It's just I'm trying to imagine what the inside of that kid's head looked like, and the best I can come up with is a swamp filled with alligators. It must have been terrible."

"Not as terrible as slipping into someone's head I actually like," I admitted.

"Did you?" Chubs said after nearly ten minutes of silence. Liam was busy testing out whether he could use Betty's car key to pry open the lids of the fruit and soup cans.

"Did I what?"

"Did you ever get inside our heads?" he finished. The way he asked reminded me of the way a kid would ask for the end of a bedtime story. Eager. Surprising—in all of my nightmares about them finding out the truth, I had pictured Chubs taking it the worst.

"Of course she's in our heads," Liam said, his arms straining to open the can's lid. "Ruby is one of us now."

"That's not what I meant," Chubs huffed. "I just want to know how it works. I've never met an Orange before. We didn't have any at Caledonia."

"That's probably because the government erased them all," I said, dropping my hands in my lap. "That's what happened to them at Thurmond."

Liam looked up, alarmed. "What do you mean?"

"For the first two or three years I was there, we had every kind of color, even Red and Orange," I said. "But . . . no one really knows why or how it happened. Some people thought they were taken away because of all the trouble

327

they caused, but there were rumors they were being moved to a new camp where they could do more testing on them. We just woke up one morning and the Reds, Oranges, and Yellows were gone." And it was just as terrifying for me to think about now as it was then.

"What about you, though?" Chubs asked. "How did you avoid getting bused?"

"I pretended to be Green from the start," I said. "I saw how scared the PSFs were of the Oranges, and I messed with the scientist who was running the classifying test." It was a struggle to push the rest of the words out. "Those kids were . . . they were so messed up, you know? Maybe they were like that before they got their abilities, or they hated themselves for having them, but they used to do terrible things."

"Like what?" Chubs pressed.

Oh God, I couldn't even talk about it. I physically could not speak. Not about the hundreds of mind games I watched them play on the PSFs. Nothing about the memory of having to scrub the floors of the Mess Hall after an Orange told a PSF to walk in and open fire on every other soldier he saw there. My stomach turned violently, and I could taste it, the metallic bitterness of blood. Smell it. I remembered how it felt to scrape it out from where it was packed painfully under my nails.

Chubs opened his mouth, but Liam held up a hand to shut him up.

"I just knew I needed to protect myself."

And, truthfully, because I was scared of the Oranges, too. There was something wrong with them. With us. It was the constant chatter, the flood of everyone else's feelings and thoughts, I think. Eventually you learned how to block some of it out, to build up a thin wall between your mind and others', but not before everyone else's poisonous thoughts were in there, staining your own. Some spent so long outside of their own heads that they couldn't function right when they finally had to return their own.

"So now you see," I said, finally, "what a mistake it was to let me stay."

Zu was shaking her head, looking distraught at the suggestion. Chubs rubbed at his eyes, hiding his expression. Only Liam was willing to look me straight in the eye. And there was no disgust, or fear, or any of the thousand other ugly emotions he was entitled to; only understanding.

"Try to imagine where we'd be without you, darlin'," he said, quietly, "and then maybe you'll see just how lucky we got."

TWENTY

THAT NIGHT, WE SLEPT IN THE VAN, EACH SPRAWLED
out on a seat. I let Zu have the rear seat, and stayed up
front next to Liam. I felt uneasy in the silence, and sleep
didn't come easy, even when I called to it.

Sometime around five in morning, just as I was about
to give into the fuzz covering my brain, I felt someone run
a light finger down the back of my neck. I rolled over onto
my other side, and Liam was there, half-awake.

"You were muttering to yourself," he whispered. "You
okay?"

I propped myself up on an elbow, wiping the sleep away
from my eyes. The rain had condensed on the windows, covering the cracked windshield like a filmy overlay of lace.
Every time a fat raindrop dislodged itself and went streaking
down the glass, it was like a tear in the fabric.

Looking out into the forest was like searching someone's
dreams, disorienting and unsettling, but inside the van,

everything was sharp. The lines of the reclining seats, the dashboard knobs—I could even read the tiny printed brand name on the buttons of Liam's shirt.

In that light, I could see every bruise and cut on his face, some just beginning to heal, and others that had long-since scarred. But what held my attention wasn't the bruise on his cheek—the same one I had given him a few days and lifetimes before—but the way his hair was standing almost straight up, curling around his ears and against his neck. The storm had turned its color to a darker shade of honey, but it didn't lose any of its softness. It didn't make me want to reach out and touch it any less.

"What?" he whispered. "What are you smiling about?"

My fingers brushed against his hair, trying to smooth it down. I realized what I was doing a full minute after Liam had closed his eyes and leaned into my touch. Embarrassment flared up in my chest, but he grabbed my hand before I could pull back and tucked it under his chin.

"Nope," he whispered, when I tried to tug it away. "Mine now."

Dangerous. This is dangerous. The warning was fleeting, banished to the back corners of my mind, where it wouldn't interrupt how good it felt to touch him—how *right*.

"I'm going to need it back eventually," I said, letting him run it along the stubble on his chin.

"Too bad."

". . . crackers . . ." a voice breathed out behind us, "yessss . . ."

Both of us turned, watching as Chubs twisted around in his seat and settled back down, still fast asleep.

I pressed a hand over my mouth to keep from laughing. Liam rolled his eyes, smiling.

"He dreams about food," he said. "*A lot.*"

"At least they're good dreams."

"Yeah," Liam agreed. "I guess he's lucky." I looked back at Chubs's curled up form and, for the first time, realized just how cold it was without the heat from Betty's vent.

Liam let his head slide down to rest against his other arm, threading his fingers through mine. He seemed to be studying the shape they made, the way my thumb appeared to rest naturally on top of his.

"If you wanted to," he began, "could you see what he was dreaming about?"

I nodded. "But those things are private."

"But you've done it before?"

"Not intentionally."

"To me?"

"To the girls in my cabin at camp," I said. "To Zu that night in the motel. I've been in your head—once. Just not in your dreams."

"Two days ago," he said, putting it together. "At the rest stop."

It was instinct to pull back, to let go before I felt him let go first, but he didn't allow me.

"Don't," he said. "I'm not mad."

He brought our hands down against his forehead, not looking at me when he asked, "Does it make it worse? To be touching someone, I mean. Is it harder to control?"

"Sometimes," I admitted. I didn't know how to explain it, because I had never wanted to. "Sometimes, when I'm

332

tired or upset, I'll pick up on someone's thoughts or a memory they're thinking about, but I can avoid being pulled in if I don't touch the person. Touching them when my head is like that . . . it's an automatic connection."

"I thought so." Liam sighed, closing his eyes again. "You know, when we first met, you used to go out of your way to avoid touching us. I kept wondering if it was something you had been trained to do at your camp, because every time one of us would try to touch you or talk to you, you'd jump like we had shocked you."

"I didn't want to hurt any of you," I whispered.

His eyes flashed open again, somehow brighter than before. He nodded to our linked fingers. "Is this okay?"

"Are *you* okay?" I countered. I recognized the look on his face—it was nearly identical to the grief he'd worn at the rest stop, talking about his own camp. "What are you thinking about?"

"I was thinking about how strange it is that we haven't even known each other for two weeks, but it feels like I've known you for much longer than that," he said. "And I'm thinking that it's frustrating to feel like I know certain parts of you so well, but other parts of you . . . I don't even know what your life was like before you went to camp."

What could I tell him? What could I say about what I had done to my parents and to Sam that wouldn't scare him into letting go?

"This is a place where we don't have to lie," he said, motioning between us. "Didn't you tell me that?"

"You remember?"

333

"Of course I do," he said. "Because I keep hoping that goes both ways. That if I ask you why you don't want to go home to your parents, you'll tell me the truth, or if I ask you what Thurmond was really like, you'll stop lying. But then I realized that it's not fair, because it's not like I want to talk about my family. It's like . . . those . . ."

I turned to look at him, waiting as he tried to piece together his thought. "I don't know if I can explain it," he said. "It's hard to put into words. Those things—those memories—are mine, you know? They're the things that the camp didn't take away when I went in, and they're the things I don't have to share if I don't want to. I guess that's stupid."

"It's not stupid," I said. "That's not stupid at all."

"And I want to talk about everything with you. Everything. But I don't know what to tell you about Caledonia," he said. "I don't know what I can tell you that won't make you hate me. I was stupid, and I'm embarrassed and ashamed, and I know—*I know*—that Charles and Zu blame me for what happened. And I know that Cole has told Mom about it by now, and she's told Harry, and the thought just makes me sick."

"You did what you thought was right," I said. "I'm sure they understand that."

He shook his head, swallowing hard. I reached over with my other hand to brush the hair out of his eyes. The way he turned his face toward me again, closing his eyes and tilting his chin, made me brave enough to do it again. My fingers followed the natural wave of his hair, tracing the strands down around his ear.

"What do you want to do?" I whispered.

"I've got to wake the others up," he said. "We have to keep moving. On foot."

My hand stilled, but it was clear that he had made his choice.

"What's the rush?" I asked, lightly.

There, at the right corner of his mouth, where his scar met his lips—a faint smile. "I think we could let them sleep, at least for a few more hours."

"And then?"

"We'll hit the road."

Two hours rolled right on by around us. We both must have fallen asleep at some point, because by the time I opened my eyes, the condensation was shrinking against the glass, and a few rays of morning light had made it to the forest floor.

As I stirred, so did Liam. For a while, we said and did nothing beyond working out the cricks and kinks from the awkward positions we slept in. When it came time to finally let go of his hand, I felt the first touch of cold air work its way in from outside.

"Wake up, team," he said. His shoulder popped as he reached back to slap Chubs's knee. "Time to carpe the hell out of this diem."

Less than an hour later, we were standing in front of the black minivan, watching as Zu did one last check under the seats. I buttoned my plaid shirt up to my throat and wrapped a red scarf I'd picked up around my neck three times—not

335

because I was all that cold, but because it helped hide the disturbing bloodstain smeared down my front.

"Yikes." Liam's expression was grim as he leaned over and pulled my hair out from where it was trapped beneath the collar. "Would you rather wear mine?"

I smiled and zipped his coat up for him. My forehead was still tender to the touch, and the stitches were as ugly as sin, but I was feeling better. "Was it really that bad?"

"*Evil Dead II* bad." Liam bent down to add a few of his clothes to my backpack. Something red appeared in his hand. "Just about gave me a heart attack, Green."

"You can't really call her Green anymore," Chubs pointed out. He was making the difficult decision about which books to abandon and which to take with him, and had seemed to settle on *Watership Down*, *The Heart Is a Lonely Hunter*, and some book I had never heard of called *Howards End*. Left behind: *The Spy Who Came in From the Cold* and *The Sound and the Fury*, which Chubs had taken to calling *The Snore and the Just Kill Me*.

"Yeah," I said. "No more Green . . ."

"All done?" Liam called to Zu. When she gave him a thumbs-up, he threw her pink bag over one shoulder and my backpack over the other. "Any day now, Marian Librarian. I thought you were the one that wanted to check out."

Chubs gave him the finger, leaning forward to put his full weight into closing the briefcase. I leaned over to help him, trying to avoid the look on Liam's face as he stood there staring at Betty's mangled black shell. Zu was crying without making a sound; Liam had his hands on her shoulders, holding her steady. Even Chubs looked at the car with a rare softness, his fingers bunching up the fabric of his pants.

I understood why we were parting ways with Betty now; the other skip tracer that had been with Lady Jane was still out there, and there was some chance that the woman had reported the car to whatever bounty network the skip tracers used. But I also understood why Liam had been so reluctant to do it. Unlike the abandoned and withered small towns we had driven through in western Virginia, the nearby cities and their populations were still holding on, which meant there would be more folks on the road, and Betty, with her bullet holes and cracked windows, was not exactly inconspicuous. Then there was the fact that we had little to no gas left, and no easy way of finding more, aside from going up and down and siphoning it from the abandoned cars along the nearby highway. There was too much traffic—too many potential eyes—running down the road to do it.

Liam had gotten us as close as he could to Lake Prince, but it was anyone's guess how long it would take us to walk there.

"It feels like we should do something," he said. "Like, send her off on a barge out to sea and set her on fire. Let her go out in a blaze of glory."

Chubs raised an eyebrow. "It's a minivan, not a Viking."

Zu pulled away from his grasp and headed for the trees to her left. Liam rubbed the back of his neck, at a loss. "Hey," he started, "it's okay, we'll—"

But when Zu reappeared in our line of sight, she wasn't empty-handed. Clutched between her fingers were four small yellow flowers—wild weeds, by the looks of it. The kind we always used to have to pull up in Thurmond's garden every spring.

She walked over to the van, stood on her toes, and lifted up the closest windshield wiper. With delicate fingers, she positioned each flower in a row, keeping them straight across the cracked glass.

Something cold and wet caught on my eyelashes. Not tears, but a misty rain, the kind that soaked through you slow and sure, driving you crazy with chills in the process. And I realized then how unfair it all was that we couldn't just crawl back inside of the car; that even if we made it to East River, we'd be soaked and sore for days.

This car—this had been a safe place for them. For us. Now we had lost that, too.

I shoved my hands in my pockets and turned away, heading for the trees. My fingers brushed again something hard and smooth in my pocket, and I didn't need to pull it out to know that it was the panic button. In the beginning, I had kept it because I wasn't sure I'd be able to protect them on my own, and now . . . . I had half a mind to drop it and let the ground claim it. Liam had confirmed everything that I'd suspected, but it seemed foolish to toss it then, when there was a chance for us to use them like they would have used us. If a PSF or skip tracer caught up to us now, I could press the button, and the agents that showed up would be more than enough distraction for us to have a chance to get away.

But it still didn't make me feel any less ashamed of how relieved I felt to find it still there—to know that Cate, with all of her promises to take care of things, was still out there, still only a touch away.

Liam thought the easiest and fastest way to navigate our small pack to East River was to travel alongside the roads that we would have taken had we still been in Betty. We were close enough to the highway to hear the occasional car whiz by, or see the flash of some long, silver-bellied semi-truck out of the corner of our eyes, but, he assured us, out of their line of sight. This was the way he had traveled after escaping the League, how he had navigated through most of Virginia—how he hoped to get home.

We were debating whether or not Chubs had broken his toe against an exposed tree root when the wail of a truck's horn shattered the silence. The booms that came next were infinitely worse—the thundering of something heavy falling and the resounding crack of metal snapping.

We all jumped—I dropped Zu's hand to cover my ears. The way the tires squealed just before the crash came was like the warning signal for White Noise.

Liam reached over and gently pried my hands from my ears. "Come with me for a second." He turned back to the others. "You guys watch the bags."

Before the sound had even settled in the air, we heard the screams. Not the desperate kind—the one you'd hear when someone was terrified or hurt or even out of their head with grief. This was a war cry. A rising rebel yell. After that, there was no chance of Zu or Chubs coming with us. They stayed behind to watch the bags as Liam and I made our way to the line of trees that separated us from the rain-soaked asphalt of the highway.

The semitruck was on its side in the middle of the road, as if it had been flung there like a toy. The smell of burned rubber and smoke curled my stomach as we crouched down, and I was concerned the trail of sparks in front of us would turn into a wall of flame.

Liam stood up and was nearly at the shoulder of the road before my hand managed to catch his elbow.

"What are you doing?" I had to shout over the sound of the rain pinging against the silver, rippled body of the trailer the truck had been hauling.

"The driver—"

Needed help, yes, I knew that, and maybe it made me soulless and horrible, but I wasn't about to let Liam be the one to do it. Trucks didn't just flip over on their side for no reason. Either there was another car and driver we couldn't see, or . . .

Or the yelling and the accident were connected.

Liam and I were still standing out in the open when the figures in black came pouring out of the trees opposite us. Every inch of them was covered in black, from the ski masks pulled down over their faces to their black shoes. There was an entire highway between us, and still the sight of them was enough to make me reach out and grab Liam's arm, squeezing it until I was sure he'd be left with a permanent imprint of my fingers.

There were at least two dozen figures in black; they moved in unison, with practiced ease. And it was so weird, but watching them flood the road and divide into two groups—one that went to the front of the truck, the other to the back where its boxed contents were spilling out—reminded me of a football team running a play. The four of them sent to the front cab climbed up and ripped the door open. The driver, who was screaming something in a language I didn't understand, was hauled down to the ground.

One of the figures in black—a big one, with shoulders the size of Kansas, pulled a knife from his belt and, signaling for the others to hold the driver down, pressed its silver blade against the man's palm.

I heard a scream and didn't realize it had belonged to me until that same black monster's head swiveled toward us. Liam jumped at the ten gun barrels that swung our way. The first bullet was close enough to nick his ear as it whistled by. There wasn't even time to turn and run. The firing stopped long enough for three of the figures to rush forward, screaming, "On your knees!" and "Head to the ground!"

I wanted to run. Liam must have sensed this, because he latched onto my shoulder and forced me down, pressing the side of my face against the cold, rough asphalt. The rain picked up, filling my ear, my nose, my mouth as I tried to bite back another scream.

"We're not armed!" I heard Liam shout. "Easy—*easy!*"

"Save it, asshole," someone hissed.

I was intimately familiar with what it felt like to have a barrel of a gun dig into my skin. Whoever was doing it this time had no qualms about dropping a knee onto my back, along with their entire weight. The gun's metal mouth was cold against my cheek, and I felt someone weave a hand in my hair and give a sharp twist. That's when I disconnected from the pain and lifted a hand, trying to twist my body enough to grab whoever was holding me. I was not powerless—we were *not* going to die here.

"Not those!" I heard Liam say. He was begging. *"Please!"*

"Awww, don't want your precious papers to get wet?" The same voice as before. "How about you try being worried about yourself or your girl here, huh? Huh?" He sounded like a jock amped up on too much juice and game adrenaline.

Someone stomped their foot down on the same hand I was trying to maneuver toward my attacker's skin. I let out a choked cry, wishing I could turn my head to see what was causing Liam to do the same.

"Doctor Charles Meriwether," the voice read out, "2775 Arlington Court, Alexandria, Virginia. George Fields—"

The letters.

"Stop it," Liam said. "We didn't do anything—we didn't see anything, just—"

"Charles Meriwether?" another voice said. Also male, this one with a heavier Southern accent. I almost didn't hear him over the rain. "George Fields—like Jack Fields?"

"Yes!" Liam made the connection a full second before I did. This was a tribe—these were kids. "Yes, we're Psi, please—we're Psi like you!"

"Lee? Liam Stewart?" There was a shuffle of feet running toward us.

342

"Mike? That you?" That, from Liam.

"Oh my God . . . stop, stop!" The gun lifted off my face, but I was still pinned to the ground. "I know him—that's Liam Stewart! Stop! Hayes, get off of him!"

"He saw; you know the rules!"

"Jesus, are you deaf?" Mike yelled. "The rules apply to adults—they're kids, you asshole!"

I don't know if Liam finally managed to throw him off, or if Mike's words did the trick, but I felt Liam rise next to me, and opened my eyes in time to see Liam drive his shoulder into the black figure on top of me. I gulped in a full chest of air.

"Are you all right?" he asked. He put his hands on either side of my face. "Ruby, look at me—you okay?"

My hands came up to grab his. I nodded.

Of the six guys gathered around us, only two pulled their knit ski caps up off their faces: the big kid—big in a Hercules kind of way—with ruddy skin and black paint under both eyes, and another one with olive coloring, shaggy brown hair pulled back into a short ponytail. The latter was Mike. He reached over and pulled the letters out of Hercules's hand and pressed them against his own chest.

"Lee, man, I'm so sorry. I never thought—" Mike choked up. Liam let go of one of my hands to clap him on the back. "What the hell are you doing here?"

Liam took the letters back from him, and reached back to draw me forward again. "We're okay now," he told me. It seemed to be true enough. The other kids in black had lost interest in us the minute Mike stepped up.

"God, Lee," he said, wiping the rain off his face. "Oh my God, I can't believe you actually made it out."

Liam's voice was tight. "I thought you were with Josh when . . ."

"I was, but I got through the fields." He added, "Thanks to you."

Another kid, this one with skin as dark as Chubs, jerked his thumb in Liam's direction. "This is Lee Stewart?" he demanded. "From Caledonia?"

"From *North Carolina*," Liam said, with surprising venom.

Mike gripped Liam's hand, his entire body shaking. "The others—did you see if any of the others made it out?"

Liam hesitated. I knew what he was thinking, and I wondered if he would tell Mike the truth about how many kids actually escaped that night.

Instead, their watches went off at once, a shrill beep.

"That's time," Hercules said to the others. "Grab the supplies and head back. The uniforms will be here any second."

A single gunshot punctuated his order like an exclamation point, thundering across the open road. Liam and I both jumped back, away from them.

The kids at the back of the truck were tossing down the entirety of the truck's load: boxes and crates of brightly colored fruit. My lips parted at the sight of green bananas, just a few days shy of being ripe.

When they moved off and started back toward the trees, I had a clear view of the truck driver being rolled, unconscious and bound, into the ditch alongside the road.

"So, you're what?" Liam rubbed the back of his neck. "Raiding anyone stupid enough to drive by?"

"It's a supply hit," Mike said. "We're just trying to bring in a little food to eat, and this is the only way that works for us. We just have to do it fast—in and out before anyone notices us and can follow us back home."

"Back home?"

"Yeah. Where are you guys headed?" Mike had to shout over the people shouting for him. "You should come with us!"

"We already have our own tribe, thanks," Liam said.

Mike's dark brows furrowed. "We're not a tribe. Not like that, at least. We're with the Slip Kid. You heard of him?"

TWENTY-ONE

EAST RIVER WAS, AFTER ALL THAT SPECULATING, nothing more than a camping ground. A big one, of course, but nothing I hadn't seen before a dozen times over with my parents. After the buildup that Mike and the others had given it, you would have thought we were walking toward Heaven's pearly gates, not some old camping spot that had been called Chesapeake Trails in its past life.

Since Mike had been the one to convince the others to take us along, he was the one stuck babysitting us as we hiked up the muddy unpaved road, saddled with boxes of fruit that were as heavy as they were tempting.

"We go on these things—we call them hits—to gather up supplies for the camp. Stuff like food, medicine, you name it. We also raid stores from time to time."

Liam had given me his jacket to wear to ward off the rain. Though it had turned to a faint drizzle as we walked, the damage had already been done to the flimsy cardboard boxes in

our arms. Every now and then, the bottom of a carton would give out completely, and whatever kid was carrying it would be forced to stuff the sodden piles of fruit into their pockets or carry them cupped in their shirts. Kids were doubling back to pick up the scattered, bright trail we were leaving behind us. Every once in a while, I would catch myself from being distracted by the bright trail we were leaving behind.

When Mike had his back turned to us, Liam snuck a hand in the top box and held an orange out in front of my face, a shy smile on his lips. When he dropped it in my jacket's pocket, he leaned over, his sweatshirt hood slipping off his head, and pressed a light kiss against my bruised cheek. After that, the cold trickle on my skin seemed to evaporate.

"Ow, ow, ow, ow," Chubs chanted behind us. "Ow, ow, ow, ow."

"You know," Mike said, "it gives me hope that, after everything he's been through, Chubs is still the same Chubs we all know and love."

"Aw, that's not true," Liam said. "This is Chubs two-point-oh. He hasn't cried once this entire walk."

"Give him a few minutes." Greg snorted. "I'm sure he won't let us down."

"Hey," I said in a low, warning tone. "Not funny."

Chubs was still trailing behind, the gap between us growing with each mile marker we passed. I stopped and waited for him, not wanting him to feel like he was being left behind.

"Need some help?" I asked as he limped up to me. "My box isn't too heavy." And his was; I could tell. He was saddled with grapefruit.

I could see in his eyes that he desperately wanted to trade, even if it was only for a few minutes. Instead, he lifted his chin and said, over the cardboard flap, "I'm fine, though I appreciate your asking."

Liam and Mike burst out laughing about something—even Zu looked back to grin at them, Liam's hat falling over her eyes. It was amazing how much better Liam looked after only a few hours; his face was animated with a kind of energy I hadn't seen . . . well, ever.

"What was he like?" I asked quietly. "When he was in camp?"

Chubs blew out a long sigh. "Well, for one thing, he was a lot more annoying with his whole, *We're gonna make it, guys, we're gonna get out one day* Pollyanna shtick. That's been dying a slow death now that he's realized just how sucky everything actually is."

He stopped to shift the box in his arms. "I mean, what do you want me to tell you? Lee is Lee. Everyone loved him, even some of the PSFs. They picked him out of all of the Blues to be a runner for the control center of our camp."

"Yeah? And what were you like in camp?" I asked, smiling.

"Ignored, for the most part," he said. "Unless I was with Lee."

As if he'd heard his name, Liam turned. "Hurry up, ladies! We're going to be left behind."

Mike was in the middle of explaining how he had hitch-hiked from Ohio to Virginia after breaking out of Caledonia, when Chubs and I finally caught up to them. Zu tugged the sleeve of my jacket and pointed through the trees to our left.

348

I had been so involved in my conversation with Chubs that I had completely missed the silky blue lake that had suddenly come into view. The clouds pulled back, revealing the sun high overhead. The water sparkled under its touch, throwing its light around the trees that lined its every side. Through them, I could see I could see a small T-shaped wood dock at the other end, and, beyond that, several wooden cabins.

"So it's more of a place to hide, then," Liam was saying. "Can he help us get in touch with our folks?"

Mike frowned. "I guess, but he usually asks that you stay and help with the camp for a few weeks in return. Plus, why would you want to go home now? It's much safer here."

I could tell Chubs wanted to press this issue, but Liam charged on with yet another question. "How long has the Slip guy had this setup?"

"Two or so years, I think," Mike answered. "Man, I can't wait until you meet him. You are going to lose your mind."

Chubs rolled his eyes heavenward, and I got the distinct impression that he and Mike were not all that fond of each other.

"And there are hundreds of kids here just roaming around unchecked?" I asked. "How has he been able to stay here so long without the PSFs catching on?"

Mike had already explained how the camp worked. All of the kids who had gathered there—some who had escaped from camps or capture, others that had been able to hide out long enough to avoid it all together—had responsibilities.

"Oh, see, now that's the beauty of being under the Slip Kid's protection," Mike said. "The PSFs can't attack him because of who he is and what he could do to them. Even ol' Gray is terrified of him."

"I know who it is!" Liam snapped his fingers. "Santa!"

Zu giggled.

"You're not too far off," Mike said. "This is going to sound super sappy, so feel free to give me shit for it, but every day here feels like Christmas."

I saw what he meant right away. Once we reached the clearing that, I assumed, had once been used for campers to set up tents, we were surrounded by dozens of kids. To our right, teens were playing volleyball—with an actual net. I heard a few shrieks of laughter and stopped to let a few little girls rush by in front of me. They were the ones that caught Zu's attention.

They all looked happy. Up and shiny and smiley. And clean. Not covered in cuts and bruises and mud like we were, but in decent clothes and shoes. A few kids lounging under the trees stopped whatever it was that they were doing and actually helped us carry the fruit boxes toward a white building marked OFFICE CAMP/SHOP without being asked or prompted.

The Office/Camp Shop was the sturdiest of the structures we had passed so far, built in a more permanent style than the smaller log cabins with their dark green doors.

"This is where we keep the food," Mike said, like it was the most exciting thing we were ever going to hear. "And where the Slip Kid runs the whole show—I'll bring you guys in for an introduction. Get permission for you to stay a while."

350

"We need permission?" Chubs asked. "What happens if he says no?"

"He's never said no before," Mike said, shifting the box onto his shoulder so he could drop an arm around Chubs's shoulder. Seeing he had my attention, he grinned ear-to-ear.

"Now, you couldn't have been at Caledonia. I would remember a face like yours." I think he thought he was being charming with those dark eyes and dimples. He looked over at Lee, who was fighting back a smile as he watched my reaction. "Where did she come from, and where can I find one?"

"Picked this one up at a gas station in West Virginia, bargain price," Lee said. "Last one on the shelf, sorry."

Mike laughed again, giving Chubs's shoulder a squeeze before he hopped up the steps, ducking under a white sheet that had been strung up over the building's small porch. I glanced at it, then had to look again.

The enormous black Ψ painted there had stopped Zu dead in her tracks and turned her face a sickly shade. I couldn't move—couldn't look away from it. Liam cleared his throat, his jaw working, as if trying to shake the words loose.

It was enough to stop Zu and me dead in our tracks, at least. Alarm lit up her face like a candle. Liam gave his friend a confused look.

"What?" Mike asked, seeing our reactions.

"Any reason in particular you've decorated this fine establishment with our mortal enemies' symbol?" Liam said.

It was the first time I had seen Mike's expression drop the entire time we'd been with him, which was close to two

351

hours. Something hardened in his eyes, something strained the muscles in his jaw. "That's our symbol, isn't it? It's Psi. It should represent us, not them."

"How do you explain the black, then?" Liam pressed. "The armbands, the shirts . . . ?"

He was right. Everyone, in some form or another, had the color on them. Most were apparently satisfied with tying a black band around their arm, but others, and not just the ones that had hit the truck for supplies, were in head-to-toe black.

"Black is the absence of all colors," Mike said. "We don't segregate by color here. We all respect one another and our abilities, and we all *help* one another understand them. I thought if anyone would be on board with that, it'd be you, Lee."

"Oh no, no, I am on board. I am, like, captain of that ship," Liam said. "I was just . . . confused, that's all. Black is the color. Got it."

The screen door creaked open again. Mike caught it with his foot. "Coming?"

Inside, I was surprised to feel a wave of heat hit my face and see the overhead lights on. Electricity—I remembered Greg mentioning something about the Yellows rigging the system to work, but did they have running water, too?

The front rooms were filled with piles of blankets and bedding, a few stacked mattresses, and a number of unidentifiable gray plastic tubs. The backroom—the Shop in the Office/Camp Shop combo—was to the right of a small, white-tiled kitchen. Mike waved to the kids inside, who were turning whatever delicious creation was inside of their pots with long wooden spoons.

The old store's wood shelves were painted a dour green, but stuffed with a rainbow assortment of canned food and bags of chips, pasta, and even marshmallows. Liam let out a low whistle at the sight of the boxes of cereal stacked high over our heads.

I thought Chubs might cry.

We left the fruit on the floor in a shady corner of the room, near a girl with cropped blond hair and a midriff-baring black shirt. She was still clapping her hands in delight, bouncing on her toes. She couldn't have been more than fourteen or fifteen and seemed to have as many piercings in the cartilage of each ear.

"I knew you'd be happy, Lizzie," Mike said, tossing her a grapefruit.

"We haven't had fruit in *ages*," she said, her pitch rising with every word. "I hope this all keeps for a few weeks."

Mike led us out of the room, leaving Lizzie to coo over the pineapples and oranges. "Let's go upstairs. He should be done meeting with the security team by now. Hayes handles hits, but Olivia—you'll meet her—coordinates watch duty around the perimeter of the camp. If you want, I can talk to her about getting you assigned there."

He looked down at Zu. "But unfortunately for you, my dear, everyone under thirteen has to sit through lessons."

That caught Chubs's attention. "What kinds of lessons?"

"School stuff, I guess. Math, a little science, some reading—depends on whatever books we were able to scrounge. It's important to the boss that everyone gets the basics down." Mike stopped at the top of the stairs and looked over his shoulder. "I know you never liked using them, but there are lessons on how to use your abilities, too."

Chubs cleared his throat behind me. "I'm fine with what Jack taught me."

"*Jack . . .*" Mike's voice trailed off. "Man, I miss that kid."

On our walk over, he had explained that there were five kids from Caledonia living in the Slip Kid's camp. Mike was the only one from Liam's old room, but there were two Blue girls, one Yellow boy, and a Green who had somehow made it all the way to eastern Virginia.

The second story of the building was more of an attic; the entire floor was one open room, but it was a nice one. Mike knocked on the door, waiting for the "Come in," before daring to twist the handle. I heard Chubs let out a nervous squeak, and I was surprised to feel my own heart skip a beat.

The door opened to the middle of the room. To the right was a white curtain, drawn all the way over to hide what I thought was probably the living area. The window behind the curtain let in enough afternoon light to hint at the shape of a bed and dresser.

The other half of the room was set up like an office. There were two bookshelves filled with binders and books of every shape and size. An old metal desk with peeling black paint sat in between. There were two simple chairs in front of the desk, and a long table pushed to the far left wall, with all sorts of electronic equipment. A TV was on, set to one of the news channels. President Gray's face filled the screen, flanked by two American flags. His mouth moved, but the TV had been muted. The only sound, aside from Chubs's sharp intake of breath, was Clancy Gray's fingers striking the keys of the sleek silver laptop.

I would have recognized him even if he had shaved his head of thick, wavy black hair—if he had tattooed his cheeks, or pierced his long, straight nose. I had spent six years staring up at every single one of his portraits at Thurmond, memorizing every mole, the shape of his thin lips—I was even intimately familiar with the peak of his hairline. But it was nothing like seeing the real thing. Those portraits hadn't captured his dark eyes, and they certainly hadn't been able to predict how striking he'd turn out to be as he aged.

"Just a sec—" He glanced up from his screen in our direction and immediately did a double take.

"Boss?" Mike said. "You okay?"

The president's son rose slowly, shutting the lid of his laptop. The rolled-up sleeves of his white shirt slid down his tan arms.

This is the Slip Kid? I thought. *Him?* Surprise was an understatement. Brain-numbing shock, the kind that reduced my train of thought to an inching crawl, was an understatement. I didn't even have a second to collect myself before the next three words passed his lips. There was no way I could have, because Clancy Gray looked straight at me and said the very last thing on earth I expected.

"Ruby Elizabeth Daly."

—⁘—

My reaction was way too strong for something as innocent as my full name. It wasn't like he had spat out three vile cusswords or screamed "Kill them now!" or "Lock them up!" I shouldn't have stumbled back, tripping over my own boots, but I was nearly to the door before I even realized it.

Clancy took a step forward, but Liam pushed him back, hard.

"Lee!" Mike sounded scandalized.

Clancy held up his hands. "Sorry—I'm sorry! My bad. I should have realized how that would sound. I was just surprised to see you." He leaned around Liam with an apologetic smile, and I paused at the door, momentarily stunned by how white and straight his teeth were. "I've read your file so many times on so many different networks that I feel like we've already met. There are so many people out there looking for you right now."

"And which one do you plan on turning her over to?" Chubs snapped.

I stood still, letting Zu keep one arm wrapped around my waist. Clancy's face flushed at the accusation, his dark eyes flicking back over to me. "None of them. I just collect information, watch the networks to see what everyone is buzzing about. And that just happens to be you, Miss Daly." He paused, rubbing a hand absently over his shoulder. "Let's see if I remember all of this—born in Charlottesville, Virginia, but raised in Salem by her mother, Susan, a teacher, and her father, Jacob, a police officer. Attended Salem Elementary School until your tenth birthday, when your father called into his station to report an unknown child in his house—"

356

"Stop," I muttered. Liam looked over his shoulder, trying to divide his attention between me and the boy reciting the sordid tale of my life.

"—but, bad luck, the PSFs beat the police to your house. Good luck, someone dropped the ball or they had other kiddies to pick up, because they didn't wait around long enough to question your parents, and thus, didn't pre-sort you. And then you came to Thurmond, and you managed to avoid their detecting you were Orange—"

"Stop!" I didn't want to hear this—I didn't want anyone to hear it.

"What's the matter with you?" Liam shouted. "Can't you see you're upsetting her?"

Clancy, maybe anticipating another hard shove, moved to the other side of his desk. "I'm excited to meet her, that's all. It's not often that you find another Orange."

A spark lit at the center of my chest, spreading quickly up to my brain. *He is an Orange. The rumors were right. He might actually be able to help me.*

"But . . . weren't you reformed?" I asked slowly. "Isn't that why they let you out?"

"You of all people should know they can't reform shit at Thurmond, Ruby," he said. "How is good ol' Thurmond, by the way? I had the dubious honor of being its first inmate— got to see them build the Mess Hall brick by brick. Did they really hang my picture up everywhere?"

A better question: Did he really think I was going to pull up a chair and shoot the breeze about the good old days?

Clancy sighed. "Anyway . . . if you're Ruby, then *you* must be Lee Stewart. I've read your file, too."

"Anything good in there?" Mike asked with a nervous laugh.

"The PSFs have been following your every move," Clancy said, leaning back in his chair. "Which means you need some place to lie low for a while, right?"

Liam hesitated a split second before nodding.

"You made a good choice coming here. You can stay as long as you need." Clancy rested his hands on his chest. "Now that I've managed to upset everyone, Mike, do you want to take them to a cabin and get them set up in the rotations?"

Mike nodded. "For the record, you didn't upset me, boss."

Clancy laughed, rich and slow. "Okay, good. Thanks for all of your hard work today, by the way. Sounds like it was a good haul."

"Like you wouldn't believe," Mike said, moving toward the door. He waved us after him, but he no longer looked at us with the same warmth. "Cabin eighteen is open, right?"

"Yeah, Ty and his guys went tribal on us," Clancy said. "I don't know that anyone has gone in to clean it since they left, though, so I apologize if it's a mess."

And then he was staring at me again, one corner of his lips turning up, then the other. A warm, fizzling sensation filled my head, sending my pulse spiking. I turned away and broke eye contact, but the image still flooded my mind, spilling in until I thought I might choke. In my mind's eye, I saw

Clancy and me alone in the same room, him on one knee, offering a rose in my direction.

Forgive me? His voice was loud in my ears, echoing as I stumbled down the stairs.

How had he done that? Waltzed right through every single one of my natural defenses. And why was my brain suddenly alive and reaching out for whoever was closest, whoever was stupid enough to let me in?

I lifted my face from where I had buried it against Liam's shoulder. When had I done that? When had we gotten outside—when had we walked all the way to the cabin?

Liam's eyes tried to catch mine as I pulled away. My head ached, physically *ached* for him. It was too dangerous to stand so close to him.

"Not right now," I whispered.

Liam's brows drew together, and his lips parted with something he wanted to say. After a moment, he only nodded and turned back toward the cabin, bounding up the steps.

I needed to get as far away from them as I could, at least until the trilling inside of my head died down. There was no plan or map involved; I just set off down a nearby path. A few kids, all strangers, called after me in concern, but I ignored them, following the smell of mud and molding leaves until I found the lake we had passed.

The trees and brush had overgrown the path down to the T-shaped wooden dock, and where there weren't plants in my way, there was a rope, along with a sign that warned DO NOT ENTER.

359

I slipped under it and kept heading down, not stopping until I sat on the edge of the old sun-bleached dock and put my head between my knees, listening to the sounds of kids laughing and yelling in the distance, wondering when the feeling would return to my legs long enough for me to stand, and when the imprint of Clancy Gray's voice would fade.

Alone, I thought, lying down on the old wood. Finally alone.

Dinner was served at exactly seven that night. There was no intercom or alarm system in the camp, but there were cowbells. Apparently that was a universal call for food, because once the first bell rang, others echoed back, spreading the noise through the cabins and trails, all the way down to where I sat studying my reflection in the dark water.

It was easy enough to find the action—two hundred–odd kids gathered around a raging bonfire to eat wasn't exactly subtle. My feet slowed the closer I came, watching as a few of the older boys threw more logs into the fire's grasping fingers. Rings of old logs provided makeshift seats for those who already had their food and didn't want to eat alone in their cabins.

The kids we had seen in the kitchen had set up a table full of what looked like slow cookers and were making runs between the office building and the fire to replenish them. Dozens of kids waited in line for their turn at the pots, their plastic bowls pressed against their chests in anticipation.

I spotted Liam straight off, standing rather than sitting on one of the logs. He had a bowl of chili in each hand and was scanning the area. Chubs would have walked right by him if Liam hadn't nudged him as he passed. He asked Chubs something, but I caught only part of his response.

"Uh, no thanks. I read *Lord of the Flies*. I know how this works—everyone starts dancing around the fire and painting their faces and worshipping a decapitated pig head and then someone gets hit by a boulder and plummets to their death—and, surprise, it's the fat kid in glasses." Liam started laughing, but even I could see how uncomfortable Chubs looked. "I think I'm going to play it safe and go read—and, hey, there's Ruby! You two can enjoy the degeneration of human decency without me."

Liam whirled around so fast his footing slipped, and he came dangerously close to dropping both bowls on the bushy-haired girls sitting beside him.

"Have fun," Chubs said as he hurried past me. I caught his sleeve and swung him back around.

"What's wrong?" I asked.

He shrugged, a sad smile curling the ends of his lips. "I'm just not up for it tonight, I guess."

I knew the feeling. After it being just the four of us alone for so long, suddenly being around so many people, even if they were kids like us, was a little stressful. If he hadn't liked it when one new person—me—had invaded his world, I could only imagine what this was doing to his nerves. "Well, if you change your mind, we'll be here."

Chubs patted my head fondly and continued up the dirt trail, back to our assigned cabin.

"What's gotten into him?" Liam asked, offering me the steaming bowl of food.

"I think he's just tired," I said, and left it at that. "Where's Zu?"

He nodded to the left, where, sure enough, Zu's smiling face appeared at the center of a small group of boys and girls her age. When she saw me, she waved. I wondered how it was possible for her face to be so vibrant. The Asian girl sitting next to her nodded as Zu gestured to her, as if knowing her every thought without her having to whisper a word. When Zu reached over to knock back the hood of the girl's "Virginia Is for Lovers" sweatshirt, she revealed a long, glossy black braid.

"Oh my God," I said, making the connection instantly.

"What wrong?"

"That kid was in your camp," I said. "I saw her in Zu's nightmare. They got separated."

"Really?" The dawning realization that spread across his face was adorable. "Guess that explains why they tackled one another to the ground earlier."

I laughed. "They did?"

"Yeah, they were rolling around like puppies in the grass—hey, Zu!" She looked our way again. "Come here a sec. No, bring your friend—"

When the two girls were on their feet, I was surprised to see the other girl stood a good four inches above Zu's head, though she looked like couldn't have been more than a year older than her.

Zu took the girl's hand and flounced over to us, grinning. She was back to wearing the hot pink dress.

"Hi there," Liam said, holding out his hand to the girl. "My name is Liam, and this is—"

"I know who you are," the girl interrupted. "Liam and Ruby." She crossed her arms over her chest. "Suzume told me all about you."

"*Told you*—told you, or . . ."

"Of course she didn't *tell* me," the girl huffed, earning a sharp elbow to her side. She turned and said something to Zu in Japanese, who, in turn, shook her head and reached up to tug the girl's braid.

"Okay, fine!" The tall girl turned back to us, flanked by the campfire. "I'm Hina. Suzume is my cousin."

"Oh, wow!" I said, looking to Zu. "Are you serious? That's amazing!"

She was bouncing on her toes, still smiling.

"And you were at Caledonia together," Liam said, slowly. "Zu, why didn't you mention it? We could have tried to track her down. Are you a Yellow, too?"

"I'm a Green," Hina said, pointing to her full head of hair. "Duh."

Zu gave us an apologetic shrug before tugging Hina away, back to the circle of younger kids who were engrossed in some kind of card game. Liam turned toward me with a look of pure amazement. "Did I just get sassed by a twelve-year-old?"

"I guess it runs in the family," I said, spinning my spoon around my bowl. The chili was warm, with a wonderful kick. I don't think I'd eaten anything other than the slop they'd served at Thurmond and junk food in almost seven years, and the fact that someone had put even the barest amount of effort into it . . . I had to go back and get seconds, thirds, until I physically could not stuff myself anymore.

363

Being so close to the fire with a belly full of delicious food was making me feel drowsy and safe. I slid down off the log so I was sitting on the ground, reclining against Liam's legs.

"That reminds me. . . ." Liam said. "Would you believe Zu actually started jumping up and down and clapping when I told her she had to get up at seven to go do some good ol'-fashioned book learnin' with the other Cubbies?"

"Cubbies?"

"Daily lessons. School." He tapped my nose with the clean end of his spoon. "Stick around, Ruby Tuesday, and you'll start picking up the cool-kid lingo, too."

When we finished eating, Liam set both of our bowls in one of the many plastic tubs floating by. The Blue controlling the one closest to us was a skinny kid, who looked like he weighed about half of what his tub did. I blinked once, twice, wondering if I was imagining it. It was the first time I had ever seen kids use their abilities so . . . frivolously. It was a strange contrast to what was otherwise a picture of normalcy. At least, what I assumed normalcy looked like. A few kids strummed on guitars or used their log as a drum set. Most were talking quietly, or playing card games.

Liam slid down behind me, finding just enough room between my back and the old log. The shimmering air around the flames, combined with the delicious heat, made my muscles turn to mush. His hand came up to brush the stray strands of hair off the back of my neck. I leaned back until I was resting against his chest, nestled between his knees.

364

"You okay now, darlin'?" he whispered in my ear. I nodded, my fingers finding the bare skin of his forearms, tracing the muscles and overlying veins there. On a discovery mission, searching for something I hadn't even realized I wanted until now. His skin was so soft, his hands warm and wide, knuckles bruised and torn with brittle scabs. I pressed my own hand on top of his, weaving our fingers together.

"I had to be alone for a little while, but I'm okay now."

"All right," he whispered. "But next time, don't go where I can't find you."

I didn't doze off so much as relax. It seemed like the longer I sat there, the quieter my head became, the more the aches and knots in my body worked themselves out, leaving me as soft as the dirt under us.

Eventually, someone brought out a decades-old boom box, and even the kids with guitars stopped playing in deference to the Beach Boys. I seemed to be the only one in the entire camp who didn't dance, but it was fun to watch the others. Zu, in particular, as she twisted her hips and threw her arms in the air—at least until she ran up to us and began to tug on our arms. I managed to beg off, but Liam didn't have nearly as much willpower.

They were both laughing when the track switched to "Barbara Ann," twirling when "Fun, Fun, Fun" came on. I should have known something was up when they both turned to me wearing identical devious looks.

Liam held up a finger in my direction, beckoning me over to him. I laughed and shook my hands in front of me. "No!"

He grinned—his first real grin in days—and I felt something tug at my belly button. The sensation was warm, tingling, and familiar. Liam pretended he was hauling a line in, and Zu actually stopped her frolicking to act it out with him. Their faces were flushed and glowing with a sheen of sweat. With nothing but fine dust and mud between us, I slid right over to them—right into Liam's outstretched hands.

"No fair," I whined.

"Come on, Green," he said. "You could use a good dance."

Zu spun around us, waving her arms in time to "Wouldn't It Be Nice." I put my hand over Liam's, letting him drop it over one of his shoulders. He took my other hand without asking, and held it lightly in his own. "Step up on my feet."

I gave him what I hoped was an incredulous look.

"Trust me," he said. "Come on, before our song is over."

Against all my better judgment, I put my feet over his, waiting for him to wince at my weight. At least his bones felt sturdy under mine.

"A little closer, Green; I won't bite."

I leaned forward, close enough that my cheek was resting against his shoulder. Liam's hand tightened around mine, and I found my other hand bunching the fabric of his shirt. And I was embarrassed because I was positive he could feel my heart hammering in my chest.

"No spinning," I said. I wasn't sure if my head or heart could take it. Up close, he was so warm, and so beautiful. I was already dizzy enough.

"No spinning," he agreed.

When we began to move, it wasn't really dancing—just some glorified swaying. Back and forth, nice and easy. For once, my brain was perfectly content to keep its hands to itself. My muscles moved slow, like honey. We were completely out of sync with the song, and then we weren't even moving at all. My cheek rested on his shoulder. The hand on the small of my back slipped under my shirt and curled against the skin there.

When the bells rang again, this time signaling lights-out across the camp, there was an audible groan, loud enough to get Liam chuckling. I didn't realize how tired I was until we separated.

"Bed time," he called, waving Zu over. She stood, brushing herself off, signaling something to the group of kids she was leaving.

The fire popped and hissed, buckling under a steady stream of water from a nearby hose. The sound it made was like an animal having the life squeezed out of it. And when the light was finally gone, settling down into a pile of unimpressive embers spread out among the ash, there was nothing but a screen of smoke to separate me from where Clancy Gray sat on the other side of the pit, watching me with dark eyes.

TWENTY-TWO

THAT WAS SOMETHING CLANCY GRAY LIKED TO DO, apparently—watch me.

Watch me while I sat out on the porch helping Zu lace her new tennis shoes before walking with her and Hina to the cabin serving as the classroom.

Watch me tease Chubs for being the first and only one to get bitten by a tick.

Watch me wait by the fire pit with Lee for Mike to arrive with what our duties would be during our time at East River.

All this watching from the window on the second story of the office, where he appeared to control everything and do nothing.

Mike had mentioned that everyone older than thirteen would be responsible for doing some work; I just hadn't realized that the assignments were chosen for you. I didn't mind helping out in the pantry, organizing and counting our supplies—but I would have so preferred being out with Chubs

in the camp's small garden, or running around the forest with Liam on security detail. It was strange not to spend my entire day with them.

The kids I worked with were nice enough; more than nice, actually. Most had never seen the inside of a camp but then again, I had never cooked a meal, so it wasn't like any of us were winning in the life experience department. What I liked most was their brand of pluck. Lizzie, for instance, had been hiding out at East River for close to two years, having narrowly escaped capture by PSFs who had pulled her parents' car over in Maryland.

"You just got out and ran?" I asked.

"Like the wind," she confirmed. "Didn't have anything on me at all, 'cept what I was wearing. I tried to meet up with my parents again, but they never went back to our old house. I got picked up by a tribe of Greens and brought here."

That was another thing: most of the kids here were either Green or Blue, with a small tight-knit group of Yellows that didn't really socialize outside of their own circle. Lizzie claimed that there used to be more, but the Slip Kid had given them permission to head out and form a tribe of their own.

"He gave them permission?" I repeated, marking down how many boxes of cereal we had left.

"Yeah, and there are other requirements, too." That, from Dylan, a small-boned kid who had only recently finished his Cubbies lessons. He claimed the nickname came from the wood shelving units Clancy had built to store all of their books and schoolwork.

369

"You have to have at least a group of five," he continued. "And then Clancy has to determine whether or not it's safe, and you have to swear on your life not to reveal anything about the camp, unless it's to another kid in need, and then you can only reveal the clue. It's to keep everyone safe. It would kill him if something happened to a kid because of him."

I felt myself soften a little then. It wasn't so much that I didn't trust Clancy's motivations; he just unnerved me. When someone takes such an interest in you, you have to wonder what it is exactly they're searching for in your face.

"What are you *doing*?"

All three of us looked over to the door, where Clancy stood stiff and still, staring at me. The wind from the open door behind him tugged at his dark hair, causing it to stand on end. Something inside of me coiled at his expression, but it wasn't fear.

"We're sorting," Lizzie said, confused. "Is something wrong?"

Clancy snapped out of whatever daze he had been stuck in. "Yeah, sorry, it's just—Ruby, would you mind coming with me for a second? I think there was some confusion on your assignment."

I passed my clipboard back to Lizzie, wondering why her eyes narrowed at me.

"I was assigned to Storage," I said, when we were standing outside on the porch.

"I didn't assign you anything," he said. "I specifically told Mike that."

I'd like to think that I wasn't the type of person to be easily intimidated by other kids—even the ones that were taller, stronger, or better armed than I was. So I'm not sure why it hit me then that I was talking to *Clancy Gray*. The son of the most powerful man in the country. A blue-blooded American prince, who wore his black polo shirt with the collar popped under a matching cable-knit sweater. He was even wearing a leather belt.

I crossed my arms over my chest. "I'm more than capable of pulling my weight."

Out in the sunlight, he was far less intimidating than he had been in the shade. And shorter. It was possible his reputation had added a few imaginary inches, but he was only a bit taller than I was, which meant both Liam and Chubs stood a nearly a full head over him. Not that it did anything to knock his title of The Most Attractive Person I Had Ever Seen.

Clancy was lean but not slight, well-kept but not groomed, composed but not comfortable. I thought, as the wind blew against us, that he might have been wearing some spicy cologne, but that seemed ridiculous.

I was glad we were out on the porch, where everyone by the fire pit could see us. I didn't think he was going to hurt me, or anything like that—why would he? I felt my hands clasp together in front of me, then move to my side, then rise up to cup my elbows, like they couldn't figure out what they wanted to be doing.

I hadn't forgotten my whole purpose in coming here, but I couldn't bring myself to ask for his help. He clearly had a good grasp on his own abilities if he was voluntarily diving into people's minds—the question should have come as naturally as breathing.

If he had these kids following his every whim and order, it had to be because he was a good guy, right? People didn't help other people just for their health. Clancy had the kind of confidence that made him the sun at the center of East River's galaxy. Everything and everyone orbited around his light.

So why couldn't I bring myself to ask? Why were my hands still shaking?

"I know you probably won't ever come around to liking me after our introduction," he said, "but I am sorry. It didn't occur to me that you were keeping that information secret."

"It's fine," I said. "But what does that have to do with my work assignment?"

For a few moments, he didn't say anything at all. He just . . . stared.

"Will you stop?" I muttered, feeling both flustered and annoyed at once. "If I say you're forgiven, will you stop doing that?"

His mouth turned up in a handsome grin. "No."

Clancy, who apparently had never been taught about respecting someone's personal space, took a step forward, and I took a step back, off the porch, my feet sinking into the sticky mud. Instead of backing off, he seemed to take it as a challenge, and came toward me again. For whatever reason, mostly the flutter of nerves in my gut, I let him.

"Listen," he said, finally. "The reason I told Mike not to assign you anything is because I'm hoping that you'll come work with me."

"Excuse me?"

"Come on, you heard me." His hand closed over my arm, and it was like a bee had been set loose inside of my skull. My brain seemed to lurch full speed back into life, flooding with milky-white images of the two of us sitting in front his desk, staring at each other as a fire devoured everything around us.

The images *he* was flooding into *my* mind.

I don't know how he did it, but it was so *real*. The image was burning me up from the inside out, blistering my lungs. Pockets of acrid smoke bubbled up under my skin, until it felt like I was about to burst open. My vision burned to black at the edges. Fire bloomed on my clothes, singeing my hair.

This is not real, this is not real, this is NOT REAL—

Clancy must have let go, or I must have found a way to twist away, because just as quickly as the fire came, it went back out, dispersing in three shaky exhales.

"You can't block me," he said, his eyes wide. "Do you even know how to use your abilities? The file the League had on you made it sound like you could control it."

Wasn't it obvious? I shook my head. *That's why I'm here*, I wanted to say. *That's why I need you*.

His gaze flicked down over me, from head to toe and back up again. When he spoke, his voice was soft. Sympathetic. "Look, I know how it is. You don't think I struggled with this, too? How lonely it is to not be able to touch

373

someone the way you want to, how terrifying it is to be trapped in somebody else's head without knowing the way out? Ruby, everything I've learned I had to teach myself, and it was awful. I want to save you from that. I can teach you things, tricks—how to use your talents the way they're meant to be used."

I hoped he couldn't see the way my hands were shaking. Oh my God, he had offered—I hadn't even had to ask—and I still couldn't say a damn thing.

Clancy's posture relaxed, and when he touched me again, flicking my braid back over my shoulder, there was no ill will behind it. "Think about it, okay? If you decide you want to, just come to the office. I'll clear my schedule for you."

I pressed my lips together, biting down hard on my tongue.

"There's nothing wrong with wanting to know how to use your abilities," Clancy added. "That's the only way we're ever going to beat them."

Beat who?

"There are so few of us left," he said. "Until you showed up in the system, I actually thought I was the only one."

"Well, there's at least one more. His name is Martin—"

"And he's with the Children's League," he finished. "I know. I accessed their report on him. Creepy kid. When I said *us* I meant the non-psychotic Oranges."

I snorted.

"I'll think about it," I said, finally. I was pinned under his dark gaze again; the hair on my arms standing on end, like a

374

whisper of electricity had run over it. I took an unknowing step closer to him.

"Listen to your gut," Clancy said, turning to head back inside the Office. A cluster of kids called out to him from where they were setting up lunch near the fire pit and, ever the president's son, he smiled and waved at them real pretty.

Listen to your gut.

So why was it at odds with my head?

I made a beeline for the wood dock I had discovered the afternoon before, needing to find some way to wash out the jitters racing through my heart. My mind felt tangled with the possibilities.

Clancy Gray had just offered me everything I could have asked for. A way to avoid repeating what had happened to my parents and Sam. A way to be with Liam, to find Grams, to not live in constant fear of what I could do to them. So why hadn't my *yes* come tumbling out, then?

I ducked under the rope tying off the path to the lake and made it all the way down the trail before I realized anything was amiss.

"Crap," I said when I saw him.

"Oh no—no, no, no," Chubs said. The goofy grin dropped off his face and he stopped throwing bread crusts out to the ducks gathered in the water. "This is *my* secret hideout. No Rubys allowed."

"I found it first!" I huffed, plopping down next to him.

"You most certainly did not."

"Try a week ago, while you were unpacking."

He balked at that. "Well . . . fine. But I got here first today."

"Aren't you supposed to be on Garden duty?"

"Got tired of hearing some girl coo about how smart the Slip Kid is for making them plant carrots." He leaned back. "Aren't you on Storage duty?"

I looked down at where my hands had clenched into fists. When I didn't answer, Chubs set the bread bag aside and sat up straight.

"Hey, are you all right?" He put a cool hand to my forehead. "You look like you're going to be sick. Are you experiencing any migraines or dizziness?"

That was an understatement. I croaked out a laugh.

"Oh." He pulled his hand away. "*That* kind of head trouble."

I lay back against the rough wood and threw my arm over my eyes, hoping the darkness might help dampen the headache. "You said Jack taught you how to use your abilities?"

"Pretty much," he said. "That was the only way I was ever going to learn—if some other kid taught me, I mean. It just took a while to decide."

"Why?"

"Because I thought that if I didn't use them, they'd eventually go away," Chubs said, quietly. "I thought everything might go back to normal. There's scientific evidence that if we stop using parts of our brains, those sections will eventually cease to function, you know." After a moment, he asked, "Did Clancy offer to help you with your abilities?"

I nodded. "I told him I'd think about it."

"What's there to think about?" Chubs smacked me on the stomach with his book. "Didn't you say that you didn't know how to control it?"

"Well, yeah, but—" *I'm afraid of how much I don't know.*

"You need to be able to control it, otherwise it'll always control you," he said. "It'll scare you and manipulate you until you go crazy, die, or they find the cure. And guess which one of those things will probably happen first."

The lunch bell sounded—two rings, for second meal. Chubs stood and stretched, throwing the rest of the bread out into the water.

"You really think they're going to find a cure?" I asked.

"My dad used to say that anything was possible when you put your mind to it." His mouth twisted into a humorless smile. At the mention of his father, my stomach clenched.

"You still haven't had a chance to send them a message."

"I've asked around, but there's only one computer in this entire godforsaken place, and only one person gets to use it."

That's right. The silver laptop on Clancy's desk.

"Did you ask him if you could use it for a few minutes?"

"Yeah," Chubs said, as the fire pit came into view. It looked like they were handing out sandwiches and apples. "He said no. Apparently it's a 'security risk' if someone other than him touches it."

I shook my head. "I'll ask tomorrow. Maybe I can convince him."

"Could you?" Chubs grabbed my arm, his face lightening considerably. "Will you tell him that we have a very important letter to deliver, but we need to be able to look up Jack's father's new address? Tell him we'll do anything—no, tell him that I will personally lick every single pair of shoes he owns clean."

"How about I just tell him that it's the whole reason we came here in the first place," I said, "and leave your tongue out of it?"

Chubs waited until I had taken my sandwich from the table before pulling me away. I thought he might want to eat back at the cabin or even the dock, but we wandered until we found Liam.

He and a few of the other guys on the security team were on a break from their rounds and had found themselves a nice clearing in the trees. It was just wide enough to square off into two small teams for a quick game of hover ball, otherwise known as football with no hands. Chubs and I found an old tree trunk to share, ignoring the small group of female spectators who had gathered to cheer the teams on.

A tall redhead with an explosion of freckles on his face levitated the old football at the start of a play. He ran alongside it, trying to keep both it and himself out of the reach of the others. Liam, at one point, had the football an inch in front of him, but his hands were too slow and his footwork too bad to catch it when it was tossed to him.

"Keep your eye on the ball, butterfingers!" I called. Liam's head whipped around in our direction. Just as his gaze locked on mine, Mike, who had the football at that point, mowed him over to get to the makeshift end zone.

Chubs and I cringed as Liam hit the ground and knocked his head against one of the old trees' roots.

"Wow," I said. "He wasn't kidding about sucking at sports."

"It'd be funny if it weren't so damn sad."

The other boys were too busy laughing to keep the ball in the air. Liam stayed on the ground, his face flushed red, but his entire body shaking with laughter. He lifted his shirt to wipe the sweat off his face, giving me, along with every other girl present, a glimpse of skin.

This time, I was the one blushing.

One of the guys I didn't recognize jogged over to Liam and helped him up, patting him on the shoulder. They laughed together like they had known each other since preschool.

But that was Liam for you—he joked about Zu making friends at the drop of a hat, but he was the same way. But Chubs and I were perfectly content to sit by ourselves, watching, waiting, but not dipping our toes into the ocean. Maybe we had just gotten too used to being alone—and maybe that needed to change.

The next morning, at exactly 9:21, I found myself standing outside of Clancy Gray's office, my hand raised and ready to knock. The only thing preventing me, besides the nerves hula-hooping my guts, was the conversation happening on the other side of the door.

"—sure we have the kind of numbers to do that. If I sent the amount of kids we'd need, there wouldn't be enough left here to maintain watch." It was a girl's voice, soft but not sweet. Olivia, most likely, if they were talking about security.

"I get what you're saying, Liv, but it would be a waste to miss this opportunity," Clancy was saying. "We're getting low on medical supplies, and Leda Corp has stopped running as many trucks up through our area."

"Are you going on another one of your trips?" she pressed. "Isn't that when you usually pick up tips about shipments?"

"Why do you ask?"

"It's just . . . you haven't gone on one in almost a year," Olivia said. "And you used to go all the time. I know we haven't been hurting for supplies, but maybe if you met with your source . . ."

"No," Clancy said, with finality. "I can't leave the camp anymore. It's not safe."

The floorboards creaked. "Did something come up on the PSF scanner?" came Hayes's gruff voice.

"They heard about the fruit stunt, obviously," Clancy said. "It would have been hard to miss, considering you mutilated that driver."

"Why d'ya have to say it like that?"

"Because you should have just left him there like I told you to. I appreciate you wanting to spread the symbol, but couldn't you have spray-painted it on the truck?"

"Are you worried this'll be bad for our *image*?" Olivia's voice dripped annoyance.

"Most people are going to have a hard enough time accepting that we're not monsters, without reports about us maiming innocent people," Clancy said. "So, please, keep spreading the black. Keep using the symbol. Just . . . try for some subtlety."

"Some what tea?" Hayes asked.

"I'm sorry to cut our meeting short, but it seems like you both have things under control and I have someone waiting for me," Clancy said. I pulled myself away from the door. "Liv, plan the hit. I'll worry about our numbers."

I took a few steps back down the staircase, but it was pointless to pretend that I hadn't been listening. The door opened, and the girl—Olivia—was the first to appear. She was tall and willowy, with legs for days and a tan that made her skin glow.

I shook my head and turned to allow her and Hayes to squeeze by. Olivia was probably about my age, but she looked so much older. She looked like what I imagined twenty would feel like. When I looked up again, Clancy was leaning against the doorframe, grinning.

"You came." He waved me inside and guided me toward his desk. Sitting down in one of the chairs, I had a fleeting look at the other side of his room, where the curtain had been restrung.

Clancy took his usual seat behind his desk, rocking the chair back as he smiled. "What made you change your mind?"

"It's . . . like you said," I mumbled. "There are so few of us left." *And I want to know how I can be around the people I love and not be terrified of erasing myself.*

"I read on the League's network that they weren't able to find any other Oranges aside from you and Martin," Clancy

381

said. "Most of the Reds were killed, apparently. That puts us at the head of the pack."

"I guess," I said. Another thought occurred to me. "How do you have access to the League's network? And the PSFs?" I gestured around the room. "*Any* of this?"

"I have friends everywhere," Clancy said, simply. His fingers drummed against his desk. "And my father leaves me alone because he wouldn't be able to stand the outrage if I expose the fact that there is no rehabilitation program, not for people like you and me."

"Me and you," I repeated.

Clancy ran a hand through his hair. "The first thing you need to understand, Ruby, is that we're not like the others. Me and you . . . everyone classified as Orange. We're different. Special. No—no, wait, I see you rolling your eyes, but you have to listen, okay? Because the second thing you have to understand, is that everyone—my father, the camp controllers, the scientists, the PSFs, the Children's League—they've been lying to you this entire time. We're special not because of what we are, but what they can't make us into."

"You're not making any sense," I said.

He stood up and came around the desk to sit next to me. "Would it help if I told you my story first?" My eyes flicked up to meet his. "If I do, you have to promise that it stays between us."

Keeping secrets. That, I could do.

"All right," he said, "give me your hand. I'm going to have to show you."

—✦—

When I had slipped into other minds, there had always been a queasy feeling of sinking involved in it. More often than not, I found myself dropped in the middle of a swamp of dimly lit memories and unrestrained feelings with no map, no flashlight, and no easy way of finding the way out.

But there was nothing frightening about Clancy's mind. His memories were bright and crisp, full of blooming images and colors. It felt like he had taken my hand there, too, and was guiding me down a long hallway of windows into his past. We only stopped long enough for me to glance inside each of them.

The office was plain, stuffed full of gunmetal gray filing cabinets, but little else. It could have been anywhere; the white paint was fresh enough that it bubbled on the wall. But I recognized the beginnings of crescent-shaped machine in the back corner and the man staring me down from across the card table serving as his desk. He was plump and balding at his hairline—and a permanent fixture in the Infirmary. I watched his lips move in a soundless explanation, my eyes drifting down to the crisp stack of papers on the desk in front of him. My eyes kept drifting down to his hand resting against the table, weighing down a sheet of once-folded paper that was trying to curl back in on itself. There at the top of it—the White House emblem. The words went into crystal focus, and I felt my eyes jump over them, drinking them in with disbelief. *Dear Sirs, You may have my permission to run tests and experimental treatments on my son, Clancy James Beaumont Gray, provided these do not leave visible scars.*

The lights in the office grew brighter and brighter, bleaching out the memory. When they faded again, I was in a much different room in the Infirmary, this one all blue tiles and beeping monitors. *No!* I thought, trying to jerk free of the Velcro restraints that held me down against the metal table. I knew what this place was.

The overhead lights were drawn down closer to my face by a gloved hand. At the corner of my vision, I saw the scientists and doctors in their white scrubs, setting up machines and computers around me. My jaw was clenched shut around the leather muzzle they had strapped to the back of my head, and hands kept my head still as wires and monitors were hooked up. I struggled again, twisting my neck far enough to catch sight of a table lined with scalpels and small drills; I saw my reflection in the nearby observation windows—young, pale with terror, a mirror image of the portraits that would later hang across the camp.

The harsh light from above grew and swelled, eating the scene. When it faded, the memory had changed again. My eyes fell first on the hand I was shaking, then slid up to the unfocused eyes of the same scientist I had seen before. The men hovering around us all had that murky quality to their expressions—blank smiles, blanker eyes. I squared my shoulders, a small thrill of victory working its way through my center as I moved through the main gate to the waiting black car. The man in the suit that welcomed me in with a perfunctory pat on the shoulder wasn't the president, but he appeared in nearly every memory that fired by next, ushering me onto stages in school auditoriums, outside domed state-capital buildings, in front of cameras at the centers of small towns. Each time, I would be handed the same set of note cards to read, be faced with the same expressions of hope and deep grief from the crowd. Always, my lips began to form the same words: *My name is Clancy Gray, and I am here to tell you how the camp rehabilitation program saved my life.*

Another light, this time from a camera's flash. When the shock of it faded, I was looking up into a face that was an older, weathered version of my own. The photographer flipped the monitor around for us to see the portrait, and I was no longer seeing myself as a boy, but a young man— fifteen, maybe even sixteen. As the photographer set up his equipment again, this time across the room, I put a hand on the president's back, guiding him around the couches, to the great dark wood desk. The rosebushes were scratching intently at the windows, but I directed his focus to the sheet of paper waiting there for him, and compelled him to pick up the pen. When he finished signing, he turned to me with an unfocused gaze and a numb, unknowing smile.

Weeks must have passed, months, maybe even years—I felt the exhaustion creep through me, wrapping itself like a heavy chain around my center. It was dark now; I couldn't place the time of night, though I saw that it was a hotel room, and not a particularly good one. I was staring up at the ceiling, half buried under the covers, when a figure seemed to peel itself out from the shadows of the closet. It was fast, almost too much for me to keep up with. A man in a black mask, the metallic gleam of a gun—I threw my covers off of me and kicked my leg out, sending the attacker stumbling back. The shot went off from his gun with a combustion of light and little sound. The smell of it scorched my nostrils.

I was flipped onto my back, one of the man's forearms braced against my neck, crushing the fragile rings of cartilage. My hands lashed out, hitting the rough carpet, the nightstand, and, finally his face. Not even the terror pulsing through every inch of me kept me from crashing into his mind.

STOP! I felt my lips form the word, but I couldn't hear myself. *STOP!*

And the man did, with the blank look of someone whose skull had just been cracked open and exposed to freezing air. He sat back, his gun on the floor at his side.

I was coughing and hacking, trying to bring air into my lungs, but I grabbed the gun and stuffed it into the waistband of my pajamas. I stopped long enough to grab my winter coat from where it had been thrown across the room's desk chair, and then I was outside, in the hallway, staring at the place where a man should have been posted outside my door to guard me. And I knew, I *knew* what was going on. I knew what would happen to me if someone were to find me alive in the morning.

I was running down the hotel's stairs, out through the kitchens, out back past the Dumpsters and through the parking lot. Running, my chest on fire, hearing the sound of voices shouting after me, boots pounding on the pavement. Running for the trees, the darkness—

"Ruby—*Ruby!*"

386

I came back to myself in Clancy's office bit by bit, with a headache severe enough that I had to put my face between my legs to avoid throwing up all over myself.

"They tried to kill you," I said, when I finally found my voice. "Who?"

"Who do you think?" Clancy's voice was dry. "That man was one of the Secret Service agents who were supposed to be guarding me."

"But that doesn't make any sense," I pressed the back of my hand to my forehead, squeezing my eyes shut against the dizziness. "If they were carting you around and using you to explain the rehab program, then why . . . ?"

"Because he figured out that I hadn't been rehabbed at all," he said. "My father, I mean. The only reason they let me out of Thurmond is because I made them think that I *had* been cured. But I got too ambitious. I tried to play my father by influencing him, and I got caught." Clancy trailed off for a moment. "He was worried that the truth about the camps would get out, I'm sure, but he couldn't just take me out of the public eye, not when he'd been the one to thrust me into it. No, I think in his mind, it was easier to just get rid of me altogether, before I could make trouble. I can only imagine what kind of spin he'd put on my murder to get back in the sympathetic graces of his fellow Americans."

I stared at him for a long while, speechless.

How did you survive that life? I wanted to ask. *How are you you, and not the monster they would have turned you into?*

"After I got out that night I met Hayes, and then Olivia, and then others. We found this place and went to work, and all the while my father couldn't put a bounty out on me, not without exposing the truth about me and his rehab program. He had to make up some lie about me attending college, to get the press off his back." Clancy smiled then. "So, you see, I did win in the end."

He rose from his chair, reaching out a hand. I took it without being conscious of it, feeling some calm wash over me as he squeezed my fingers. My head was silent. I felt myself lean forward.

"When I heard your story, I knew I had to meet you. I had to make sure that you knew the truth about what was going on, so you wouldn't be caught in the dark the way I was."

"The truth?" I looked up, startled. "What do you mean?"

Clancy didn't release my hand; he only sat on the edge of his desk in front of me. "The woman who broke you out of Thurmond—the League agent? What did she tell you about the White Noise they used that day?"

"That the camp controllers had embedded a frequency in it that only Oranges, Reds, and Yellows could detect," I said. He must have known about that—they used the same method to broadcast the location of the camp. "That they were trying to pick out any of the dangerous ones that were still hiding out."

Clancy released my hand and reached back to turn his laptop so it faced us. On the screen was a snapshot of my face on the morning they had brought us into camp, but the text beside it wasn't my history.

"Read the second paragraph aloud."

I looked up at him, confused, but did as he asked. "'Camp Controller Harris discovered the discrepancy in the Calm Control at 05:23 the following morning, after noticing an underlying frequency that had been added without his consent.'" I paused, licking my dry lips. "'Upon further investigation of the recording devices in the Mess Hall, he came to the conclusion that the outbreak of violence there that resulted in the use of the Calm Control at approximately11:42 was directly provoked by undercover operatives from the terrorist group the Children's League. He believes these same operatives planted an identification frequency in the Calm Control. Psi subjects 3285 and 5312 who were taken from camp boundaries at approximately 03:34 by a Children's League operative, are now believed to have been mistakenly identified as Green upon their initial classification. . . .'"

"Keep going," Clancy said, when my voice trailed off.

"'Subjects 3285 and 5312 are believed to be highly dangerous. Orders have been issued for their immediate recapture and reprocessing'—*reprocessing?*" My eyes flew up again. "But the way this is written . . . they didn't know . . . they didn't . . . Are you trying to tell me that they had no idea I was an Orange until *after* I got out?"

Clancy nodded. "It sounds that way."

"Then I wasn't in any danger after all? They wouldn't have killed me?"

"Oh, you were definitely in danger," he said. "They had all of the pieces, and it just took one curious mind to put it all together. But if you're asking whether or not you would have been caught if the League hadn't planted the frequency—then the answer to that is no, probably not."

"Then why did they do it?" I demanded. "It seems like a huge risk to take to only get a few kids."

"A few extremely valuable, *rare* kids," he corrected. "Kids that would have been killed otherwise."

Seeing my expression, he added, not unkindly, "You didn't really think they let any of the kids like us live, did you? Not Oranges. Yellows, yes, because their threat can be contained, but not Oranges."

I passed a hand over my face. "What about the Reds, then? They were killed, too?"

"No," Clancy said. His voice became quiet, hesitant. "They had a much worse fate."

I waited for him to continue, hands twisting in my lap.

"The president's classified program." Clancy crossed his arms over his chest, leaning back. "Project Jamboree. Dear old Dad's been training himself a special army using all of the Reds they took from the camps. So you can see why . . ." He cleared his throat. "You can see why the League would be interested in finding any particularly dangerous kids for their own."

I shook my head, dropping my face into my hands. Of all of the scenarios I had imagined—of all the things I thought had happened to those kids—this was too insane for me to have ever dreamed up.

"How could they force them into this?" I asked, my voice sounding hollow to my own ears. "Why did they agree?"

"What other choice do they have?" Clancy asked. "They were made to think that if they didn't cooperate, something would happen to their families. They underwent a special conditioning program to make them think that they were needed and cared for absolutely. Before my father and his advisers figured out I was influencing them, I was able to supervise enough of the program to ensure that they *would* be cared for—better than if they had been in camps, at least." He shook his head. "Don't be afraid for them. They'll get out from under my father's control one day."

And they're not dead, I thought; there's that.

"Ruby."

I looked up, feeling cold down to my guts.

"Let me show you what I know," he whispered, his other hand rising to brush the hair off my cheek. The clenched mass of nerves in my stomach eased at the touch, and I felt what few suspicions I had left about him unwinding. We were the same, in the ways that mattered. He wanted to help me, even though I had nothing to offer him in return.

"No one will be able to hurt you or change you if you can fight them off," he said, softly.

It wasn't depression that drove me forward—it wasn't even self-pity. It was a pure, distilled strand of hatred, weaving its way through my core. I thought the Slip Kid would be able to help me reclaim my old life, but now I knew that wasn't enough. I needed him to help me protect my future. When I spoke, my words burned the air between us.

"Teach me."

TWENTY-THREE

JUST BECAUSE CLANCY HAD ALL THAT POWER, IT didn't mean he actually used it. It was strange to me that someone who could influence the thoughts of others had been born with a personality that naturally drew people to him. I witnessed it firsthand, when he offered to give me a tour of the camp.

Clancy waved at the few kids in black around the fire pit. His presence sent a buzz through the air. Smiles bloomed on every face we passed, and there wasn't a single person that didn't wave at us or call out some kind of greeting, even if it was just a quick, "Yo!"

"Do you ever talk to any of them about what you've been through?" I asked.

He glanced at me out of the corner of his eye, as if the question had startled him. I watched as he tucked his hands in the back pockets of his pants, his shoulders slumping with his thoughts.

"They've put their trust in me," he said, with a small, sad smile. "I don't want to worry them. They have to believe I can take care of them, otherwise our system wouldn't work."

This "system" was something else. It's one thing to carve the Psi symbol into the side of buildings and string up banners over porches, but to actually internalize the message?

My first true example of this came when the girl in charge of the camp's gardens stomped up to us on the main trail and demanded that Clancy punish three kids who she believed had been stealing fruit under her nose.

It took me two seconds of listening to Clancy talk the situation out to realize that the way of life at East River wasn't built on a foundation of hard and fast rules, but rested almost entirely on his good judgment and what everyone under him perceived to be fair.

The accused were three Green boys, only a few months out of Cubbies. The girl in charge of the Garden had left them sitting in the dark dirt like ducks in a row. Each wore black shirts, but their jeans were in different states of disarray. I stood off to the side as Clancy knelt in front of them, completely unbothered by the wet earth staining his own pressed pants.

"Did you steal that fruit?" Clancy asked gently. "Please tell me the truth."

The three boys exchanged looks. It fell on the larger one sitting in the middle to answer. "Yes, we did. We're very sorry."

I raised my brows.

"Thank you for being honest," Clancy said. "Can I ask you why?"

The boys were silent for a few minutes. Finally, through some coaxing, Clancy got the truth again. "Pete has been really sick and hasn't been able to come to meals. He didn't want anyone to know, because he thought he'd get in trouble for not coming to Cleaning Duty this week, and he—he didn't want to let you down. We're sorry, we're *so sorry*."

"I understand," Clancy said. "But if Pete is really sick, you should have told me."

"You said at the last camp meeting that the med stuff was low. He didn't want to take any medicine, in case someone else needed it."

"It sounds like he needs it, though, if he's too weak to come to meals," Clancy pointed out. "You know that when you take food from the garden, there's a chance that it could throw off the meals we have planned for everyone."

The boys nodded, looking miserable. Clancy looked up at the kids gathered around us and asked, "What would you like them to do in return for taking the fruit?"

The girl in charge opened her mouth, but an older boy stepped up and leaned the rake in his hands against the simple fence surrounding the garden. "If they're willing to help weed for a few days, a couple of us will take turns sitting with Pete and making sure he gets meals and medicine."

Clancy nodded. "That sounds fair. What does everyone else think?"

I thought the girl in charge was going to stamp her foot in anger when everyone else agreed on that "punishment." She was deeply unhappy with the outcome, if the red in her cheeks was any indication. "This isn't just a one-time problem, Clancy," she said, walking us out of the garden. "People think they can just come in here and take what they want, and it's not like we can lock it like the storeroom!"

"I promise I'll put it on the agenda at our camp meeting next month," Clancy said with one of his smiles. "It'll be right at the top of new business."

That seemed to satisfy her, at least for now. With one curious look flung in my direction, the Empress of Vegetables turned on her heel and marched back into her domain.

"Wow," I said, "she's a real gem."

He shrugged, absentmindedly fiddling with his right ear. "She has a valid point. If we start running low on food in the storeroom, we have to lean on the gardens, and if that's been picked over, we're in trouble. I think everyone here has come to understand how interconnected life is at East River. Hey—do you mind if I stop by and visit Pete?"

I smiled. "Of course not."

The little boy was buried under a mound of blankets—if the bare mattresses around it were any indication, the other boys had gladly donated theirs to his pile. When his flushed face finally emerged from the covers, I said hello and introduced myself. Clancy stayed to speak with him for a good fifteen minutes, but I waited outside in the fresh air, watching the comings and goings of the camp. Kids waved and smiled at me, like I had been there for years, not a few days. I waved back, something tightening in my chest. I don't know when it had dawned on me, or if it had been a slow, creeping realization, but I had begun to understand that black—the color that I had trained myself to fear and hate—was the same thing that allowed these kids to feel a small measure of pride and solidarity.

"You'll never feel alone here," Clancy said, shutting the cabin door behind him. We walked to the laundry building next, then made a stop by the wash houses to test the faucets and make sure the lights were still working. Every now and then, someone stopped Clancy to ask a question or air a complaint, but he was never anything other than patient and understanding. I watched him unravel a misunderstanding between cabin mates, take suggestions for dinner, and give his opinion on whether the security team needed more kids assigned to it.

By the time we reached the cabin that served as the Cubbies' classroom, I was dead on my feet. Clancy, however, was ready to give his weekly lesson on U.S. history.

The room was small and crowded, but well lit and decorated with colorful posters and drawings. I spotted Zu and her pink gloves even before I saw the teenage girl at the front of the room tracing a finger down the length of the Mississippi River on an old map of the United States. Hina sat next to Zu, of course, frantically scribbling down notes. I suppose it shouldn't have surprised me, but the kids actually cheered when Clancy appeared in the doorway. The girl relinquished the front of the room to him immediately.

"Alllll right, alllll right," Clancy began. "Who can tell me where we left off?"

"Pilgrims!" a dozen voices chimed in.

"*Pilgrims?*" he continued. "What are those? How about you, Jamie? Do you remember who the Pilgrims were?"

A girl about Zu's age sat straight up. "People in England were being mean to them because of their religion, so they sailed to America and landed at Plymouth Rock."

"Can anyone tell me what they did after they got there?"

About ten hands shot in the air. He picked a little boy close to him—he might have been a Green, but he could just as easily have been a Yellow or Blue. My usual method of distinguishing kids from one another was failing me now that we were all mixed together. Which, I suppose, was the point.

"They set up a colony," the boy answered.

"You got it. It was the second English colony, after the one set up in Jamestown in 1607—not too far from where we are now, actually!" Clancy picked up the map the teacher had been using and pointed out both places. "While they were on the *Mayflower*, they created the Mayflower Compact, which was an agreement that guaranteed everyone would cooperate and act in a way that would be beneficial to the colony. When they arrived, they faced a lot of hardships. But they all worked together and created a community where they were free from the English crown's rule and could practice their faith openly." He stopped pacing for a moment, casting his dark eyes out over his audience. "Sound familiar?"

Beside me, Zu was all wide eyes. I was sitting close enough to see the freckles on her face, but, more importantly, feel the happiness radiating off her. I felt my own heart lift. Hina leaned over to whisper something in her ear, and her smile only grew.

"Sounds like us!" someone called, from the back of the room.

"You bet," Clancy said, and talked for the next hour and a half about how the Pilgrims interacted with the native tribes, about Jamestown, about all the things my mother used to teach at her high school. And when he had used up all his time, he took a small bow and motioned for me to follow him outside amidst all the groans and complaints from the Cubbies. We were both still chuckling as we walked to the fire pit, where they were just starting to set up for dinner. I felt a number of eyes latch onto us immediately, but I didn't care. I actually felt a small thrill of pride.

"So?" Clancy said, as we stood beside the Office's porch, listening to the bells calling everyone to dinner. "What do you think?"

"I think I'm ready for my first lesson," I said.

"Oh, Miss Daly." A smile curled at the edges of his lips. "You already had your first lesson. You just didn't realize it."

Two weeks passed like a page tearing from an old book.

I spent so many hours of so many days locked inside Clancy's room, pushing images into his mind, blocking him from trying to do the same, talking about the League, Thurmond, and White Noise, that we both fell out of sync with the camp's schedule. He had his daily meetings, but instead of asking me to leave, he had me wait on the other side of the white curtain, where we were now conducting most of our practice sessions.

There were times he had to go out and inspect the cabins, or handle an argument, but I almost always stayed up in that musty old room. There were books and music and a TV at my disposal, which meant I never once had the opportunity to be bored.

I still saw Chubs at some of our meals, but Clancy often had food brought to us. Zu was even harder to track down, because when she wasn't in class, she was with Hina or one of the older Yellows. The only time I really spent with the two of them was at night, before the camp's lights were shut off. Chubs, more often than not, was a ghost—always working, looking for ways to catch Clancy's attention by stitching up the kid who'd split her lip or suggesting a more efficient way of harvesting the garden. The longest I sat with him was when he took out my stitches.

Zu, for her part, delighted in showing me what she had learned in school, and the tricks the other Yellows had taught her outside of it.

After a few days, she stopped wearing her gloves. It only really hit me one night, while she was brushing out my hair. I had pulled away to go switch off the lights, but she beat me to it—she snapped her fingers, and the overhead light blinked out.

"That's amazing," I gushed, but it would have been a terrible lie to say I didn't feel a pang of jealousy in how much progress she had made. I had only been able to block Clancy out of my mind once, and not before he had found out about what had happened to Sam.

"Interesting" had been his only comment.

While I saw Zu and Chubs every day, Liam was a completely different matter. The security team had him scheduled for the second watch—five p.m. to five a.m.—all the way at the far west end of the lake. He was usually too tired to stumble back to the cabin after his shift, and spent most of his days sleeping in the tents they had set up near that entrance. I saw him once or twice talking animatedly to a crowd at breakfast, or visiting with Zu at Cubbies, but it was always from the window of Clancy's room.

I missed him to the point of a real, physical ache, but I understood that he had responsibilities. When I had a thought to spare, it usually went to him, but I was so focused on my lessons that it was hard to let my mind drift to anything else for too long.

Clancy laughed, drawing my attention back to him from the window, and I suddenly wasn't sure *how* I could let my thoughts wander. He was wearing a white polo shirt that emphasized the natural glow of his skin, and pressed khaki pants casually rolled at the ankle. Whenever he was out with others, he was properly buttoned up, his clothes clean and ironed within an inch of their lives—but not with me.

Here, we didn't have to put on any show. Not for each other.

When we first started these lessons, it had been from either side of his ridiculous desk; it felt like I was squaring off against a school principal, not being guided through a Psi lesson by my freak guru. Next, we had tried the floor, but after a few hours of sitting, my back felt like it was ready to crumble. He had been the one to suggest sitting on his narrow bed. He had taken one end and I had taken the other. Then, we started inching closer. Bridging the distance on his red quilt, nearer to each other with each lesson, until one day I snapped out of whatever haze Clancy's dark eyes had put me in and realized our knees were pressed up against one another.

"Sorry," I mumbled, when I turned back toward him. "Can we go from the top?"

He found everything about me amusing, apparently. "Take it from the top? Are we rehearsing for a play? Should I get Mike in here to start building props?"

I'm not sure why I laughed at that—it wasn't even all that funny. Maybe trying to throw my brain at his for the last twenty minutes had made me loopy. The only thing I seemed sure of was how big and reassuring his hand felt as it took mine and squeezed.

"Try again," he said. "This time, try to imagine that those invisible hands you were telling me about are actually knives. Cut through the haze."

Easier said than done. I nodded and closed my eyes, trying to fight back the flood of color in my cheeks. Every time he used my lame way of explaining how my brain seemed to work, I felt embarrassed, even a little bit ashamed. He had laughed the first time I made the comparison, waved his fingers in front of my face like he was casting a spell over me.

He had tried a number of different methods to try to demonstrate how to do it. We'd gone down to the pantry so I could watch him slip into Lizzie's mind and, for no other purpose than to make me laugh, ask her to cluck like a chicken. Clancy had tried to show me how easy it was to affect the moods of multiple people at once, settling an argument between two kids without saying a single word. At one point, we'd sat on the stoop of the Office and he'd read me the thoughts of everyone who passed by—including poor Hina, who was, apparently, harboring a desperate crush on Clancy.

The truth was, he could do everything and anything. Block me out, push in an image, a feeling, a fear. Once, I was sure, he had even passed on a dream to me. I didn't want to feel like I was disappointing him, not when he was giving me so much of his precious time—the thought made everything inside of me clench with fear. He told me to take it slow, that it had taken him years to master all of this, but it was impossible *not* to want to rush through the lessons, to get a grip on my abilities as soon as possible. It seemed to me that the best way to repay his kindness was to master myself to the point where I could stand beside him and feel pride, not shame, in what I could do.

Until I could unlock his secrets, we were never going to be equals. He had called me his "friend" several times, during our lessons and in front of other kids, and it surprised me how much I recoiled at the term. Clancy had hundreds of friends. I wanted to be more than that—I wanted him to trust me and confide in me.

Sometimes, I just wanted him to lean closer, to tuck my hair behind my ear. It was a repulsively girly thought, though, and I wasn't sure what dark corner of my mind it had come crawling out of. I think my head was playing tricks on me, because I knew what I really wanted was for *Liam* to do that—do more than that.

But every time I tried to slip into Clancy's mind, I was thrown back. Clancy had so much control over his powers

402

that I didn't even have time to feel the usual disorienting rush of thoughts and memories. Every single time, it was like he had drawn a white curtain around his brain. No amount of tearing could bring it down.

That didn't mean I didn't try, though.

Clancy smiled, reaching over to brush my hair back over my shoulder. His hand lingered there, sliding over to cup the back of my neck. I knew he was staring at me, but I couldn't bring my eyes up to meet his, even as he leaned closer.

"You can do this. I know you can."

My teeth clenched until I felt my jaw pop. A muscle twitched in my right cheek. I tried drawing the hundreds and thousands of wandering fingers together, focusing them into something sharp and lethal enough to penetrate his wall. I squeezed his hand, increasing my grip until I'm sure he felt pain, and threw the invisible dagger toward him, diving in as fast and hard as I could. And still, the moment I brushed up against that white wall, it felt like he had reached over and slapped me across the face. He sighed and dropped his hand.

"Sorry," I said, hating the silence that followed.

"No, I'm the one that's sorry." Clancy shook his head. "I'm a terrible teacher."

"Trust me, you are not the problem in this equation."

"Ruby, Ruby, Ruby," he said, "this isn't an equation. You can't solve it in three easy steps, otherwise you wouldn't have accepted my help, right?"

I looked down as he began to rub his thumb over my upturned palm. A slow, lazy circle. It was strangely calming, and almost hypnotizing to watch.

"That's true," I began. "But you should know I haven't exactly been . . . honest."

That got his attention.

"The others—they were looking for you because they thought you were some magic man that could get them home. But I wanted to look for you because I was banking on the rumors that you were an Orange, and that you might be willing to teach me."

Clancy's dark brows drew together, but he didn't let go of my hand. Instead, he rested his other palm on the sliver of space between our crossed legs. "But that was before I told you what the League was planning for you," he said. "What did you want me to help you with? No—let me guess. Something to do with what happened to your parents, right?"

"How I erased myself," I confirmed. "How to keep it from happening again."

Clancy closed his eyes for a brief moment, and when he finally opened them, his eyes seemed darker than before, almost black. I leaned in closer, picking up on a strange mix of sadness, guilt, and something else that seemed to be seeping through his pores.

"I wish I could help you with that," he said, "but the truth is, I can't do what you can. I have no idea how to help you."

I have no idea how to help you. Of course. Of course he didn't. Martin was an Orange, too, but he didn't have the same abilities I did. I wonder why I'd assumed the Slip Kid would.

"If you . . . tell me about it, and explain how you think it works, I—then I might be able to figure something out."

It wasn't so much that I couldn't talk about it; it was that I didn't want to. Not right then. I knew myself well enough that I could predict the choked words and teary explanation that would follow. Every time I let myself think about what had happened, I always came out the other end exhausted and shaking, feeling every bit as scared and hopeless and horrific as I did when those moments had actually occurred.

He watched me from under those dark lashes of his, a look of understanding quick to come. His thumb hovering over the pulse point in my wrist. "Ah. It's a Benjamin. I should have expected that, I'm sorry." Seeing my look of confusion he explained, "Benjamin was my old tutor back— well, back before everything went to hell. He passed away when I was very young, but I still can't talk about it. Still hurts." One side of his mouth curled up in a rueful smile. "Maybe you don't have to say anything at all, though. We *could* try something else."

"Like what?"

"Like you blocking me this time, not the other way around. I bet it'll be easier for you."

"Why do you say that?"

"Because you're not vicious enough to put up a good offense—trust me, that's a compliment." He waited for me to smile before continuing. "But you are guarded. You don't show your cards to anyone. There are times that you're impossible to read."

"I don't mean to be," I interrupted. Clancy only waved me off.

"It's not a bad thing," he said. "In fact, it'll help you."

Well, it certainly hadn't helped me fend off Martin.

"Can you sense when someone is trying to break into your head?" he asked. "There's a tingling sensation. . . ."

"Yeah, I know what you're talking about. What should I do when I feel it?"

"You have to push right back up against them, throw them off whatever track they might have been on. In my experience, the things you really want to protect, like memories or dreams? They have their own natural defenses. You just need to add another wall."

"Every time I tried to get into your head, it was like a white curtain blocked me."

Clancy nodded. "That's the way I do it. When I feel the sensation, I push back the image of that curtain and I don't let up, no matter what. So what I want you to do is bring to mind some kind of secret or memory—something you wouldn't necessarily want me or anyone else to see—and I want you to drop your own curtain down to protect it."

I must not have been doing a good job of hiding my hesitation, because he took both of my hands in his again, lacing our fingers. "Come on," he said. "What's the worst that could happen? I see some embarrassing moment? I think we're good enough friends now that you can trust me when I say I won't tell a soul about any falls or public puking."

"What about streaking and eating playground sand?"

He pretended to consider it for a moment, grinning. "I suppose I could refrain from sharing that with the entire camp at dinner."

"What a fair, just leader you are," I said. After a moment, I added, "Do you really consider me a friend, or are you just saying that because you want to see me get my four front teeth knocked out when I tried to play soccer?"

Clancy shook his head and laughed. His favorite stories always seemed to be the ones that involved me trying to pretend I was a boy, or the fast-food binges my dad used to take me on when my mom was out of town at a teacher's conference. They were so completely foreign to his experience, I realized, that I must have seemed like an alien.

"Of course I consider you my *friend*. Actually . . ." he began, his voice low. When he glanced at me again, his dark eyes were burning with a kind of intensity that made me feel like my head was full of air, ready to float away. "I consider you a lot more than that."

"What do you mean?"

"You may have been looking for me, but let's just say that I was waiting for you. It's been a long time since I felt like someone understood what I was going through. Being an Orange . . . you can't compare it to what the others are. They don't understand us or what we can do."

It's only us, came a small voice in my mind, *it's just the two of us.*

I squeezed his hands. "I know."

His attention seemed to wander, his eyes carrying over to the other side of the room, toward his computer and TV. I thought I detected a glimmer of sadness in his eyes, a real kind of pain, but just as quickly, it was gone, replaced by his usual confident expression.

407

"You ready to try?"

I nodded. "I promise I've been trying. Please—please, don't give up on me."

I was surprised when I felt his hands pull free from mine. Stunned, when I felt them glide up my bare arms and over my shoulders. I didn't stop him. This was the thing about Clancy—the thing I was quickly coming to terms with. With him, I didn't have to be afraid, not of what I could do intentionally or by mistake. I didn't have to throw up every defense I possessed to keep my brain's wandering hands still, because Clancy was more than capable of keeping me out of his head.

But Liam . . . he was something precious, something I could break with a single misstep. Someone I couldn't be with, not right then, not the way I was.

Clancy leaned forward to begin his work. I leaned forward, too, right up against his chest, where it was warm and smelled of pine and old books and thousands of possibilities I had never known.

I didn't block him on the first try—I didn't even block him on the fifth try. It took three days and his witnessing almost every sour, cheek-reddening memory in my head for me to finally throw up some kind of defense.

"Think deeper," he told me. "Think about something you wouldn't want anyone else to know. Those memories will provoke your strongest defenses."

There wasn't anything left that he hadn't already seen. I swear, the kid could have been a brain surgeon for how sharp and accurate his pokes and prods were. Every time I brought to mind a memory or thought and tried to put an invisible wall around it, my defenses crumbled, as flimsy as waxed paper. Still, he didn't get frustrated.

"You can do this," Clancy kept repeating, "I know you can. You're capable of more than you'll admit to yourself."

It was his strange badgering for some kind of juicy memory that finally produced my first actual result.

"Does it have to be a memory?" I asked.

He seemed to consider this. "Maybe you should try something else this time. Something you imagine." It could have been my mind playing tricks, but his face suddenly appeared much closer to mine. "Something you want. Or . . . someone?"

The way he said it made me think it was a question, a serious one cloaked by a casual voice. I kept my face impassive.

"Okay," I said. "I think I'm ready."

Clancy didn't look so sure. But I was. This particular fantasy had been creeping up on my dreams for weeks, invading the slips of time when I wasn't holed up practicing my abilities.

It came to me in the middle of our third night at East River, right at the hour that separated day from night. I startled awake in bed, confused as I listened to Chubs snore and Zu toss and turn. Every inch of my skin had tingled as I tried to process what I had just seen, if any of it had actually happened—if any of it *might* actually happen.

This was a dream I could never share, one I carried deep inside my heart, tucked so far down that I hadn't

409

even realized it was there until it sprang out of me, fully formed.

I must have dreamed we were in spring. The cherry blossom trees at the end of my parents' street in Salem were in full bloom. We drove past them in Black Betty—Liam and I, sitting up front together, listening to a Led Zeppelin song that might not have even been real. Outside of my parents' house were white balloons, tied off on either side of the white fence's gate, floating arrows that pointed us up to the open front door. Liam took my hand, wearing exactly what he had worn the day I had met him, and together we walked straight down the house's main hallway, through the pale yellow kitchen, until we found the door to the backyard and everyone outside waiting.

Everyone. My parents. Grams. Zu. Chubs. Sam. All sitting around a blanket my parents had spread out over the grass, eating whatever it was my dad was grilling. Mom was running around, tying up more balloons, her hands still stained with dark dirt after planting all of the new, pale flowers that flooded over what once had been a yard of plain grass. We said hello to everyone, I hugged Sam, I pointed out the birds up in the trees to Zu, and introduced Chubs to my mother.

And then, Liam bent down and kissed me, and there were no words to describe that.

Clancy's intrusion came like all the others had before, first with a tingle, then with a roar. I had been so lost in thinking about the dream that I hadn't even felt him take my hand to start that trial run.

I liked Clancy a lot. More than I ever expected. But he didn't have a place in this dream. There was nothing there I wanted to share with him.

I clenched his hand back, hard, and threw everything I had into sending my other set of hands out from inside me, like a shove.

His curtain strategy hadn't worked for me, but this one? Using offense as defense? This one was maybe a little too effective. Even before I opened my eyes, I felt Clancy jerk back, sucking in a hiss of what sounded like pain.

"Oh my God," I said, when I finally shook the haze from my mind. "I'm so sorry!"

But when Clancy looked up, he was smiling. "Told you," he said. "Told you that you'd figure it out."

"Can we do it again?" I asked. "I want to make sure it wasn't a fluke."

Clancy rubbed at his forehead. "Can we give it a rest for a little while? I feel like you just tackled my brain."

But Clancy didn't get a rest. Almost as soon as the words had left his mouth, we both heard a very different kind of warning. There was a shrill wail from the other side of the room, one I had never heard before, almost like a car alarm. He winced, tucking his head down to escape the noise, even as he jumped up from the bed.

He made his way to his desk, flipping open his laptop lid. His fingers flew as he typed in his password, the blue-white screen of the laptop illuminating his pale face. I came to stand behind him just as he clicked open a new program.

"What's happening?" I asked. "Clance?"

He didn't look up. "One of the camp's perimeter alarms was triggered. Don't worry—it might be nothing. We've had animals step a little too close to the wires before."

It took me a minute to realize what I was looking at. Four different color videos, one in each corner of the screen; four different viewpoints of the camp boundaries. Clancy leaned forward, bracing his hands on either side of his laptop.

He reached across me to get to the wireless black radio sitting on the other side of his desk. He never once took his eyes off the screen.

"Hayes, do you read me?"

There was a moment of silence before Hayes' gruff, "Yeah, what's up?" came crackling through the speaker.

"The southeast perimeter alarm was triggered. I'm watching the feed now, but—" I think what he was going to say was, *I don't see anyone or anything,* but his next words had me ducking under his arm to take a look at the screen myself. "Yeah, I see a man and a woman. Both in camo—unfriendlies, by the look of it."

And there they were. They looked well into middle age, but it was hard to be sure. Both were wearing what could only be described as hunting attire, head-to-toe camouflage. Even their faces appeared to have been painted brown.

"Got it. I'll take care of it."

"Thanks . . . get them to back off, will you?" Clancy said carefully, then turned the volume of the radio all the way down.

Southeast perimeter—good, not Liam's area. I let out a grateful sigh.

412

My eyes were still on the screen when Clancy shut the laptop lid. "Let's get back to work. Sorry for the distraction."

I could feel my surprise betray me. "Don't you need to go out there?" I asked. "What's Hayes going to do to them?"

Clancy only waved me off. Again.

"Don't worry about it, Ruby. Everything is under control."

One crack might not be enough to bring a fortress's defenses down, but it was enough to splinter into two cracks, and then three, and then four. After the initial breakthrough, it became a mission of mine to find different ways to slip into Clancy's mind. I never got to stay for very long before I was unceremoniously tossed out, of course; but every small victory spurred me on to achieve another, and then another. I could catch him when his thoughts were focused on something else, trick him into trying to protect one memory when I was really going after another. It surprised Clancy, but I thought it also, in a secret way, excited him. Enough, at least, to have me start practicing on others.

It was like running downhill in a way; the momentum carried me through all sorts of experiments, big and small. I made a spectacular mess of dinner one night when I pulled each of the six kids working on it aside and planted six very different ideas about what they were supposed to be making for the meal—all at the same time. I had one girl so convinced her name was Theodore that she began to cry whenever anyone told her otherwise. It became so easy, in fact, to convince someone to do what I asked, or suggest that

413

they had done something they really hadn't, that Clancy told me it was time to move on to trying to do the same without having to touch the unsuspecting test subject first.

I was getting there, slowly, and maybe not entirely surely, but there was something almost delicious about feeling the same powerful swell of abilities that had once terrorized me corked and controlled. Every aspect of them became sharper, easier.

But on the Tuesday that followed, we were interrupted again.

One of the older Yellows, a girl named Kylie, came pounding on Clancy's door. She didn't wait to be let in; I actually fell off the bed with the force of her entrance.

"What's this about you denying our request to leave?" Tangles of dark curls flew around her face. "You let Adam leave, you let Sarah's group leave, you even let Greg and his guys go, and you and I both know they have the collective brainpower of a fly—"

The floorboard squeaked as I took a step back toward the bed. Clancy had left the curtain open when he went to answer the door, so Kylie had a full view of me. She whirled back toward Clancy, who had put two pacifying hands on her shoulders. "Oh my God! Are you in here fooling around? Did you even *look* at my proposal? I spent days on that!"

"I read it three times," Clancy said, motioning me forward with his hand. He looked at her with the same calming smile and patience he had shown me since our lessons began. "But I'm happy to discuss why I had to decline now. Ruby—tomorrow?"

And just like that, I found myself outside in the morning sunshine.

The spring weather was still sporadic—cold and dismal one day, perfectly warm the next. Spending two weeks holed up with Clancy had made keeping up with the season's bipolar tendencies even harder. I stripped my sweatshirt off and pulled my hair up in a messy bun. My first thought was to check in on Zu, but I didn't want to interrupt her lessons. I tried to find Chubs in the gardens, but the girl in charge told me—in her bossiest voice—that she hadn't seen him in a week, and she was going to rat him out to Clancy for the punishment he deserved.

"Punishment?" I repeated, bristling, but she didn't elaborate.

I found him in the next logical place.

"You know," I called as I stepped onto the dock, "bread is actually bad for ducks."

Chubs didn't so much as look up. I sat down next to him, but it only prompted him to stand up and stalk away, leaving his bag and book behind.

"Hey!" I called. "What's your problem?"

No response.

"Chubs—*Charles*!"

He whirled back around. "You want to know what my *problem* is? Where do I even start? How about that it's been almost a month, and we're still here? How about the fact that you and Lee and Suzume are all off making friends and skipping around even though we're supposed to be working to learn a way to get home?"

415

"Where is this coming from?" I asked. Maybe he hadn't fit in as naturally as Liam and Zu had, but I saw him talking to other kids as he worked. He seemed okay—maybe not happy, but, then again, when was he ever? "This place really isn't that bad—"

"Ruby, it's horrible!" he burst out. "*Horrible!* We're told when to eat, when to sleep, what to wear, and we're forced to work. How is this any different from camp?"

I sucked in a sharp breath. "You're the one that wanted to come here! I'm sorry it's not living up to your high and mighty expectations, but it works for us. If you'd just try, you could be happy here. We're safe! Why are you in such a hurry to leave?"

"Just because your parents didn't want you, it doesn't mean that the rest of ours don't. Maybe you're not in a hurry to get back, but *I am*!"

He might as well have shot me straight through the chest; I felt all of the blood leave my heart as one of his hands came up to clutch his dark hair. "I've been working so hard, I've been *trying*, and God, you didn't even ask him, did you?"

"Ask him—?" But I knew. As soon as the words left my mouth, I knew exactly what promise I had neglected to keep. The anger in me deflated. "I'm so sorry. I've been so wrapped up in lessons that I forgot."

"Well, I didn't," he said, and left me standing alone in the sunlight.

An hour later, I was under a stream of warm water, hands pressed to my face.

The camp's wash rooms—one for boys, one for girls—were about as glamorous as an outhouse. The floors were beveled concrete, the shower stalls wood planks and plastic curtains crawling with black mold. We used the rooms every night to brush our teeth and wash our faces, and, once or twice a week, to shower. But today, without floral shampoo and conditioner perfuming the air, I realized the cavernous room smelled like sawdust.

I stayed in there until I heard the bells signal the end of lunch. I still hadn't formulated a plan for the rest of the day when I walked outside—and into the one person I hadn't realized I was desperate to see.

Liam stumbled back a few steps at impact, his wet hair clinging to his cheeks, longer than I remembered.

"Oh my God," I said with a laugh, pressing a hand to my chest. "You scared the hell out of me."

"Sorry about that." He smiled, extending a hand toward me. "Hey—I don't think we've had the chance to meet. I'm Liam."

TWENTY-FOUR

I DON'T KNOW HOW LONG I STOOD THERE STARING at his hand, bile rising in my throat as fast and steady as a scream.

Oh my God, no, I thought, taking a step back. *No, no, no nonono . . .*

"See, you look exactly like a friend of mine, Ruby, but I haven't seen her in *ages*, so I'm . . ." His voice trailed off. "Okay, was that joke really that bad?"

I turned around, pressing my face against my towel so he wouldn't see my tears.

"Ruby?" He looped his own towel around my waist and drew me to his side. "That was the Liam Stewart way of saying, *Hi, darlin', missed you something fierce.* Oh, wow, bad enough to make you cry?"

He smoothed his hands down over my hair. "Okay, that's it—" He bent down, and before I could stop him, lifted me over one shoulder.

Liam didn't let me wiggle free until we were back at cabin 18. He dropped me on the folded futon that Zu and I had been sharing, making a quick stop at his bed for a blanket.

"I'm not cold," I said, when he wrapped it around my shoulders.

"Then why are you shaking?" Liam sat down next to me. I turned so my face was resting in the crook of his neck and I was breathing in his clean, woodsy smell.

"I'm just pissed at myself," I said when I found my voice. "I told Chubs I'd ask Clancy if he could use his laptop, but I got distracted and forgot."

"Hmm . . ." Liam's fingers were busy untangling my wet hair. "I don't think he's upset at you. I think he's upset that I'm keeping us here. It's just reinforcing his fears about not getting home."

"How do I make it up to him?"

"Well, for one thing, you could ask about the computer," he said, his other hand taking mine. "Though I still don't really understand how you're in the position to ask to borrow it. I feel like I haven't seen you in ages."

"You haven't," I said. "You're always on watch."

He laughed. "It's lonely sitting up in a tree without you."

"I want to hear about what you do all night," I said. "Have you tried talking to anyone about freeing the camps yet?"

"I brought it up with some of the guys on my watch, and Olivia. She's trying to get us in to see Clancy about it. I think . . . I think it's going be great, I really do. It *could* work."

"Clance said that the western gate is the one that used to give them the most trouble," I said, twisting to look up at him. "You're being careful, right?"

Liam went very still beside me, so still that he seemed to forget to breathe.

"Clance, huh?" he said in an unnaturally light voice. "I guess you *are* in the position to be asking favors."

"What's that supposed to mean?"

Liam sighed. "Nothing, sorry. I didn't mean for that to come out like that. It's great that you guys are friends." I tried to look up at him, but he was looking at the other end of the cabin, where a set of drawers with our things rested against the wall. "So he's been giving you lessons?"

"Yeah," I said, wondering how much, if anything, I should hold back. "He's been teaching me how to keep others from prying into my head."

"What about tricks to keep you from slipping into others' heads?" Liam asked. "Is he helping you with that, too?"

"He's trying to," I said. "He said that if I strengthened my control over my abilities, that would come naturally."

"Well, you can always practice that with me," he said, resting his forehead against mine. I felt the trickle start at the back of my mind, the warning before the flood. Clancy had told me that when I felt it coming on, I needed to break all physical contact and imagine a white curtain sweeping between me and whomever I was with.

But I didn't want to do either.

I felt his lips travel from my forehead, whispering something against my eyelids, my cheeks, my nose. His thumbs

420

stroked the length of my jaw, but even they stilled as I pulled back and turned away from him.

"What are you so scared of?" he whispered, his voice laced with hurt.

Had this boy really once just been a stranger?

Had I really once thought that I'd be able to live a life without him in it?

"I don't want to lose you."

He made a noise of frustration, his eyes clear and bright as he spoke. "Then why are you the one that keeps letting go?"

I never got the chance to answer. A moment later, Hina burst through the cabin door, Zu in tow, and told us they were leaving.

"Okay, okay, slow down," Liam said. Zu was darting around the cabin, collecting her things, as Hina's mouth ran a mile a minute. I wasn't sure whom I was supposed to be paying attention to—my friend or the girl she had, apparently, elected to speak for her. Every time Hina opened her mouth, Liam and I reverted back to the same state of shock.

Zu. Leaving.

Leaving.

I caught her on her way to the drawers, steering her to the futon and forcing her to sit. She must not have picked up on our shock, because her face was bright and glowing. I studied it, the way her smile seemed to crackle with her own brand of electricity, and felt something inside of me shrink in defeat.

"Us and three others," Hina said, breathlessly. I wondered if she had run all the way over from class. "Two Blues and a Yellow. Kylie *finally* got permission to leave the camp."

Liam twisted around to look at Zu when he said, "And go . . . for a hike?"

Zu made her *Are you serious?* face.

"Help me out here. Tell me what *you* want to say."

Hina was finally silent, and for a moment, one crazy second really, I thought Zu was actually going to open her mouth and have out with it. Liam's entire body tensed, as if he was expecting the same thing. But Zu only slipped her notebook back out of her pink duffel bag and wrote in her neat, looping handwriting. When she flipped it over, she was looking him right in the eye.

I want to go with them to California.

I know I should have been happy for her. I should have been celebrating the fact that she was finally able to come out and tell us exactly what she wanted. I just never imagined what she'd want would be a future without us.

"I thought Clancy turned down Kylie's request to leave?" I asked Hina.

"He did, but she said she finally wore him down."

"What's in California?" Liam asked, leaning against a cabin wall.

"My parents have a house there," Hina explained, "and they're waiting for us. The West Coast government isn't going to turn us back over to the camps."

"What about Zu's parents?" I asked. "They—"

To her credit, Hina knew what I was trying to ask

without my having to ask it. "My father has not been on speaking terms with my uncle for some time."

"Zu, that's a long trip," Liam began uncertainly. "What if something happens? Who else is going? That Talon kid?"

She nodded, and all of a sudden her eyes were on me. I tried to give her an encouraging smile, but I was worried I might burst into tears instead. We all waited as she scribbled out another hasty note and showed it to Liam again.

You don't have to worry about me anymore. Isn't that good?

"I like worrying about you." Liam put a hand on her head. "When would you be leaving?"

Hina at least had the decency to look guilty. "We actually have to leave right now. Kylie is worried Clancy might change his mind. He wasn't . . . all that happy."

"That's a little fast," I choked out. "Have you really thought about this?"

Zu looked right at me when she nodded. The next note was for both of us. *I want to be with my family. I just don't want you to be mad at me.*

"*Mad?*" Liam shook his head. "Never. Ever. You're my girl, Zu. We just want you to be safe. It would kill me if anything happened to you."

There was a knock at the door. Talon, an older Yellow with his hair woven into intricate dreadlocks, appeared first, followed by a wide-eyed Chubs. Liam stood.

"Good," he said. "I was hoping to talk to you."

Talon nodded. "I figured. Kylie and Lucy are here, too." She stuck her head inside and waved. "Do you want to talk outside?"

423

Liam's hand reached out and touched the small of my back. "Help her pack?"

"Are you nuts?" I heard Chubs say. "You barely know these people!"

"Excuse me," Hina protested, her hands on her hips. "In case you've forgotten, she's my *cousin*."

I'll miss you, too. Zu stopped piling her things into her pink suitcase and tore the sheet of paper out for Chubs to keep. He sat so suddenly that he almost missed the futon. For several moments, he couldn't do anything other than stare at her. I knew the feeling.

"Did Kylie say why you guys had to leave tonight?" I asked, sitting beside Chubs.

Zu only shrugged.

"I mean . . . are you guys just going to *walk* to California?" Chubs said, his voice rising with each word. "Do you have some kind of plan?"

"Maybe you'll find a new Betty," I said, but the moment I uttered her name Zu stopped packing and shook her head. The next note took some time for her to write.

No, there's only one Betty.

"And apparently she wasn't enough for you," Chubs said, with a shocking amount of hurt. "I guess everything is replaceable, even us."

Zu took a deep breath, walking over to him with her pink bag at her side. He tried to look away, but she was standing right in front of him, wrapping her arms around his neck. All he could do was hug her back, his face hidden in the fabric of her jacket.

The camp's bells began to ring, a frenzied sound that didn't cease until it had driven everyone outside. I let Zu and Hina lead us, pushing a path through the gathered kids. This was the first time their black garb seemed remotely appropriate.

Kylie handed a piece of paper to Lee, and he nodded at whatever she was telling him. Lucy was next to them, as tiny and quiet as ever, but she reached up and patted Liam on the shoulder in what I guess was supposed to be a reassuring way. All happy pretenses were gone. The only way to describe the look on his face was stricken.

"—borrow that pen?" he asked Talon. The boy began to pat down his black cargo pants, searching the pockets until he came up with a blue-capped pen. With it in hand, Liam knelt down in front of Zu and tore off half the sheet of paper Kylie had given him.

I wished I could have seen what he had written there, but it wasn't for my eyes. When he was finished, he folded the paper over several times and pressed it into her palm.

The bell fell silent. Everyone's eyes shifted to the right, where Clancy appeared at the head of the path, Hayes towering beside him. His face, which I had grown used to seeing relaxed and proud, was pinched with what was either annoyance or anger.

"Kylie has decided to go tribal and will be leaving immediately."

A murmur of surprise rippled through the crowd.

"She will only take these four with her," he shouted over the noise. "There will be no more requests to leave granted until our numbers are full. Is that understood?"

425

Silence.

"Is that understood?"

Chubs jumped beside me at the noises and shouts confirming that, yes, it was.

Clancy turned sharply on his heel without another word, heading back in the direction of the office. As soon as he reached the white building, the kids around us seemed to exhale the collective breath they had been holding, turning to each other with confused whispers.

"That was weird."

"Why didn't he give them bags, like he usually does?"

"He's worried if our numbers get down too low, there won't be enough people here to protect the camp."

My eyes floated up toward the office until they fixed on Zu waving me over.

No gloves, I thought, watching her hand fall back to her side. Hopefully never again.

"Do you really have to leave now?" I asked when I reached where she and Liam were standing. The clusters of kids swarmed Kylie and the others, wishing them good luck and offering up blankets and bags of food.

Zu put on a brave smile, wrapping her arms around my waist.

"Please be safe," I told her.

The next note was for me and me alone. *When all this is over, will you come find me? There's something I want to tell you, but I don't know how to say it yet.*

My eyes traced every inch of her face. It was so different from the girl I had met only a few weeks ago. If she had

426

changed this much in so little time, how could I even be sure I'd recognize her years down the line, after the dust of all this hell finally settled?

"Of course," I whispered. "And I'll miss you every day until then."

Just before they stepped off the trail and into the untamed forest, Zu turned and gave us one last wave. Beside her, Hina did the same. Then, they were gone.

"She'll be okay," I said. "They'll take care of her. She should be with her family. Her real one."

"She should be with *us*." Liam shook his head, his breath catching in his throat.

"Then maybe we should follow her."

Liam and I turned back. Chubs was trailing behind us, his eyes hidden as the drooping sunlight caught his glasses.

"You know we can't," Liam said. "Not yet."

"Why not?" Chubs advanced toward us, his voice losing all semblance of calm it held before. Feeling the curious eyes on us, I drew them both off the main path.

"Why *not*?" Chubs repeated. "Clearly we aren't going to get the help we need to track down our parents *or* Jack's. It'd be better for us to just go now, before anyone misses us. We could still catch up with her."

"And do what?" Liam asked. He ran a frustrated hand through his already mussed up hair. "Wander around until we just so happen to stumble on them? Hope that we don't get our asses caught and thrown back into camp? Chubs, it's *safe* here. This is the place we're supposed to be—we can do so much good from here."

427

I saw, maybe even before Liam did, that this was the wrong thing to say. Warning alarms went off in my mind at the sight of Chubs's nostrils flaring and his lips twisting with anger. I knew that whatever was about to leave Chubs's mouth would not only be sharp, but cruel.

"I get it—I get it, Lee, okay?" Chubs shook his head. "You want to be the big hero again. You want everyone to adore you and believe in you and follow you."

Liam tensed. "That's not—" he began, angrily.

"Well, what about the kids who followed you before?" He slapped around the pocket of his trousers before pulling out a familiar folded piece of paper. Chubs's grip on the letter nearly crushed it. "What about Jack, and Brian, and Andy, and all of them? They all followed you, too, but it's easy to forget about them when they're not around, isn't it?"

"Chubs!" I said, stepping between them when Liam advanced, his right fist swinging up.

I'd never seen him look so perfectly furious before. A wave of crimson washing up from Liam's throat to his face.

"Can't you just admit you're doing this to make yourself feel better, not to actually help anyone else?" Chubs demanded.

"You think . . ." Liam almost couldn't get the words out. "You think they're not in my head every goddamn second of every goddamn day? You think I could ever forget something like that?" Instead of hitting his friend, Liam hit himself, banging his fist against his forehead until I finally caught his arm. "Jesus Christ, Charles!" he said, his voice breaking.

"I just . . ." Chubs stalked past us, only to stop and turn back again. "I never believed you, you know," he said, his voice shaking, "when you talked about us getting out of camp and getting home safely. That's why I agreed to write my letter. I knew most of us wouldn't make it, with you in charge."

I stepped forward the same moment Liam did, holding my hands out in front of me to keep him from doing something I knew he would regret. I heard Chubs storm away behind me, heading back in the direction of our cabin. Liam tried to take another step forward, but I pressed back against his chest. Liam was breathing hard, his fists balled up at his sides.

"Let him go," I said. "He just needs to blow off steam. Maybe you should think about doing the same."

Liam looked like he was about to say something, but instead, he let out a frustrated grunt, spun on his heel, and started toward the nearby trees, in the exact opposite direction Chubs had taken. I leaned back against the trunk of the nearest tree and shut my eyes. My chest was too tight to do anything other than take in shallow, short breaths as I waited.

It was nearly dark by the time he emerged, rubbing his face. The skin on both hands was torn and bleeding from smashing them into something solid. His face was drawn in the twilight, as if the flush of anger had been ripped out of him and he'd been left with nothing more than gray sadness. I held out an arm to him as he came near, wrapping it around the solid warmth of his waist. His arm settled down

429

over my shoulders and he pulled me close, pressing his face against my hair. I took in a deep breath of his comforting smell—wood smoke, grass, and leather.

"He didn't mean it," I said, walking him over to a fallen log. He was still shaking, and looked unsteady on his feet.

Liam didn't sit so much as collapse down onto it, leaning forward to brace his elbows against his knees. "Doesn't make it any less true."

We sat for a long time—long enough for the sun to disappear behind the trees, and then below the horizon. The silence and stillness between us became unbearable. I lifted my hand and guided it lightly down the length of knobby bones between his shoulder blades.

Liam sat up slowly, turning to look at me. "Do you think he's okay?" he whispered.

"I think we should probably go check," I said.

I don't know how we made it back to the cabin, only that when we arrived, Chubs was sitting on the porch, silent tears streaming down his face. I could see the apology written there, the wretched guilt, and was surprised to find my heart could break even that bit more.

"It's over," he said as we sat on either side of him. "It's all over."

We didn't move for a long time.

TWENTY-FIVE

IT SHOULDN'T HAVE SURPRISED ME THAT LIAM THREW himself back into watch duty, but it took a generous amount of coaxing from the others for his mind to refocus on the camps. I sat by his side more than once as he and Olivia talked through possible ways of breaking through camp defenses, offering suggestions here and there as they discussed how to bring up their ideas with Clancy.

The thing about enthusiasm—especially Liam's particular brand—was that it was catching. There would be nights I would simply sit back, watching, as he became more and more animated with his hands as he spoke, as if trying to shape his ideas out of the air for the rest of us to see. His words were coated with such unyielding hopefulness that it visibly inflated everyone around him. By the end of the first week, interest in the project had spiked to such a level that we had to move the meetings out of our small cabin, to the fire pit. Now, when Liam went anywhere, it was always

431

with a loyal pack of kids around him, trying to catch his ear.

Chubs and I were less enthusiastic about getting back into the swing of things. He forgave me, maybe because a miserable person can only stand to be alone with their misery for so long. He never went back to work at the Garden, but that girl, the bossy one, never ratted him out, either.

I went back to lessons with Clancy. Or at least tried to.

"Where is your head at today?"

Not invading his, that was for certain. Not even cracking it.

"*Show* me what you're thinking about," he said, when I opened my mouth. "I don't want to hear about it. I want to *see* it."

I glanced up from the pool of sunlight spilling from his window to the floor. Clancy leveled me with a look of annoyance that I had only seen him wear once, after realizing one of the remaining Yellows couldn't zap one of the camp's few washing machines back to life.

Never at me, though.

I closed my eyes and reached for his hand again; I brought to mind the memory of Zu's backpack disappearing into the wild thicket of trees. Over the past few weeks, fewer and fewer of our conversations had involved words. When we wanted to get a point across, we shared it our own way—spoke in our own language.

But not today. His mind might as well have been encased in concrete, and mine might as well have been made of jelly.

"Sorry," I mumbled. I couldn't even muster the strength to feel disappointed. I could feel myself slipping into a strange funk, one in which every little noise or sight outside the window was enough to distract me. I just felt tired. Confused.

"I do have other things I could be doing," he continued, something simmering beneath his words. "I have rounds to make and people to talk to, but I'm trying to help *you*. I'm here with *you*."

At that, my stomach did a strange flop. I sat straight up against his headboard, ready to apologize again, when he rolled off his bed and moved across the room to his desk.

"Clancy, I really am sorry." By the time I came to stand in front of the desk, he was already typing away at his laptop. He let me stand there in silent, gut-twisting worry, for what felt like nearly an hour before he bothered to look up from whatever he was doing. He seemed tired of pretending now, too. Annoyance had taken a sharp turn into anger.

"You know, I really thought that letting your Yellow go would help you focus, but I guess I was wrong." Clancy shook his head. "I was wrong about a lot of things, apparently."

I bristled, but I'm not sure if it was because of the way he said *your Yellow* or the implication that I wasn't capable of mastering the things he was trying to teach me.

I needed to leave. If I stayed a second longer, I might say something that would ruin our friendship. I might tell him that Zu had a name, that of course I'd be worried about her out in the world without me there to protect her. He should have realized that I could have spent the last few weeks spending time with *her*, but instead I had agreed to work with *him*. Spend time with *him*. Comfort and support *him*.

433

Maybe I had learned a lot, and maybe I had a better grip on my abilities, but staring at him, my fists clenched and shaking, I couldn't justify it. What was the point of being holed up with someone who didn't believe in me when I had people out there who did?

I turned sharply on my heel and stalked toward the door. As I opened it, Clancy called, "That's right, Ruby, run away again. See how far you get this time!"

I didn't look back and I didn't stop, though some part of me recognized that this might be it—that I was walking out on the one chance I had to learn how to manage my abilities. Sometime in the last ten minutes, my head had disconnected itself from the stubborn muscle beating in my chest and, honestly, I wasn't sure which was guiding me outside and away from him. But what I did know, with dead, absolute certainty, was that I didn't want him to see the way my face crumpled, or for him to glimpse whispers of guilt and sadness circling around inside of my head.

I couldn't hide anything from him, but this was the first time I had ever wanted to.

It took a few days for me to realize that Zu's leaving wasn't the only event that had shifted the rotation of the earth. Once Chubs had pointed out East River's similarities to camp life, I couldn't go back. Where I had seen kids in jeans and black T-shirts, I was now seeing uniforms. Where I had seen kids waiting in line for their food, I was now seeing the Mess Hall. When the lights turned out in the cabins at nine p.m. sharp, and I watched a few members of the security team stroll past our window, I was back in Cabin 27, staring up at the belly of Sam's mattress.

I began to wonder if the supposedly dead security cameras in the office and around the facilities were actually on.

I did try to go see Clancy a few times to apologize, but he always sent me away with a stern *I don't have time for you today.* I got the sense he was punishing me, but I wasn't sure what I had said or done to warrant it. In any case, it quickly became clear that I needed him in my life more than he needed me. That, combined with my stinging pride, made me feel even worse.

It was a Wednesday, only an hour before Liam and the others were meeting to discuss a new camp liberation strategy, before Clancy was finally ready to see me.

"I'll be back in a little while," I told Liam, squeezing his hand at breakfast. "I'll just be a few minutes late."

But when I walked into Clancy's office and saw the state of it, I wondered if I should have come at all.

"Hey, come in—just watch your step. Yeah, sorry about the mess."

Mess? *Mess?* His office looked like someone had detonated a bomb and unleashed a pack of wild wolves to pick over the salvageable remains. There were piles of paper everywhere, printouts, torn maps, boxes . . . and then there was Clancy himself, his hair falling into his face, wearing the same rumpled white shirt I had seen the day before.

In the weeks I had known him, I had never seen Clancy as anything less than impeccable. It was actually a little scary how put-together he was. I'm sure some of it had to do with

435

the way he was raised. That even if his father hadn't taught him himself, some crotchety old nanny had waxed poetic on the value of tucking your shirt in, polishing your shoes, and combing your hair. He looked like he was fraying at the edges.

"Are you okay?" I asked, shutting the door behind me. "What's going on?"

"We're trying to coordinate a hit for med supplies." Clancy settled down into his chair but was back on his feet a moment later, when his laptop began to chime. "Hang on just a sec."

I toed one of the paper piles on the floor, trying to peek at what was written on it.

"Those are reports of the usual nightly activity at a nearby truck stop," Clancy said, as if reading my thoughts. His fingers flew over the keyboard. "And League intelligence about PSFs in that area. It seems that Leda Corporation is now employing the government to protect their shipments."

"Why the PSFs?" I asked.

Clancy shrugged. "They're the largest military force the government has now, and, thanks to dear old Dad, the most organized."

"I guess that makes sense." I leaned back, but staring at the glowing symbol on the laptop lid reminded me of Chubs. "Can I ask you a favor?"

"Only if you let me apologize first."

I sat down and studied my hands. "Can't we just forget it ever happened?"

"No, not this time," he said. "Hey, will you look at me?"

The expression on his face alone made my heart swell to

twice its usual size. It was dangerous how handsome he was, but today his pained look was absolutely lethal.

He does care, a little voice in my head whispered. *He cares about you.*

"I'm sorry for losing my temper," he said. "I didn't mean the things I said about your friend Suzume, and I definitely didn't mean to imply that you haven't been trying."

"Then why did you say that?"

Clancy rubbed a hand over his face. "Because I'm an idiot."

"That's not an answer," I told him, shaking my head. *You really hurt me.*

"Ruby, isn't it obvious?" he said. "I like you. I've only known you for, what, a month? And you're probably the only real friend I've had since I turned ten and figured out what I was. I'm an idiot for getting so upset that you were focused on someone else when I wanted you to be focused on me."

I was almost too stunned to move.

"I didn't let Suzume and the others go because I thought it would help you focus. I let her go because I thought it would make you happy. I didn't even stop to think that, yeah, of course you'd be worried about her, especially after how hard you worked to protect her."

He more than cares about you.

I had to look away now. Play the situation off. My brain had turned to mush, and my heart wasn't much better. "I *guess* I could forgive you. . . ."

"But only if I do you that favor?" I could hear the smile in his voice. "Sure. What?"

"Well . . . I know you don't allow it, but I was hoping

437

you'd make an exception in this case," I said, finally looking back at him. "My friend . . . he needs to use your computer to try to contact his parents."

Clancy stopped smiling. "Your friend Liam?"

"No, Chu—Charles Meriwether?"

"The one who's been skipping Garden duty?"

Okay, apparently that girl *had* ratted him out.

Clancy was silent as he shut the laptop and stood. "I'm really sorry, Ruby, but I thought I made it clear that no one else could leave."

"Oh no!" I said, forcing a laugh. "He just wants to check in with his parents to make sure they're all right."

"No," Clancy said, moving around so he was sitting on the edge of the desk in front of me. "He wants to make arrangements to leave and take you with him. Don't try to cover for him, Ruby. It's the same for everyone. I don't doubt for a second that he's desperate enough to tell his parents the location of this camp."

"He would never," I said, getting riled up on Chubs's behalf. "Really."

"You were there when we had intruders a few weeks ago. You saw how easy it could be for someone to slip past our defenses. What if they hadn't triggered the alarm? We would have been in serious trouble." Clancy's face was dark, worried. "If Charles wants to contact his parents, tell him he needs to fill out a request with instructions on how to do it, just like everyone else. I have to base my decisions on what might threaten the camp's security—no matter how much I want to help you help your friend."

438

It was no good. Chubs would rather not contact his parents at all than grant a stranger access to his only means of safely communicating with them.

"Though," Clancy said after a moment, sitting down next to me and kicking his legs up on the desk. "There is something that could persuade me."

I couldn't look at him.

"Fifteen minutes, Ruby. You teach *me*."

What could I possibly know that he didn't?

"Do you think you could walk me through how you erase someone's memory? I know it's not something you're proud of, and I know it's caused you a lot of pain in the past, but it seems like a useful trick, and I'd be interested to learn it."

"Well . . . I guess?" I said. Like I could deny him after all that he had done for me. But it wasn't something I knew how to teach. I'd barely managed to figure it out for myself.

"I think understanding how you do it will also help me figure out how to prevent you from accidentally doing it again. Sound good?"

That sounded great, actually.

"If you'd let me," he continued, "I'd like to walk through your memories and see if I can find any clues. I just want to confirm a suspicion I have."

I don't think he expected the request to give me pause, but it did. He had been in my head multiple times, seeing things I'd never spoken about to anyone. But I'd been able to keep him from seeing the things that really mattered, the dreams I wanted to protect.

I kept thinking about what Liam had said before, when he told me about his sister. *Those memories are mine.*

But if I wanted a future with my family—with Liam— then I had to relinquish my control. I had to let Clancy in if it meant I could avoid the same thing happening in the future.

You can trust him, said the same voice at the back of my mind. *He's your friend. He would never overstep.*

"Okay," I said. "But only those, and, afterward, Charles gets to use your computer."

"Deal."

Clancy knelt in front of me, hands cupping my jaw, fingers weaving through my hair. I tried not to squirm at his proximity and his assumption that I would be fine with it. We'd sat this close before, but somehow this felt different.

"Wait," I said, sitting back. "I told Liam and the others I'd meet with them about something. Can we maybe do this later? Or even tomorrow?"

"It'll only take a second," Clancy promised, his voice soothing and low. "Just close your eyes and think about the morning you woke up on your tenth birthday."

Come on, that same voice said. *Come on, Ruby. . . .*

I swallowed hard and did as he asked, imagining myself back in my old room, with its blue walls and enormous window. Bit by bit, the room reassembled itself. Blank walls bloomed with cross-stitch samplers Grams had sewn, pictures of my parents, and a map of D.C.'s metro system. I could see all six of the stuffed animals I slept with, on the floor next to my bright blue comforter. Even things I had

440

completely forgotten—the lamp on my small desk, the way the middle shelf of my bookcase sagged—suddenly came back into clear focus.

"Good." Clancy sounded far away, but I felt him near, closer and closer. His breath was warm across my cheek, an unexpected touch. "Keep . . ." He sounded breathless. "Keep thinking. . . ."

I saw his face through a glossy haze, his dark eyes burning the shimmering air. I saw only him, because for those few passing moments, he was the only thing that seemed to exist in my world. Every part of me felt slow and warm, like honey. Clancy blinked once, then again, as if to clear his own cloudy gaze, to remember what he was supposed to be doing. "Just keep . . ."

And then his lips—his lips were so close, smiling against mine. Fingers wove their way through my long hair, thumbs gliding along my cheeks. "You—" he began, his voice hoarse. "You are—"

At the slightest pressure, something hot and dark sparked there, sending a wave of desire straight into my core. His hands slid down over my neck, my shoulders, down my arms, down . . .

And then there was nothing gentle about it.

His lips pressed against mine hard, with enough force to drive them apart, to steal breath, and sense, and the feel of the bed under me. The skin of his face was smooth and cool against mine, but I was warm—too warm. The fever that swept up over me made my body go limp, and I was pressed back against the bed, sinking into the pillows there like I was falling through clouds. The blood had left my head, and all that was left there was a low, throbbing pulse. My hands came up to tangle in his shirt—I needed to grasp something, to hang on before I fell too far.

"Yes," I heard him breathe out, and then his mouth was on mine again, his hands at the hem of my top, edging it up over my stomach.

You want this, a voice whispered. *You want this.*

But it wasn't my voice. I wasn't saying that—was I? In that instant, a flash of his black eyes gave way to a light blue. That was I wanted, what I really wanted. My mind felt slow, drugged with the strain of thought. *Liam.* But here was Clancy. Clancy, who helped me, my friend, beautiful in a way that made me lose trains of thought. Clancy, who more than liked me. . . .

Who was also an Orange.

My eyes flew open as his hands slipped up to my neck, his fingers tightening slightly around the skin there. I tried to pull back, but it felt like he had flooded my veins with concrete. I couldn't move. I couldn't even shut my eyes.

Stop, I tried to say, but when his forehead found mine, the pain that exploded behind my eyes was enough to make me forget everything.

TWENTY-SIX

THE COMPUTER'S FRANTIC BEEPING WOKE ME FROM A dreamless sleep, tugging at me until my eyes drifted open. I was lying in darkness.

My body felt heavy, and though someone had pulled off my sweater, my shirt was plastered to my skin with a thin sheen of sweat. If I had been alone, I might have taken it off, or at least kicked my jeans off my legs to let my body breathe, but I knew better. I was still in his room, and if I was here, then so was he.

The light on Clancy's dresser was on, and I could hear the voices of kids below at the fire pit. Night, already? It was insane that my blood could run as frigid as winter at the same moment my heart started to squeeze out a panicked rhythm.

The creaking of the old mattress was drowned out by the TV. For a while, I did nothing but listen to President's Gray baritone voice give his nightly address. My legs seemed to be the last part of my body willing to wake up.

"—assure you that the jobless rate has declined from thirty percent to twenty percent in this past year alone. I gave you my word that I would succeed where the false government would not. As much as they would like you to believe they have influence on the world stage, they can barely control their terrorist branch, this so-called Children's League—"

The TV set turned off with a hiss of static. Footsteps.

"Are you awake?"

"Yes," I whispered. My throat felt sore, my tongue swollen.

The bed dipped as Clancy sat down beside me. I tried not to wince.

"What happened?" I asked. The sound of the voices below grew louder, getting trapped between my ears.

"You passed out," he said. "I didn't realize . . . I shouldn't have pushed so hard."

I raised myself up on my elbows in a vain attempt to pull away from his touch. My eyes were fixated on his lips, the white teeth gleaming behind them. Had I imagined it, or had he—?

My stomach clenched. "Did you find anything out? Did it prove your theory?"

Clancy sat back, his face unreadable. "No." He stood again and began to pace between the window and the white curtain. I caught a glimpse of the other side of the room, and was unsurprised to find that it was awash in the blue light of the open laptop.

"No, see, I've been going over this again and again in my head," Clancy said. "I thought maybe you erased their memories intentionally because you were angry or upset, but you didn't go all out and erase their entire memories, just . . . *you*. And again, with that girl Samantha. Samantha Dahl, age seventeen, from Bethesda, Maryland. Parents Ashley and Todd. Green, photographic memory . . ." His voice trailed off. "I've been thinking around and around and around in circles, trying to understand how you do this, but walking through your memories doesn't tell me what's going on inside of your head. No cause, only effect."

I wondered if he even realized he was rambling, or that I had managed to get myself off the bed, with my only thought to get the hell out of that room and away from him. The pain came back to me in pieces.

What did he do to me? I brought a hand to my forehead. My head ached like all the other times he had been inside of it, but the pain was sharper. He hadn't just looked in, he had made me want him—made me want to kiss him.

Hadn't he?

"It's late," I said, interrupting him. "I need to . . . I need to go find the others. . . ."

Clancy turned his back on me. "Find *Liam Stewart*, you mean."

"Yes, Lee," I said, taking a few slow steps back toward the door. "I was supposed to meet him. He's going to be worried." The white curtain caught in my hair as I passed it.

Clancy shook his head. "What do you even know about him, Ruby? You've known him for, what, a month? A month and a half? Why are you wasting your time with him? He's a *Blue*, and not only that, but he—he had a record, even

445

before camp. Even before he killed all of those kids. A hundred and forty-eight. Over half of their camp! So you can cut all of your bullshit and hero worship, because he doesn't deserve it. You're too valuable to be screwing around with him."

He whirled around just as my hand touched the door, and slammed it shut.

"What is your problem?" I yelled. "So what if he's a Blue? Aren't you the one that keeps going on about how we're all Black and how we should respect each other?"

The smile that curled his lips was as arrogant as it was beautiful.

"You need to accept the fact that you're Orange and that you're always going to be alone because of it." A measure of calm had returned to Clancy's voice. His nostrils flared when I tried to turn the door handle again. He slammed both hands against it to keep me from going anywhere, towering over me.

"I saw what you want," Clancy said. "And it's not your parents. It's not even your friends. What you want is to be with him, like you were in the cabin yesterday, or in that car in the woods. *I don't want to lose you,* you said. Is he really that important?"

Rage boiled up from my stomach, burning my throat. "How *dare* you? You said you wouldn't—you said—"

He let out a bark of laughter. "God, you're naive. I guess this explains how that League woman was able to trick you into thinking you were something less than a monster."

"You said you would help me," I whispered.

446

He rolled his eyes. "All right, are you ready for the last lesson? Ruby Elizabeth Daly, you are alone and you always will be. If you weren't so stupid, you would have figured it out by now, but since it's beyond you, let me spell it out: *You will never be able to control your abilities*. You will never be able to avoid being pulled into someone's head, because there's some part of you that doesn't want to know how to control them. No, not when it would mean having to embrace them. You're too immature and weak-hearted to use them the way they're meant to be used. You're scared of what that would make you."

I looked away.

"Ruby, don't you get it? You hate what you are, but you were given these abilities for a reason. We both were. It's our *right* to use them—we have to use them to stay ahead, to keep the others in their place."

His finger caught the stretched-out collar of my shirt and gave it a tug.

"Stop it." I was proud of how steady my voice was.

As Clancy leaned in, he slipped a hazy image beneath my closed eyes—the two of us just before he walked into my memories. My stomach knotted as I watched my eyes open in terror, his lips pressed against mine.

"I'm so glad we found each other," he said, voice oddly calm. "You can help me. I thought I knew everything, but you . . ."

My elbow flew up and clipped him under the chin. Clancy stumbled back with a howl of pain, pressing both hands to his face. I had half a second to get the hell out, and I took it, twisting the handle of the door so hard that the lock popped itself out.

447

"Ruby! Wait, I didn't mean—!"

A face appeared at the bottom of the stairs. Lizzie. I saw her lips part in surprise, her many earrings jangling as I shoved past her.

"Just an argument," I heard Clancy say, weakly. "It's fine, just let her go."

I burst outside, completely out of breath. My feet were drawn toward the fire pit, but I forced myself to stop and reconsider. There were so many people still out, gathered around the food tables. I wanted to find Liam and explain why I hadn't been there, to tell him what had happened, but I knew I was a mess. I needed to calm down, and there was no way I could do it here. There were too many potential questions. I needed to be alone.

So of course when I backed up a few steps, I managed to walk right into Mike.

"Hey, there you are!" His hair was pulled back into a ponytail, a black bandana tied around his head. I could smell gasoline on him, and something metallic. "Ruby? You okay?"

I bolted, heading past the Office, down the path to the cabins. Eventually, I found what I thought was the path we had walked Zu out on, but it turned out to be nothing more than an old side trail, overgrown and unforgiving to bare skin. Fine. It would do. There was no one around. That was my only criterion.

I walked until I lost the light from the fire pit, clawing at my T-shirt, trying to pull it away from my skin. It smelled like his room. Like evergreens and spice and old, decaying things. I pulled it over my head and threw it as hard and far

448

as I could, and still—still—I couldn't shake the smell. It was everywhere: my hands, my jeans, my bra. I should have run straight for the lake, or even the showers. I should have tried to soak his venom out.

Calm down, I thought. *Calm down!* But I couldn't pick apart exactly what was pulsing through me. Anger, for sure, that I had been lied to, that I had fallen for it. Disgust, for the way he had touched me and invaded even the pores of my skin. But something else, too. An ache inside of me that expanded and twisted, turning me to stone.

Liam was standing right in front of me, and I had never felt so alone.

"Ruby?" His hair was pale silver in this light, curled and tangled in its usual way. I couldn't hide from him. I had never been able to.

"Mike came and got me," he said, taking a careful step toward me. His hands were out in front of him, as if trying to coax a wild animal into letting him approach. "What are you doing out here? What's going on?"

"Please just go," I begged. "I need to be alone."

He kept coming straight at me.

"Please," I shouted, *"go away!"*

"I'm not going anywhere until you tell me what's going on!" Liam said. He got a better look at me and swallowed, his Adam's apple bobbing. "Where were you this morning? Did something happen? Chubs told me you've been gone all day, and now you're out here like . . . *this* . . . did he do something to you?"

I looked away. "Nothing I didn't ask for."

449

Liam's only response was to move back a few paces back. Giving me space.

"I don't believe you for a second," he said, calmly. "Not one damn second. If you want to get rid of me, you're going to have to try harder than that."

"I don't want you here."

He shook his head. "Doesn't mean I'm leaving you here alone. You can take all the time you want, as long as you need, but you and me? We're having this out tonight. Right now." Liam pulled his black sweater over his head and threw it toward me. "Put it on, or you'll catch a cold."

I caught it with one hand and pressed it to my chest. It was still warm.

He began to pace, his hands on his hips. "Is it me? Is it that you can't talk to me about it? Do you want me to get Chubs?"

I couldn't bring myself to answer.

"Ruby, you're scaring the hell out of me."

"Good." I balled up his sweater and threw it into the darkness as hard as I could.

He blew out a shaky sigh, bracing a hand against the nearest tree. "*Good?* What's good about it?"

I hadn't really understood what Clancy had been trying to tell me that night, not until right then, when Liam looked up and his eyes met mine. The trickle of blood in my ears turned into a roar. I squeezed my eyes shut, digging the heels of my palms against my forehead.

"I can't do this anymore," I cried. "Why won't you just leave me alone?"

"Because you would never leave me."

His feet shuffled through the underbrush as he took a few steps closer. The air around me heated, taking on a charge I recognized. I gritted my teeth, furious with him for coming so close when he knew I couldn't handle it. When he knew I could hurt him.

His hands came up to pull mine away from my face, but I wasn't about to let him be gentle. I shoved him back, throwing my full weight into it. Liam stumbled.

"Ruby—"

I pushed him again and again, harder each time, because it was the only way I could tell him what I was desperate to say. I saw bursts of his glossy memories. I saw all of his brilliant dreams. It wasn't until I knocked his back into a tree that I realized I was crying. Up this close, I saw a new cut under his left eye and the bruise forming around it.

Liam's lips parted. His hands were no longer out in front of him, but hovering over my hips. "Ruby . . ."

I closed what little distance was left between us, one hand sliding through his soft hair, the other gathering the back of his shirt into my fist. When my lips finally pressed against his, I felt something coil deep inside of me. There was nothing outside of him, not even the grating of cicadas, not even the gray-bodied trees. My heart thundered in my chest. *More, more, more*—a steady beat. His body relaxed under my hands, shuddering at my touch. Breathing him in wasn't enough, I wanted to inhale him. The leather, the smoke, the sweetness. I felt his fingers counting up my bare ribs. Liam shifted his legs around mine to draw me closer.

I was off-balance on my toes; the world swaying dangerously

451

under me as his lips traveled to my cheek, to my jaw, to where my pulse throbbed in my neck. He seemed so sure of himself, like he had already plotted out this course.

I didn't feel it happen, the slip. Even if I had, I was so wrapped up in him that I couldn't imagine pulling back or letting go of his warm skin or that moment. His touch was feather-light, stroking my skin with a kind of reverence, but the instant his lips found mine again, a single thought was enough to rocket me out of the honey-sweet haze.

The memory of Clancy's face as he had leaned in to do exactly what Liam was doing now suddenly flooded my mind, twisting its way through me until I couldn't ignore it. Until I was seeing it play out glossy and burning like it was someone else's memory and not mine.

And then I realized—I wasn't the only one seeing it. Liam was seeing it, too.

How, how, how? That wasn't possible, was it? Memories flowed *to* me, not *from* me.

But I felt him grow still, then pull back. And I knew, I knew by the look on his face, that he had seen it.

Air filled my chest. "Oh my God, I'm sorry, I didn't want—he—"

Liam caught one of my wrists and pulled me back to him, his hands cupping my cheeks. I wondered which one of us was breathing harder as he brushed my hair from my face. I tried to squirm away, ashamed of what he'd seen, and afraid of what he'd think of me.

When Liam spoke, it was in a measured, would-be-calm voice. "What did he do?"

"Nothing—"

"Don't lie," he begged. "Please don't lie to me. I felt it . . . my whole body. God, it was like being turned to stone. You were scared—I *felt* it, you were scared!"

His fingers came up and wove through my hair, bringing my face close to his again. "He . . ." I started. "He asked to see a memory, and I let him, but when I tried to move away . . . I couldn't get out, I couldn't move, and then I blacked out. I don't know what he did, but it hurt—it hurt so much."

Liam pulled back and pressed his lips to my forehead. I felt the muscles in his arms strain, shake. "Go to the cabin." He didn't let me protest. "Start packing."

"Lee—"

"I'm going to find Chubs," he said. "And the three of us are getting the hell out of here. *Tonight.*"

"We can't," I said. "You know we can't." But he was already crashing back through the dark path. "Lee!"

I went back to find his sweater, and pulled it on, but not even that could keep away the chill as I followed him out of the woods, back in the direction of the cabin and fire pit.

When I got to the cabin, Chubs was already there, propped up on his bed reading. He took one look at me and snapped his book shut. "What in the world happened?"

"We're leaving," I told him. "Get your things—what are you staring at? Move!"

He jumped down off the bed. "Are you okay?" he asked. "What's going on?"

I had only just finished telling him everything that had happened with Clancy, when Liam came bursting through the door. He took one look at the two of us together and let out a shaky breath. "I got worried when I couldn't find you," he told Chubs. "Are you ready?"

I pulled on a baggy T-shirt and took Liam's jacket when he threw it to me. Chubs tied up his shoes, snapped his suitcase shut, and didn't put in a word of protest as we switched off the cabin lights and headed out into the darkness.

The smell of smoke from the fire pit followed us down the main trail longer than the light or the voices from it. I caught Chubs looking back toward it over his shoulder, just once; the distant orange glow reflected in the lenses of his glasses. I knew he wanted to ask what we would do next, but Liam hushed us both and started down a side trail that I had never seen before.

It was well-worn but narrow enough that we had to walk single file. I kept my eyes on Liam's shoulders until he reached back to take my hand. The trail grew darker the farther we walked into the thick layers of young trees.

And then we were out, and there was light—so much of it, that for a moment I had to hold up a hand to cover my eyes. I felt Liam tense and stop, his hand tightening around mine until it hurt.

"Told you," I heard Hayes say. "Told you he'd try to get out this way."

"Yes, good call."

"*Damn*," I heard Chubs swear behind me, but I was too shocked to do anything other than step out from behind Liam, and see where Clancy, Hayes, and the cluster of boys from Watch stood blocking our only way out.

454

TWENTY-SEVEN

THERE WAS A SINGLE MOMENT WHEN NO ONE MOVED at all.

I recognized where we were now that the area was lit up with flashlights and lanterns. I had seen it once before, on Clancy's computer screen. This is where, days before, the skip tracers had tried to slip through the camp's wire fences and Hayes had "taken care" of them. Much like how he seemed poised to take care of us now.

The boys in front of us stood where the path met the silver wire marking East River's boundaries. Clancy was at the center, looking infinitely more pulled together than he had a few short hours ago.

"I think we need to have a talk," Clancy said, his voice pleasant. "It seems like something dangerous is about to happen."

"We're heading out," Liam said, the anger in his voice barely contained. "And we don't want trouble."

455

"You can't just *go*." Hayes pushed his way to the front of the group, looming at Clancy's side like a cannon waiting to be aimed. "We have a system here, and you haven't earned your keep yet."

The words had just left his mouth when we heard the sound of footsteps and voices crashing through the dried brush of the other, bigger trail behind them. Olivia appeared first, followed by Mike and four of the other kids Liam had been working alongside the past month. They reacted the exact way we had—first, cringing away from the light, then stopping short in shock.

"What's going on?" Olivia demanded, cutting around the line of kids in black until she was standing right in front of Clancy. "Why didn't you radio me?"

"Hayes and I have it under control." Clancy crossed his arms over his chest. "You should head back to your posts."

"Not until you tell me what's happening—" She whirled around to face us, taking in our bags. "Are you *leaving*?"

"Lee," Mike said, making the connection at the same time. "What are you doing?"

"It seems that Liam Stewart is staging another break-out," Clancy said, "or at least was attempting to. Looks like it'll be just as successful as the last."

"Go to hell," I cut in, grabbing Liam's arm before he could have a go at Clancy. He was shaking with anger, but we were outnumbered—didn't he see that?

"Ruby," Clancy said quietly, with all of the familiarity of the kid I had thought was my friend. "Come on, can we at least talk things through?"

456

Yes, a voice whispered in my ear. *Wouldn't that be for the best?* The tightly wound anger in my chest began to unravel, slowly at first, then in a strange, cool rush. My fingers slid from Liam's. All of a sudden, it did seem like talking was the best option—the only option. I had been so angry and afraid before, but this was Clancy.

It was *Clancy*.

I took a step toward him, toward that smile. I could . . . I could forgive him, couldn't I? It would be easy. Everything with Clancy was easier. My feet moved on their own, knowing exactly where I needed to go. Where I was supposed to go.

But Liam didn't let me, and Chubs wasn't about to, either. I felt the latter's hands grab my backpack. The moment Liam stepped back in front of me, Clancy disappeared from sight, and I couldn't remember why it had felt so important to go to him, to let him walk me back to camp.

"Stop it!" Liam yelled. "Whatever you're doing to her, *stop it!*"

"He's not—" Mike began, looking between Liam and Olivia. I saw her just beyond Liam's shoulders, her face a grim mask. Behind them, the other kids from Liam's watch detail were abuzz, unsure of where to look.

"I'm not doing anything," Clancy said, his voice taking on an edge of ice. "You're the one that's jealous of the relationship she and I have."

The boys around him began to nod in agreement, their faces strangely expressionless.

"You're the one that's trying to break the rules here," he continued. "Because it is a rule, isn't it, Liv? If you want to leave, you have to ask me, right?"

She hesitated, but nodded.

Liam's arm dropped from in front of me slowly. His brows drew together, and he seemed to incline his head toward Clancy, as if listening to something the rest of us couldn't hear. I felt, rather than saw, the tension leave the lines of his shoulders. He took a step back, and then another away from me, one hand going to his forehead. "Sorry . . . I just . . . I didn't mean . . ."

"You're happy here, aren't you?" Clancy asked, pleasantly. "There's no reason why you can't go back to feeling that way. There are rules here. You know them now, and you won't break them again, will you?"

"No," Liam said, his voice hoarse. He was staring at me, but his eyes had taken on a milky quality that I recognized at once. And so, apparently, did Chubs. His own eyes narrowed, zeroing in on Clancy with pure, razor-sharp fury.

"Let me tell you what I think about your fucking *rules*," he said, his voice dripping with venom as he pushed past Liam. "You sit up in your room and you pretend like you want what's best for everyone, but you don't do any of the work yourself. I can't tell if you're just a spoiled little shit, or if you're too worried about getting your pretty princess hands dirty, but it sucks. You are fucking awful, and you sure as hell don't have *me* fooled." The full force of Clancy's cold gaze fell on Chubs, but he went on, undaunted. "You talk about us all being equals, like we're one big happy rainbow of peace and all that bullshit, but you never once believed that yourself, did you? You won't let anyone contact their parents, and you don't care about the kids who are still trapped in camps *your*

458

father set up. You wouldn't even listen when the Watch kids brought it up. So what I want to know is, why *can't* we leave?" He took another step forward, cutting off Clancy before he could start speaking. "What's the point of this place, other than for you to get off on how great you are and toy with people and their feelings? I know what you did to Ruby."

The others stood by in silence, but the longer Chubs spoke, the clearer their eyes became; Mike, in particular, shook off Clancy's influence with a look like he was about to be sick. The other kids' eyes flicked around, nervous and unsure.

Clancy had been perfectly still the entire time Chubs had torn into him, but now that Chubs was finished, Clancy leaned in close, as if he were about to whisper a secret to him. Only, when he spoke, his voice was loud enough for us all to hear. "I toyed with more than her feelings." His eyes flicked to Liam's face. "Didn't I, Stewart?"

The sweep of furious crimson that washed up over Liam's throat to his face was enough to tell me exactly what kind of image Clancy had pushed into his head.

"Don't!" I screamed, but it was too late for that.

What happened next passed so fast that half of the people gathered there must have missed it. Liam raised his fist, ready to launch it into Clancy's smug face, but his hand got no farther than his shoulder. Every part of him—every muscle, every joint, every sinew—went board-straight, like he had received a great electric jolt. He froze, and a breath later, he was on the ground and Hayes's fists were slamming into his face.

"Stop!" I begged, ripping free of Chubs's grip. I knew what Clancy had done to him, and why he couldn't even raise a hand to protect his face. I saw a spray of blood hit the dirt, and it was more than I could take.

It was more than any of us could take.

"Clance," I heard Olivia say, "that's enough. You made your point. *Hayes*—you'll kill him!"

Again and again and again, on whatever surface of skin he could find, Hayes drove his fist into Liam, like he could pound his fury into him. The blows didn't stop until Clancy put a hand on his shoulder, and even then, Hayes made sure to get one last punch in across the face. He heaved Liam up by the front of his shirt, and when Clancy nodded to him, Hayes slammed Liam back against the ground and stood up, leaving him a limp mess of raw skin facedown in the dirt.

The moment the two of them were out of sight, Chubs and I both lurched forward, pushing through the circle of kids that closed around Liam. We got maybe two steps before Mike blocked us from going farther.

"Don't," he said. "You'll only make it worse."

"What are they going to do to him?" Chubs said.

"Go back to your cabin," he told us. "We'll take care of him."

"No," I said, "we're not leaving without him."

Mike rounded on me. "I don't know what the hell you said to him or made him think, but Lee was happy here. This is exactly what he needed, and you've screwed him over—"

"Don't you dare," Chubs snapped. "Don't you *dare* blame her for this. Your head is so up the Slip Kid's ass you can't see anything that's going on around you!"

460

Mike bared his teeth. "We all put up with you at Caledonia because Liam asked us to, but I don't have to do that here."

"Whatever," Chubs said. "Do you think I care about that? The only thing I care about is what's going to happen to Lee—you know, the one that put everything on the line to get us out in the first place?" His words had the desired effect. Mike paled in the darkness. "You can have your stupid Slip Kid, but don't expect us to let you keep Lee."

We threw ourselves forward again, trying to claw our way through to reach him. A pair of arms wrapped around my chest, another around my legs, and it didn't matter how hard or loud we were screaming, the kids dragged us away from Liam all the same.

Chubs and I sat on Liam's bunk, not speaking, not moving, not doing anything but watching the cabin door. Through the windows, we saw curious faces—gawkers and guards alike, all trying to figure out exactly what had happened. Lights-out had come and gone, but it wasn't like either of us was going to be able to sleep. Judging by the two figures in black standing directly in front of our door, it didn't seem like we'd be able to leave, either. Not after our failed escape attempt, and certainly not after Chubs had rained down a verbal hailstorm on Clancy.

"Where did you learn to talk like that?" I finally asked, but he only shrugged.

"I tried to imagine what Lee would have said, and went from there." Chubs rubbed the top of his head. "Did I really say he had pretty princess hands?"

461

I let out a strangled laugh. "All that and more."

The seconds ticked by at half the speed of my thoughts.

"Why weren't you affected?" I wondered aloud. "He did try it on you, didn't he?"

"He *tried*; I definitely felt it. Little did he know . . ." Chubs tapped his forehead. "Steel trap. Nothing gets out *or* in."

I had a fleeting thought that what he was saying could very well be true, and that it might even explain why his was the only head I had managed to avoid slipping into, but we heard a loud shuffle of steps on the path, and everything else flew straight out of my head.

Olivia and another kid came stumbling in, one of Liam's arms over each of their shoulders. His face was turned down, and I could see where mud had caked into his hair. The rain had started about an hour after we had left him.

"Lee," Chubs was saying, trying to get him to rouse. "Lee, can you hear me?"

We helped them lay him out on the futon. It was dark enough in the room that I didn't see the extent of his beating until Olivia set a flashlight lantern down on the floor beside him.

"Oh my God," I said.

Liam's face turned in my direction, and for the first time, I realized he was actually awake—his eyes were swollen shut. I let my hand fall on the arm hanging off the side of the futon, and moved it so it was across his chest. The breath escaped his lips in wheezing sighs. There was a thick layer of gummy, dried blood caked around his nose, his mouth,

462

down to even his chin. Daylight would reveal the rest of the bruises.

"He needs antiseptic," Chubs said, "bandages, something—"

"If you two come with me," Olivia replied, "I'll walk you to the supply room. No one will be out to bother us."

"I'm not going to leave him," I said, still crouched beside Liam on my knees.

"It's all right." I barely felt Chubs's hand on my shoulder as he brushed by.

The screen door creaked open and shut behind us; I waited until I heard the shuffling footsteps of the other kid follow them out before I looked back down at Liam's face. I moved my fingers, feather-light across his face, as gently as I could. When I came to his nose, he let out a sharp hiss, but he didn't try to twist away until I brushed his swollen split lip.

I don't know if I had ever cried as much as I had in the past month. I had never been like the other girls in my cabin at Thurmond, who cried every night, and then again every morning when they realized their nightmare had been real. I wasn't even a crier as a kid. But there was no way to hold them back now.

"Do I . . . look as pretty as I feel?" His words were slurred. I tried to get him to open his mouth, to make sure all of his teeth were still there, but his jaw was too tender for me to touch it. I leaned forward to press my lips against where my hands had been.

"Don't," he said, one eye just barely cracked open. "Not unless you mean it."

"You shouldn't have gone after him."

"Had to," he managed to mumble out.

"I'll kill him," I said, anger flaring up inside of me. "I'll *kill* him."

Liam started to chuckle again. "Ah . . . there she is. There's Ruby."

"I'll get you out of here," I promised. "You and Chubs. I'll talk to Clancy, I'll—"

"No," he said. "Stop—it'll make things worse."

"How could things possibly get any worse?" I asked. "I messed everything up for you. I ruined everything."

"God." He shook his head, mouth twisting into a shadow of a smile. "Did you know . . . you make me so happy that sometimes I actually forget to breathe? I'll be looking at you, and my chest will get so tight . . . and it's like, the only thought in my head is how much I want to reach over and kiss you." He blew out a shaky breath. "So don't talk about getting me out of here, because I'm not leaving, not unless you're part of the package, too."

"I can't go with you," I said. "I won't put you in that kind of danger."

"Bull," he said. "Nothing's going to be worse than being apart."

"You don't understand—"

"Then *make* me," Liam said. "Ruby, give me one reason why we can't be together, and I'll give you a hundred why we can. We can go anywhere you want. I'm not your parents. I'm not going to abandon you or send you away, not ever."

"They didn't abandon me. What happened to them was my fault." The secret had slipped out of me like a long

464

exhale, and I'm not sure which of us was more surprised by the admission.

Liam settled into silence, waiting for me to continue. It occurred to me then that this was it. This was really the moment I was going to lose him. And all I could think about was how much I wished I had kissed him one last time before he started fearing me for what I was.

I leaned my head down on the cushion beside his. In a whisper, because I wasn't brave enough to say it any louder, I told him about going to bed the night before my tenth birthday, about how I woke up expecting my usual birthday pancakes. About the way they locked me in the garage like some wild animal. And when that story was over, I told him about Sam. How I had been her Chubs until I wasn't, until I was nothing at all.

My throat burned when I was finished. Liam turned his face toward mine. We weren't even a breath apart.

"Never," he said after awhile. "Never, never, never. I am never going to forget you."

"You won't have a choice," I said. "Clancy said I won't ever be able to control it."

"Well I think he's full of it," Liam said. "Listen, what I saw in the woods, when you . . ."

"When I kissed you."

"Right. That . . . that really happened, didn't it? What he—what that asshole—did. That happened to you. He kept you there, frozen, like he did to me."

Yes, but also no. Because a small part of me had wanted Clancy to do it. Or had he only made me want him, played my emotions with a single touch? I nodded, finally, my insides still squirming with revulsion at the memory of his skin against mine.

"Come here," said Liam softly. I felt his fingers' light touch run along the crown of my head, feather-soft as they came down to cup my cheek. When I lifted my face, he met me halfway and kissed me. I was careful not to touch his face, only his shoulder and arm. When he pulled back, I seemed to follow, my lips searching for his.

"You want to be with me, right?" he whispered. "Then *be* with me. We'll figure it out. If nothing else, I trust you. You can look inside my head and that's all you'll see."

His warm breath spread over my cheek like another kiss. "Mike worked it out. He's going to try and find a way to sneak us out, and then you, me, and Chubs? We're gonna hit the road. We're going to find Jack's father, we're going to find a way for Chubs to reach his parents, and then we're going to talk about what we want to do."

I leaned over and pressed a kiss to his forehead. "You really don't hate me," I breathed out. "You're not scared— not even a little?"

His battered face twisted with what I thought was supposed to be a smile. "I'm scared to death of you, but for a completely different reason."

"I'm a monster, you know. I'm one of the dangerous ones."

"No you aren't," he promised. "You're one of us."

TWENTY-EIGHT

CHUBS RETURNED A FEW MINUTES AFTER LIAM faded into a restless sleep. He stirred again when we began cleaning the cuts and gouges on his face, reaching for my hand at the first touch of stinging antiseptic. When I felt his grip began to relax, and saw his eyelids flutter shut again, I finally released the breath I had been holding.

"He'll live," Chubs said, seeing my expression. He was stuffing away the rest of the supplies in my backpack. "He'll have a wicked headache in the morning, but he'll live."

We took turns sleeping, or at least pretended to. My body was thrumming with anxious unspent energy, and I could hear Chubs muttering to himself, as if trying to work through the night's events.

And then came the sound of feet slapping against the concrete steps of the cabin once more, and we gave up pretending altogether.

"Lizzie—" I heard one of the boys outside our door say. "Are you—"

She pushed past them, throwing the screen door open so hard that it slammed against the wall. Liam startled awake, more confused and disoriented than he'd been before.

"Ruby!" Lizzie was looking straight at me, her face ashen. Her hair had caught in her dozens of piercings, but it was the blood on her hands that stopped the flow of blood to my head.

"It's Clancy," she gasped, clutching my arms. "He just . . . fell and starting shaking all over like crazy, and bleeding, and I didn't know what to do, but he told me to get you because you'd know what was going on—Ruby, please, please help me!"

I stared at her hands, the wet blood.

"It's a trick," Liam croaked from the futon. "Ruby, don't you dare . . ."

"If he's really hurt, *I* should go," Chubs told Lizzie.

"Ruby!" she cried, like she couldn't believe I was standing there. "There was so much blood—Ruby, please, *please*, you have to help him!"

He really thought I was stupid, didn't he? Or did he just think his influence extended that far—that I could ever forget what he had done to Liam and go rushing to his side? I shook my head, anger rippling over my skin. Too *immature* and *weakhearted* to use my abilities, was I?

We'd see about that.

Liam pushed himself up into a sitting position. "You know him," he was saying. "Don't do it, don't—"

"Show me where he is," I said, over Chubs's protests. I turned to him. "You have to stay with Liam, understand?" *You have to watch him because I can't.* "I'll take care of everything."

I would get us out. Not Mike, not a burst of random luck—*I* would get us out, and seeing Clancy's face slack with my influence would be well worth the effort it would take to break into his mind. Hadn't he taught me everything I needed to know to do it?

"Ruby—" I heard Liam say, but I took Lizzie's arm and guided her outside, past the confused kids, past the cabins. Outside, the temperature had dropped almost twenty degrees.

Fat tears dripped down her chin. "He's in Storage—we were talking about—about—"

"It's okay," I told her, putting an awkward hand on her back. We ran through the garden and up the office's back steps. She fumbled to put her key in the lock, only to have it jam. I had to kick it in; Lizzie was too far gone to do anything but sprint inside. The hall and kitchen were empty. The whole building smelled like garlic and tomato sauce. Everyone must have been out setting up for dinner.

Everyone except Clancy, who stood in the middle of the storage room, leaning against a shelf of macaroni boxes.

Lizzie ran to the back right corner of the room and dropped to her knees. She pawed at the ground, her trembling hands clutching only air. "Clancy," she cried. "Clancy, can you hear me? Ruby is here now—*Ruby*, come here!"

My stomach turned violently, and I was surprised by how sad it made me feel to have my worst suspicions confirmed.

469

Why does it have to be like this? I thought, looking at him. Why?

"You came, you really came," Clancy said in a bored, flat voice. He sounded like he was reciting the words from a script. "Thank you, Ruby. I appreciate your help in my hour of need."

"Why are you just standing there?" Lizzie wailed. "Help him!"

"You're sick," I said, shaking my head. Clancy came toward me, but I moved to the opposite end of the room, where Lizzie had her face buried in the ground. "Stop it, I'm here. There's no reason to keep torturing her."

"I'm not torturing her," Clancy said. "I'm just playing around." And then, as if to prove his point, he barked, "Liz, shut up!"

She stopped mid-gasp. A trickle of blood escaped her lip from where she had bitten it. I took her hands, turning them over. The blood was coming from *her*, from two neat cuts across her palms.

"What do you even want?" I asked, whirling around. "I've told you everything, and what I didn't say, you went ahead and saw!"

It was only then that I noticed what Clancy was wearing. Nice, pressed black slacks, a white button-down shirt without so much as a speck of dust on it, and a red tie, trailing down over his stomach in the exact same way the blood was dripping down Lizzie's chin.

"I'm just keeping you in here for a little while," he said, "then we can go."

"And where, exactly, are we going?" My eyes fixed on the shelf behind his head, the one full of metal spoons and mixing bowls.

"Anywhere you want," he said. "Isn't that what that Blue promised you?"

I tried to stay calm, but the way he spat the word out—*Blue*—rankled my already frayed nerves. I don't know if Lizzie sensed the sharp change in my mood, but Clancy did. He was smiling, that perfect Gray smile, the same one that had followed me across Thurmond's grounds.

Good, I thought. Let him think I'm helpless. Let him think that there was no real threat from me, not until he was flat down on the ground, unable to even remember his own name.

"Do you have a better offer?" I asked.

"What if I did?"

"I'd find that hard to believe," I said, inching closer, trying to distract him, "considering you care so little about me. If this situation had been reversed, you wouldn't have come running, would you have?"

He shrugged. "I would have come. I just would have walked."

"Please let Lizzie go," I said. It scared me the way she was acting, like a little kid. What was it about being Orange that turned people into such monsters?

"Why? If she stays you won't think about trying anything, because it might mean her getting hurt, or worse." He said it so casually that I actually thought he was kidding.

"How can you be sure?" I hoped my voice sounded stronger than it felt in my throat. "I don't know her that well."

471

"I've seen your memories. You're what shrinks call 'overly empathetic.' You won't do anything if it means hurting others—not intentionally at least."

He said it with the utmost confidence, which made the shock on his face when I lunged at him that much sweeter. For once, he hadn't predicted my response, hadn't pulled me under his sway. I slashed across his face, heard him grunt as my nails bit into his cheek.

The connection was instant and powerful. It seemed that some part of what he had said was true, after all. I needed to *want* to use my abilities. I had to *want* to have control over them. And God, did I want to. I wanted to tear his brain to shreds.

The images that churned up from the dark waters of his head were so unlike what I had seen before. Instead of the bright glare and the sharp, controlled edges, they were sketched in a kind of watery charcoal. Unfocused, fuzzy. I saw faces, bloated and distorted, rise up from the murky surface. His mind had gone limp; I felt like I could reach both hands up and reshape him.

"Let her go," I said, my grip on his throat tightening. I threw the image of him sending Lizzie away, and a moment later he was mumbling the words, "Lizzie, go . . . outside."

She bolted for the door, and I felt a thrill run through me. He was shaking under my hands, his eyes blinking, but I held on to him.

"Now," I said. "Now you're going to let us go, too."

But even as the words left my mouth, I felt the unraveling. I gripped harder, my fingers digging into his skin. *Not yet*, I begged, *not yet, I need—I need to—*

472

As quickly as I had slipped in, I was thrown out, and that damn white curtain swept between us. I tried to throw myself at it again, but Clancy's hand lashed out to snatch my wrist, and I felt every muscle in my body thicken to stone.

"Nice try." Clancy let me fall to the ground like a board, and actually stepped over me to examine his scratched cheek in a pot's reflective surface. "Didn't even draw blood."

I couldn't even move my jaw to tell him off.

"Good to see my lessons were of some benefit to you," Clancy snarled, raking a hand through his disheveled hair. He turned back to face the shelves, hiding his face, but I saw his hands clench at his side, bunching up the fabric of his pants. I hadn't ruined him, but I had rattled him. "I like to see my students applying themselves, but don't mistake a few weeks of practice for years of it."

I focused on trying to untangle whatever mental block he had thrown on me. I started with my toes, imagining them moving one by one. And . . . nothing.

Maybe I could erase memories, but he could turn people into living stone.

The first scream came only a second after I heard the first whirring engines. An unnatural wind stirred up the trees outside. Their branches scratched against the side of the building, insistent, as if to get our attention. I saw Clancy cringe at the high-pitched shriek of sirens, too, but he straightened himself up from his core. His face was lit with eagerness, and that's what frightened me most of all.

"That's it, then," he said, brushing his jacket off. "They're finally here."

I couldn't squeeze my eyes shut. The air was burning them, and then the air itself was burning. The telltale smell of smoke filtered in through the open windows. Gunfire, more screaming, more struggling. I imagined myself moving, on my feet and running for the door, to the others, to safety, but I got no farther than a blink. But that was something. I could work with that.

"You're okay," Clancy told me as he sat down next to me. One of his feet began to tap out a rhythm against a stool. "I won't let anything happen to you."

The blood roared in my ears. The kind of yelling that was coming from outside didn't sound human; more like live animals having their skin torn clear off the bone. It sounded like pain, and terror, and desperation. The pitch of the metallic whine coming through the walls increased in intensity as each minute ticked on.

Rabbits need dignity and above all the will to accept their fate.

I felt, rather than heard, the footsteps thundering down the hall. I couldn't tell how many there were. They were all moving in perfect time. The storage room door burst open in an explosion of smoke and heat.

I had never been so grateful for anything in my life as I was that I was looking at his face when the PSFs barged in. The anticipation there gave way to blank incomprehension and then to pure, unadulterated rage. Whatever Clancy had been expecting, it wasn't two Psi Special Forces soldiers.

He didn't even have to touch them. "Shut up!" Clancy hissed, throwing a hand out in their direction. "Get out! Tell your superior that there was no one here!"

The man in front, his body hidden under layers of fabric and body armor, held a gloved hand against the device in his ear and said, in a monotone voice, "Building clear." The signal he gave to the other two was a simple, mechanical wave. As they jogged out of the room, I realized that they were the ones that had been letting off the smoke.

That the fires had started with them.

"Damn it—God *damn it!*" Clancy was shaking his head. A fist flew out and smashed into the nearby shelf, its impact drowned out by the rattling of gunfire outside. "Where are my Reds? Why didn't he send *them*?"

He brought a bruised knuckle to his lips and began to suck on it, pacing the short length of the room. His breath came out in short bursts, and seemed to reflect the rapid turning of his thoughts.

My Reds. His—the way that he spoke about them left no doubt in my mind what the implication was there. Project Jamboree, his father's program.

No, I thought. Not his father's.

I could see the different shards of the fractured full picture in front of me now. When he had first explained the program, I hadn't known him all that well, or seen what he was capable of doing—not enough to piece together the clues he had unintentionally left for me to uncover.

There really wasn't a single person in the world that was immune to his abilities, not even President Gray.

Clancy was still stalking across the room like a caged panther, the muscles of his back rippling with each spray of gunfire. Then he stopped, looking up at the windows and the smoke that was swirling against them.

"Who told you, you bastard?" he said, in a low enough voice that I wasn't sure he knew he was speaking aloud. "Which one of them broke my influence and figured it out? I was *so* careful. So goddamn careful—"

He turned on his heel and stalked back toward me, and I saw the truth of it all written on his face. The same hand that bled with newly split skin had been the same one to coax his father, his advisers, anyone and everyone it took, to consider Project Jamboree. Hadn't he said that before his father realized he was controlling him, Clancy had had some hand in making sure the program ran smoothly, and that the kids were treated well?

He clearly could have done more than that. If he had all of East River under his sway, what's to say he couldn't have controlled a small army of Reds, too?

Clancy must have seen the realization in my eyes, because he let out a low, humorless laugh. "I forget sometimes, you know, that he's not stupid. Even after he finally figured out I was manipulating him, he never put it together that Project Jamboree came from me. I made sure of it after I escaped—I even left East River to check on them from time to time, to make sure my influence was still there. I timed the leak of East River's location *perfectly* with the end of their training program."

One hand came up to fist in his hair, and there was something breaking in his voice when he spoke again. "I grew up idolizing him, but when I saw what he really was—what he could do to his *own son*—" His words choked off slightly. "*Who* was it? Who tipped him off? How would he have known to send the PSFs instead? I should be controlling my Reds right now—and we should all be marching up toward New York to take him down—"

Clancy bent suddenly, grabbing the front of my shirt and hauling me up from the floor. He shook me, hard enough that I almost bit my tongue clean off, but he didn't say a single word. The bullets and screams outside didn't touch his stony features, or his thoughts. Smoke began to crawl along the floor, rolling, heaving, seizing everything in its path. With no warning, Clancy's hands released my shirt and glided up my shoulders in a lover's caress; his fingers closed around my neck, and I was sure, so damn sure, that he was either going to kiss me in his rage, or kill me.

More footsteps, lighter than before, but no less urgent. Clancy looked up, annoyance creasing his forehead.

I didn't see what happened next, only the aftermath. Clancy went flying back into the shelves, hard enough that there was an audible crack as his head connected with the back wall. His body tore down the shelves of pasta and flour, landing in a messy pile on the floor.

Chubs's upside-down face appeared over mine. His glasses were scratched and bent, and his face and shirt were stained with soot, but he didn't look like he was hurt.

"Ruby! Ruby, can you hear me? We need to run." Why did he sound so calm? Gunfire roared in my ears, an endless stream of tiny pops and explosions. "Can you move?"

I was still too stiff to do anything other than shake my head.

Chubs gritted his teeth and slipped his arms around me, making sure he had a good hold. "Hold on, I'm getting us out of here. Move when you can."

Outside the safety of the Office, there was no escaping the noises. My heart lurched to life, pounding against my rib cage.

Tear gas and smoke coated the air in thick layers. Everywhere there was fire—on the ground, climbing the trees, dropping onto cabin roofs. My face and chest felt like they had caught, too. The wind blew the fire so close to us that Chubs had to pat my jeans down so I wouldn't go up in flames. He grunted, and I knew he was struggling to keep us going under my weight. I wanted to tell him to drop me, to take the letters in Liam's jacket and run.

Liam. Where is Liam?

Through the swirling ash I saw the lines of black uniforms marching the kids from camp down the path to the cabins. I saw a girl thrown out of her cabin and into the dirt, only to be yanked up by her hair. Two kids I recognized from the camp's security detail raised their guns at the PSFs, who blew them away in a cloud of fire.

"STOP WHERE YOU ARE!"

The air was knocked from my chest as Chubs dropped me to throw that same soldier up into a tree. When his arms circled my chest again, we were moving faster than before.

And then we were falling, tumbling down the hill. Chubs let out a surprised croak as we rolled, picking up brush and embers along the way. The back of my hand smacked against a tree, but I couldn't see where we were going. The smoke blinded me.

I came to a slow stop at the base of the hill, sinking face-first in the muddy bank. My hands and legs all convulsed as the feeling began to return to them.

I felt hands on the back of my jacket. Chubs dragged me on my back, choking and coughing.

We are going to die. We are going to die. We are going to die.

Rabbits need to accept their fate, rabbits need dignity and above all the will to accept their fate, their fate, their fate, their fate—

The water was freezing and swallowed me whole. Shock cut straight through my limbs, waking them with a slap. I struggled against the water, flapping my arms to break to the surface. The orange-stained sky was waiting as I broke into the night, coughing up water and poisoned air.

Chubs found me again. One hand clung to a wood post, the other reached out for me. *The dock*, I thought, *our dock*. I kicked toward him and let Chubs draw me under the cover of the old wood. The helicopters flying overhead beat the lake into a frenzy of waves and patterns. I could barely keep my head above the cold water, but I was alert enough to see the searchlights from above dancing over the lake's surface.

I kept one arm around Chubs's shoulders and used my free hand to reach up and grab hold of the dock's algae-slick supports. He did the same, and waited until the sound of boots and guns had cleared from overhead before whispering, *"Oh my God."*

479

I moved my arm to draw us closer together, and hugged him as hard as my muscles could. We didn't dare to speak, but I felt him shake his head. He knew what I was trying to say, I knew what he wanted to ask, and neither of us could find the words to choke out amid the smoke and screams.

TWENTY-NINE

MY LEGS WERE HALF FROZEN WHEN WE WERE FINALLY brave enough to move. It had been silent for some time—since the sun began to warm the sky. The helicopters disappeared first, then the sound of gunfire. Between the two of us, there was only breathing and whispered fears about what had happened to the others—to Liam.

"I don't know," he said. "We split up. He could be anywhere."

I had wanted to get us out of the water two hours before, but we kept hearing the sound of falling trees and the crackling remnants of the terrible firestorm.

My muscles were so stiff that it took me three times as long to pull myself onto the dock than it normally would have. Chubs collapsed beside me, shaking with each cold breeze that slashed over our wet clothes. We crawled our way back up the path, staying low to the ground until we were sure, positive beyond measure, that we were the last ones left.

Most of the cabins were gone—piles of charred wood and stone. A few still stood, burned out and hollow or missing their roofs. Ash flew around us like snow, collecting on our hair and sticking to our wet clothes.

"We should go to the Office," I said. "Get inside. We can gather up supplies and then try to go out and search for Lee."

Chubs's feet slowed beside me, and I saw for the first time how red his eyes were. "Ruby . . ."

"Don't say it," I warned, my voice sharp. It wasn't an option. "Don't."

I didn't want to think about Lee. I didn't want to think about Zu or the other kids who had gotten out of camp. We had to keep moving. If I stopped now, I knew I would never be able to start again.

The front rooms were clear. The boxes and tubs had been removed. I forced Chubs to walk behind me when I slipped into the storage room, but it was empty.

"Maybe they got him," Chubs said, rubbing his head.

I grimaced. "When have we ever been that lucky?"

Upstairs, the bedroom was perfect. Before he left, Clancy had made his bed, put away the stacks of paper and boxes, and, it appeared, dusted. I ripped the white curtain back, joining the two halves of the room while Chubs fussed with the TV, clicking the power button on and off.

"They cut the electricity," he said. "Want to bet they cut the water, too?"

I collapsed down in Clancy's office chair and pressed my face against the dark wood. Chubs tried to peel Liam's wet jacket off my shoulders, but I wouldn't let him.

"Thank you for coming to find me," I said, closing my eyes.

"You dumbass," said Chubs affectionately. He patted me on the back. "Always running right into trouble."

When I didn't move, I felt his hand still on my shoulder. "Ruby?"

"Why did he do this?" I whispered. Everything in this room reminded me of Clancy, from the smell to the way he had organized the books by color on the shelves. "He just threw them all to the wolves."

Chubs squatted down beside me, his knees cracking like an old man's. His hand never left my arm, but he seemed to struggle with what he wanted to say next.

"Far be it from me to even approach untangling that hellhole of a mind," he said, carefully. "But I think he just liked being in control. In charge. It made him feel powerful to manipulate people because he knew outside of this place he was just as vulnerable as the rest of us. There are some people like that, you know? The darkest minds tend to hide behind the most unlikely faces. He put on a good leader act, but he wasn't like . . . he wasn't like Lee—or Jack. He didn't want to help kids because he believed everyone deserved to feel strong and protect themselves. Clancy was only ever thinking of himself. He would never have jumped in front of another person and . . . He would never have taken a bullet."

At that, I sat up. "I thought Jack was shot escaping?"

Chubs shook his head. "Jack was shot protecting me, and he protected me because—" He took a deep breath.

483

"Because he thought I couldn't protect myself. He didn't realize how much he had taught me."

"I'm so sorry," I said, feeling tears prick at the back of my eyes. "For everything."

"Me too," he said after a minute, and I didn't need to look back to know that he was crying, too.

The laptop was stored in the top drawer of his desk, the note taped to the top of it glaringly yellow.

Ruby,
I lied before. I would have run.
—CG

"Chubs!" I called, waving him over. The power-on chime was oddly sweet. Little bells.

"He just left it here?" Chubs asked, tapping his fingers against the desk. "Is the wireless card still there?"

It was, but Clancy had taken care to wipe everything else from the computer. Only the icon for the Internet was left, sitting in the middle of the screen.

"Why does the clock in the corner say fifteen?" Chubs asked, sitting down in the chair. I leaned over to see what he was pointing at. The battery life. We only had fifteen minutes.

"That *asshole*," I fumed.

Chubs shook his head. "It's better than nothing. As long as the connection holds, we can use it to try to figure out a way out of here. We can even look up Jack's father's new address."

"And post your message to your parents," I said, feeling a frail wave of happiness cut through me.

"It's okay. I'd rather use these . . . fourteen minutes to find Jack's dad," he said. "I might even be able to put a call through to him if the computer has a microphone."

He didn't dare try to call his own parents.

"Seriously," I began. "It'll take you two seconds to post the message. Do you remember it?"

"Enough to make it work," he said.

I moved around the room listlessly, listening to him type, taking in the room's stale smell. My feet drew me over to the side of Clancy's bed, where I finally stopped, my anger at him overwhelming even the anxiety I felt.

The window was coated in soot and protested bitterly when I tried to throw it open. The flood of fresh air that rushed in made it worth the fight; I leaned forward, bracing my arms against the sill. The camp was spread out before me in piles of ash and scorched earth, but it was all too easy to imagine where the clusters of kids had once stood, waiting to get their food by the fire pit. When I closed my eyes, I could hear the laughter and radio drifting up to me, taste the spice of chili and wood smoke on the air. I saw Liam below, the firelight turning his hair pure gold as he bent his head in quiet conversation with the others.

And when my eyes opened, I was no longer just imagining him.

I tore out of the room, ignoring the way Chubs's voice followed me. I stumbled down the stairs, trying to take too many at once, flew through the entryway and out the door that was barely hanging from its frame.

He was down the trail, back toward the cabins, struggling to get around the maze of fallen trees and buildings. His battered face was twisted with grief and fear, and he could barely limp through the wreckage.

"Lee!" The word exploded out of me. He dropped the charred wood from his hands and struggled over the tree, blindly fighting his way through its leaves and branches. Seeing me. Believing and not believing it all at once. "Oh my God!" I threw my arms around his neck and nearly took us both down.

"Thank you," he was whispering, "thank you, thank you. . . ." And then he was kissing my face, every inch of it he could find, wiping away the tears and soot, chanting my name.

Liam wasn't the only one who escaped, but he was the only one who came back.

He had relived the night for us as we sat in Clancy's office, eating what food was left in the supply room. Chubs had the laptop at his side, checking every few minutes for a message from his parents, or rechecking the address he had found for Jack's dad.

When the fighting had broken out, it was enough of a surprise that most of the Watch kids couldn't get to the cabins from the outer gates in time to make a real difference. The ones who were off duty came to our cabin and forced him—"Carried me, is more like it," Liam said, bitterly—away, running for one of the hidden side trails that had been marked for this exact purpose. They moved until morning, not stopping until they reached that same stretch of highway that they had picked us up on.

"There were maybe twenty of us at most," he said, gripping my hand. "All in bad shape. Liv and Mike found a working car and piled the ones that were scary bad into the back, to go find a hospital, but . . ."

"What about the rest of them?" I asked.

"They split." Liam rubbed at his eyes and winced. The skin there was still tender, blooming to black.

"And why didn't *you*?" Chubs demanded. "What the hell is the matter with you that you'd come back here, knowing that there could still be PSFs?"

Liam only snorted. "You think that mattered to me for a second when there was a chance the two of you were still here, too?"

We didn't have time to waste; we all knew the PSFs well enough to know that there was a chance they would double back and check for survivors. The two of them went to work immediately in the supply closet, trying to figure out how much food we could carry with us. I tried to be useful, too, but I could feel my attention drifting upstairs, to Clancy's desk.

I finally gave into my restlessness and left the two of them locked in an argument over canned food. I made my way back upstairs, patting the inside pocket of Liam's jacket to make sure Jack's and Chubs's still-damp letters were there.

There were two minutes left of the laptop's battery. The power icon was flashing, warning that reserves were low. The screen dimmed and the lights in the keyboard switched off. I typed as fast as I could, searching the online White Pages for Ruby Ann Daly, Virginia Beach.

No results.

I tried again, just with her name but no location. A listing did pop up, but it was for Salem. I hadn't lived there in close to a decade, but I recognized my parents' address when I saw it.

A minute and fifteen seconds. I looked in the Web-site history for the site Chubs had talked about, the one that let you make calls, and typed in the phone number. I lost two seconds with each ring.

I don't think I wanted to talk to her so much as to hear her speak. Going to her wasn't an option for me anymore. There were more important things to take care of. But I needed to know that she was still out there—that there was one more person in the world who remembered me.

It clicked. My heart jumped up into my throat, my fingers curling against the desk.

My mother's voice.

Hello, you've reached the residence of Jacob, Susan, and Ruby Daly . . .

I don't know why I started to cry then. Maybe I was exhausted. Maybe I was tired of how hard everything had become. I was happy that the three of them were together, that Mom and Dad had fixed their family and replaced one Ruby with another. The thing I'd realized most over the past few days was how important it was for us to take care of one another and stick together. And they were taking care of each other. Good.

Good.

But it didn't mean that I wasn't going to close my eyes and pretend, if only for a few minutes, that I was the Ruby who still lived on Millwood Drive.

488

THIRTY

Hours later, when it was just the three of us back on the road, we finally had a chance to tell Liam exactly what had happened to us the night before.

"Thank God Chubs found you," Liam said, shaking his head. "You knew him better than any of us, and you still went."

"I really thought I could control him," I said, leaning my forehead against the cool window. "I'm an idiot."

"Yes, you are," Chubs agreed. "But you're *our* idiot, so be more careful next time."

"Cosigned," Liam said, hooking his fingers over mine on top of the armrest.

We'd found the car abandoned along a side road a few miles west of East River, and picked it only because it still had a quarter tank of gas. Driving in this car was nothing like driving in Betty. Chubs's long legs dug into the back of my seat, and the car smelled like old Chinese food. Still, it was running. After a while, it would become ours.

"There's another one," Chubs said, tapping on his window.

I opened my eyes and craned my neck back, catching a quick look at the white pole. On top of it was a white box, and on top of that was a small antenna. Cameras, everywhere.

"Maybe we should get off the highway," Liam suggested.

"No!" Chubs said. "We've seen two whole cars since we got on the sixty-four, and it'll take us twice as long to get to Annandale if we get off again. They'll be watching for Betty, anyway, not this car."

Liam and I shared a look. "Tell me again what your mom's message said?"

"She said to make a reservation at my aunt's restaurant and wait for them in the kitchen," Chubs said. "I did that from East River, so we should be set to meet them there tonight. My aunt will probably even feed us."

"Let's drop you off first, then," Liam said.

"No," Chubs said. "I want to deliver Jack's letter."

"Chubs . . ."

"Don't *Chubs* me," he snapped. "I owe Jack a lot. I want to do this."

The address for Jack's father was a Days Inn motel, far away from Annandale's neighborhoods of sprawling homes. Liam seemed to think that the motel had been converted to a temporary housing complex for the workers rebuilding D.C., but there was no way to prove his theory until a rickety old bus pulled up alongside our car in the parking lot and unloaded a dozen dust-covered men, clutching neon vests and hard hats.

"Room 103," Liam said, leaning over the steering wheel. He squinted with his good eye. "The guy in the red shirt. Yeah, that's him—Jack looked a lot like him."

The man was short and square, with a graying moustache and a wide nose.

Chubs reached between us and plucked the wrinkled letter out of my hand.

"Slow down, Turbo," Liam said, clicking the car locks on. "We haven't even checked to make sure he's not being watched."

"We've been out here for almost an hour—do you *see* anyone? The only other cars in the parking lot are empty. We lay low, like you wanted, and it worked." He reached over and pulled the lock up manually. Liam stared at him for a moment, before relenting.

"All right; just be careful, will you?"

We watched him scurry across the parking lot, glancing around. Making sure there really was no one out watching room 103. He tossed a *told you so* look over his shoulder.

"Nice," Liam said. "Real nice."

I reached over and rubbed his shoulder. "You know you'll miss him."

"It's insane, isn't it?" he said, with a light laugh. "What am I going to do without him telling me how dangerous it is to open canned food the wrong way?"

Liam waited until Chubs had raised his hand and knocked before unbuckling his seat belt to lean over and give me a light kiss.

"What was that for?" I said, laughing.

"To get your mind on the right track," he said. "After we take him home, we have to figure out how to find Zu and the others before the PSFs do."

"What if—"

The door to room 103 cracked open, and the face of Mr. Fields appeared, tired and suspicious. Chubs lifted the wrinkled letter and extended it out to him. I wished Chubs had turned at an angle so we could have made out what he was saying. The man's face flushed crimson, so dark that it matched his work shirt. He yelled something, loud enough that his next-door neighbors opened their curtains to see what was happening.

"This is bad," Liam said, unlocking his door. "I knew I should have had him practice with me first."

The door shut in Chubs's face, only to open again all the way. I saw a flash of silver, saw Chubs raise his hands and take a step back.

The gunshot tore through the sunset, and by the time I screamed, Chubs was already on the ground.

We ran toward the room, screaming for him. All the complex's residents were standing outside now, mostly men, some women. Their faces were monstrous blurs.

Jack's father raised his shaking gun toward us, but Liam threw him back into his room and pulled the door shut with a sweep of his hand. My knees slid across the loose asphalt as I dropped down beside Chubs.

His eyes were open, staring at me, blinking. *Alive.*

He tried to tell me something, but I couldn't hear over

492

the screaming from inside 103. *"Fucking freaks! Get out of here you goddamn freaks!"*

Bright red blood bubbled up from just below Chubs's right shoulder, spreading out over his shirt with hundreds of gliding fingers. I couldn't do anything at first. It didn't look real. Liam diving for the man's gun, pointing it at 104 and 105, not real.

"It's okay," someone said behind us. Liam whirled around, his finger on the trigger, his face set in stone. The man raised his hands; he was holding a small phone. "I'm just calling nine-one-one, it's okay; we'll get him help."

"Don't let them call," Chubs gasped. "Don't let them take me." He choked on the words. "I need to go home."

Liam looked back over his shoulder. "Grab his legs, Ruby."

"Don't move him," the man from 104 said. "You're not supposed to move him!"

Jack's father appeared behind us again, but the man with the cell phone tackled him back into the room and kicked the door shut behind him.

"Grab him," Liam said, tucking the gun into the waistband of his jeans.

I slipped my arms under Chubs's, carrying him the same way he had carried me. One of the other men stepped forward—maybe to stop us, maybe to help.

"Don't touch him!" I screamed. They backed off, but only just.

Chubs pressed his own hands against the wound, his eyes wide and unblinking. Liam took his legs, and together we carried him. The men called after us, telling us the

493

ambulance would be there any minute. The ambulance, along with every PSF. The soldiers wouldn't save him; they wouldn't. They'd rather see a freak kid die.

"Don't let them take me," Chubs squeezed out. "Keep my legs below my chest, Lee, don't lift them so high, not for chest wounds, breathing difficult—"

It wasn't the babbling that sent the spikes of fear straight into my heart, but the unending pulse of blood leaking out from behind his hands. He was shaking, but not crying. "Don't let them take me. . . ."

I climbed into the backseat first, pulling Chubs in behind me. His blood soaked through the front of my shirt, burning against my skin.

"Keep . . . pressure on it," Chubs told me. "Harder . . . Ruby, harder. I'm going to try to . . . hold it in with . . ."

His abilities, I think. The blood did seem to slow somewhat when his hand covered it again. But how long could that actually last? My hands covered his, shaking so hard they probably did more harm than good.

"God," I was saying, "oh my God, don't close your eyes—talk to me, keep talking to me, tell me what to do!"

The car squealed as we turned out of the parking lot. Liam hit the gas as hard as he could, slamming his palms down against the steering wheel. *Shit, shit, shit!*

"Take me home," Chubs begged. "Ruby, make him take me home."

"You're going—you'll be fine," I told him, leaning over so he could see my eyes.

"My dad . . ."

494

"No—Lee, *hospital*!" I wasn't speaking in sentences, and Chubs wasn't either, not anymore. He made a sound like he was choking on his own tongue.

When the glimpses came, they were washed in the same bright red as his blood. A man sitting in a large armchair, reading. A beautiful woman leaning across a kitchen table. A cross-stitch pattern, an emergency room sign. The black at the edge of my vision was curling up. Someone had taken a knife and driven it straight down into my brain.

"Alexandria is a half hour away," Liam shouted, turning back over his shoulder. "I'm not taking you there!"

"Fairfax Hospital," Chubs wheezed out. "My dad . . . tell them to page Dad. . . ."

"Where is it?" Liam demanded. He looked at me, but I had no idea, either. It occurred to me then that there was a chance we would be driving around so long that Chubs would die. He would bleed out right here, right now, in my lap. After everything.

Liam whipped the car around so hard I had to brace Chubs and me from flying off the seat. I bit my tongue in an effort to keep from screaming again.

"Keep talking to him!" Liam said. "Chubs—*Charles!*"

I don't know when and where he had lost his glasses. His eyes were red at the edges, staring up at my face. I tried to hold his gaze for as long as I could, but he was trying to hand me something. Chubs lifted his hand from where it had fallen across his stomach.

Jack's letter. Its edges soaked in wet, sticky blood, but open. Waiting to be read.

495

The handwriting was small and cramped. Each letter had a ghostly halo around it from the time it had spent submerged with the two of us in the lake, and some were gone completely.

Dear Dad,
When you sent me to school that morning, I thought
you loved me. But now I see you for what you are. You
called me a monster and a freak. But you're the one
that raised me.

"Tell him to read . . ." Chubs licked his lips. I had to lean down to hear his voice over the wind outside. "Tell Lee to read my letter. I wrote it . . . it was for him."

"Charles," I said.

"Promise—"

Whatever lodged itself in my throat made it impossible to speak. I nodded. A rush of blood bubbled up under our hands, coming faster than before.

"Where is it?" Liam was shouting. "Chubs, where is the hospital? You have to—you have to tell me where it is!"

The car began to quiver, then howl, sounding more beast than machine. Liam hit a pothole in the road that sent the front hood flying up, along with a cloud of gray-blue smoke. We got another ten, maybe twenty feet, before the car jerked to a dead stop.

I looked up, meeting his gaze.

"I can fix it," Liam swore, his voice breaking, "I can fix it—just—just—keep him talking, okay? I can fix this. I can."

I waited until I heard the door slam behind him before I closed my eyes. Chubs had gone so still, so pale, and no amount of shaking or yelling would bring him back out of it. I felt his blood leak past my hands, scarlet under the overcast sky, and I thought about what he had said the night Zu left us. *It's over. It's all over.*

And it was. The unnatural calm that settled over me told me as much. All along, I'd been fighting. I'd been fighting the moment I left Thurmond, struggling against the restraints everyone wanted to wrap around me, kicking and clawing against the inevitable. But I was tired now. So tired. I couldn't deny what a part of me had known from the moment the PSFs had burned my world down. What a part of me had known all along.

What had Miss Finch said, all those years ago? That there were no do-overs, no comebacks? That once someone was gone, they were gone forever. Dead flowers didn't bloom, and they didn't grow. A dead Chubs wouldn't smile, spout off rambling sentences, wouldn't pout, wouldn't laugh—a dead Chubs was unimaginable.

I reached into the pocket of Liam's jacket and pushed the panic button. Twenty seconds clicked by, each one feeling longer than the last. It gave a little vibration, a little acknowledgment, and I released it.

Outside, Liam was banging metal against metal—growing more helpless and angry by the second. I wanted to call him back to us, to have him next to Chubs, because I was sure this was it. I was sure he was going to die right there in my arms, less than twenty-four hours after he had saved me. And I couldn't do anything for him other than hold him.

"Do not die," I whispered. "You cannot die. You have to take calculus and go to football games and go to prom and apply to colleges and you absolutely cannot die. You can't—you *can't*—"

I detached completely. A familiar numbness took hold of my entire body. I was vaguely aware of Liam shouting something outside. My arms tightened around Chubs's chest. I heard feet shuffling against the loose asphalt outside; all I could smell was smoke and blood. All I could hear was my own heartbeat.

That's when the door across from me opened, and Cate's face appeared.

And that's when I began to cry, really cry.

"Oh, *Ruby*," she said, anguished. *"Ruby."*

"Please help him," I sobbed. "Please!"

Two pairs of hands reached in to lift me out. My arms were still wrapped around Chubs. I couldn't move my hands. There was so much blood. I kicked and butted against whoever was trying to pull us apart.

"Ruby, sweetheart," Cate said, suddenly next to me. "Ruby, you have to let go now."

I had made a mistake. This was a mistake. I never should have called them. A terrible noise filled the air, and it wasn't until Liam was there, holding me back, his arms around my shoulders, that I realized I had been screaming the entire time.

There were three cars surrounding our smoking, useless hunk of metal. All SUVs.

"If you get him help, we'll go with you," I heard Liam tell Cate. "We'll go with you. We'll do whatever you want."

"No," I cried. *"No!"*

Liam was holding me steady, but I felt the way his arms shook. We watched them load Chubs's still form into the back of one of the SUVs, and the door had barely shut before it tore off down the highway. Chubs's blood was still warm on my skin, cooling every second, and it made me want to crawl out of it.

"Please," Liam said, his voice breaking. "Calm down. You have to calm down. I've got you. I'm right here."

There was a pinch on the back of my neck; there and gone, faster than taking a breath. All at once, I felt my muscles relax. I was being dragged forward on limp legs, the image of the nearest white SUV swimming in and out of focus. *Lee?* I wanted to say, but my tongue was too heavy. Someone slid a dark hood over my face, and I was being lifted—up, up into the air, like my father used to do when I was just a kid. When I thought I could grow up and fly.

And then the real darkness came.

THIRTY-ONE

IT WAS THE COLD WATER THAT WOKE ME, MORE THAN the woman's soft voice. "You're all right," she was saying. "Ruby. You're gonna be fine." I'm not sure who she thought she was fooling with her sweet little B.S., but it wasn't me.

The smell of rosemary was back, filling my nose with a memory that felt both ancient and new. Which was it?

When I felt the press of her hand against mine, I forced my eyes open, blinking against the sunlight. Cate's face swam in and out of my vision. She stood and crossed the room, drawing the gauzy curtains shut. It helped somewhat, but I was still having trouble fixing my sight on any one thing. It was glancing off bright, shiny surfaces. A white dresser, pale purple wallpaper, a flashing alarm clock, a mirror on the opposite wall, and our reflections there.

"Is this real?" I whispered.

Cate sat at the edge of my bed, the exact same way she had at Thurmond, only now she wasn't smiling. Behind her,

Martin leaned against the wall in camo pants and boots. He looked like a completely different person to me. I hadn't fully recognized him at first glance. The roundness in his face had thinned out, sinking his eyes further into his skull. Someone had been dumb enough to give him a gun.

"We're in a safe house outside of Maryland," she said.

"Lee?"

"Safe here, too."

Not safe, I thought; never safe with you.

I felt the urge to run rise up deep from my bones; it was instinct now. Exhaustion and pain had stripped every other sensation away from me. My eyes scanned the room—two windows, the only other exit aside from the door. I could break the glass. I force Cate back with a single brush of my mind, get Liam, and we could be gone before anyone noticed. It could work.

"Don't even try," Cate said, following my eyes. She slipped a small silver object from the back pocket of her jeans and held it out to me, the rough pattern of the speaker face up. "Even if you could get past me, every single one of the agents downstairs is carrying one of these on them. Judging by your last hit of Calm Control, you're not going to be of much use to Liam when they take him out and shoot him for your insubordination."

I jerked away. "They wouldn't—" But I saw the truth of it in her eyes. They would. They risked everything to break me out of Thurmond. They fought off skip tracers to get me back. I had already seen in Rob's mind that despite what they claimed their mission was, they didn't have any qualms about offing a few kids if it meant getting the ones they wanted.

"How could you even think about it?" Martin hissed. "Do you know how much time she wasted looking for you?"

Cate waved him off. When she leaned toward me again, I saw there were splatters of blood across the front of her shirt. Dark. Dried.

The memory came into painfully sharp focus. "Chubs—what happened to Chubs?"

Cate looked down at her hands, and something in me clenched.

"Honestly," she said, "I'm not sure. We haven't been able to contact the group of agents that took him, but I know they reached the hospital." Cate reached for my hands, but I wouldn't let her take them. The thought turned my stomach. "He's safe. They'll make sure he's taken care of."

"You don't know that," I said. "You said it yourself."

"But I believe it," Cate said.

I wanted to tell her that her beliefs weren't worth a damn thing when she spoke again. "I've spent the last month looking for you. I stayed in this area, hoping you'd eventually show up, but Ruby, where were you? Where did you go? You look like—like—"

"East River," I said.

Cate sucked in a sharp breath. So the League had heard about what happened.

"Oh, that's perfect," Martin said, pushing himself up off the wall. He slid the strap of his rifle over his shoulder and stalked toward me. "Sitting around on your ass for weeks

502

doing nothing? Figures. I've been actually making a difference. I've been part of something."

He made as if to touch my leg, but I grabbed his wrist tight in my hand. I wanted to see what he had gone through for myself—the training, the screaming instructors. I latched on to the strongest of his memories and spread it open in my mind. I wanted to glimpse our future.

Martin's memory bubbled up like hot tar, forming and shaping itself until I was standing where he had stood. The package that had been in his hands was now heavy in mine. I felt the weight of it cramp my fingers, but my eyes were focused only on the climbing numbers on the elevator's display: 11, 12, 13 . . . The bell dinged as it passed each floor, heading to 17.

I cast a sly look to the girl standing next to me, dressed in a skirt suit, her young face caked with enough makeup to age her well beyond her years. She clutched her leather tote bag to her side like a shield, and it was only when she released it that I noticed her hands were shaking.

I was wearing a FedEx uniform; I could see myself through Martin's eyes, reflected in the elevator's silver doors as they slid open.

We were in an office building of some kind. It was dark out, but there were still men and women working, tucked away in their cubicles, their eyes glued to their computer screens. I didn't stop, though, and neither did the girl at my side. Her face had broken out in a sweat, heavy enough to smear her makeup, and I felt a stab of irritation go through me at the sight of it.

The largest office was located at the far back corner of the building, and that was where I was headed. The girl all but let out a sigh as I left her by the drinking fountains. She was there for backup. This was *my* mission.

The door to the office was closed, but I could see someone's shape behind the frosted glass. *He's still here.* And so, thankfully, was his executive assistant. She looked confused at the sight of the package, but all it took was a single stroke at the back of her hand. Her eyes went glassy, unfocused, and I knew I had her. The elderly woman got up from her chair and turned toward the office door. I left the package right on her desk.

Free of that weight, I hustled back through the maze of cubicles, catching the eye of the girl by the fountain. When I jerked my head toward the elevators, she followed, looking back and forth between the elevator bank and the office floor, her lip caught between her teeth.

She didn't do anything stupid until we were outside, though. I jogged down the steps, heading for the waiting FedEx van and the dark-haired man sitting in the driver's seat. I was already at the door when I realized she wasn't behind me. The girl was frozen at the top of the marble steps, her eyes wide and her face as pale as the stone beneath her feet.

She was going to run back into the building to warn them about the explosive, to warn them. *Weak.* The words shot through my mind, as crisp as if they had been drilled there. *Ditch and die. Double-cross the League and die.*

I took the handgun from under my seat and leaned out the open window. But I never got a shot off. Upstairs, high on the seventeenth floor of the building, an explosion blew out a shower of glass and concrete, and she had disappeared under their weight.

Martin's hand stayed at my side, and he stopped moving. This is what it means to be one of them, I thought. This is what they will turn us into. I had slipped into his mind to confirm my suspicions, but even I was surprised at how easy it had been. Weeks ago, when we first got out, I hadn't been able to fend him off. Now, all he had to do was brush by me and I overpowered him. With a single touch.

Clancy had taught me well.

I looked at Martin again, feeling a strange sort of pity for him. Not because of what I was about to do, or the way I would be using him, but because he thought he knew what it meant to be powerful and in control. He honestly still thought he was stronger than me.

I put a finger on the back of his hand, just one.

"What's your name?" I asked him.

The reaction from him was priceless. There wasn't an ounce of color left in his cheeks, and his lips began to smack against one another, trying to form the word, trying to call up a memory that was no longer there.

"Where are you from?"

I could see the panic now; it caused his eyes to bulge. But I still wasn't finished.

"Do you know where you are now?"

I almost felt guilty—*almost*—when I saw the moisture began to gather at the corner of his eyes. But I also remembered how helpless and afraid he had made *me* feel, and I regretted not having done more. A plan was forming at the back of my mind, and it was almost too terrible to acknowledge as my own.

"I don't—" He gasped the words out. "I don't—"

"Then maybe you should leave," I said in a cold voice.

I barely had to push the image of him doing it. He bolted from the room, slamming the door behind him. Running from the scary monster.

Cate stared after him, an unreadable expression on her face. "Impressive."

"I thought he could do with an attitude adjustment," I said. I kept my voice cold and flat, just the way I thought she'd want it. I had seen enough to know the viciousness these people demanded, and I needed them to want me. "Since it seems we'll be spending a lot of time together now."

Her pale blond hair fell over her shoulders as she bowed her head, but Cate didn't deny it. We were trapped here. She had accepted Liam's deal.

"I guess it was never really a choice to begin with," I continued. "Eventually, you were going to have to bring me in."

"You are a valuable asset to the resistance." Cate lifted her hand toward me, only to drop it before it could touch my face. Smart lady. She knew what I could do. "I hoped you would come to see that on your own terms."

"What about Lee?"

"He's a security risk now that he's seen this safe house and the agents here. He's safer with us, Ruby. The president wants him dead. I'm sure he'd come to see that . . . eventually."

My hands twisted against the pale bed sheets. A weapon. Liam as a weapon. Liam, who could barely lose his temper without feeling guilty. He had fought so hard to escape this violence, and I'd turned him right back toward it. They'd put their hands on him and press him into their mold, and he'd come out the other end of it as the same dark creature he had struggled to avoid becoming.

I was breathing hard now, though inwardly I was as calm as the waters on East River's lake. All at once, the final piece clicked into place, and I knew what I was going to do.

"Okay," I said. "I'll stay and I won't fight you or manipulate you. But if you want me to do as you say . . . if you want to use my abilities, or do testing on me, I have one condition. You have to let Lee go."

"Ruby," she began, shaking her head, "it's too dangerous, for everyone involved."

"He's a Blue. You don't need him. He won't ever be a fighter, not like you want."

And if he stays here, you will kill him.

You will kill every good part of him.

"I can do so much now," I told her, "but you won't see another hint of it until you let him go. Until you swear you will never chase him down."

Cate watched me for a moment, a hand pressed to her mouth. I could see the indecision in her face. I had used Martin to show her exactly what I could offer them, and he, apparently, had already proven to them how valuable an Orange could be. These were not, however, the terms she would have chosen.

507

"All right," she said, finally. "All right. He can go."

"How do I know you'll keep your promise?" I asked.

Cate stood and reached again into her pocket. The silver Calm Control device, the only thing keeping me out of her head, was still warm when she pressed it into my palm. My fingers closed around hers.

"So help me God," I said slowly, clearly, when Cate looked up at me. "If you go back on your word, I will tear you apart. And I won't stop, not ever, until I've destroyed your life and the lives of every single person in this organization. Believe me, you may not always keep your promises, but *I* do."

She nodded at me once, and there was something almost like pride in her eyes.

"Understood," Cate said, and we did.

They kept Liam in the bedroom at the other end of the hall, in a room painted a soft blue. The kind of color you'd only find in the sky just before sunrise, maybe. It might have been a nursery once. There were clouds painted on the ceiling, and the few pieces of furniture left seemed too small for an average adult.

Liam sat on the tiny bed with his back to me. At first, as I shut the door behind me, I thought he was staring out the window. As I came closer, I saw he was actually fixated on the wrinkled sheet of paper in his hand.

The bed dipped as I crawled across it, wrapping my arms around his chest from behind. I pressed my cheek against his, letting my hands wander until they found his steady heartbeat. He shut his eyes and leaned back.

508

"What are you looking at?" I whispered.

He handed me the paper wordlessly as I moved to sit beside him. Jack Fields's letter.

"You were right," Liam said after a moment. "You were so right. We should have read it. We would have known not to bother."

It was the dead way he spoke, so flat, so coated with grief, that made me crumple the letter and throw it across the room. He only shook his head, pressing a hand over his eyes.

I fumbled with the inside pocket of his jacket, where I had stashed Chubs's letter all those days ago. Liam watched me pull it out, and sagged beside me.

"He told me he didn't write it for them," I said. "He wrote it for you. He wanted you to read it."

"I don't want to."

"Yes, you do. Because when you get out of here, you'll want something to say when you see him again."

"Ruby." Now he sounded angry. His arm dropped from around my shoulders, and he stood up. "Do you really think that if he lives, they're going to let us see him? Do you think they're even going to let *us* stay together? That's not how these people work. They're going to control our every move, right down to who we see and what we eat. Trust me, it'll be some precious piece of luck if we even find out if he's alive, never mind if they've brought him in for training."

Liam paced the room once, twice, three times, and it felt like an hour had passed before I worked up the nerve to open Chubs's letter myself.

The room was silent for a long time.

"What?" Liam asked, finally. His voice was laced with fear. "What does it say?"

It was blank. There was nothing written on the sheet of paper aside from Chubs's parents' name and their address, and there had never been. Not a single drop of ink.

"I don't understand . . ." I said, passing it to him. That couldn't have been right. Maybe he had lost the original letter, or was carrying the real one? When I looked up again, Liam was crying. One hand destroying the letter in his fist, the other pressed against his eyes. And then I realized I already knew the answer.

Chubs hadn't written anything because he didn't think he had to. He thought he was going to be able to tell his parents everything he wanted to say in person. He believed he was going to get home.

Liam's knees seemed to buckle out from under him as he sat back down on the bed. His forehead came down to rest against my shoulder, and I wrapped both arms around him. *He did believe you*, I wanted to say. *All along, he believed you.*

I felt so much older, then. Not sixteen, not sixty, not even a hundred, but a thousand years old. Older, but not brittle. I felt like one of the oak trees that grew along the highway overlooking the Shenandoah Valley, with deep roots and a strong core.

He gets to go, I thought. He gets to go home.

For a long time I did nothing but hold on to him. I wanted to memorize the way his hair curled at the ends, the scar at the edge of his lips. I had never felt time's sting as sharply as I did then. Why did it only ever seem to freeze or move forward at a barreling speed?

"The crazy thing is, I had all of these plans," he whispered. "What we were going to do. All the places I was going to take you. I really wanted you to meet Harry." The window breathed in afternoon light. I felt his hand trail down the length of my arm. "We'll be okay," Liam said. "We just can't let them separate us."

"They won't," I whispered. "I was thinking . . . I know this is going to sound so corny, but . . . if there's one good thing that came out of all this, it was that I got to meet you. I would go through it all again—" Tears pricked my eyes. "I would, as long as it meant I'd met you."

"You really think that?" Liam sat up and pressed his lips against my hair. "'Cause, frankly, the way I see it, you and me? Inevitable. Let's say we didn't get stuck in those god-awful camps—no, just listen. I'm going to tell you the amazing story of us."

Liam cleared his throat again and turned to fully face me. "So, it's the summer and you're in Salem, suffering through another boring, hot July, and working part-time at an ice cream parlor. Naturally, you're completely oblivious to the fact that all of the boys from your high school who visit daily are more interested in you than the thirty-one flavors. You're focused on school and all your dozens of clubs, because you want to go to a good college and save the world. And just when you think you're going to die if you have to take another practice SAT, your dad asks if you want to go visit your grandmother in Virginia Beach."

"Yeah?" I leaned my forehead against his chest. "What about you?"

"Me?" Liam said, tucking a strand of hair behind my ear. "I'm in Wilmington, suffering through another boring, hot summer, working one last time in Harry's repair shop before going off to some fancy university—where, I might add, my roommate will be a stuck-up-know-it-all-with-a-heart-of-gold named Charles Carrington Meriwether IV—but he's not part of this story, not yet." His fingers curled around my hip, and I could feel him trembling, even as his voice was steady. "To celebrate, Mom decides to take us up to Virginia Beach for a week. We're only there for a day when I start catching glimpses of this girl with dark hair walking around town, her nose stuck in a book, earbuds in and blasting music. But no matter how hard I try, I never get to talk to her.

"Then, as our friend Fate would have it, on our very last day at the beach I spot her. You. I'm in the middle of playing a volleyball game with Harry, but it feels like everyone else disappears. You're walking toward me, big sunglasses on, wearing this light green dress, and I somehow know that it matches your eyes. And then, because, let's face it, I'm basically an Olympic god when it comes to sports, I manage to volley the ball right into your face."

"Ouch," I said with a light laugh. "Sounds painful."

"Well, you can probably guess how I'd react to that situation. I offer to carry you to the lifeguard station, but you look like you want to murder me at just the suggestion. Eventually, thanks to my sparkling charm and wit—and because I'm so pathetic you take pity on me—you let me buy you ice cream. And then you start telling me how you work in an ice cream shop in Salem, and how frustrated you feel that you still have two years before college. And somehow, *somehow*, I get your e-mail or screen name or maybe, if I'm really lucky, your phone number. Then we talk. I go to college and you go back to Salem, but we talk all the time, about everything, and sometimes we do that stupid thing where we run out of things to say and just stop talking and listen to one another breathing until one of us falls asleep—"

"—and Chubs makes fun of you for it," I added.

"Oh, ruthlessly," he agreed. "And your dad hates me because he thinks I'm corrupting his beautiful, sweet daughter, but still lets me visit from time to time. That's when you tell me about tutoring a girl named Suzume, who lives a few cities away—"

"—but who's the coolest little girl on the planet," I manage to squeeze out.

"Yup," Liam said. "Wanna try for the ending?"

By then, I couldn't help myself. I brought both hands up to my face, pressing my fingers against my eyes.

I had to do it now, or I never would. We couldn't hide up here forever. They could change their mind about his leaving as quickly as they had the first time.

I sat up and wiped the tears off my face, gritting my teeth. Liam pushed himself up so that he was sitting beside me on the edge of the bed, a concerned look on his face. For a moment I was terrified that he knew what I was about to do.

He tilted his head to the side, a small smile turning up the corner of his lips. I tried to smile back, but inside I was breaking apart. "What?"

When they brought us to the camps, they took everything. They stripped away our friends and family, took our clothes, took our future. They only thing we got to keep were our memories, and now I was about to take those from him, too.

"Close your eyes," I whispered. "I'm going to finish the story."

I felt the trickle at the back of my mind and let it turn into a roar. And when I kissed him, when my lips pressed against his one last time, slipping inside of his mind was as easy as taking his hand had been.

I felt him jerk back, heard him say my name in alarm, but I didn't let him get away. I pulled myself from his mind, day by day, piece by piece, memory by memory, until there was nothing of Ruby left to weigh him down or keep him bound to my side. It was a strange unwinding sensation, one I had never felt before, or maybe one I never recognized until that moment.

The problem of Chubs rose in the back of my mind, and I had a split-second to make a decision. If he was alive—and he had to be, there was no alternative for me—the League would bring him in. But if Liam knew that, he'd come back to find a way to get him out, and the deal would be for nothing.

I would take care of Chubs. *I* would be the one to help him give the League the slip. There was no reason why Liam couldn't think that his friend had made it home to his parents; no reason he needed another distraction from getting home himself. It was a simple adjustment, a quick patch over an ugly memory. . . .

And then I was out of air and out of time. The door behind me opened and I pulled away from Liam. He stayed board stiff, his hands resting on his knees, his eyes shut tight. Cate looked back and forth between us, her brows drawing together. I stood and moved to her side.

A moment later, Liam's bright blue eyes opened, and he was seeing me. He just wasn't seeing Ruby.

"What happened?" he asked, looking between Cate and me. He reached up to touch his face, which was still swollen and battered.

"You had a car accident," I said. "The League picked you up."

Cate stiffened beside me; I caught the sudden comprehension fall over her features, out of the corner of my eye.

"The League . . ." he repeated, his eyes narrowing.

"Yes, but if you feel well enough, you can go," Cate said, when she recovered. "Your brother asked us to give you some money for a bus ticket."

"I bet he did," Liam grumbled as he searched the ground for his shoes. "Why can't I remember the accident?"

I'm not sure Cate realized how plainly she was wearing the shock on her face. Her hand floated up toward my shoulder—to steady me, or herself, I wasn't sure—but I stepped away.

"Does your head still hurt?" I managed to choke out. I

was still wearing his jacket. I couldn't bring myself to take it off. "You hit it pretty hard."

"A little," he admitted. I didn't like the way he was looking at me, his brows drawn together in concentration. "And the League is just letting me go?"

Cate nodded and threw him an envelope. Liam threw it right back to her.

"I don't want your money."

"The procedure to contact your parents is also in here," she said.

"Don't want it," he said. "Don't need it."

"What am I supposed to tell Cole?"

Liam drew himself up on unsteady legs. "Tell him to come home, and then we can talk." He turned to me. "What about you? Are you really one of them? You look like you have a lot more sense than that."

Wordlessly, I took the envelope from Cate. When I pressed it into his hand, he didn't toss it back at me. "You'd better get going."

"I'm not going to thank you," he told us. "I didn't ask for your help."

Cate led him out into the hall. "You didn't have to, and you never need to."

He started down the stairs.

"Hey—" I called. Liam stopped, turning back up to look at me. "Be careful."

His blue eyes flicked back and forth between Cate and me. "You too, darlin'."

I watched him go, from the window overlooking the

street, following his familiar shape as he stepped outside and closed the door behind him. No car, no one to watch over, no one to help. He was completely free.

And he looked happy. Sure of himself, at least. His feet instinctively knew what direction home was. Now there was nothing left to keep him from getting there.

Liam passed through the white fence surrounding the house and stepped onto the sidewalk. He flipped the sweatshirt hood up over his head and glanced both ways before jogging across the street. I watched him grow smaller and smaller with each step.

All the world will be your enemy, Prince with a Thousand Enemies, I thought, *and whenever they catch you, they will kill you. But first they must catch you, digger, listener, runner, prince with the swift warning.*

Be cunning and full of tricks, and your people shall never be destroyed.

Cate came up behind me, stroking a hand through my hair. "You'll be happy with us," she said. "I'll take care of you."

I drew the gauzy curtains shut, my fingers sliding over their silky surface. I watched her for a moment, searching for the tell that would reveal her lie. I wondered if she still thought I was the girl she had carried out of Thurmond, who had cried the first time she'd seen the stars.

Because she didn't know that there were two of me now; split between everything I had wanted, and everything I would now have to be. One of me, the hardest, angriest part, would stay with these monsters and slowly find herself

517

twisting into their shape. But there was another, secret Ruby. This one was as thin as a wisp of air, and had struggled for so long just to be. This was the one that Liam carried with him, without knowing. The one that would ride in his back pocket, whisper words of encouragement, tell him that he was born to chase the light.

For the first time in months, I heard Sam's voice whisper in my ear: *Don't be scared. Don't let them see.*

I turned from the window, and I didn't look back.

ACKNOWLEDGMENTS

As the old song goes, "I get by with a little help from my friends," and that's definitely the case here. My thanks to:

My family, of course, for a lifetime of love and support. You inspire me every day.

Merrilee Heifetz, my amazing agent, who worked tirelessly on behalf of this project and was behind it in an amazing way from the start. Likewise, thanks are owed to Genevieve Gagne-Hawes for her early feedback, all of which helped shaped the story into what it is today.

The whole team at Hyperion, especially my editor, Emily Meehan. Both she and Laura Schreiber have taken incredible care of this story, and not a day goes by that I don't stop and think how lucky I am to work with such talent.

My early readers, in particular Sarah J. Maas, who cried and laughed in all the right places, and Carlin Hauck, who helped back my imagination up with actual science.

Everyone at RHCB, for their unwavering support, interest, and understanding.

And, finally, there are no adequate words in the English language to convey how thankful I am to Anna Jarzab for loving this story as much as I do. I'm blessed to have you as a champion, but even more privileged to call you my friend.

Also by
ALEXANDRA BRACKEN

THE DARKEST MINDS SERIES
The Darkest Minds
Never Fade
In the Afterlight
The Darkest Legacy
Through the Dark
The Rising Dark

THE PASSENGER SEQUENCE
Passenger
Wayfarer

THE PROSPER REDDING SERIES
The Dreadful Tale of Prosper Redding
The Last Life of Prince Alastor